In honor of the

MILLENNIUM
CHRISTMAS

2000

BOOK DESIGNED & PRINTED BY:
C. JOHN COOMBES

EBOOK ISBN 9780982221310   0982221312
PRINT ISBN 9780982221365   0982221363

CLAUS

A CHRISTMAS INCARNATION

A novel by
C. J. COOMBES

Escape to a time
When life was an adventure.

Our nation was young,
And so were her people.
A time of struggle and setback,
Of pain and perseverance.

A time also of freedom, joy,
And the birth of new traditions.
The future was fearful and uncertain,
But no more so than for the children.

For them, let us say,
Fate brought forth a man.
He was wealthy and influential,
He was good-hearted and generous.
A man of conjecture and mystery.
He was there for them, a savior,
A second chance, a hope.

Only one person may have known him.
A person who struggled to understand him
Through the eyes of a child,
Through the heart of a woman.

A disciple named Elizabeth.

ILLUSTRATIONS BY:
C. JOHN COOMBES

It would be preposterous
To assert that
Fact is born of myth.

Conversely…
It has been proven
Myth is a child of truth.

BOOK TWO

The woman

PART ONE

THE M HART EDITION

Lady Rebecca Memorial Foundation

CHARITY AFFAIR

The Public
is Invited to Attend
an Evening of Entertainment
to Include Dinner and Guest Speakers

Proceeds Donated for the Betterment of the Less Fortunate

ONE

Wednesday, January thirty-first, eighteen-ten marked the day of Mary's return from her honeymoon. Since the date of her departure shortly before Christmas, she had been away enjoying a warmer southern climate with her husband, Dr. Sawyer. Out of touch for almost a month and a half, only conscience kept them from further enjoying the raptures of sunny paradise and sexual intimacy.

Dr. Sawyer understood the necessity of arriving back home by the first of February as promised in order to reopen the doors of the infirmary. It was not an easy thing to go on holiday and leave the sick and ailing behind—even if it was a honeymoon. The consequence of such departures was apparent, and no more so than now, as they viewed the line of afflicted souls waiting impatiently at the office door for his return. His patients felt abandoned and believed they had suffered long enough by making do with whatever home brewed elixirs they might muster.

"They're back! They're back! Thank god," exclaimed one man with a sigh of relief.

"Yes! Yes! I can see 'em! Here they come now," chimed in another.

"Where?" asked a local drunkard.

"Right there, fer cryin' out loud! How can ya miss 'em? They got a ton o' luggage atop their coach."

"Good Lord, man, they're comin' down the middle o' the road," said a fellow patient.

"I can miss 'em cuz I'm blind as a bat, ya idiot. Why d'ya think I'm here for?"

"If ya weren't always lookin' through the bottom of a bottle, ya wouldn't be so blind. You old sailors are one an' the same. Ya don't know when to quit," exclaimed a disgruntled old woman.

19

"I hain't 'ad a drop 'n days." The drunkard protested.

"Ha! Them ain't waves making ya rock like that," said an old salt who knew better. "Good thing he can't see himself."

"Good thing he can't *smell* himself," mumbled the old woman.

"Ahh shuddup, all o' ya!"

The drunkard shuffled away wounded. The rest of the crowd, pushy and hopeful, waited anxiously as if it were President Madison himself who was about to pull up to the curb. Instead, Mary and Dr. Sawyer stepped out into the winter air to face the welcoming party. The scruffy bunch was an insufferable lot, mostly men, mostly homeless, a sobering sight for eyes so soon returned from a honeymoon perfectly satiated by passion and bliss.

Dr. Sawyer reached up toward the driver who was bent awkwardly over the cabin roof and struggling to lower their trunks. The doctor took each from the driver and placed them one by one on the sidewalk, where Mary attempted to muscle them away in spite of her husband's objections.

"Mary, for the love of god, leave this be. The last thing I need is for the town to hear that I am tending to your sprains and pulled muscles after having carried *my* baggage. How would that make me look?" He kidded. "Please, leave them be, *Mrs.* Sawyer, you married a *husband*, not a heathen."

"Mrs. *Sawyer*. I like that. I like being called Mrs. Sawyer, but did you think you made me a wife or a weakling? I have pushed and pulled more luggage for the Claussens than you'll ever know. With all due respect, *Mr. Sawyer*, remember it was I who traveled around the world, not you."

After two or three loving jabs to Dr. Sawyer's lapel, Mary dismissed both his concerns and expression. She plowed a path through the maze of languishing bodies as she dragged the heavy trunks from the curbside to the doorstep.

Dr. Sawyer had no desire to dwell before the gathering, and so stood fast on Mary's heels with bags in hand. Wishing to be polite, but not encouraging, he nodded coolly to those folks milling about the walk. He refused to meet the many desperate eyes staring in hopes of stealing his attention. He kept them at his back, choosing instead to focus on the front door while working his key to release the lock. The crowd pressed in upon him and his patience. He was entirely unprepared to deal with their issues and complaints at this time. He struggled with a mounting annoyance as he turned to speak to Mary in a voice muffled by clenched teeth.

"I ask you, Mary, how do these people know I'm back even before I know I'm back."

Although Mary humored him, returning to Boston prompted Dr. Sawyer to feel as though he were going back to war—all the way to the front lines. His honeymoon was suddenly being snuffed out prematurely by an onslaught of maladies, obligations, and a particularly gloomy and depressing winter day that could sink one's disposition lower than the freezing temperatures that pained his fingers and toes. There had been no foot warmer in the coach, and he doubted anyone could knit a glove or sock to save his hands and feet from the chill that, once started, crept up his bones to shake him silly. Boston's weather was a brutal contrast to the soothing southern climate of Savannah now left to memory.

He stared at the door handle. At this moment his wants were few. He wished only for a hot cup of coffee and to sit a spell before the warmth of a fire. His want grew stronger as another gust of wind worked its way beneath the collar of his coat. He pulled it tighter about his neck and turned about to face the crowd, his impatience having surfaced.

"Ladies, gentlemen, please! I *beg* you give us room. We are tired. We are cold and tired, and very much would like to get settled in before—." Dr. Sawyer was immediately interrupted by a man speaking in an overbearing and garbled tongue due to a fist full of fingers jammed deep into his wide-open mouth.

"But doc, if ya don' look at this here'n tooth, it'll be the death o' me, I swear. I won't make it another night. It's this—."

"Sir, I assure you that you will live to see the morrow, and should you suffer a little, consider it penance for your sins. Please, see here." He pointed to the door glass. "For those of you who cannot read, which I assume must be everyone, the sign clearly states that we shan't be open for business until tomorrow the *first* day of February, not the *last* day of January.

It is for this reason, I ask you to please call upon your patience and consideration. You may rest assured, beginning first light tomorrow I shall be busy attending to your needs, but for now we require what little time it takes to set down our baggage and call on family and loved ones. I am sure you understand how they await word from us, wishing to know that we are returned in good spirits and health, and no less so than our own desire to see them, so please...."

"Hey, doc, have you seen Mr. Claussen?" asked one of the spurned patients. "Did ya get a chance t' talk to 'im?"

"Yeah, how's he doin' anyway?" asked another.

"No one's seen hide ner hair of 'um since 'er death," exclaimed yet another.

To be asked anything about Mr. Claussen in such a direct manner was most unusual. It caught both Mary and Dr. Sawyer completely off guard. Mary frowned, feeling a cramp of uneasiness driven by the sound of the word 'death'.

"Whose death?" she asked, for the word had a jarring effect.

"They say 'e ain't set foot off that ship in over a month."

"I 'eard 'e looks ter'ble. That's what da mates aboard are sayin'."

"I 'eard the same thing. Hear tell, 'e ain't eatin' a thing fer a month. Nutin' but teeth an' bones."

" I heered 'e's been doin' some hard drinkin'," offered the drunkard who had now wandered back.

"Whose death?" Mary asked again, this time feeling more reason for concern, but the crowd had turned into itself, swept up into a new rush of conversation over this issue that had gripped the hearts of an entire city.

"I 'eard there was better'n a thousan' sailors at the funeral. She was a fine lady, wasn't she? Everyone said so."

"Yeah, down on the docks they loved 'er. She always put out a good meal, she did; I'll give 'er that."

"I think I ate there. Yeah, I ate there a lot," the drunkard noted.

"The tents ain't been up since. Lot a people goin' hungry again. It's sad to see it."

Mary felt a dreadful crush of apprehension move over her. It was pressing down upon her and causing a tingling sensation that tightened the skin about her arms and neck. She raised herself upon the doorstep to better look over the crowd. With a demanding and far less respectful voice she admonished the crowd for ignoring her question.

"Pardon! Pardon me! Hey, listen up! Listen to me! Who has died? Who is this you speak of? Will you please quiet your-selves and tell me who it is that has died!" Even the doctor had stepped back from the door to pay closer attention.

The commotion on the sidewalk suddenly stopped. The patients turned toward her with a look of surprise. A sole voice answered.

"Lady Claussen, of course."

"*Lady Claussen.*" The crowd echoed in unison a split second later.

"Lady Rebecca Claussen, surely *you* must know."

Their eyes exhibited not only the mixture of astonishment that still existed in their hearts, but also a show of surprise that the Sawyers had no knowledge of the tragedy.

Mary went ghost white. The man's response clobbered her, knocking the breath from her breast. Instinctively, she reached out to her husband for support. Dr. Sawyer took hold of her at once.

"That cannot be," she countered. "You are most certainly mistaken," she said, shaking her head in denial.

"No ma'am, no mistake. 'Tis true," the voice returned.

"Oh! It's true." The crowd agreed. "She's gone an' buried."

"No, that is impossible, I tell you—I only saw her just a few—ah…. It's…." It was more than just a few; yet, this was beyond belief, a vicious rumor. She knew it had to be a rumor, as were most dreadful stories that circulated about the docks. Yet, a certain fear was creeping about her soul and keeping her from wanting to know anything more.

"She's dead, Mrs. Sawyer. Died, Chris'mas eve, a month ago. I's there an' sawr 'em lay 'er t' rest wit' me own eyes."

"Me too. Lot's 'o mates went t' pay respects."

"Yeah, they all sang that song. Ya know—the one 'bout 'Rebecca, darlin' dear', 'member me an' I'll be near'. That one about the lady of the Thames, you know the one. Everybody's always whistling it."

"Yeah, we were all singin' it. Sounded purty good," said the drunkard.

It's been the talk o' the town fer weeks. Nobody knows what's happened t' Mr. Claussen, 'e's disappeared."

"'E hain't dis'peared nothin'. 'E's on board ship, ya idiot. E's drinkin' 'ard, ever'body knows that." The drunkard insisted.

"That's what you say. That's what they say, but nobody's act'shlee seen 'im. Anyways, it was ter'ble. She burned up."

Mary stared blindly into the faces before her, absorbing one verbal strike after another. Their combined response to Mary's question left her stunned and defenseless to face a devastating truth. Their voices began to recede into the distance. Her knees grew weak and as she started to fall away faint hearted. A sharp cry startled her back to her senses.

"*Shut up!* Shut up all o' ya. Shut up and get back! Get back, I say! Get, get, get! Move along now."

The crowd quickly stepped aside before this harsh and brassy trumpet of a voice. Mary was fully in shock by the time the large frame of Mrs. Pennington broke through the ranks of the patients.

"Oh, Mary, Dr. Sawyer!" She half curtsied. "I am so sorry you had to find out this way. We've been watching and waiting for your return, and I swear, I ran out the second I heard you were back. I hoped to break the news myself, but I see I am too late, and I am just furious with myself."

"Don't be, Lydia. I have no doubt that you've done your best, but what is this that we hear? What is all this about?" asked Dr. Sawyer.

"Please, sir, let us get Mary inside. By the look of her, she is faint and needs to sit."

Dr. Sawyer and Lydia helped Mary inside to the waiting room and eased her into a chair. She was lifeless. Distraught and disbelieving, she foundering in her thoughts. She searched Lydia's face for a sign of sanity in a world suddenly overturned by madness.

"Oh, Lydia. Say it isn't true. My god, what has happened during my absence, what has happened? What is this I hear? I have scarcely been gone a month. How can this be?" Mary looked deep into Lydia's eyes for answers, her tears beginning to show. "This cannot be true. Tell me it isn't. I have so waited to see her. I have so much to tell her—the honeymoon—the wonderful things that have happened. I brought her back a most splendid gift. Why didn't somebody send word?" Tears suddenly burst forth from Mary's amber eyes, spilling across her freckles and flowing down her still chilled and now colorless cheeks. Lydia kneeled beside the chair and took her arm.

"I am sorry, Mary. I am so very sorry. I know this comes as a terrible shock, but we had no idea how to reach the two of you, and besides, what could you have done? There was nothing anybody could do. It was out of our hands. It was God's will. Do you understand? It was best you enjoyed your honeymoon and keep those memories, but now that you are back, I will tell you all you wish to hear."

"Please, everything, I must know everything."

"And so you shall, but take hold of your strength for this is most unpleasant to recount. It was a terrible tragedy, Mary, terrible as you might ever imagine." Lydia took a breath and began. "Lady Rebecca died at the Boston Community Church in a fire on the eve of Christmas. I was there, and I can say the fire came upon us with such speed and ferocity that we barely escaped with our lives. Within moments the whole of the church was engulfed in flame. The entire roof collapsed in one enormous crash. Why we were spared, I can't begin to know. But for whatever His reason, the Lord led us through the burning timbers and showed us the way out. It was surely a miracle that anyone survived.

"The fire started while we were in the meeting room opening gifts. We had no idea of the danger, until someone opened the door to the church and the smoke and heat poured in. We had no time to think, but gathered up the children and made a run for it. Unfortunately, in all of the confusion and terror, one of the little girls, Annie Lynn Wagner, was somehow separated and left inside.

"We discovered her missing soon after reaching the safety of the street when taking a head count. Lady Rebecca was frantic. You know how she was, always thinking of others first. My word, before we even knew what was going on, she had raced back inside that church, flames and all, and that was the end of it. They both perished. It happened so fast. In a matter of moments it was all over. The church, everything, burnt to the foundation—gone. Lady Rebecca and Annie Lynn were trapped in the back room, you know the room I speak of, the lean-to—."

"Yes, but I don't understand. There is a door to the back yard. Why didn't they—."

"Indeed there was, but it was frozen shut, blocked by ice on the step."

"Are you saying the door opened outward?" asked Dr. Sawyer. Mrs. Pennington was distracted by his question. She looked at him somewhat confused.

"Apparently, so."

"For the love of god! What idiot—never mind, never mind. Please, go on. You were saying."

"Yes, well then—you see, we had a fire burning all day for the children's comfort. The heat inside melted the snow off the roof, and the run-off collected upon the porch where it froze once again into a large mound at the door's sill. There was no way out but through the church, which by that time was wholly aflame and impossible to enter. It was the most tragic—well, I don't know what to say, tragic is hardly the word to describe the horror of it."

Lydia did her best to comfort Mary, who was physically sickened at hearing of the disaster, appalled at the thought of someone dying such a ghastly and fearful death. She was riddled with guilt at being alive and well, knowing that she surely would have

27

accompanied Lady Rebecca and Elizabeth on their Christmas rounds under normal circumstances.

The guilt was not eased by the additional news of Mr. Claussen and Elizabeth. The emotional foundation of her world had been busted out from beneath her. Over and over, she pushed aside the tide of tears that streamed across her cheeks.

"Is it true, then, that no one has s-seen anything of Mr. Claussen?"

"Pretty much so. He shut himself in their cabin aboard REBECCA the night of her death and no one has seen him since."

"Well, is he all right? Has anyone looked in on him t-to see?" Mary became anxious, but was settled by Lydia's assertive reassurances.

"I have spoken with Captain Ward, who was summoned from Baltimore by the crew. He has taken it upon himself to stay nearby should he be needed. I believe they came to be good friends, at least that is what is said."

"Oh, thank god. Yes, yes, it is true. They are the best of friends. He will care for him as a brother," spoke Mary through a wadded handkerchief.

"It appears so, for I am told it was he who finally talked Mr. Claussen out of the bottle and convinced him to clean up and eat. This is one of the reasons I have come looking for you. I have word from Captain Ward that Mr. Claussen wishes to meet with you the moment you are first able. He says Mr. Claussen believes it most urgent he speak with you, for it has to do with young Elizabeth."

At the mention of Elizabeth's name, Mary dropped her face into her hands and sobbed. She heaved without control as Lydia held her arm and continued to speak in as gentle a manner as possible.

"I hear tell she is doing poorly, sick from her grieving. I must warn you, Mary, the poor child was witness to the worst

28

of it. She broke through the crowd and was in view of Lady Rebecca's outreached arm as she perished. It must have left a scar of unimaginable proportion. How she will ever overcome such a memory is beyond me. They say she screams all hours of the night, unable to escape her endless nightmare. Mr. Claussen was supposed to have departed for the Orient, but for her sake, he has instead awaited your return."

"Oh, my god, my god, my dearest Elizabeth. The p-poor child must be s-suff-ering beyond all reason. I must go to her. She needs me; I k-know she does. I must go to her now without fur-ther delay. We m-must go to her Allen." Mary's eyes spilled tears anew.

"At once my dear." Dr. Sawyer attempted to console his wife.

"W-Wh-ere is she, at the Barrington?"

"I believe she is, yes," said Mrs. Pennington.

For a moment, Mary regained her composure. She let out a breath and calmed herself so to think more clearly.

"All right, Allen, what are we to do, what are we to do? I think—I think, before Elizabeth, we should see Mr. Claussen. Yes, yes, let us go to Mr. Claussen at once. We must see him first. We must seek his advice in this matter. I believe it best. I must hear what he has to say. Poor Elizabeth, imagine her grief. My heart hurts to think of it." Mary dropped her head back into her hands.

"By all means, darling." Dr. Sawyer kissed her gently and then turned to Mrs. Pennington. "Lydia, would you join us? I would appreciate it."

"Certainly."

Dr. Sawyer moved away and stepped back out onto the street. He had hoped to further use the coachman's services, but was too late. The street was empty except for the crowd which, in spite of their aches and pains, was nosy enough to linger about in the cold and watch Mary's suffering. He quickly offered a fee to anyone who would run to the livery and inform the stable master that he was in immediate need of his buggy. The drunkard was off at once, shuffling away at his best speed.

Dr. Sawyer returned to wait at Mary's side, leaving only one time more to fetch blankets from their bedroom upstairs. He kept them draped across his arm as he stood beside her and stared down the street with impatience for a sign of his buggy. As soon as it arrived, the three set off for the docks.

The air inside the lobby of the infirmary was every bit cold as the air outside, but free of the wind. As Dr. Sawyer pulled the door closed behind him, what drafts remained settled out and the room returned to its month-long winter stillness. The only sign of an interruption, besides diminishing echoes, was that of baggage containing numerous curios, gifts, and mementos suddenly forgotten and left suspended indeterminately upon the wooden floor a few feet inside the front door.

TWO

The moment Dr. Sawyer's buggy rounded the corner and came into view of REBECCA's vermilion hull; he and Mary sensed the mournful state of misery about the waterfront. Gone were the large food tents that produced so many a tantalizing aroma, so many a hot meal. Gone were the canvas harbors that fostered an atmosphere of festivity and friendship to reach out and beckon the hungry and homeless.

The customary crowd of sailors and those colorful lost souls 'down and out' were nowhere to be seen. The chatter of the unemployed, and the laughter and cursing of old sailors no longer drifted through the crisp winter air. No longer were the regulars to be seen huddled around barrel fires drinking hot cider and warming their hands. The place stood barren, desolate, and empty of life. Only the Mistress of Winter haunted the docks, her breath blowing loosened rigging to slap eerily against frozen ship masts as swirls of snow spun in ghostly circles upon the wharf.

Dr. Sawyer brought the buggy to a halt at the base of REBECCA's boarding plank. Mary had asked to speak to Mr. Claussen alone, and so he and Lydia prepared to await her return. Drawing up scarves about their faces, they slid together upon the seat and wrapped the blankets tightly to ward off the wind blowing inland from the bay. At the same time, they watched with concern until Mary, now making her solemn ascent up the slippery plank, was safely aboard. Dr. Sawyer sensed how the wind pushed at her back, seeming to hurry her pace aftward along the ice-covered bulwark, and rush her toward the broken heart of Mr. Claussen.

Mary entered the pilothouse and pulled the door shut behind her. She sealed out the whistling wind and noises that sought to disrupt the crush of her recollections. She felt utterly alone as she waded into a stream of yesteryear's memories. She slid her gloved fingertips along perfectly polished panels of wood that now replaced once chipped and scarred bulkheads damaged by the blast of pirate's fodder. She looked up at the wiped slate board and read invisible words written in chalk, long since erased. Scenes aplenty passed by as her footsteps echoed with hollow resonance along the darkened corridor that led to the Claussen stateroom.

At last step, she faced the cabin door now closed to conserve heat. She stood before it, biting her lip, staring at the hinged plank of wood that separated her from the universe of Mr. Claussen. She wondered what she would say. She watched the fog of her breath hang thick in the still air. It was cold inside; it was cold outside; it was cold everywhere, and the lack of warmth seemed a curse that enforced the upheaval within her heart. Finally, she raised her fist and rapped lightly. The response was instant and commanding.

"Enter!"

Filled with apprehension, she adjusted herself and then slowly opened the door. She peered nervously into the cabin before making any move to cross the threshold. Christopher had heard the approach of a visitor and although prepared, had not imagined at this moment it would be Mary. He knew her return was imminent, but was greatly surprised nonetheless.

"Mary? Mary, my word, you are back! Praise the Lord! I heard your carriage upon the wharf but never thought to look outside" He rose to his feet at once, his face moved by an expression of relief and joy at first sight of her freckled face. "Oh, my dearest Mary, it is good to see you home." He stepped out from behind the table.

"Mr. Claussen, am I bothering you? I have only just returned. I came as quickly as I could. I have left my baggage sitting at the front door so I might come straight away."

"Bother me, good Lord, I should say not! I have been sitting here anxiously awaiting your return. Come in; come in from the cold. Bother me, what a thing to say. When is it ever a bother to look upon you, to hold you in my embrace?"

Mary entered the cabin. Christopher reached out for her, but looked beyond.

"Are you alone? Is Allen not with you?"

"He waits for me outside."

"You must ask him in. I insist. I would be embarrassed to have him wait in the cold."

"No, no, Mr. Claussen. He is with Mrs. Pennington. He is fine. He remains outside at my request. I thought it better. I wished to speak with you in private."

"As you wish. Come, my dear, sit."

"I brought you and Lady Rebecca gifts, but—but—. She stammered, as her heart again came apart.

"Sshhh." Christopher consoled her. Her tears affected him deeply. "I know, I know. It is hard."

"I can't believe all that I am hearing. I am swimming in confusion and grief. I so want you to tell me it isn't true, Mr. Claussen, for the sake of god, tell me none of what I hear is true. Tell me Lady Rebecca is here with you safe and sound."

Mary shook her head, her voice breaking and failing her. Unable to speak further, she raised a fresh handkerchief to her eyes. Christopher took her firmly into his embrace, as might a brother to a younger sister. She rested upon his shoulder.

"I so wanted to see your face, Mary. I must say with heavy heart, it is true, all of it. How I wish it could be different."

He gave her time to regain her composure and then led her back to the table where he offered her a chair. He wrapped her in a thick blanket to warm her and then went on to pour hot tea. He asked of Mary's health and accounts of her honeymoon, but she would have none of it.

She observed the gaunt look of him. He was bundled up against the cold as though he had little ability to warm himself. He appeared half the man she knew. He had been devastated, and yet he only asked of her and Allen. It was his nature to keep his burdens to himself, and so with respect, Mary pressed him to reveal something of his feelings and needs.

"Lemon?" he asked.

"Yes, yes, yes, lemon," she answered with impatience. "Now please, Mr. Claussen, let us not waste precious time discussing lemons and my Allen. Let us not discuss my honeymoon. It brings me no pleasure to share my joys at a time such as this. I am sick with worry for you, for your well-being. I can only imagine how you have suffered during my absence. I see it in your face. I see it all about you. I see it on the docks. The whole town has been mourning while I have been off frolicking. I feel terrible. I feel terrible for you. Tell me what I might do. Please, just tell me what I might do."

He avoided the issue no more. "You are kind, Mary, but I insist you not speak of your honeymoon as mere frolicking. It was never meant to be a time of reflection on the hardships of the world. It was meant to be a time of happiness and if I had heard anything different I would have been guilt ridden forever.

Having said that, I am thankful for your concern. It has been a difficult time, difficult indeed. Difficult not only for me, but for all of us as I am sure you can imagine. Rebecca's passing happened so fast that I scarcely am able to accept the truth of it myself. My only consolation is a belief that she was of such kind heart that the Good Lord wished her to be at his side for some nobler cause."

"Forgive me, Mr. Claussen. I have no idea what to say. What words—what does one say?"

"What can be said? This is the hand of fate, the will of Providence. We are but mortals. We are powerless to change it. I am bitter, Mary, bitter to the point of ruining my life by the anger within which I drown. I seem destined to be deprived of love. I am never given a choice, but to accept such fate, and you must try as well to accept these trials that have befallen us.

"Drink your tea and warm yourself. We haven't the luxury to cry further, for there is much we need to discuss, and nothing more important than the health of dear Elizabeth. That is why I have called for you. That is why I have waited. I am deeply worried for her, Mary. She is not at all in a good way. I know full well she believes I have abandoned her."

"And I as well." Mary closed her eyes as if avoiding a reflection of her guilt. She looked out the window until Christopher continued to speak.

"Arla came by a fortnight past, and advised me of young Elizabeth's condition. She received word that I was to weigh anchor on the first—tomorrow actually, as soon as you returned. I planned to make way for China, but she feared that my leaving would be the ruin of Elizabeth, should she find out. She pleaded would I reconsider my departure, or at least promise to await your return should you be delayed, or until the child regained a measure of her strength.

I took Arla's words to heart and promised I would remain in port for as long as need be, this much to her relief. However, I am unsure of what else I might do to ease the child's suffering. Obviously, my first thought was of you. Elizabeth asks for you often, and…." Christopher took pause for a moment then winced. "I haven't gone to her, Mary. At first it was because of the bottle. I drowned myself in drunkenness. I was unfit to be human. But after that, I'm not sure. I don't know why I didn't go to her. I guess I felt no good could come of it. I have nothing to offer the child but further pain. I cannot stand by her side. I cannot console a heart that I shall leave behind with all certainty. She will never understand how I must leave my memories if I am ever to escape this torment. The child is too young to comprehend the often-cruel complexities of life. I pray you do."

"I do, Mr. Claussen, I do understand. But—leaving? I can imagine nothing worse. I am not at all pleased to hear of such plans. They seem so—so sudden. I can't imagine you—I don't know—being gone, I guess. China! My word, sir; why must it be the other side of the world? Why so far away—and for how long? We are the ones who love you. We are the ones who stand by your side. I can't say it at all pleases me to hear of this. I am certain that Elizabeth and I are of the same mind in this matter. I confess you may have given my hand away in marriage and Allen is everything I have dreamed for, but to have you gone so soon from my life and—and so far away…."

Mary was truly filled with unease. Indeed, she was happily married, but it would still take time for her to fully switch her loyalties and confidence from Mr. Claussen to her husband Dr. Sawyer. Passion was instant, but trust could only be earned over time. Mr. Claussen had provided her care for many years, and the security of his presence was deeply embedded.

"You fill me with pride, Mary. I was pleased to give your hand away to Dr. Sawyer. He is a fine man, well rooted, established, and he will do you honor. As for me, I must go. It isn't that I love you or Elizabeth less. The fact is, I cannot move, I cannot breathe, I cannot lay eyes upon one harbor, one street, one church along this coast of Massachusetts without enduring years of memories bent on tearing me apart. I fear to know what would have become of my life had it not been for Captain Ward and his sense of discipline. I have come through the worst of it, but I am not strong enough to remain. I must go, Mary. I am desperate to escape this pain. I must put these emotions behind me if I am to keep my sanity.

"I did see Elizabeth once—just after the funeral. I sent for her so I might prepare her for my departure. I tried to explain my need to leave the best I knew how, but she just looked at me with those eyes. She was lost, utterly lost. To merely look upon the child releases from my heart a torrent of emotion that would suffer any man to display in public. Elizabeth became so much a part of Rebecca's heart that when I look into her eyes, I only see a reflection of Rebecca's love. I don't know...." He shook his head, and Mary could see the frustration building within him. He continued.

"I know the bonds shared by you and Elizabeth are as strong as those between any two sisters. I know you care and worry for her, as do I. I hope you are able to see the child, without breaking—it brings—." He suddenly turned away as if to clear his throat. He avoided her eyes. "She suffers, Mary. I fear you think the worse of me; I fear you think me cruel for not standing by her side, but I know in my heart to do so will only prolong her agony, for I leave with the tide come hell or high water. This she will never understand, and I refuse to give her false hope. It would be heartless. It would be unforgivable. You must believe this, Mary. The sooner she weathers the storm, the sooner she finds the sun. Do you understand what I say?"

"I understand, Mr. Claussen, honestly I do."

36

"Either way, it is the future that we must now address, Elizabeth's future, and yours as well. I beg you hear me out, Mary, for I wish to propose to you and Dr. Sawyer an arrangement that would ease my concerns for Elizabeth immensely, and at the same time provide a generous income for the both of you.

I understand that you are only just married, and this next year should be a time of privacy and intimacy. I respect your union, Mary, and I am most sensitive to this matter. If after giving my proposal due consideration, you choose not to accept my offer—you have my word, I shan't hold the decision against you.

However, I assure you that my financial offering will be most generous. I have made it purposely difficult to refuse. It would allow you and Allen to buy or build the home of your dreams, a home that would provide all of the privacy that newlyweds deserve, a home that would meet all your needs, and yet, give Elizabeth the support and love she deserves, the support and love that was promised her by Rebecca and myself. I can't impress upon you all that such an arrangement would mean to me. Would you at least hear my offer?"

"Mr. Claussen, I have every intention of caring for Elizabeth, whether at the Barrington or in my home. I wish no money for doing what eases the pain in my heart. There is no choice in this matter. Allen would certainly understand. He cares a great deal about Elizabeth and knows well my love for her.

Liz was greatly distressed to see me leave over Christmas. It is as you have said. She feels abandoned. I am keenly aware of this and discussed this very issue with Allen on numerous occasions during our time away. I explained to him how she feels hurt and believes that she has lost me to his love. He has already agreed with a sincere heart that she is to visit us regularly, and stay as long as she pleases. She is as you say, a sister to me, Mr. Claussen. You needn't pay me for her care. I love her dearly, sir."

"Mary, you bring me such happiness and peace of mind." Christopher's eyes went moist. He turned to look out the window, to catch his breath, to hide his fragile emotions. "Elizabeth means the world to me, as do you. The two of you are what I have of family, and as for you, I can't imagine anyone having a heart of greater virtue. It is because I am confident that you will give Elizabeth the best of care that I thrill to give you the funds to further that cause. You will never know of want or worry, this I promise you."

"No, no, Mr. Claussen. I wish you wouldn't promise such things. It makes me feel cheap. It isn't necessary, believe me."

"Mary, please allow me this honor. You know very well that the money is of no concern to me. I know the goodness in your heart, and you have no reason to fear that I might feel you entertain sinister motives or a lack of conscience. I beg you allow me this, it would ease my mind, it would bring me peace while I am away."

"I—I don't know. What if Elizabeth discovers that I am being paid to care for her? What would she think? Wouldn't she always wonder if I truly loved her or if it was only for the sake of money? I don't—oh, I don't know, Mr. Claussen."

"Have no fear, Mary. For one thing, your relationship with Elizabeth goes back a good many years. For another, Elizabeth will have her own account, and when she reaches an age whereby she might seriously wonder about these things, she will have the resources to leave if she should so choose.

"I would encourage you to tell her of the arrangement as soon as she is well enough to listen. Hide nothing from her, for she is a bright child. It would work out best for everybody if you will just allow me to do this. Please say yes, Mary. I am at your mercy in this matter. Please, I beg—say yes."

Mary squirmed. In every way, the idea of the money went against her moral conscience. She sat torn between Mr. Claussen's wishes and what she felt in her heart was the only right thing to do. However, she looked at his once handsome face and despaired over the ravaged appearance of him. It saddened her, and so determining that Mr. Claussen had endured enough, she decided if this arrangement would ease his troubled soul, then so be it.

"All right, I will agree if Allen so does, but know as for money; I do this only for you, only because it is what you wish."

"I never doubted it, Mary, not for a moment. Thank-you, thank-you, thank-you, you have the heart of a Saint." Christopher closed his eyes, rolled his head back and expelled a cloud of worry. "Ohhhh. I feel so much better already." He looked back at Mary and smiled.

Being much relieved, he went on to ask about other issues. He directed the conversation toward her and the events surrounding the honeymoon, while Mary steered them back to Mr. Claussen and those matters concerning his well-being. After all, it had been her place to care for him during those same years he had cared for her. She reiterated her disappointment regarding his plans to leave for China, and attempted at every chance to change his mind, though she realized the futility of her efforts.

She remained with Christopher for nearly an hour before being torn away from his side by the knowledge that Allen and Lydia were out in the cold and waiting on her. She accepted the terms of his arrangement, his good-bye, his final embrace, and greatly saddened, she closed the cabin door behind her leaving him again alone to himself. She moved through the pilothouse and out onto the wind-blown deck. The gusts stole away her breath as she stepped along the waterway of a snow-covered and seemingly abandoned ship.

As Mary descended the plank, the signs of grief and hard crying were all about her. She was unable to speak, other than to ask her husband in a shattered voice if he might drive her to the Barrington Hotel immediately. Her grief was such that he asked no questions. They dropped Lydia off en route and, having calmed down somewhat, Mary began to convey to Allen what she knew of Elizabeth's poor condition.

"My god, Allen, the child has utterly succumbed to her grief. I fear she may never recover from this tragedy. First, it was her mother,and now the one person who was most devoted to her has been taken. I must go to her at once. I am all she has, Allen. She needs me. She needs us. We must do all we can to mend this innocent child's broken heart."

* * *

Their buggy halted behind a panting Morgan relieved to be free of the demands placed upon it. As Dr. Sawyer walked around to assist Mary down from her seat, a delivery wagon that had been parked in front of them pulled away from the curb leaving Lady Rebecca's vermilion coach in full view. The sight of it came as a terrible jolt to Mary. It was too personal a possession. It was Lady Rebecca's signature, her calling card.

Mary was compelled to avert her eyes. She was filled with sadness and tremendous guilt that worked to deepen her misery, guilt for having her time of bliss while living blind to the horrors in Boston. She felt guilty for being alive, guilty for having been gone. She felt ashamed and wished to avoid these troubling thoughts, and so urged her husband to hurry. Impatient to do what good she might, she took Dr. Sawyer's hand and stepped down to the street. She then led him by the arm, pulling him along quickly beneath the canopied entrance of the hotel.

They entered the plush lobby directly. Inside, a world of memories lingered, memories of the grandest party Boston had ever experienced. Wonderful memories close to Mary's heart. Recollections that only further reminded her of the tragedy and unfairness in life.

She and Dr. Sawyer ascended the wide carpeted circular stairway, past the second-floor ballroom where before all of Boston, Lady Rebecca had placed her mark on Elizabeth. In Mary's mind, she was able to see past the closed doors. She overlooked the empty chairs and unclothed tables that filled a now dark and silent room, and instead relived the bright lights, the festivities, and the one crowning moment of glory.

She shivered with goose flesh, recalling how Lady Rebecca's hands laid the magnificent gold and diamond necklace about Elizabeth's small neck. She could still hear the gasp from the crowd, the look of shock upon their faces. She knew well the ridicule Elizabeth had endured, and knowing the justice Lady Rebecca had inflicted upon the child's tormentors put a smile on Mary's face even now.

Lady Rebecca had knocked the ego out of the arrogant as effectively as if she had clubbed them with a coal shovel. Oh, how they talked. It was in all the papers, in all the coffeehouses, at every sewing circle and quilter's guild. Young Elizabeth, the lowly maiden, had been raised to the ranks of lords and ladies, the well heeled, the powerful. She was to become a Claussen and command a fortune second to none.

Mary harbored no envy. The Claussens had generously provided for her, and now more than ever by this morning's arrangement, Mr. Claussen had made her and Allen undeniably wealthy. However, the wealth came with a price. It bothered her. It made her feel dirty even though she knew in her heart that money didn't sway her feelings, and it certainly couldn't buy love or happiness.

She knew in her heart that before this morning she was blissfully happy, she was newly wed, madly in love, and most of her thoughts were about having children. She understood with compassion the love and need that Lady Rebecca fostered for Elizabeth. It was the same love she herself held for her near-sister, and riches would never alter her heart.

At the third-floor landing, there stood an attendant ever watchful behind a drawn and secured red velvet rope that prevented the general public further passage along the east corridor. Against the wall and near the rope's fixed end stood a highly polished mahogany side table. It was positioned tastefully beneath

41

the center of a beautiful Italian tapestry trimmed in silk fringe that depicted an old wooden table covered with wine and food, fading into a rich background of autumn trees woven in vivid oranges, brilliant reds and deep maroons. It was affixed overhead to a sturdy brass rod fitted with ornate end caps fashioned of hand-worked alabaster.

The table displayed a simple but elegant brass plaque atop a small easel, flanked by white and gold china vases, each overflowing with the color and fragrance of fresh-cut flowers. The plaque noted in a superbly engraved calligraphy, that one had reached the residence of Claussen. It was here that they halted before the attendant.

"Doctor Allen Sawyer and wife, Mary."

"Yes, sir. You are expected—please pass."

The attendant removed the velvet barricade at once, and then swung his arm, directing them down the hall toward the Claussen entry doors. They walked briskly along the plush hallway, in and out of the glow of each tiny gaslight until they reached the end, where they faced the imposing double doors that heralded the main entrance to the Claussen suite. Allen reached past the gargoyle eyes staring down at him from above the bronze door-knockers and grasped the bell rope alongside the jamb. Lightly, he pulled at it.

THREE

My dreams were now my reality. I had given up the excruciating pain of the real world for the gut wrenching fear and anxiety of my mind's aimless wanderings. There seemed no sense to its manner of healing. It may have been attempting to protect me from further pain by sealing me away forever from the light of day.

And yet, I would relive visions of Lady Rebecca's out-stretched arms reaching for me from a fire and cause me to explode emotionally. I would erupt from the deep, forced awake suddenly by my own screaming as if I were burning up in the mournful agony of invisible flames.

More often my dreams seemed to deal with facing fears. I would find myself standing upon fragile floating islands in the sea. They were like glass, thin, flat and transparent, easily broken apart. Always, there were cracks. There were always things looking up from below, things trapped, things drowning. I struggled for my breath.

Dazzling shops stocked with every delight covered the islands and served to beckon me from one to another, but they were separated by stream-like canals, each precisely a width that left me to wonder whether or not I was able to leap across. Prowling shark-like creatures slipped by silently beneath the water's surface followed by the alarm of cracking glass.

I stared at the brightly painted signs of the stores. I stared at the dark shadows swimming below. I was always undecided. Should I jump, or should I not? I was perpetually torn between the light and the dark, the desire and the fear. Sometimes, the shops were Mr. Claussen; sometimes, he was the shark.

In my half-conscious state, I took little notice of the small doorbell sounding its tinkle through the apartment. I never heard the large doors open wide to offer a full view of Arla, the head servant, whom I knew would express her profound relief by gushing freely with gratitude. Her chatter drifted into my room through the silence that was now prevalent since Lady Rebecca's death.

"Oh my, my, my! Mazza Sawya, Iz so gla' you come! Iz so gla'. I jez so gla'. Come in! Come in! Please, you too, Missus Sawya, come in this mi'nt!"

I heard the Sawyers step into the parlor where Arla moved to take their coats. All the while she continued to prattle. "The chile, she sick an' all, I bin prayin' fo'er. Buh da Lor' he ain' lisnun. No suh! I bin prayin' harr an' she jez getin' poorer an' poorer by da day. Make 'er well Mazza Sawya, she a goo' chile, but she got a brokun 'eart, po' thing. She jez dyin' a brokun 'eart. You know, I swear, it jez' make me gonna cry."

In some form of distraction, I imagined how Arla shook her head and wrung her hands. I knew she was genuinely concerned for me. I imagined Mary was beside herself at hearing this, and had to exercise restraint from leaving Allen to run to my side. Their voices directed my dreams.

"Take us to her, if you would, please," Dr. Sawyer requested.

"Oh! I would! Yessuh, Mazza Sawya, I wou' indee'! Jez follow me thiz way. I brin' ya to 'er thiz mi'nt. We don' wanna be wasin no time. No suh! We don' wanna be doin' dat. I'z jez so sad, Missus Sawya, I'z so sad, I jez gonna cry, I jez know it."

I dreamed Arla was talking to herself and beginning to sob. I dreamed Mary was crying. I dreamed the whole world was crying in my room. I felt the presence of Dr. Sawyer sit upon the edge of my bed. He disrupted my sleep, disturbing me like a wave crossing a placid sea. My eyes were barely open and refused to focus. He picked up my lifeless wrist as if to lead me back to a distant shore.

"It's weak, but it's there, regular as a clock. Mary, help me turn her over onto her back."

"Her eyes are so dark and hollow, Allen. She looks as though she hasn't eaten for days."

Mary could not control her tears. She wiped her eyes to better see me as she assisted her husband. I was now awake, but despondent and confused after having been turned over. I moved more and more out of my dreams and into their world. I began to pay some attention to what was going on about me. My eyes let in some light. About the room, I saw words floating through the air, words with meaning that slowly fell into place.

"Arla, how long has she been down?" Dr. Sawyer asked.

"Oh! Two weeks, leas'! Buh, sinz day fo yezzaday, she don' wake up now. I'z scared Mazza Sawya. She don' eat. She ain' touch' a morsal fo mo'n a week! Ah makes up da bez griddle cakes n' scrapple, wit lozza surip n' jelly, buh no matta, Mazza Sawya, she ain' gonna ea' fo nutin. Ah bin beggin' 'er, I'z sayin', Please! Lizzy, ya gots ta ea' chile. She won' lizun. No suh! She jez don' lizun. Un uh! She jez lay there doin' nutin an' don' talk fo' no un. She lookin' terble. She bin scarin' me alf t' death! Yez suh! She scarin' me goo!" Arla removed a white handcloth from behind her apron and mopped her face.

Dr. Sawyer looked into the pupils of my eyes and spoke to me in a soothing voice.

"So tell me my precious Elizabeth, what is this nonsense about not eating? We all have to eat or we get weak and sick. You will eat or I will be left with no choice but to give you some of the worst, most god-awful medicine your young tongue has ever tasted. You hear me?"

He then turned toward Mary and spoke to her slowly and with confidence. He understood himself to be attending the needs of more than just a child.

"Oh, I'm sure she'll be fine, Mary. She's weak and in bad need of a meal. I expect she's a good fifteen pounds below her weight. I can feel those ribs sticking out, but then children seldom come with any extra fat to tide them over. She needs to start eating, and she's past the point of doing that without some encouragement.

"I would say that what she needs more than anything right now though, is a good dose of down to earth love and affection, and maybe a spoonful of honey in warm water to start." Dr. Sawyer poked and pulled at me.

45

"She is dehydrated. She needs water more than food at this time. Knowing how fond she is of you, Mary, I believe you can probably do her a great deal more good than I. So, why don't we wrap her warm in the blankets, remove her to the buggy, and bring her home with us as we have discussed."

Mary was unable to answer. She only passed her attention back and forth between Dr. Sawyer and me. She wiped her eyes repeatedly and then shook her head in agreement, swallowing hard and showing a sign of relief.

Dr. Sawyer lifted me into his arms effortlessly. My head floated about in a thick fog. I stirred, trying to shake myself free of this cloudy cover. I kept my eyes on Mary and tried to focus.

"Mary?"

"Yes, Liz. Yes, yes, it's me, honey. I'm here. Don't worry, I'm here, I won't leave again, I promise." she sobbed.

"Lady Rebecca is dead," I whispered.

"Yes, yes, I know."

I drifted away as Mary lowered her flooding eyes. I was soothed by the sound of her voice, the sound of her sobs.

Dr. Sawyer led the way downstairs and through the lobby, holding me firm within his arms. The hotel staff had taken to me from the start, and was intensely concerned for my well-being. I had become their sweetheart, wealthy and now above their rank, but still a maiden servant at heart who knew their work well and hadn't forgotten her roots. Because of this and their worry for me, they were quick to offer both blessings and a hand with baggage, blankets and doors. Mary trailed behind us, following through the large windowed doors as we exited the hotel.

Once outside, the brisk winter breeze worked to diminish my drowsiness, and I found myself reaching out for Mary. She had been distracted. She held back a moment under the canopy while Dr. Sawyer, followed by the hotel staff, stood at the curb. I saw her gaze upon the vermilion coach. She stared at the gold calligraphy that announced to all, the identity of the spirit concealed inside. A spirit she must have believed now watched in quiet judgment. She stared at the curtained cabin windows then lowered her eyes, feeling the weight of Lady Rebecca's presence. She spoke under her breath.

"She'll be fine, milady, I promise. I'll care for her myself. I give you my word. You must believe that my love for her equals your own. Rest in peace, milady, rest in peace."

Mary's words did as much for me as for Lady Rebecca.

FOUR

The ability to adapt is a blessing bestowed especially upon children, and it is assuredly a god-given form of survival in a world as hard and unforgiving to a child as the American frontier. Here, 'sudden death', heartbreak, and despair were the brutal realities of daily life in the best of times.

Fortunately, for young eyes like my own, there were also great numbers of new and remarkable sights to be seen, new and remarkable experiences in growing up that contributed immensely toward my recovery from the memory and pain of my past. I was swept away from things dark, and lifted up so I might marvel at all that was bright and fresh.

Understand, I saw nothing of these wondrous things at first, for I was locked deep within misery's dungeon, and all the change in the world was ineffectual until the moment Dr. Sawyer placed me in Mary's arms on that cold and dreary January day. Held firmly within her embrace, we rode away in the Sawyer buggy leaving behind the Barrington Hotel along with its scrambled assortment of memories and emotions, all overwhelming and much too powerful for my hopelessly shattered adolescent spirit.

From that afternoon on, Mary took to her own agenda. Her actions were beyond my control, and I was given no choice, but to accept the tenderness, the fragrance, and the feel of her love and affection. Her concern for me was undeniable, and she worked with determined persistence to coax me out of the gloom.

Oftentimes, Mary would lie down beside me in my bed. She would draw up the covers about us and wrap her arms tightly around me. It was easy then to dismiss the world. I would lay there with the warmth of her gentle breath washing over me as we slept. Her closeness brought me back to the safe haven I once knew in the cramped berths aboard the REBECCA. In those days we weathered out storms of a different kind.

Many a time, Mary and I lay together engaged in intimate conversation, she giving me the direction I needed to find my way back from a discouraging world, a world filled with new-found worries that worked hard to keep me wary.

"But what if *you* die?"

"We all die sometime, Liz, but I surely intend to be around long enough to raise my own family and watch over you."

"But what if Mr. Claussen dies?"

"Mr. Claussen can take care of himself. I wouldn't worry about him."

"I miss him so much, Mary. I just wish I could see him."

"I know Liz, but he is very far away—the other side of the world."

"He said he wanted to be my father. Why would he leave me?"

"Sometimes, love is so very painful, one is unable to face it."

"How can love be painful? I don't understand. Are you saying it hurts him to see me?"

"In a way, yes. It isn't anything that you do. He knows you wouldn't want to cause him pain, but when he looks at you, he sees all the things that are good and loving, and it reminds him of Lady Rebecca and her death, and all that he has lost. That makes him cry and hurt the same way that it made you cry and hurt. Love can be very painful, Elizabeth, and that is why he left. He needs to put that pain to rest so he can once again find happiness in his life."

"But I don't understand how he could leave me if he loves me as you say. Maybe he just wants to forget about me as well. Do you think he wants to forget about me? Would you ever leave me?"

"Of course not! Never, never—, never!"

"I would never leave you either. I would never have left him. I would never have wanted to forget him. I know that."

"He doesn't want to forget you, Liz. He just needs time. He'll keep you in his heart, I promise."

"I don't think I will ever be happy so long as he is gone."

Mary looked at me thoughtfully. "I never realized how close you felt to him, Liz."

"I miss him. I wish he would come home. We wouldn't have to talk about any of this. I wish he would come home now."

"Maybe so, but I don't believe that will happen for a very long time. I am certain he thinks of you often, but we must accept his being gone and go on with our lives. At least you are here for me, and I am here for you. We have each other, and I love you, Elizabeth. I love you very, very much."

"I love you too, Mary."

* * *

It seemed unlikely I would ever recover from the nightmares of Lady Rebecca's hellish death. Nights were bad for me. But as for her passing, I found comfort in knowing she went to heaven. Obviously, I couldn't reach out and touch her or feel her embrace as I might with Mary, but I felt she was always there for me, always present at my side. I spoke to her frequently during my days and religiously at night.

On the other hand, I found no comfort whatsoever in Mr. Claussen's passing. He was alive, and regardless of how many reasons or excuses given, I found his decision to leave incomprehensible and in my childish mind unforgivable. I felt he had lost sight of his home and all those who loved him. I felt he had lost sight of me. I was both broken-hearted and frustrated by my inability understand his motives or reach out to him. I was tormented by his absence. His departure tore open a wound in my heart that refused to heal.

The more I felt rejected, the more I obsessed with finding fragments of his existence for which to cling. Emotionally, he held me captive. He always had. I was drawn forcefully to him from the first day I saw him—from the first time I served him coffee at the Claussen estate. The power of his attraction never faded, not by time nor distance, and even now my desire to know of his whereabouts was often unbearable.

In spite of my anguish over this matter, I did begin to show signs of improvement in other ways. My thoughts of Mr. Claussen were bound to become less and less, as I invested my time putting my new surroundings to the test. I found Mary's home to be stable and supportive, and in time I regained my footing. I regained my appetite, my strength, and most important, a child's optimistic outlook on life—though still very much guarded. Time was what I needed most, and now having risen from the ash, my spirit barely noticed how the months passed me by.

50

* * *

Mr. Claussen trusted Mary implicitly. Aside from being Lady Rebecca's first maiden servant, he knew well how Mary had taken to me from the start. He knew that we had formed strong bonds during our journey from Sweden, bonds that had proved much to my good fortune.

And so, as soon as Mary thought me in good health and spirit, she made a point of fully explaining that Mr. Claussen had presented her and Dr. Sawyer with a generous gratuity in return for taking me into their household and seeing to my comfort and security. Her words sounded much more like an apology than an explanation. Mary was worried sick that I might feel her caring was done only for the money. It was absurd, even comical that I should be reassuring her about anything, and yet, it took some effort on my part to put her mind at ease.

This matter of the money troubled her to such an extent that it was only put to final rest on the day that I leaned over her lap as she sat fretting at her kitchen table. I placed my hands upon her shoulders and stared directly into her eyes.

"You had room for me in your heart long before a room in your house, Mary." She gazed upon me with wonder. A smile crept across her face, and I felt her relax. Her eyes were suddenly moist.

"Thank you so very much for saying that, Elizabeth."

Because of the arrangement made in my behalf, the burden of grief that I was obligated to carry from my past to my future was greatly diminished. In becoming Mary's charge, I would not become an orphan of means. Through her, I had regained one strongly forged link that anchored me to my history and to someone who understood who I was and from where I had come. I would maintain a sense of family. It allowed me to resolve my grief with someone close to my heart, someone who also had

51

been deprived, someone who understood my need for answers to questions never asked.

The arrangement removed me forever from the cold business-like atmosphere of the Barrington Hotel with its hallways and lobbies crowded full of souls, but empty of hearts. It placed me into a warm and cozy environment of gardens and puppies, the smell of dinner and the sound of bedtime prayers. I was to be protected by a family and raised on a foundation of love.

FIVE

Lady Rebecca's passing opened my eyes wide. It was common knowledge that her pregnancy had shaken me, leaving me insecure, but it hardly compared to the way her death had stripped me raw of a misguided belief that the world revolved around me.

In a brutal manner, fate forced me to understand that I was no more center of the universe than was a mudlark on the River Thames, and that I was no more capable of protecting myself from pain or injury than that scarred and downtrodden creature of a child. I had discovered through Lady Rebecca's death that I too was mortal.

It was hard to make sense of all the fearful things that now streamed into my young mind. When troubled, I often went out to sit in the grass beside Mary's garden where I focused my thoughts on Lady Rebecca and confided in her spirit. I couldn't understand why she had to be taken from me.

I couldn't understand as I looked across patches of varied color why the miserable weed, drab and unbecoming, a pest to all, was blessed by God to withstand the wildest of wind and gale, and yet the gentlest rain destroyed those flowers that offered Him only beauty. Was it His way of gathering a bouquet? Was Lady Rebecca beautiful to Him? Was she to be collected?

I was confused about this and so much more. My young mind suffered under the weight of mistrust and concern that accompanied my premature entrance into adulthood. There were questions—many, many, questions. Who in my life might become sick or die next? What was Small Pox and Measles? What was Consumption? What was Cholera and where was 'Out West'? Where was China for that matter?

Where was Mr. Claussen? And, what kind of man was President Madison, and who were the War Hawks, and why were they always demanding that we go to war? Who was this fearsome Shawnee Chief Tecumseh, and why was he killing all the god-fearing settlers?

To my eyes, life appeared a terrible thing, akin to images in warped mirrors that reflected half-truths and illusions ready to mislead me. It was fraught with lies and ever-changing trickery. The air was filled with warnings. Everybody seemed to be running from one frightful thing or another. Whether it be the Indians or the English, disease, or disaster, I could see now that it was necessary to let go my childish ways and learn how to protect myself from the unexpected—the sooner the better.

And so, I said good-bye to my make believe world where dolls were ladies and lords, and dreams were reality. I determined to change my course and pay closer attention to real-life people and real-life events that surrounded me. I felt pressed to learn how these things might affect me. I wanted to know more about the world of adults so I might comprehend where I was to fit into the scheme of things, and how best to prepare for the horrors that seemed inevitable.

Fortunately for me, it wasn't necessary to go to 'China' or even walk the streets of Boston in order to learn what was on the mind of grown-ups. Simply hanging about the infirmary offered me all of a lesson I might ever need. I spent many an hour listening in on the conversations that occurred in Dr. Sawyer's office and the front lobby museum. Eventually, I was able to gain a feel for their world and the state of affairs, not only about Boston, but also across much of the country.

The infirmary was small, but far better informed than most of those places frequented by the general public. Whether people stopped in to marvel at the artifacts in Dr. Sawyer's museum, or to pick up their medicine; they were bound to receive a good dose of advice from visiting patients or '*regulars*' regarding their health— and the health of the nation.

Few stepped back out onto the street without leaving a little 'piece of their mind' in return for 'whatever it was worth.' There was never a lack of opinion to be sure; and because the patients represented all walks of life from the 'well-heeled haves' to the 'hopeless have-nots', it proved to be a good starting place for me to acquire a rather broad and evenly balanced view of the adult world that up to this point I had paid little if any mind.

Oftentimes, as on this day, voices of our friends and patients could be heard in the lobby adding to the air of controversy regarding the English. I learned quickly that all conversations pretty much boiled down to the English at one point or another. I came to understand that in America the English were held responsible for all that was good or bad in our lives.

* * *

"Mr. Johnson, what I am saying to you, sir, is that you must try and calm yourself. You are much too tense for your own good. You need to settle down, or you will no longer have need for these stomach pills, for you will have no stomach, or worse, no need for a stomach."

"Settle myself! Surely, you jest, doc. How can anybody be settled now days with the current state of affairs? Just look out your window; look down the street, look aroun' town.

54

Everyone's walkin' faster, talkin' faster—hurry, hurry, hurry—scramblin' 'bout like headless chickens. Commotion, that's all there is, commotion and confusion at every corner. Anyone with a brain is gonna be worried, doc, and for good reason. My only fear is half of 'em out there still got no idea how bad things are really gettin'. Ya know what I'm sayin'?

"There's plenty of talkin' and whisperin' goin' on, but if ya listen, ya realize half of them folks still think this is a great ado about nothing. They're illiterate fools, ya know what I'm sayin'? If they knew half of what I know, they would all be in here gettin' stomach pills. Mark my words, they'll be finding out soon enough and you'll be gettin' rich. My advice to you, doc, is to start stockin' up on your pills." With a certain air of arrogance, Mr. Johnson resigned himself to the futility of trying to enlighten the ignorant masses.

"An' tell me, Josh, what is it that you know so well an' figuah the ra-est of us have a lack of wit t' unduhstand?"

"I'll tell ya what I know, Hubert. We're on the doorstep of war! War, I say! Trouble is, everybody's talkin' it, but few are believin' it. I'm here to tell you, I've been listenin' to them War Hawks, an' they are leanin' hard on the Congress—mighty hard. Make no mistake, I've heard enough of their ranting to realize that we're about to push the king too far, and we'll be payin' for our stupidity."

"You worrah too much, Josh. A war-ah is pointless."

"Ya see, doc? That is exactly what I'm talkin' about. Nobody appreciates the gravity of our position. It isn't like we have the greatest navy afloat and the ability to call the king's bluff, ya know what I'm sayin'? But, I promise you this; we will surely have the greatest collection of English marines ever assembled, and once they land on our shores, you can bet there'll be plenty o' hell to pay.

"Not to worry if you're a War Hawk! Lord, no. You won't see any marines landin' down south in Louisiana or out west in

St. Louis where they all live to stir up a ruckus, no sir! They'll be landin' right here in our harbor an' firing rounds across our front yards. And should they decide not to get their hands an' feet dirty, I guarantee they will simply double or triple the number of ships in that bloody blockade that is already starvin' us half to death as it is.

"You sound just like them folks in the street, Hubert. *'Nah, nah, nah, there ain't gonna be no war. We whipped their asses once, an' we can do it again.'* They're all out there in the street a braggin' 'bout how we fought hard and won our cherished independence. Independence? What independence? We have no independence. Ya hear what I'm sayin'? We-have-no-in-de-pen-dence, Hubert."

Mr. Johnson made a face as though he had bitten into a sour apple. His pudgy little body seemed to wrinkle all at once. "Whether you care to believe it or not, we live under the influence of a king and an empire that controls the seas and that's a fact. We may have had our revolution, won our battles and all matters of principle, but we are not nearly so independent as we would like to believe and don't kid yourself to think different.

"We were, we are, and we'll always be joined hand and hand with the king, his cronies and colonies. That is, if we have any hope of turnin' a profit and puttin' food on the table. I say with all due respect, it ain't the bible, it's business that determines what shall an' shall not be. Ya hear what I'm sayin'? Business determines who succeeds and who fails, who lives an' who dies, not a preacher or a mob of Bostonians who raise arms an' do a lot of saber rattlin', but can't hit the broad side of a barn." Mr. Johnson gasped for a breath of air.

"Mebbee, so, Josh, but—."

"No, no, listen, Hubert. I have heard those War Hawks and their misinformed cries. Freedom! Freedom, at any cost! The farther away from the coast they live, the louder they scream to be heard. No wonder! What do they have to lose? They are too busy grabbin' land and plowin' fields for profit, ya know what

I'm sayin'? Why would they care about our relations with the English? Why should they care about a harbor town?" Mr. Johnson was nearly panting when Dr. Sawyer stepped in to calm him.

"I'd advise you to let these things work themselves out on their own, Mr. Johnson. I stand here and watch the pressure of your blood build in your face as you sit talking about such affairs, none of which you have any power to change. You are going to pop your top, my friend, and you'll have no reason to worry yourself about an Englishman again in this life."

"Now, you heeya me out, Josh," said Hubert. "You just slow yo-ah ha-art down a minute and heeya me out. If a Warh Hawk cries out fo-ah justice against English tyranny, it is because he believes in his h'art by all that he has seen, that you an' yo-ah kind arh mo-ah concerned with the bottom line of yo-ah ledger sheets than the impressments of ou-wa boys by the British navy. I have seen—."

"Me and my kind!" cried Josh. "I beg your pardon, Hubert, but it might do you well to know that it isn't *'me and my-ah kind'*, but the commoners in this town who prefer to see the impressments carried out. It is not I who feel that the flood of English immigrants to our shore has driven my wages down to nothing. It's those folks in the streets who want them outta here, be it impressments or whatever—not me and my kind."

Hubert countered, "I don't know, Josh. It seems to me everuhwhe-uh 'cross the country people arh up in ahms demanding justice 'cept fo-ah heeya in Boston. Heeya we arh—the ha'dest hit of all, sufferin' the most, an' the powahs-that-be seem mo-ah concerned with smoothing the fe'thers of the crown fo-ah the sake o' profit than keeping ouwah boys at home with their-uh wives an' family or-ah standin' up fo' ouwah own country."

"I beg to differ—."

"Shush, Josh. Shush! Just shush. You've had your say. Now, heeya me out. Ther-ah is plenty of ha'dship, I agree, but I also believe ther-ah arh a numbah o' folks in yo-ah league who arh making out handsomely with this blockade by means of favorable, an' I might add, hypuh-critical contracts with the English, an' they don't want their-ah boat rocked —."

"Oh, hogwash, Hubert! That is pure malarkey, and I take offense to it. Mark my words; a few boys taken for runnin' the blockade'll seem like child's play after you've been here to see the fall of the city. And don't think it can't happen. I'm already down forty percent for the year, and have had to let many a good man go for lack of work. Last year I was off by a full thirty per-cent. Who do you think that is killin'—me—or the man at the bottom?

"I'm tellin' ya, business is being hard hit by these ongoing disputes, and financial devastation is in the comin'. Confrontin' the navy or needlin' the king'll only irritate an already sensitive wound. It's bad all along the East Coast, but it's god-awful here in Boston, and it's gettin' worse by the day. We need the English, my friend. Think what you will, fool yourself as you wish, but we need them, ya know what I'm sayin'?

"Everyone thinks because I'm in the business of importing, it's only my problem. Not true! It starts with shipping and then like a disease it works its way inland. Pretty soon there are no wares left in the city and there'll be no need for your services, Hubert, because who in hell needs to fill a wagon when you can't even fill your own pockets?

"Mark my words, the street'll be teemin' with folks wishin' t' be impressed upon a ship of His Majesty for the sake of a hot meal. Food won't be found easily in Boston by the end of the year. You'll see, you'll see, mark my words, you'll see!" Mr. Johnson shook his finger at Hubert. "Tell him, doc. You seem to have a pretty good handle on what goes down. What do you think? Am I right or wrong?"

"I think you are both right, and understand I am not trying to sidestep the issue to avoid taking sides. I view England much the same as a rich mother-in-law. She is family, and we put up with her because there could be much to gain, but she always feels like she has a duty to meddle in our affairs. We love the gifts, but hate it whenever she stops by."

"Well put, Doc, but—we should pay a lot more attention to the rich mother-in-law and gifts part, an' what we stand to gain, ya know what I'm sayin'?" Mr. Johnson concurred.

"Doc, I couldn't agree with you mo-ah, so long as I live in Boston, but I've been a wainwright fo-ah goin' on thirty some ye-ahs, an' I've made wagons fo-ah haulin' wares as far-ah west as the sun'll set. Have ya any idea how many of those wagons make return trips from the fronteeya fo' one reason or anoth-uh? I talk t' them folks on a daily basis, an' I'm heeya to tell ya that they have nothin' good t' say 'bout the English whatso-evuh. They'd just as soon shoot an Englishman as look at 'im. The Warh Hawks will have their-ah way. You may mark my words. It's an enormous country we live in. It's about mo-ah than just Boston, and out there-ah the Warh Hawks rule.

"Out there-ah, them folks arh dealing with the Indians, just as you said, Mr. Johnson. Out there-ah, they arh being butch-ahd in their'ah beds by the redskins an' it's the English who's been supplyin' the whiskey and weapons and workun' 'em up. Let us not kid ouwahselves, the English have no desi-ah to lose their-ah grip on the furring trade an' they desperately want ou-wah migration no-arth an' westward t' be stopped. Of course, they would gladly pay the Indians to do their-ah dirty work an' the proof is in the amount of weapons flooding in from no-arth of the bo-arder. You should talk to those folks in Michigan or Illinois and Ohio. They want the English out by bully or-ah ball, what-evuh works the fastest, an' I can't say I blame 'em one bit.

"I also think you ovuh-look the numbuh of French that popu-late this land from he-yuh to St. Louis, from the mouth of the Mississippi to Canada. I suggest you stop by an' pay them a visit. We do a tremendous amount of trade with the French an' I hear it is quite profitable. I think you will find right off, some may suppo-art Napoleon, some may not, but none of the French will take kindly to any notion of becoming British subjects, on that you can count, sir-ah."

* * *

Mary and I were heading down the stairs on our way to market. All morning, we had little choice but to listen to the men arguing their passions, for their raised voices sounded throughout the infirmary, up and down, end to end.

"Will you listen to those men," she whispered across her shoulder as I followed her along the hall. "It's a wonder they aren't hoarse." I was still giggling over the remark when we entered the lobby. Mary spoke up at once unabashed.

"As the Lord is my witness, I am of a mind to go and see Johnny the carpenter and hire him to build a podium that I might place right here in the middle of this lobby. You gentlemen ought to hear yourselves. It gets louder down here than in Parker's coffeehouse. I'm willing to bet, should I start selling coffee; I would do a better profit than do you in doctoring, Mr. Sawyer." She walked up to her husband and kissed him on the cheek. The men about the room chuckled heartily.

"My dear, somebody has to work out the problems of the world. If not us then who? From all that you have heard, do we not at least exercise our right to opinion, do we not stand for social justice and freedom of speech?"

"On the surface it appears so, but underneath I can't help to ask if it has more to do with social justice or just socializing to avoid an honest day's work.

"Ouch, but those arh mighty unkind words fo-ah men with such noble cause as ow-ahs, Mrs. Sawyah." Hubert feigned a wounded heart, but Mary continued.

"Besides which—, freedom, I have discovered, can also be a catchall term for doing whatever one chooses—right or wrong. Have you never noticed that scoundrels locked up in the brig protest that their rights and freedom have been trampled?"

A tiny bell over the front door rang out. In walked Sal Carter. He was another importer like Mr. Johnson and they were good friends, but poles apart both physically and in their views. Mr. Johnson did most of his business with the English, whereas Mr. Carter did his with the French. Mr. Carter was a handsome man.

"Good day, all." The greeting was returned.

"Good morning, Mrs. Sawyer, Miss Elizabeth."

"Good morning, Mr. Carter," we answered.

"Is it not a most pleasant morning? A great day for a walk." The cheery look upon Mr. Carter's face suddenly turned pensive. He looked about the room. "Such poor response—do I sense a certain tension in the air? Ah-haa! Surely, I have interrupted a good debate. Wonderful! Who wishes my point of view?" Everyone laughed. Hubert spoke up.

"Mar-uh is setting us straight on some o' ouwah misconceptions."

"That is not true, Hubert," said Mary.

"She has raised the possibility that as a nation we may have too much freedom fo-ah ou-wah own good."

"I never said that!" Mary was horrified to be accused of such a scandalous statement.

Sal jumped right in.

"One can never have too much freedom, Mary. Look at how we thrive. This country is built on freedom, and who can dispute the way in which it flourishes. Freedom is the blood of the land. Freedom is the character of this country. No one can deny it or ever take it away."

"Ya know, judging by the count of ships off our shore, I believe the King begs to differ." Mr. Johnson countered.

"Blah! The king's a bloody idiot. You think he will take away our freedom? Never! I will tell you what he will do. He'll continue harassing us until he whips up the anger in the best of us and then we'll do him in. Those English bastards, I have had a gut full of their kind. Oh—I beg your pardon, Mary, Elizabeth. My emotions get ahead of my manners, forgive me my foul mouth."

"You're forgiven, but are they really so different than us, Mr. Carter? I mean, Johnson, Carter, Sawyer, to me they sound like good family names that are very English." Sal couldn't be bothered with the obvious. Instead, he looked straight at her and spoke out with conviction.

"Mary, let me tell you a little secret about the king. He is too arrogant to see that we Americans are aware of our free state and all that it represents. He still believes us to be stupid unthinking commoners accustomed to bending on one knee. He believes we have no brains, and so makes statements like he hasn't returned the Great Lakes because of our war debts. What nonsense! He is scrambling to profit from furring those waters in order to fill his coffers, and we all know it.

"The war debts are only his. His campaign against Napoleon must be funded. He needs money, but he would bleed us dry if for no other reason than to spite us. Let him scramble as he might, let him demand we give allegiance to the Church of England, let him demand we pay taxes to the crown, let him block the passage of our ships. The more he tries to chip away at our freedom, the more he tries to box us in—the more he points out all that we have to lose."

"Joshua seems to feel we should work to improve ouwah relations with the King—maybe considuh conforming to some of his demands."

"Blah! Hubert, pay him no mind. Josh says stuff like that when his bottom line gets meager. It clouds his vision and he starts spewing nonsense."

"I beg your pardon!"

"I feel for your poor profits, Josh, I told you before, stick with the French, but you're not one to listen."

"I don't have to listen—."

"In fact, look to the French and remember that no one has ever successfully petitioned for his freedom. The French were the only ones who tried, and it got them nowhere, so they took it by force. God bless them all. They taught us well.

"No, Mary. I say, there's no such thing as too much freedom, so long as your actions aren't injurious to others. Ask yourself, why it is that those red skinned savages, who are primitive by nature, fight like the devil while enlightened Europeans tend to succumb to their masters no matter how oppressive their rule.

"Europeans are too passive by nature. They avoid confrontation until pushed into a corner with no place left to go. Before their eyes, you may take something from them, and they turn away and live with less. That's the trouble. All Europeans except for the French, have been raised to take their beating and bow to their master without complaint. They're all slaves of a sort; they just don't know it. In this country only slaves are slaves. We know it, and we fight like wildcats for our freedom. We stand up smartly for what we believe and bow to no one. To hell with kings and masters!"

"Hallelujah! To hell with kings masters! Hear ye, hear ye! Well said Mr. Cahtah." The men chimed in together. I followed Mary as she rolled her eyes and walked over to Dr. Sawyer.

"To hell with kings and masters. My word, such talk is old hat. We women have been saying that about you gentlemen for as long as I can remember. I am off to the market, Allen," she embraced him. "Come along, Liz." The room was suddenly silent. Her comment squashed the discussion flat. We stepped outside, leaving the men, their grins and passions behind a closed door.

Yet, all about town in the streets there resounded echoes of the same arguments for or against the crown. Between the local tavern walls, I would hear men bellowing their points of view over pints of beer. They eagerly fueled already heated conversations and forced their impassioned convictions into opposing faces. It was hardly uncommon to hear or see overworked emotions howling behind swinging fists, leaving Mary and I to sidestep a brawl.

What I would not see in the lobby, but was also commonplace in the street, were the spokesmen pitching political differences to whatever crowds might gather and listen at the center of town or at the many middle-of-the-road markets. They were hard to miss, for they risked life and limb in order to perch themselves as high as humanly possible atop mountains of crates or barrels where they might holler out their declarations a little louder and a little farther. The brave souls or underpaid fools would scale anything that would give them the advantage of a head's height over their opponent.

Oftentimes the criers moved their bellowing down the lane in gigantic strides as they balanced atop walking stilts, stirring up passels of kids, each rascal daring the other to run between the crier's wooden legs. It added a good deal of cursing to the pandemonium, but didn't stop the town criers from leading their converts forward in hopes of gaining strength through numbers.

These boisterous characters marched up and down the streets, collecting new supporters and scaring the devil out of the cattle and chickens in the road as they paraded banners, posted fliers, and expressed hardened opinions. Groups sympathetic to either side of the issue paid out good money to employ the loudest of town criers—the bigger the mouth the better the pay.

Commotion and concern about war swirled about me daily. The papers were filled with commentary and reports of unrest, and although hostilities did occur, even massacres in the north, it never seemed to actually touch any one of us personally. The closest I ever felt to the conflict was when the local militia put on a display of military might for our benefit at the public grounds with all the trappings and fanfare that could be afforded. We generally laughed and hoped we wouldn't have to count on them for our defense.

There were other signs to be noted however, such as news of neighbors, who were forced to pack up and travel to stronger economies—those free of the blockade. The business community was indeed taking a beating, and everybody appeared to suffer except for a select few like Mr. Claussen.

I was very sensitive to any matter that concerned Mr. Claussen. We were known about town to have a close relationship with him, and word of his success reached our ears regularly, most generally in hopes we would convey how someone had been outwitted and suffered unfairly—in their opinion—by his prowess. To hear all told, his ships were sailing free upon the open sea much to the disbelief, amazement, and disgust of his competitors.

It was precisely this matter being discussed in the infirmary when Mary and I returned from the market. Mr. Claussen probably ranked second only to the British on the list of topics for discussion in Boston's shipping community. As with the British, I had heard arguments about Claussen many times before, and I wasn't surprised to hear them now considering both Mr. Johnson and Mr. Carter were importers, and still conversing in the lobby upon our return. Mary went on to the kitchen, but I held back. I always wanted to know what was being said about Mr. Claussen.

"You're dreamin', Sal, ya know what I'm sayin'? Even if the sea swallowed up Boston, it wouldn't make the least bit of difference to Claussen. Who cares if the Claussen Wharf is bigger or smaller that the India or Central Wharf? Mark my words, Boston is nothing more than a stop point on a globe covered by his fleets, a place to drop anchor, have a pint, and take a piss!

"It isn't like we don't have enough trouble with the English or that godforsaken Embargo Act, lets just pile on a heap of competition from Claussen. His ships suck up every profit that can be chocked in a hold. He's just about done this city in. Look around; the consequences are hardly invisible unless you happen to be standing in Claussen's shoes. I mean, I don't know how he does it. I mean, on his docks you'd swear there was a rummage sale every day of the week. Yet, India Wharf as I hear tell is barely one quarter filled. Ya know what I'm sayin'".

"That's probably true, Josh, but why take it out on Claussen? Face it, he's smart, brilliant I suppose. He simply out thinks you. He switches his base of operations as easily as he switches his flags."

"Ah of-tun see the Swedish mahrquee flyun' on his masts", said Hubert.

"That's right, and he switches his cargo. One minute his holds are filled with English imports, the next it's east coast lumber. He's a clever man, Josh, clever. The man makes fools out of us for sure, but in whatever business of shipping he engages, he is always legal and on top, and in the right place at the right time. Sometimes all his ships disappear at once, not a one to be found. I hear they go to New York, or New Haven, or farther south yet. Who knows? He makes a killing, and I admit I have never seen anything like it, never, but I don't hold it against the man."

"Say what ya like, Sal. He doesn't play fair. He's got a deal going with the English and God only knows whom else. I don't know exactly what it is, but it ain't fair for the rest of us. And you know what I'm sayin'."

Dr. Sawyer was supporting his chin as he looked up at the ceiling and voiced his thoughts aloud. "You are right in what you say, Josh. I remember Claussen mentioning on more than one occasion that he had a special article of non-intervention given to him by an English Captain or Admiral, or something of the sort. I can't remember. Stowington! That was it. Yes,

66

Captain Stowington. The English won't touch him because of it. But, I firmly believe it isn't just Claussen or his articles. He has the best of the best working for him, top-notch traders and speculators under his employ, and they know their business."

"I am certain what you say is true," said Mr. Carter. "I have heard of those articles many times myself over the years. According to scuttlebutt, Claussen actually rescued Stowington's man-o'-war if ya can believe that, but then who can dispute such a story after seeing him time and time again sail through the blockade straight into port. I say proof is in the pudding."

"Ya know, it's more than that," said Mr. Johnson. "I mean, I've heard tell that when he returns from England, he sails directly for the English ships first and gives them their pick of the goods before dropping anchor here in port. We worry about our ships getting sunk, and the English worry about *him* getting sunk. Ya know what I mean? It is incredible, preposterous—all of it. If it wasn't for the way he smooths over relations with the English, I'd say it was almost un-American."

"Actually, its very American. He profits enormously at British expense by shipping Maine timber to England on those special lumber ships he builds. Those trees are ready-made masts, three feet in diameter, a hundred tall, and only Claussen has a fleet of ships with decks that can handle them."

"I don't wanna hear it. Him and his special ships. He's a pain in my ass."

"Now, Josh, I'm just telling you, don't be getting yourself worked up over Claussen like you do over the English. No good will come of it."

"Please, doc, spare me the advice. You have done well by his acquaintance, not so the rest of us."

"Lo-ard, you arh a-whining!" Hubert broke his silence. "Did you evuh stop to considuh where-ah this town would be if Claussen wasn't bringin' in shiploads o' goods. There-ah 'd be no Boston. You said so yourself, Josh, the India dock is practically empty of store-ahs. You all see the money he makes on his ventures, and you all despise him for it, but you fail to see the money that evruhone else down the line is making from his success.

"It is like you said befo-ah, Josh, 'it starts with shipping and then works it's way inland'. He could veruh well be the only solid trade connection we have to the outside world. I think you should give the man a little mo-ah credit. If the poor-ah aren't poor-ah enough, think of the misery they would enjoy without the profits of his success. He puts food into the mouths of many. Besides, the kids love him. They ar-uh always runnin' about his docks looking fo-ah handout."

"I commend you for voicing such an unpopular opinion, Hubert. I must say I'm inclined to agree with you," said Dr. Sawyer. "I for one feel we owe a great deal to the man. Fact of the matter is, the community owes much to him and there can be no denying it. I must say again, having known Mr. Claussen personally, I found him to be a fine upstanding individual, who fears the Lord and pays his taxes. I have never known him to knowingly do a soul harm. He is generous to a fault with family and friends. He is a man of good will and reputation, and he deserves our respect regardless of what he appears to be in the eyes of his competitors."

To hear Dr. Sawyer speak in Mr. Claussen's behalf was all it took to set loose my heartfelt loyalties, and I spoke up fiercely in defense of Mr. Claussen without invitation.

"I wish you all to know that if you knew Mr. Claussen as I know him, you would never question his character. He thinks nothing of himself, only of others. He thinks of the homeless and the hungry. He thinks of children. He thinks of orphans and people like me. Oh, what a curse it should be to live among men with character such as his. The day Mr. Claussen sailed from our shore was indeed a sad day for us all, and I for one miss him dearly."

I found myself glaring at Mr. Johnson, daring him to dispute me, but he said nothing, nor did anyone else. From the corner of my eye, I saw Mary moving in my direction with a look of concern in her expression. If I had been closer, she probably would have yanked me out of the room. Women never spoke freely on such issues among men. It was not their place, and although most anyone was allowed to voice an opinion within the infirmary, it was considered highly irregular for a woman to speak in such a bold fashion. It was even less acceptable for a young girl such as myself to voice anything at all without being viewed as entirely disrespectful. But, any statement that I perceived to be contrary to Mr. Claussen's good name easily annoyed me, and I showed little restraint in charging off in his defense.

Mr. Sawyer always had the final word in these debates, and being aware of my sensitivities, made no excuse for my outburst. Quite possibly, he was grateful to simply let my remarks dissipate as the front door opened with the ring of the bell, and Mrs. Covington stepped into our midst.

"Good morning," said she.

"Good morning," said Dr. Sawyer and the debaters.

"You have made your point clear as crystal, Elizabeth," said Dr. Sawyer to me quite suddenly. "And with that, I am now called to duty. Please, Mrs. Covington, if you will follow me."

Dr. Sawyer removed himself from the conversation and escorted Mrs. Covington to his office. Sal, Josh, Hubert and the others having passed too much time and coffee resigned themselves to return to their duties, and the air of the infirmary was once again quieted.

"Come along, Elizabeth."

"Coming."

There was only the slightest hint of discomfort in Mary's voice, though merely calling me Elizabeth instead of Liz often spoke volumes of what was on her mind. I did as she asked, but as I followed her upstairs, my mind moved in a different direction.

Saying nothing further, I was focused on the extent to which Mr. Claussen influenced our lives. I thought it phenomenal considering that he was never to be seen, let alone found doing business in Boston. He remained aloof and unencumbered by the politics of our world. His concerns were monitored and controlled by subordinates. To those of us in Boston, Mr. Claussen existed in places of rumor, places unreachable at opposite ends of the earth. He was only close to home when his competitors brought to light an accounting of profits made by him in their backyards.

All of these discussions and issues contributed to my lessons in adult affairs. True to Mr. Johnson's predictions, war had been declared and President Madison eventually gave one William Harrison command of the entire Northwest region with orders to clear it of both the British and the Indians. Harrison was a Kentucky military hero, who had been given ten thousand men to lead, but late season rains and mud bogged them down. The entire war campaign seemed to fizzle. So too did our glorious Boston.

New York overtook our impoverished town as the place of growth and commerce, and worst of all, it overtook our historic command of the sea. Even in cultural matters, Boston lost out to Philadelphia. I saw the prosperity of Boston crumble about us, and I tried to stay prepared for whatever ill fate should befall me during its demise.

However, to my good fortune, I was blessed with no further tragedy. And so, in spite of war and our town's financial and cultural woes, in spite of its loss of pride and the fatigue of surviving day to day, at the infirmary my life progressed peacefully and in a most pleasant fashion under Mary's care and Mr. Claussen's distant hand.

SIX

As my guardian, one of Mary's earliest decisions in my behalf was to remove me from the misery of the private school that I had been forced to attend. She had listened with compassion to each and every tearful tale of my schoolroom experience. I knew that on more than one occasion Mary had approached Lady Rebecca hoping to win me some relief, but her efforts were hardly successful. Her arguments fell upon deaf ears because Lady Rebecca believed learning to stand on my own two feet and face the world was every bit as important as my learning to add or subtract. And school was the perfect place to learn both.

It may have been Lady Rebecca's dogged insistence about my attending school that opened Mary's eyes to her own lack of knowledge. Or it may have been her marriage to Dr. Sawyer, an intelligent, well-known and respected individual, upon whose arm she was escorted through the homes of Boston's prominent families that caused her to voice a hint of her insecurity.

For whatever her reasons, one thing was clear. Mary was committed to improving her position through education, and although she had been quick to remove me from the classroom, she was equally determined that nothing would cause me to suffer her apparent embarrassment, which she must have found every bit as humiliating as the teasing I suffered in class. Learning was to be a priority in our house.

"Do you mean it?" I asked, fearful of a joke.

"Done. Finished. No more. I asked Mr. Claussen specifically about the issue of school, and he said I was to decide what was best for you. I decide—no more."

"Yes! Oh, thank-you, thank-you, thank-you, Mary!"

"Now understand, that doesn't mean no more book-learning; it means no more school."

"I understand, and I promise you I will study. I will study everything, and I will do so dutifully, so long as I don't have to go back to class."

"You don't have to worry about that; it's over, no more class. I aim to bring private tutors here to the house."

"Can we employ Mr. Gaines? He was so good to me. He was fair and honest. He stood in my favor on every occasion, even to face Lady Rebecca."

"Really."

"I swear."

"In that case, I'll pay him a visit. I'll extend my offer when I see him."

"Who else will you ask?"

"At this point I am not sure. If you must know the truth of it, this is not all that it seems. It isn't as easy as one, two, three. First of all, it has been pointed out to me quite clearly on more than just one occasion that book learning beyond basic reading and arithmetic is considered immoral for women. Most instructors won't even discuss teaching women anything above the basics."

"What?" I stared at Mary. "What are you saying? We can't be taught? We're not supposed to learn anything?"

"Does that surprise you? There are many things you have yet to discover about this world you are entering. It is a man's world, and never think different. It's a man's vote, a man's decision, and a man's wrath that you'll face."

"Am I not supposed to learn anything?"

"Oh, you can learn all you want, so long as it involves scrubbing laundry, washing dishes, raising children and how to make a husband happy in his home. That is encouraged, I assure you. But when it comes to other things in life, things beyond that, things that you might find very interesting, then it's a different story."

"Do men think we are stupid?"

"I don't think stupid is the word. Fragile might be a better term. Most men believe subjects such as the discipline of long division too easily overwhelm the female mind. They contend that there is a risk run, should you do a taxing problem in division for example, whereby you might faint, or worse go insane." Mary contorted her face to imitate a lunatic.

"You can't be serious." My eyes never left her. I was watching for some sign of a game. It could only be this, otherwise how was I to believe the absurdity of what I was being told.

"You know how much you enjoy watching Allen do his work, how curious you are about it? Well, medicine is considered too indelicate and entirely inappropriate for a woman's gentle quality. It makes no difference that we have stomach enough to midwife or go through the grizzly ordeal of childbirth ourselves. That somehow is different. I would love to see how one of those tutors might hold up to such an experience.

"Geography, it is said will cloud our minds and distract us from the teachings of the bible. And then there is music, beautiful music, considered to be frivolous and inarguably sinful by a good many of the religious congregations about this area. god forbid we should sing, let alone learn to read notes."

"You mean all those songs we learned to sing aboard the REBECCA were sinful? We were actually in sin all the time we sang? Does that mean all sailors are sinful?" I was astonished.

"Stop, stop! I don't know." Mary laughed. "I would wager most all sailors are indeed sinful, but I hardly feel it has anything to do with their songs. However, there are plenty of folks who believe singing is as bad as drinking. I for one, don't. I believe singing is good for the soul."

73

"So do I!" I was indignant. "Tale of a whale, and what about Lady Rebecca's song? That is sinful? I thought it was beautiful."

"I agree, Liz. The world is a strange place, filled full of strange people. It makes for some interesting situations. Unfortunately, we women are all too often on the short end of the stick."

"So what do we do?" I asked.

"Well, we do what we can. Where there is a will there is a way. Talk has been going around about opening a public school for those who are privileged enough to attend, but so far it is mostly talk, and I question whether there will be a free seat for a woman or a girl for that matter. And in all honesty, I would be rather embarrassed to attend school with a class of young-sters. I would much prefer to learn in private by a tutor who thinks of me as a project worth completing, or a truckload of tutors, if that's what it takes."

"I thought you just said they won't teach us book-learning."

"I did, but we have one weapon in our arsenal that reigns supreme."

"What's that?"

"Money. Lots and lots of money," Mary laughed. "Terrible isn't it, but I can't wait to listen to all the reasons why they feel they might set a bad example by teaching us anything of value as I keep increasing the amount of money I place on the table. The first lesson will be theirs for the learning, for they are pompous fools and if they don't prove it to themselves, then I will."

"I can't imagine Mr. Gaines to be like that."

"And I am not saying he is. He may be the exception. There are always exceptions."

"So what does all this mean? Because I am about to become a young woman, I can no longer do whatever it is I want? I can't study what interests me?"

"That's pretty much it."

"I don't understand, Mary. As long as I am a girl, I can do whatever I want, but when I grow into a woman and start taking my studies seriously, I can't. Even if I am only two or three years older?"

"You can thank men and their intellect for such remarkable absurdities."

"But, Dr. Sawyer and Mr. Claussen never seemed to hold that view. I always thought they wanted me to learn as much as I could."

"They always have. It's like I said; there are always exceptions. Never forget how fortunate we are to have such forward thinking men in the family. We have been spared."

"This is crazy, Mary. I don't get it. Why was Lady Rebecca so insistent that I attend school and study? She of all people must have known I wasn't supposed to learn anything. It seems a waste of time."

"Liz, honey, Lady Rebecca never took a second seat to anybody. She brought herself up by her own bootstraps. She learned to read at an early age. She understood the power of knowledge. She was self-taught by all she read while in the orphanage. Remember, it was Lady Rebecca who kept pounding into your head the need to stand up and face the world? Never back down. Believe in yourself. Take charge of your life. Well, as you get older you will better see why she pushed you so."

Mary was correct. I remembered those lessons clearly. They were often painful events from my past, but for the first time ever, I was suddenly feeling something of admiration for Lady Rebecca instead of my usual feelings of love and affection or dismay.

I spent a number of days mulling over this fact that as a woman I was prohibited from reaching out for whatever stars I wished to hold. For a good long time, I could only look at Mary and shake my head over the idea of being relegated or pressured into some backward bastion considered to be the female domain. This had been a revelation that I was completely at a loss to understand.

What I did understand, was how I was only to be saved by the persuasions of money. Money, I was quick to learn, was an all-powerful tool. It was an equalizer that made the weak as powerful as the strong. It made women as fearsome as men. I watched Mary use it quite effectively to steer our tutors in whatever direction she pleased.

And so, in the end, I did study long division and geography. I also studied music, manners, and basic medicine among many other subjects, all without restriction. I was spared nothing, and not only did I escape insanity, but I never fainted once. I enjoyed everything and refused only one suggestion, the study of French. It was a foolish and stubborn decision, but I had inherited a low opinion of Napoleon from Mr. Claussen, and believed it would do nothing other than hinder me in my attempts to speak fluent English.

From those days on, all my education, both primary and higher was received at home. The private instruction not only provided me with the very best in learning, but it also gave Mary an opportunity to gain the education she so longed to possess. She was an eager student and this only encouraged me to study harder, for I was blessed to have at the same time a wonderful classmate and a determined guardian.

As for our tutors (apart from Mr. Gaines, who proved to be every bit as sensible as I believed), if they were raising eyebrows, they did so in the dark of night. I doubt they made any mention of their activities because they would have been held equally accountable by their peers for passing on such knowledge to the 'feeble sex' and thereby contributing to the corruption of the moral fiber of our nation. It was amusing what ideals people would sacrifice for the want of money.

* * *

Dr. Sawyer took kindly to me from the start and held no ill feeling toward my boarding in his house. A gratuity could never foster a genuine affection. I knew in my heart that he enjoyed having me. I could feel it. He always asked about my health and well-being. He always paid attention to how my studies were progressing. He appreciated the opportunity for learning that my schooling brought home to Mary by being in my company. He was honest, and as Mary had said, he was a very forward thinking man in comparison to most.

My schooling did much more than enlighten me. It brought into my life a structure and discipline that required my full attention and effort. In other words it prevented me from being distracted by thoughts of Lady Rebecca's death. The days of impossible suffering that followed the church fire in eighteen-and-nine were fading into the past as time turned weeks into months, and finally into years.

The tranquility of my life with Mary and Dr. Sawyer eventually healed my wounds, ended my nightmares, and erased many of the scars. It placed those horrible memories of Lady Rebecca's death into a perspective I was able to manage. I was maturing into an intelligent young lady and with Mary's help, I was learning to accept the hand of fate, no matter how harsh or unfair.

SEVEN

There were certain things about city living that were very specific to the lifestyle. One of those things was the times at which we ate. In the city, people ate breakfast early, followed by a light lunch, and usually a supper later in the evening, say between six and eight. Such schedules seemed odd to those folks raised in the country.

Country folk always ate an early breakfast, but it was customary to sit down to a large meal between noon and three. It was the hottest part of the day and a good time to take a break from the sun in the open fields. The main meal was followed later with something light at about eight, just before retiring for the night.

This change in an ages old custom came about because so many people were either living or coming into the city for work. It was impractical for them to return home in the middle of the afternoon for the sole purpose of eating. Instead, they remained in the city and ate a light lunch at their job to tide them over until they left their workplace and returned to the farm.

So it was, I stood in the kitchen helping Mary prepare a light lunch for Dr. Sawyer, we having long since adopted the city dweller's eating habits, when from up front came the double ringing of the door bell as it opened and closed. A moment passed before Dr. Sawyer called down the hallway.

"Mary?"

"Yes?"

"Would you come here for a moment, please?"

"Coming."

"Would you finish slicing up this bread, Liz? I'll be right back."

THE LETTER

"Mmm hmm." I agreed.

A few moments later, Mary returned as promised and sat down at the table. I glanced her way and noticed she was studying me. I smiled at her.

"Why are you looking at me like that?"

"I don't know. Do you know how much I enjoy having you here?"

"Oh, oh. I'm in trouble. What is it now?"

"No, not trouble. I have something for you." She handed me a sealed letter.

"What's this? One of the orphans?" I asked noting an air of mystery. We were always getting posts from the orphans, especially during the Christmas season. I might have thought it a late arrival, but for a sense of apprehension about Mary.

"What is it?" I asked, wearing a humorous face. I flipped the envelope over to read the return address and my heart stopped dead.

It was the wax stamp of *Christopher Nicholas Claussen*!

The letter came as a complete surprise, and my first feeling was one of utter shock. I took a seat. My stomach instantly twisted about until beneath the table my ankles were wrapped, one around the other, toes curled up and rubbing hard. Adrenaline burned my insides. The feel of the letter in my hands catapulted me back to Lady Rebecca's death, and a flood of emotions engulfed me. I sat staring at the envelope, momentarily frozen in place, unsure of how to approach it.

"Are you all right, Liz?"

"Yes." I nodded my head. "I am surprised," I laughed nervously, "very surprised, maybe even a little afraid."

Mary was aware of the impact this letter might have upon me. So too had been Dr. Sawyer. This was why he had first called her

81

to the lobby. They had no idea of what news the letter brought, but discussed the matter in order to be prepared for whatever my reaction. I placed the letter on the table and continued to stare at it. My fingers, my toes, my thoughts, all came to a numbing halt. Mary and Allen had received an occasional word from Mr. Claussen over the years, but not me, not one word until now.

"Are you not going to open it?" asked Mary.

I didn't answer, but instead nodded my head, as I cautiously moved to free the flap from the wax impression that sealed it. I wondered if Mary could see the slight tremor in my hands. I removed the sheet of paper. It had been written almost two months earlier. Having unfolded it, I fell hopelessly into his words. I found it difficult to breathe.

15 October 1812

Dearest Elizabeth,

It has been so long.

I fear I would be lost should I again walk the streets of Boston. Take heart in knowing the very man you believed had courage enough to face down a raging sea has walked the decks of REBECCA years on end before working up the courage to write this little girl.

I am sure you have come to realize I was not nearly as strong as you had hoped. I fear you will reject my letter, I fear you will reject me, and I shall understand should you toss my words to the sea, setting them adrift as am I.

I ask only you believe that I speak truth when I say, since having seen you last, not one day has passed whereby my thoughts weren't with you. I remember your tears. I remember the feel of your face cupped in my hands. I am haunted by the memory of your eyes looking up to me for answers, for direction, for the hope I was uable to bestow. I had lost my way, Elizabeth. I am both sorry and filled with regret for having failed you.

I have prayed every night that God watch over you, and put into your heart a reason you might see to forgive me my leaving.

I am thinking that I have addressed you as my little girl, and how far that must be from reality. I pray my letter arrives in time to convey my best wishes for your fifteenth birthday and the Christmas season. I know in my heart that you have blossomed into a creature of beauty. I envy the boys who have the privilege of seeing your face. I envy the lad who will soon take your hand, leading you into his world and out of mine forever.

You might wish to know that I have come to terms with Rebecca's death, and I have managed to put my life back in order. It is because of this that I have found myself thinking so much of you. At last, I have been able to separate my feelings for you from those I held for Rebecca. I am able to deal with the pain of her passing, but I doubt it will ever subside entirely.

My thoughts of you do quite the opposite these days. They fill me with joy and a longing to return home. I can never bring back my beloved Rebecca, but I would fight mightily to earn the chance of having you in my company again. I think of you often, Elizabeth. Please remember me.

Christopher N. Claussen

The rush of emotion was unbelievable.

Even after these years gone by, the words he penned drove straight to my heart. I reread the letter time and time again. With each pass I drew more emotion. He had resurrected feelings that I thought were buried deep and beyond reach, but instead surfaced explosively. My eyes showed what was in my heart and tears streaked my cheeks with glistening trails. How could I be so moved after such a long passing of time?

"Are you sure you are all right, Liz?" Mary was concerned.

"Would you like to hear what he has to say?"

"Only if you wish."

"He remembered my birthday."

I conveyed all he had written. At first we sat there in silence, unsure how to accept this unexpected letter. Afterwards we began to discuss those tragic times past and reflect on how we felt about Lady Rebecca's death then, and how we felt about it now. We talked about his leaving.

"He was a wonderful man, Liz."

"I hear you say that, Mary, and I suppose it is true. I tried so hard to understand why he left me. Please don't get me wrong. I don't believe I could have been any happier than I am with you and Dr. Sawyer. I know it was for the best. I just—I just—I guess I was completely overwhelmed by him. I was so taken by his presence. He was a god to me. I remember how I craved his attention. Maybe I craved it because Lady Rebecca gave me all of hers and Mr. Claussen seemed so distant that I had to work for his. I don't know. I only know whatever life was left in me died the day he told me he was leaving."

"I know. I remember. So often I wished you had been just a couple years older, just as you are now, so that you would have seen him for what he truly was. He was distant for sure, but he was most gracious. He was generous and kind. I believe all that he says in his letter is from his heart and truthful. You are blessed to have someone such as he to care so deeply and provide so freely for your well-being."

"He is good to me, I'll never deny it. I haven't a clue what it means to want, but back then it was different. I only barely understood the meaning of wealth, Mary. I only wanted the one thing money couldn't buy, *his attention*. I still feel that way at times."

After making sure everything was calm and I was composed, Dr. Sawyer came into the kitchen to have lunch. I was pleased that he joined our conversation because his comments and opinions were always so sensible. During the three years passed, I had gained enough maturity to view my past in an objective light, made all the brighter by Dr. Sawyer's compassionate ear and gentle direction.

That is not to say that our discussions eased the impact of the letter upon me. In fact, the remainder of the day I preferred to be left alone to my thoughts. During those hours, I forced myself to relive hurtful memories and not be crushed by the feelings of loss. I dared to peer into dark places from my past and view unsettling recollections from the safe distance of time. I was encouraged to discuss my feelings openly with Mary and Allen if I so chose, but there was no longer any need, and by day's end I felt as though I had at last truly closed the longest chapter of my childhood.

As for Mr. Claussen—at fourteen, I was probably more mystified by the man than ever. I was even annoyed to admit to myself that I still longed for his attention in the worst of ways. I never would have admitted this to Mary or Dr. Sawyer, but in my heart there was no escaping the truth of it. I had no choice, but to write him a letter in return. I thought of him the whole of that night, and the following morning I literally jumped out of bed in a run for paper and quill. He had reached out to me, and my arms were as wide open and wanting as was my heart.

So began the correspondence that healed wounded hearts. He wrote to me infrequently, and yet, from the beginning I could sense his disappointment should I fail to write him regularly of my accounts. I soon realized the pattern to his postings. I could expect one to arrive in response to every four or five of mine. I knew it wasn't due to his indifference toward me, but his inability to send letters. He might arrive in port to find five of my letters awaiting ashore, and then he would read them all at once and set about writing one in return, generally many pages, well written with careful thought and full of heartfelt feeling and sincerity.

From letter to letter we strove to learn all we could about one another. We discussed personal needs, intimate feelings, dreams of the future, and delicately touched on the painful issues of our past. I found myself drawn ever closer to his words. Our separation brought me nearer to him in my heart than I had ever imagined possible during my time spent in his home.

Mr. Claussen's attentiveness to my well-being never faltered. I had become more than a child in his mind. I had come to be the salve for his wound, a source of love and affection that bridged time and distance across oceans to fulfill his need for peace. I was the potion for the insufferable pain within his soul. I was a place he frequented in order to cry or carry on. A place he protected. I sensed he thought of me as some form of sacred tabernacle that housed his most personal memory.

Aside from philosophies and feelings, Mr. Claussen also made it quite clear that an account remained open for my use, and he encouraged me to use it, if for nothing more than my own pleasure. There was no limitation ever imposed upon my requests financially. He claimed he would have spoiled me regardless of whether he had been living in Boston or not. Still, I kept modest my withdrawals and remained very respectful of his generosity. Many times I preferred not to accept his assistance, but he would dress me down severely if he became aware of it.

"...where is the sanity in all my effort, if you fail to make advantage of these rewards for my labor...."

He would get very upset.

EIGHT

No doubt by design, Lady Rebecca had instilled within me her regard for the welfare of others, especially the orphans. It was that part of society for which she had lived and died in an attempt to improve. With a conscience built from such foundation, I entered into an incident that forever marked the direction of my life and the esteem in which I would be held.

It happened in May of eighteen-thirteen when I was four months into my fifteenth year. Mary and I were picnicking in the midday sun at a small commons just between the Battery and Winnesimmet Ferry at the River Charles. It was a great place to observe the many keelboats doing business upon the river. With the continuous movement of rivermen and passengers, stevedores and stowage, the place was guaranteed to offer a stage of activity that would keep one engaged and entertained for many an hour, day or night. This was in addition to the main attraction of young sailors crossing over from the navy yard on the opposite bank.

It was yet early spring when nights were prone to hard freezes, but days were set ablaze with brilliance and sunshine, and views of such clarity in a cloudless sky; it simply awakened every sense. I believed we might see forever beyond the horizon, and the sounds of birds, nature, couples strolling about, and especially the laughter of children seemed to carry for miles. It was the kind of day that brings out the best in everyone. The greens were dotted with people rushing to enjoy the first taste of summer and witness how the sun forced leaves out onto the branches.

Mr. Gaines, our primary instructor, had been kept from his obligation to administer our lessons. For reason of some unexplained emergency, he was not to return before the week's end, three days off or more. Taking full advantage of our unexpectedly open schedule, Mary saw to it that our time was to be enjoyed, and on this day she wished to show me off.

87

I had just finished devouring two slices of freshly baked cornmeal bread covered with a generous spread of butter, between which were layered thinly sliced pieces of smoked ham. This, to be enjoyed with a mild mouth-watering swiss cheese, all prepared by Mary's hand and carefully packed into our basket. There was applesauce to follow and fresh lemoned tea to wash it down—and last, but not least, a chunk of chocolate to be had for desert—a dreadfully large chunk of chocolate donated to our cause by Dr. Sawyer with a devilish smile. No woman in her right mind could view it without a worry for her figure. I knew, because at fifteen *'appearances'* were everything.

We were spending our day in sinful laziness, taking turns reading to each other from Lady Harrison's *'Guide to a Proper Lady'* and conversing about the inadequacies of my love life.

"It isn't a great thing. It isn't a shipwreck. My life isn't over, Mary."

"I know Liz, and I am not insinuating any such thought. I just wish you would make yourself more available. I mean if I didn't take it upon myself to bring you out into the public and show you off, I believe you would stay forever at home reading. There are many fine men in Boston and I know for a fact that they watch your every move. You are a beautiful, beautiful girl. You should be thinking about marriage before—."

"Before I am, what I am—*a spinster*. I know—*'soon to be sixteen and still unmarried.'* I don't have a clue how I might make myself more *'available'* as you put it. Men don't approach me, Mary. It's like—well, do you remember when Lady Rebecca would tell us how Mr. Claussen could never find his one true love because of all his wealth? I think it's something like that. A lot of people think the Claussens adopted me and that I am fabulously well-heeled. I think it puts men off. I think they feel inferior or else they are afraid of me."

"You must try, Liz. I want you to be in love. I want you to have babies."

"You should be having babies, not me."

"Don't you be concerned about my babies. They'll come in time, you tart."

"Yes, *dear*."

The day was supremely peaceful, and I lay upon our blanket listening to Mary fret over me, while watching the reddish glow of sunshine from behind closed eyes. As the grass warmed and dried out beside me, I seemed to hear it snap and pop while working itself up from the still chilly winter earth below.

And so, blissful was our tranquil setting until that moment when the most wretched wail ever, rolled across the green. I sat up with a start and looked about but was unable to see anything so soon after opening my eyes. I was forced to shield my view from the bright light of day as I tried to search out across the park for this person in distress.

"What was that all about?" I asked somewhat unnerved.

"I don't know," Mary responded. She also was looking nervously about.

Again the scream, only this time I turned my head to face the origin of the cry. As my eyes adjusted and I began to focus more clearly, a young girl of maybe ten or eleven in years came into view. I saw her drop to her knees. She was now huddled along-side a storage building on the lane at the upper edge of the common, just above us from the river.

I saw her fall back into the building and throw up her arms as if to protect herself. Then to my alarm, I next saw an older man strike her, then strike her again and again. The roar of his anger followed her cries for mercy. As the echo of his voice reverberated across the green, it reminded me of the bellowing of the rummies, those old sailors who no longer went out to sea, but forever washed themselves in grog. Frantic, I turned to Mary for direction, ready to assist her in whatever manner possible to rescue the young girl from her attacker.

"Help her, Mary! Help her! We must do something!" I cried out. "Did you see that? Mary! Stop him! Stop him!" I urged.

Mary sat next to me bearing witness. She was clearly concerned, but showed no sign of going to the girl's rescue. I looked to her for a signal, expecting her immediate direction, but saw only a face gripped in the agony of indecision and despair. I realized at once that she had no idea what to do, and the ruckus I now raised only served to heighten her anxiety.

"Quiet, Elizabeth!" she snapped. "It's not our concern. I am sorry. I am sorry we have to be witness to this, but it is a private matter and it will pass. I implore you leave it be so he isn't further angered by provocation."

"But, Mar—."

"Leave it be, Elizabeth! Pay it no mind and it shall soon be over."

Mary had given me fair warning, but what I saw for the first time was how my basic instincts were much different than hers. I was ready to act and ask questions later. Mary must have sensed this, for I believed she more afraid of what I might be possessed to do.

She looked away, but I could not. I turned in time to see the man strike the child again. He was brutal. It wasn't a slap or spank; it was the type of blow one man might expect to deliver to another. The young girl pleaded for mercy. Whimpering, she rolled into a little ball and, with her hand outstretched, attempted to ward off his anger. I was just rising to my feet, unsure of what I was about to do, when to my horror I saw the man kick her so hard that she left the ground she was cowering upon. That was the last straw.

"Stop it! Stop it, you beast! Stop it at once!" I screamed.

"Elizabeth!"

I was not only on my feet, but broke forward into a run as Mary reached in vain for me with a great gasp. I headed in his direction, utterly unconcerned for my safety or the outcome of my actions. I was screaming hysterically at the man, trying to expose his brutality before all who might listen.

"Look! Look! He's beating a child! He's beating a child! You're cruel! Leave her be! Leave her alone! Look at him! He's beating her! He's kicking her!"

Verbally, I launched a particularly vicious assault at the stranger. I hurled my accusations fearlessly for all to hear. I was unrelenting. I was reprimanding and indifferent to his motives. I screamed as loud as I could, all the while pointing at this man who now turned to face me. He was quite shocked—a shock that quickly turned to rage.

"Shut yer mouth, hussy, or I'll wring yer miser'ble neck!" he roared.

I cared not and continued to assault him, screaming out my revulsion for such barbarity, all to the horror of Mary, whom I had left behind upon the blanket.

"He's a monster! He's beating a child! He's kicking her! He's a monster; he's a monster! Stop him! Somebody stop him!"

"Shuddup!" he threatened.

"Help! Somebody help!"

"Shuddup or I'll break yer bloody neck, child!" He started for me, but suddenly halted as he took notice of the many people, especially the rivermen, giants of their gender, gathering about to investigate the disturbance. I could see the veins on his neck standing out, pulsing with rage, but I found within myself strength beyond his, a strength I never knew I possessed. I stood my ground and screamed for all I was worth.

A group of sailors and rivermen started quickly in my direction and broke into a run to assist me. The brute now looking about, and being a good judge of the situation taking shape, turned at once and fled. The men arrived full of concern for our well-being and ready to give the man a sound thrashing. They departed only after my assurances that I would care for the young girl.

I attempted to gather my wits, for I was still breathing hard and shaking nervously. My body was flooded with adrenaline. I walked what distance remained in order to speak to the girl, who was only a few years my younger. I knelt beside her. She was covered with welts that were blackening upon her face even as I looked upon her. I placed my hand on her shoulder and attempted to console her. She withdrew immediately.

"It's all right. He's gone. You've nothing to fear now."

"Go away!"

"You're hurt."

"Leave me alone! Go away! Just leave me be!" She looked at me with eyes like daggers. Instead of being put off, I found myself hardened to the ordeal.

"Never!"

"Go!"

"No!"

Sensing my resolve, the girl broke down into tears and wept.

"Please, go away. He will beat me for talking to you. He is watching. He will know. He will beat me terrible. Please, I beg of you, leave me be." The girl cried out so hard in sobs that my heart wished only to reach out for her, but I restrained myself for her sake.

"I will do as you wish, if you will promise me one thing only."

"Anything, please leave," she pleaded.

"What is your name?" I asked.

"Caroline."

"Caroline, I am Elizabeth Dennison. If you are in trouble, promise me you will go to Doctor Sawyer's office on Summer Street. That is where I live. Just ask and someone will tell you where to go. Do you promise?"

"Yes, please go. Please go away."

"Promise me."

"I promise, now go away, please go away." The girl buried her face in her hands and continued to sob. I rose to my feet and looked down upon her. The image was seared into my memory, a scene that would forever haunt me.

I turned back and noticed right off that Mary had walked away from our blanket. A quick glance about found her off in the distance speaking to a stranger sitting up against a large oak tree. I watched as she then continued on past the man, walking slowly away and looking out to sea. She never once looked back my way, and that made it obvious she was upset with me.

I didn't call out to her or go to her side, but instead returned to lay face down upon our blanket, my chest to the earth. I watched Mary for a moment more before closing my eyes. I tried to relax. I was still very agitated over the incident and willed my heart to slow its pace. I could feel it pounding into the ground beneath me. I was also now very nervous about Mary's return.

Opening my eyes a time or two, I watched as she paced back and forth along the hillside. Yes, I thought to myself, Mary was most certainly upset. I knew we would have to face each other sooner or later, and because it was I who lay upon the blanket, it was up to Mary to decide when that time would be.

I was given ample time to settle myself, for it was nearly half an hour's passing before Mary strolled back toward our picnic, now a distant memory of what had been a wonderful afternoon. Her look was one of stress.

I closed the book that I pretended to read, set it aside, and looked to greet her, however awkward that might be. I wasn't without worry. I had no recollection of ever seeing Mary even remotely upset with me before this day. I feared for my actions and the consequences in store for me within the Sawyer household. I had repeated my apologies over and over in my head while awaiting her return. She walked up to the blanket and looked down at me. She hesitated.

"Hi." I began to speak, but Mary raised her hand to shush me and I was quick to obey.

"Is the girl all right?" she asked.

"I believe so. Badly bruised for certain, but nothing more that I could see."

"Very well." Mary paused, "Elizabeth, there is something I must say." She lowered herself next to me and took a deep breath, but would not look directly at me. She fixed her eyes on her hands.

"I was beside myself with anger over the scene that you made, your intent to intrude into the private affairs of another. So angry in fact, I couldn't bring myself to face you upon your return. Actually, if the truth be known, I was in such a state of rage I never even bothered to watch for your safety, believing you would get what you deserved for such unbecoming behavior. A lady never meddles, Elizabeth." Mary paused for a moment as if to ensure her words were picked carefully.

"I had to leave, to walk, to sort out my own thoughts and settle myself. And in doing so, I came to ask myself why I felt so angered." Mary turned her head away. She couldn't meet my eyes. "Elizabeth—, I discovered I was angry with myself. I was angry with myself for being the older and supposedly wiser, yet entirely failing to act with even a hint of the courage you so readily dispense. I was embarrassed for my inability to stand up to the stranger, to the brute, as did you without a second's thought.

94

I would like to have found an excuse to save myself from such shame, but there is no excuse. I wanted to believe screaming, as you did, was a spectacle so unladylike, so unpolished that no moral woman would exhibit such behavior in public. But it isn't true, no matter how hard I hoped different. The fact is, you did exactly what should have been done." She turned and looked directly at me with her moist amber eyes.

"I saw in you that same special gift of courage, Lady Rebecca possessed in everything she did. It is the look I would have seen the night she ran back into the church had I been there. It is something in your character, something both of you share that I lack." Mary dropped her eyes to her hands. A tear flashed in the sunlight as it fell to her lap. "I hope you can forgive me, Elizabeth. I will live with this humiliation for a long time."

She sat silent, and for a moment I was speechless. It hadn't been what I expected, and her eyes laid bare the truth of her shame. I was at once flooded with a feeling of love and compassion, for Mary was everything to me. I wished only to ease her embarrassment, and so I rose to my knees and wrapped my arms around her neck. I tried to console her.

"You shouldn't fret so, Mary. After all, I am still free to scream like a brat. Remember, I am unmarried. I am still allowed some childish acts at my age. It would have been different if I were you. I mean, how would I have looked carrying on in such a manner if I were the wife of a respected doctor? They would have said it was the old man's private affair and you were acting like a complete ninny with no mind to the disrespect you brought Allen. It was in God's hands to be done as he saw fit, Mary. If He had wanted you to scream, you would have screamed your heart out, you can be sure."

Wholly disheartened, she heard me out. It was a fair stretch and hopefully true, but at the very least sharing the blame with God eased her remorse. She was grateful for my words and the reprieve.

"Now it's my turn to read to you." I picked up the book.

NINE

It was dead of night when a slow and forceful pounding at the back door disrupted our dreams and caused us to awake at once with a start. Dr. Sawyer was brought quickly to his feet by the disturbance, for a man was in the back yard yelling mightily for us to awake.

"Open ze door! Open ze door! Vake up, doctor!"

We were still living over the infirmary, and after-hour calls were not so uncommon. Babies in particular seemed to gain great pleasure in arriving after the rest of the world had settled down to take a rest. It was all in a day's, or in this case, a nights' work for a doctor.

"I'm coming! I'm coming! Hold on! There's no need to break the door!"

I listened to Dr. Sawyer holler out from his bedroom as he stumbled about trying to find his slippers and senses. I sat up on the edge of my bed just in time to catch a glimpse of his shadow racing across the landing toward the staircase.

Mary always said that her husband slept with one eye open ever ready to face an emergency, but I found it questionable as I listened to him bumping into this and that. At any rate, he couldn't be blamed for the good sleeping weather that drugged us on this cold spring night. I stood up from my bed and worked to open my eyes and close my mouth, whereafter I walked out to meet Mary who was already at the top of the landing.

"My word, what's hatt'ning?" I asked with a yawn.

"Sounds like baby Gerber has finally arrived."

Mary struck a match and the darkness retreated. She touched the flame to a candle, and after handing me the holder, started her way down the staircase in preparation for whatever need might arise. We watched attentively, fully expecting to see the desperate face of Mr. Gerber, a local German immigrant whose wife was a week overdue. He had been in to see Dr. Sawyer earlier in the day and was plenty nervous about his wife's condition, as her labor had started late in the pregnancy. Now he would not only be nervous about her labor, but embarrassed as well for having called at this early hour in hopes of gaining a helping hand with the delivery.

"Open ze door, doc. Hurrreee!"

The pounding continued even as Dr. Sawyer opened the door a crack to look outside. Nary a word was passed before he lifted the chain and swung it open wide. From out of the darkness, the German sprang into our midst carrying a blanket-wrapped woman in his arms.

"She is bat."

"Follow me, this way."

"Bring the light, Liz!" said Mary in an anxious tone. "Hurry!"

The base of the candleholder cast a shadow upon the floor below us and so I was quick on Mary's heels as we headed down the staircase to better illuminate the back entrance.

Something was wrong. The thought of a difficult delivery filled my head as it cleared of sleep and I strove to overhear what might next be said. The man hurried down the hallway beneath us, his stocky frame protected from the cold by a sizable great-coat and hat, which blocked most of my view.

I knew instinctively that the situation was serious. I tipped the candleholder to cast a brighter light upon this person when suddenly it was a child's face that rolled back away from his shoulder to stare up at me deathlike. I was riveted with shock at seeing what had come to us from the night.

"It's Caroline! Oh, my god, Mary, it's Caroline!" I gasped.

I missed whatever Mary might have said, for I was crushed, believing at once I had made a grave mistake, maybe the worst mistake of my life. As I tried to grapple with what was taking place, Mary turned to race back up the stairs, snatching away the candle before disappearing into her bedroom.

I stood alone and numb in the darkness until the soft glow of an oil lamp within the infirmary made its way along the corridor to reach the staircase. Mary was in her room getting dressed, which left me and a devastated conscience to descend slowly one step at a time. Keeping to the shadows, I crept up behind Dr. Sawyer and the stranger who were standing shoulder to shoulder over the patient.

Dr. Sawyer then stepped away to light a second and third lamp. Instinctively, I covered my eyes in order to prepare myself for the scene now open before me. Caroline lay still as death upon the table. Peering between my fingers, I watched as Dr. Sawyer approached her and removed the blanket.

I took in the full measure of the savagery. I could hardly bear to look. Her blood-covered clothes stood in stark contrast to the white linen of the examination table. She had been butchered. She was now delirious, shaking uncontrollably from shock and exposure to the cold night air. How long had she been out wandering? What had she endured? I couldn't imagine.

I stood motionless, adjusting my fingers as though trying somehow to filter out the worst of what was before me. My ears were filled with sounds no one else could hear. Her pleas came back to haunt me with a vengeance. Inside my head, over and over I heard her cries to be left alone. She told me the price she would pay for my interference, but I had brushed her fears aside.

She was unaware of Dr. Sawyer as he attempted to remove her dress. He was unable. It was adhered to the dried blood and wounds upon her back. She was shaking violently. Mary rushed in and began stoking the fire to heat the room and prepare hot water. She laid out the towels that would be needed to begin softening the blood-soaked garments. Her words were gushing as she pointed out to Dr. Sawyer that this was the girl who was beaten at the green.

I should have helped. I wanted to help, but I couldn't. I remained hidden in the shadows, also shaking beneath my night-clothes from the chilly air, but even more from the shock. I stayed to myself, unseen in the background wishing no attention, for I believed without question that my own doing brought about the misery now before me. I strained to hear every word of the conversation that took place between the stranger who called himself Werner Reinhardt and Dr. Sawyer as they hovered over Caroline's lifeless form.

The German removed his hat and nervously kneaded it with both hands. His head was bowed as though he had done some-thing wrong, as if he had failed by not doing enough. He went on to tell how he had watched Caroline stumbling about aim-lessly at the outskirts of town.

"Yas, sir. Gell...I hat just unloatet a couple cort of oak over at Kinberlant's Bakery for ze morning stoke, und vas heting back to my cabin vhen, gell...I come to pass zis fraulein heting tovart town. She vas down on Derry arroad, na ja, down by ze olt Harper fence line.

"Arright avay, I vas suspicious. Gell—nobodys vat's up to any goot vill be seen vandering arrount town at zis hour...espe-cially not sat far out. I mean it is verry dark, sie wissen, ja? Und it goes vitout saying come ze early morning, it's verry kalt outside. I see ze fraulein out zere valking about vit nutting on, but dis dress.

"I sink sometink vas amiss. I coult tell by ze light of my lantern sat she vas not arright, sie wissen? I sink she vas valking in her sleep, maybe. So, I stop my vagon to look, sie wissen, ja? I vas vondering vhat she is toing, yah? Und she valks arright past an' never looks at me. Verry strange, I sink. I calt out to her, but she vas babbling on und never see me.

"I sink dis fraulein neets help, so I climb down und valk up behind her mit ze lantern. I vas sinking she be one of zose poor alten souls, sie wissen, ja? I sink maybe she lost her mindt und such, so I calt out to her again, but she keep on valking, just talkink to herself und valking avay.

"I tell you, doc, I vas about to reach for her, to take her by ze shoulder vhen I see ze back of her dress. Gell—I sought it vas filt from layin' on ze grount, or sometink. Zen, as I got arright up close mit ze lantern, I started sinking diff'rent. I see her back. Oh! Jesus Maria." The man shivered. "I reached arrount in front of her like dis, for fear of touchink her back." He threw his arm out and made a hook out of it to show us how he stood behind Caroline and stopped her from walking any farther. "She stop't right zere und stoot before me shakin' ter'ble, und I say, my eyes sey vere sopping vet once I see vhat happened to ze poor childt. Sie wissen, I never seen nicht's like zis, Doc. Who coult do such a sing?" He turned his face away momentarily.

"Nun, she vas askin' for you by ze name, und zen I try to get her in ze vagon und all, gell—I guess you know ze arrest. I come here. Vhat t'you sink, doc? She look bat, yah. Dis not goot, not goot, no?" The stranger shook his head, visibly concerned.

Dr. Sawyer listened to the account as he began the process of soaking the dress and cutting it free.

"You found her a half hour ago, more or less?"

"Yah, sats arright. Half hour, yas. I cover her mit ze blanket. I keep it for my legs in ze vinter. It is goot und varm."

"She is very lucky you found her. Her hands and feet are like ice."

Carefully, Mary raised the cloth as it released itself from the softening blood, thereby enabling Dr. Sawyer to ease the scissors up along Caroline's spine. He pulled the separated dress away from her, exposing the raw meat of her flesh and at once, I began to retch. It was as though someone had opened her inside out. She had been whipped mercilessly with something similar to a belt, maybe narrower like a buggy whip.

Mary covered her mouth. She had to look away. She had experienced much blood and injury working alongside her husband, but it was never the same as when it was a child. She was hoping for children herself, wishing to start a family, and so Mary's outlook was far closer to that of a mother than a nurse.

Mr. Sawyer was a well-trained and seasoned doctor, and he maintained his professionalism without falter. He knew his patient's lives depended on it, but I could still see something of the crime in his face. He reached for Caroline's wrists and looked at them carefully.

"She was tied, struggled. Probably hung by her wrists. I suspect her father pulled her dress up over her head and whipped her. The man should be shot."

"Oh my Lord, Allen." Mary whispered. "Tell me you can help her, you must help her, you must...." Mary's voice trailed off. She was visibly distraught. She couldn't look at Caroline, but she couldn't turn away. "Can you help her, Allen?" She pleaded out loud, while Dr. Sawyer studied the wounds.

"Hard to say—this is not good.... I don't know, Mary, she's young. Her youth is her best chance. Children heal fast. Unfortunately, she is extensively lacerated and these wounds will fester profusely. I can't make any promises. The wounds are too severe. It is mostly in God's hands, but I will say this, it is important that we keep her bathed and as clean as possible, changing her dressings every hour or two. For now, I will administer some opiates to relieve her pain. It must be intense and will only get worse. I assure you, her agony will put us to the test. We must be strong for her sake." Dr. Sawyer stopped to think. He shook his head in disgust. "Even if she recovers, she will carry these scars to her grave."

Caroline shook in an inhuman manner as her body began to warm and the sight of it was more than I could bear. I backed away from the room, my self-esteem shredded as severely as Caroline's back. I retreated to the shadows of the stairwell and sat down to cry in private. I was deep in my misery when

101

surprised by Mr. Reinhardt, who had come back down the hall to let himself out. He put his hand on my shoulder and I looked up, my face awash in tears.

"Now, now childt. You musn't cry. It is not your toing. You must pray."

"No, it is my doing. She told me to stay away, b-b-but I-I wouldn't listen." I wiped my nose.

"You know ze fraulein?"

"Yes. Well, not really. A man was beating her, and I started screaming to draw attention to him until he ran off. I thought she would be grateful that I came to her rescue, but she was put out. I think it was her father. She feared he would return to beat her because of my meddling. She pleaded for me to leave. She begged me, but I wouldn't have any of it. I stayed and this is the result. It is now just as she said."

Mr. Reinhardt studied me at length in the glow of his candle. He seemed to be determining whether or not I was worth the effort he suddenly made to sit down alongside me at the bottom of the staircase.

"Vhat's your name childt?"

"Elizabeth."

"Elizabet, may I tell you a story? Vould you mindt? I sink it vill help."

"All right."

"A long time ago, vhen I vas just a small boy, I vas valking down ze lane by my house. It vas ze middle of vinter, und it vas verry kalt outside. A lot kalter zan it is tonite, sie wissen, ja? Vhile I vas valking past ze Guntherhaus, I still remember ze name, I saw diz cat sitting on top of a post. I sink ze cat is kalt und maybe hungry, but I sink it is a cat und smart und it vill be all right. Vhy should I bother to help such a smart animal as a cat, yah?

102

"Gell—ze next day I vas valking back along ze lane und vhen I came to ze post ze cat vas gone. I vas not surprised until I lookt down und zere covert mit ze snow vas ze cat. He vas deadt. I stoot zere und looked at him for a verry long time. I vas sure I might have done sometink to help sat cat. It made me feel very bat. It has been forty jears since sat night und I never forget. It vas only a cat, but I never forget.

"Elizabet, vhen you sink you should help, und you feel it here inside, to it, even if you feel foolish. Ze rest of your life you vill know you dit right. To you understand vhat I say?"

"Yes, thank-you. Your words will help me, I am certain." I wiped my eyes on my nightie.

"I must go now. I have vork to do und I am late. Don't cry, yah?"

"I won't." I was beyond good manners, and kept wiping my nose on my sleeve. Mr Reinhardt rose to his feet, and I did still possess enough composure to rise as well and see him to the door.

"Thank you for your kind words, Mr. Reinhardt."

"You dit goot, chidt, but now you must pray for her, yah?"

"Yes."

"Goot night, Elizabet."

"Good night, sir."

He handed me his candle and I closed the door. I went back upstairs to my room and extinguished the tiny flame of light. I collapsed onto my bed in the darkness of night so I might cry freely once more without being seen or heard as I suffered to relieve myself of shame.

"You dit goot. You dit goot."

I tried to believe what Mr. Reinhardt had said. I was so proud of my action in preventing her a further beating at the park, but the memory of her voice haunted me.

"Leave me. Leave me."

Her pleas ran through my head over and over again. Maybe I should have listened. I was too stubborn, too pigheaded at times. Why couldn't I have listened to what she was saying? I buried my face deep into my pillow to stifle my sobs.

"You dit goot, you dit goot."

Mary had been right after all. Interfering had only further angered the man, exactly as she had predicted. She had been thoughtful, whereas I had been rash. I relived her words as well.

"Leave it be. Leave it be."

She had first anticipated the outcome, whereas I had moved in spite of the outcome. My face was scorched with self-consciousness. I felt as if the whole world was pointing at me. It was entirely my fault, and run as I might wish, I had no place to hide outside the folds of my pillow.

"You dit goot, you dit goot."

I lay there and the more I thought of the man who beat her the more I started to burn. He became the focal point for my anger, and then boiling up from within me, from my very core, I felt myself being overcome with a hardening resolve to fight back. The feeling was not unlike my feelings earlier in the day. I sat up in my bed and wiped away my tears with the sheets. I felt the heat of my humiliation begin to change into the fire of anger, the flames stoked with dogged determination to fight my way out of this incorrigible state of miscalculation.

"I did the right thing. I know I did the right thing. I would do it again."

I spoke aloud through the blackness in my room and I heard my voice return to me from the walls. I was feeling belligerent, and so I rose from the bed and walked over to my study desk. I reached about in the darkness until I felt the still warm candle. I put a lucifer to it, and in the glow of a new flame, I fanned through my numerous collections of papers placed in neat order upon the shelves. I removed a packet of slips, carefully kept bundled and securely tied with ribbon. These scraps of paper formed the hub of a web that was first built upon by the fifty orphans who came to America aboard the REBECCA.

As Lady Rebecca had hoped, the children kept in contact with her and with one another the best they could. Milady knew books were extremely difficult to obtain on the frontier, much more so than in Europe, and so she encouraged the orphans to practice reading and writing by posting letters, especially during the Christmas season and dead of winter when fields lie fallow and frozen. Not only was it then that time was more apt to be found for letter writing, but it added much to the joy of the season by keeping everyone up-to-date on the latest news.

By the time of Lady Rebecca's death, hundreds of cards and letters were sent at Christmas time, solidifying new relationships and rekindling old friendships. Mr. Claussen had promised to pay for postage, and to this day even though he was nowhere to be found, his promise remained good. These letters and cards represented links that reached out to the lives of children and families spread out as far as the rivers flowed and beyond. At Christmas, Lady Rebecca, Mary, and I would display all the cards, and we marveled at the irony they presented. That is to say, the farther in miles traveled, the closer in heart they felt.

Even all of our friends and neighbors began to partake in the ritual and soon the whole community was trading season wishes on cards, and delivering them to one another. I tried hard to keep the tradition alive with Mary's help, and it had become quite the Christmas affair with many of our close friends and neighbors pitching in.

Now, I grabbed the inkbottle, and after sharpening a quill, I penned away the hours. I heard Dr. Sawyer climb the stairs in order to take in a few hours of sleep. Mary remained downstairs at Caroline's side. He stuck his head in my room.

"Shouldn't you be asleep?"

"I tried."

"Are you all right? I thought I heard you crying earlier tonight."

"I'm fine."

"So—this was the little girl, you helped today."

"Yes." I kept my eyes glued to my hands. I bit my lip and struggled to keep from bawling.

"It was a wonderful thing you did today. I am very proud of you."

"Wonderful!" I was horrified. I looked up to meet his eyes. Mine were filling with tears. "How can you say that? Look at her! She told me not to meddle. She told me what would happen. Even Mary knew what would happen." I choked on a sob and immediately dropped my eyes. I felt the heat of Dr. Sawyer's gaze above me.

"Listen to me carefully, Elizabeth. What happened to Caroline tonight would have happened no matter what. It would have happened whether you came into her life or not. All you need believe is this. Because you came into her life, she came into yours, looking for you, looking for help. After all is said, that may be the only thing that saved her life"

His last words brought a rush of emotion. I jerked with silent sobs that squeezed out my tears. I would not look up from my desk, but the tears that dropped from my cheeks glistened as they fell through the soft glow of the candlelight.

"What is it you're doing?"

I nodded my head as if to say 'nothing', while trying to regain my composure and a speaking voice. At last I uttered, "writing a letter."

"Hmm. Well, do try and get some rest. You did good, Elizabeth. I am proud of you—very proud."

"Yes, sir."

From that evening on, we took it a day at a time. Even when given the copious amounts of opium, Caroline whimpered continuously from her pain. She was mostly incoherent. The wounds healed with difficulty. They would scab over preventing sufficient drainage and then would fester terribly as Dr. Sawyer had predicted. Mary would have to soak her in mild solutions of saltwater, which were unbearably painful, but both opened and cleansed the wounds. The baths were kept as hot as possible to force the wounds to expel their pus. The sight was both agonizing and sickening. The signs of scarring were all about. What kind of parents could subject a helpless child to such brutality?

TEN

On the sixth day of Caroline's care, a woman entered the infirmary almost as soon as the door had been unlocked for morning hours. The tinkle of the bell announced her arrival, and she introduced herself as Mrs. Beyers. She appeared common in her heavy corduroy dress, bonnet, and woolen shawl.

She seemed very anxious and went on to explain to us that she was searching for her lost daughter. The name Caroline barely rolled off her tongue, and we were frozen in place. The room went silent. We stood there unmoving, lost for words, staring at this person before us.

The woman was quick to note our expressions. "Did I say something wrong? It's Caroline! She's here! She's here, isn't she. Oh! Praise the Lord. I have been worried sick, looking for that girl."

"You are Caroline's mother?" Dr. Sawyer asked trying to conceal his astonishment.

"Oh, yes, I am! She's here isn't she." The woman grew excited.

"Would you please have a seat, Mrs. Beyers?"

"What is it? You know something. Is she here? If she is, you must tell me. I must see her. I want to see her now. I've been worried sick." The woman became lightly agitated and somewhat demanding.

"Please! Mrs. Beyers, have a seat." Dr. Sawyer spoke with an authoritative voice and took control of the situation. She did as he demanded.

"Yes, she is here. She is very sick and under heavy sedation."

"Sick? I must see her! I must! Please, let me pass!" The woman jumped to her feet and attempted to sidestep Dr. Sawyer, who reached out to restrain her.

"Mrs. Beyers! I am afraid I must ask you to take control of yourself. Please! I implore, take hold of yourself and be seated!" Mrs. Beyers cowered before Dr. Sawyer's demands and began to sense the gravity of the situation. Slowly, she sank back into her chair. Her eyes began to glass over.

"What's become of my baby?" she mumbled.

"I will waste no time, but state frankly that Caroline was whipped so severely that she nearly died. She still may, if we fail to keep her wounds cleaned out. She is permanently disfigured; of this, I have no doubt. Mrs. Beyers, I must ask, of what do you know about this matter?"

Mrs. Beyers sat motionless and gazed around the room as though in a trance. Her head rolled about as her eyes welled up with emotion, then dropped into her upheld hands. She hid herself from our view.

"You must think the very worst of me, but I love my daughter." She shook her head. "I love my daughter. She's my first. The first is always special. If I stay, I lose her, and if I leave, I lose her." She cried through her hands. She sobbed and the tears fell.

"Mrs. Beyers, has this happened before?" She looked up and nodded affirmatively to the fact.

"Yes, but never so bad she required the service of a doctor."

"Do you have other children?" Again, she shook her head.

"Yes. Three others, but he never pays 'em mind. It's different between him and Caroline. There's this bond between 'em that tears 'em apart. There's no middle ground. He adores her, and can never do enough to please her, but when he goes into a rage, he vents his fury at her. It's some kind of insanity the two of them share. I can't leave with four children, and I can't stop the madness."

Dr. Sawyer studied the woman, while Mary and I stood still and silent. I could see he was making a judgment of this mother. He stood up and spoke to her quietly.

"You may come with me now, Mrs. Beyers, but I must warn you to prepare yourself, it will not be a pleasant sight."

We followed as he escorted her upstairs to Caroline's room and let her enter. Caroline was lying on her stomach with her back bared and covered with a salve to keep the wounds soft. Mrs. Beyers gasped. She turned at once to face the wall. She slid her hands about as if to find her way out of a cage.

"Oh, god forgive me! What has he done? What has he done?" She spoke to herself. She turned around and cowered before the sight of her daughter. "What can I do, I don't know what to do." It was a plea of sincerity. It was at this point; I spoke up, much to the surprise of all in the room.

"Leave her, Mrs. Beyers."

"What?"

She turned to look at me through grief-stricken eyes.

"Leave her and she'll live. Take her back and she'll die. You know that. You've seen for yourself, and there can be no denying it." I spoke my mind with firm conviction. Mary moved forward intent on hushing me—hoping to soften so outrageous a proposal, but she cut herself short, undoubtedly thinking over her regrets involving our first incident with Caroline.

"I—I don't understand," she stammered.

I held up three posts, and without taking my eyes off her, I made my point. "I sent out sixteen letters across this country to families who I thought might take Caroline and give her a good home. It has only been four days, and already I have three families who are willing to take her in and provide for her. You have to let her go if you wish her to live. You see here in my hand, it can be done. Whether Caroline lives or dies is a choice you will now make."

"Elizabeth!" Mary was unable to restrain herself.

"I speak the truth, Mary, and Mrs. Beyers knows better than we."

Dr. Sawyer kept silent.

"I—I—I don't know if I could do that. She's my first. She's so special to me."

As she bemoaned her situation, I moved toward her and took her arm. I led her to the bedside.

"Look at her. Look at her closely, Mrs. Beyers. You can if you love her. You can leave her with me and know in your heart she will be safe. Look at her, Mrs. Beyers. Take a good look with your heart. Is this what you want?"

"N-n-n-n-noooo," she wailed in desperation.

"You must leave her. Leave her with me."

Mrs. Beyers summoned up the strength to look long and hard at her daughter's wounds. She wept openly and the tears disappeared into her daughter's hair. She leaned over to kiss her baby's head. Caroline was too heavily drugged to respond. Mrs. Beyers then stood up and prepared herself to leave. She looked directly into my eyes and expressed a love and frustration that could not be put into words. She turned away and stepped toward the door, but before leaving the room, she turned back to face us one last time.

"I know what kind of person you think I am. I will know that until the day I die."

She burst into sobs, her cries echoing in the stairwell as she descended the steps in haste to take her leave. The trail of her wailing was cut off by the slam of the front door and the protest of a hard struck bell. We three were left to ourselves, standing still in the silence once again, a silence more notable for our loss of words and the labored breathing of a drugged Caroline.

The issue had been brought to conclusion in a matter of moments. It was done with such suddenness and with such boldness on my part, that it felt unsettling even to me. The entire event was short-lived but intense, and like all other calamities, it too would pass.

Yet, not before shaping up to become a milestone in my life, for the incident reawakened within me a persuasion to engage once again in the helping of those in need. I was suddenly compelled to resume an earlier lifestyle that had been interrupted by Lady Rebecca's death. I had thought many times of the cat on the post, and in my heart, I felt I had done the right thing. I also felt there were many more suffering creatures awaiting my help.

The week had also taught me another lesson about life. That being, no matter how brutal some acts of violence, they weren't always as simple as people inflicting pain upon others. They were also manifestations of problems deep-rooted in relation-ships that matured into distorted visions of love. Love was a difficult thing to understand at best, and for me this insight was both perplexing and frightful, for it seemed we hurt most the ones we love. I thought of Mr. Claussen.

Caroline went on to regain her strength, but suffered from the loss of her family. Even in light of the beatings she endured, they being the near death of her, she was fraught with anguish for having been separated from her father. Arrangements were made for letters to be passed back and forth through me from Caroline to her mother, Mrs. Beyers, and vice versa. I made no attempt to hide the fact I was opening Caroline's letters and reading them to assure myself at no time did she attempt to reveal her whereabouts.

Her feelings for her father were apparent to all. Through her letters, I could see, she found no fault in his action. She was the sole focus of his being and she thrived on that attention. The arrangements made for her safekeeping gave rise to much emotional pain and suffering, for she was unable to see the signs of her own demise. It was a strange dark love, mysterious and incomprehensible, a love that beckoned death.

ELEVEN

The 'whipping,' as it came to be known in our conversations, marked a watershed, a point beyond which I would never return to the relationship I formerly enjoyed with Mary and Dr. Sawyer. The consequences of my intervention changed not only the life of Caroline, but mine as well, for without realizing it at the time, I essentially removed myself forever from that selfish and irresponsible world of children.

On that day in particular, by my own accord, I was determined to right a wrong at whatever cost. Not only had I chosen to do so in behalf of another with no thought given to reward or personal gain, but I also had readily jumped into a situation that would have given the most confident, conscientious and mature of adults reason to pause. My actions that afternoon clearly heralded my coming of age with no less fanfare than one might find in a hall half filled with trumpeters. All of a sudden, at least to the rest of the world, I had grown up.

Mary and Dr. Sawyer now approached me in a manner much more direct, more up front and straightforward. Mary still showered me with affection, for she knew my needs, but she was far less protective. Her love and affection was more that of a close friend and less that of a guardian. She encouraged me to get out more, to go into the city and be seen, to find a man.

Mary no longer was so apt to question my activities in order to pass judgment or give permission because for the most part she and Dr. Sawyer respected my decisions. They had determined I could hold my own if the burdens of fate were upon me. Taken as a whole, the changes generated by the event were profound and apparent, taken in part, they came with subtlety and sometimes unexpected.

"Elizabeth?" called, Dr. Sawyer.

"Yes."

"I would like to ask something of you that might seem rather strange at first, but I am sure you will understand my request once you have heard me out."

I looked up from my book to see Dr. Sawyer smiling at me. It was obvious he wasn't upset or concerned, so I was all ears and curious.

"What would that be?" I returned the smile, for we were all in good humor.

"I have discussed this a number of times with Mary as of late, and she has finally insisted I take the matter up with you and not her." Mary was listening and nodding from across the room.

"What?" Now, I was more than curious.

113

"I wondered if you would object to addressing me as something other than Dr. Sawyer. I find it awkward. Actually, my preference is Allen."

"Allen?" I laughed. I understood the implications at once and I was embarrassed. Dr. Sawyer went on to explain himself.

"I am serious. My feelings have always been somewhat— what shall I say—*hurt*," he kidded. "I was never privileged enough to be called your 'father', and I know you address me as 'Doctor' out of respect, but try and imagine how bizarre that must feel to me when I consider you to be family. Of course, I don't expect you to call me father—that would be ludicrous, but Doctor or Mister Sawyer is just as unfitting from my point of view. It was awkward when you were twelve, but now that you are about to be sixteen, and we think of you as an adult, it seems even worse.

I feel very strongly that the time as come for us to be on a first name basis. Not to mention that I have never heard you address Mary as Mrs. Sawyer. You are now an adult, Elizabeth, and I am an adult, and for the rest of our lives, whether you remain here in our house or are happily married in some other state, you will always be like a sister-in-law to me or at the very least, a dear friend. Friends, who go though life as close as we, address each other by their first names. So, having spoke my piece, tell me, is that a problem for you?"

"No, sir. I am flattered, honored, really I am. I am happy to call you Allen if that is what you prefer, but it will take some doing to break me of my habits. I think it will take a lot of getting used to— much like those days when I first called Lady Rebecca *mother*."

"Oh, have no fear, Elizabeth. If you continue to call me Dr. Sawyer, I will simply respond by calling you Miss Dennison," he paused and turned to look at Mary, "or maybe I should say Miss *Claussen* seeing as how that is what everyone else in Boston calls her."

* * *

We three chuckled, but it was true. By announcing their intent to adopt me, the Claussens had given birth to a common misbelief that had taken on a life of its own. As I grew, so too did the misunderstanding. Within hours of Lady Rebecca's death, Mr. Claussen and I disappeared from public view leaving nothing but rumor and the assumption I had been adopted. Because of a grand party and one ceremonious announcement days before her death, Lady Rebecca ushered in a fallacy that was widespread and deeply embedded. The myth was hopelessly beyond anyone's ability to correct or control; this, to an extent, I was only now beginning to appreciate.

The 'whipping' had launched me once again into the limelight, and gossip regarding my readiness to defend Caroline traveled about Boston in record time. Along the way, facts became fiction as reality was riddled by rumor. The episode had been embellished to the point of legend, and unfortunately for me, Caroline no longer lived in the Boston area where she might be called upon to bring some sagacity to the stories.

One version had me jumping into the Charles to rescue a drowning child after a cruel father had thrown her into the river. In another particularly colorful account, I suffered brain damage during a battle to the death as I fought to protect Caroline from a renegade Indian molester. The more I attempted to assert the simple truth; the more I looked like Joan of Arc. I had become nothing short of a saint, and many viewed my coming out into public as the long awaited resurrection of Lady Rebecca's spirit. Again and again I would hear faces in a crowd call out a most unsettling announcement.

"She is the chosen one!"

"She is the chosen one!"

115

One thing was for certain, I found myself suddenly swamped by requests to attend community affairs. If I wasn't busy enough with projects of my own, others were constantly chasing me down, seeking and pleading for my support in their own cause, if only to stop by and make an appearance.

After years of being absent from social work, I was again traveling down paths I knew as a child. Past familiarities awaited my return, none more so than the faces of old friends long since seen. Even these people, who should have known better, stepped up to state in public that I was the adopted Claussen child, and they did so in droves with unabashed pretense. I was met everywhere with great fanfare and ado.

Swirling afresh now, was talk of the day and manner in which Lady Rebecca announced my adoption at the Barrington Hotel. Common folk from every corner reveled in re-telling how milady had an axe to grind, and how she uplifted a simple maiden to the ranks of lords and ladies. They retold the tales of how her announcement was made in a great and dramatic fashion in order to make clearly understood my standing not only in her heart and home, but also among her peers. In truth, they could hardly embellish the story or stretch the facts for the event in its entirety made all the daily journals. It leveled the upper crust of Boston. Now, I realized how effective was her action, for it was still remembered with passion among the poor in spite of the years gone by.

At first, as with the rumors about Caroline, I tried my best to dispel the adoption misunderstanding, but after correcting people day to day, every step of the way, I finally shut my mouth in silent protest and set free the myth to run its course. It became astonishingly obvious to me that people didn't wish to hear the truth. They didn't care to investigate the facts. People absolutely wanted me to be a Claussen. I found this amazing, but in time I came to understand why.

What those in the charitable groups remembered from the past, which I was only now beginning to fully grasp, was this:

whenever one used the Claussen name—*things happened*; they happened fast and without question. The Claussen years had been the golden years in the community for social work. They were times when everyone came together for a cause, and everyone wanted those times back.

For these reasons, no matter what my endeavor, no matter how indecisive my direction, no matter how frivolous my request, I was taken dead serious, as though my word was gospel. I merely had to whisper the name Elizabeth Claussen and the seas parted. People expected me to spread the Claussen name, even abuse it to my advantage; whatever was necessary to further my cause and hopefully theirs.

And this I did. At first, the inner me felt somewhat belittled, as though I were merely a vassal shouldering the weight of an immense fortune, which was the only thing that mattered to anyone. Thankfully, I was not an insecure woman by nature, and I pressed on working hard to make 'Elizabeth' the only thing that mattered. Through effort and dedication, I was making headway and a name synonymous with success and accomplishment, one with promise as well as power—power to make change.

Not that I could separate myself from Claussen's wealth in the eyes of others, they weren't fools, but at least I could attempt to keep it within perspective. If by conscience, I was reluctant to use the Claussen name, I was more reluctant to spend the Claussen resources recklessly. It was as Mary had explained, when conferring with the tutors, money was a tool. It could be an instrument of pleasure or punishment, of welfare or war. It was persuasive; it was pervasive. It should be used judiciously.

I worked to set goals for myself while the community worked out its own agenda. Theirs were ambitions and hopes that I would be the person to fill Lady Rebecca's shoes. It seemed remote that anyone could do that, but I was pleased to rediscover that charitable work was as natural for me as taking my next breath. It was an activity and an arena where I felt welcome and at ease. And why shouldn't I? My familiarity with the ins and outs of social work were learned early, since age nine at Lady Rebecca's side.

For certain, there was plenty of opportunity for me to prove myself because after a decade of ongoing decline, Boston still awaited recovery. Her glory years seemed behind her and the future looked bleak in the best of light. It was disheartening, depressing actually to realize how many of her citizens suffered as they struggled to hold on. There was little room to turn, for Massachusetts as a whole was in a poor way. Her dories, her shallops and sloops were beached. Her cod and mackerel fisheries all but destroyed. Her land forever rocky, unproductive, and serving only to put the strongest willed souls to test.

Contrary to common belief, in hard times such as this, the very wealthy always gave to the poor. It was the moderately wealthy families that might or might not. Oftentimes you could sense their embarrassment for enjoying good fortune while so many went without, and for that reason they shied away simply to avoid guilt.

Common folk saw misery frightfully close, living as they did one step ahead of the impoverished. From their point of view, if the well-heeled of the world could do little to make a differ- ence in the bloated ranks of Boston's poor, then what chance was there for the average struggling person to make a difference?

They failed to understand that a person's labor was often needed more than their money. Whether rich or poor, time was the hardest thing to give up for another, especially if there was no clear sense of direction or personal satisfaction to be realized. When one wasn't working sun-up to sunset, then one was col- lapsed in bed.

Mr. Claussen was keenly aware of this, and pointed out how Lady Rebecca earned her reputation by understanding these obstacles. He reminded me how she was able to overcome them by reaching out to all classes and making them feel good about becoming involved.

Lady Rebecca motivated Bostonians out of bed with balls, banquets and social activities. Her affairs were most attractive and missed only with the deepest of regret. Through such interaction, Lady Rebecca made each individual feel a crucial element to the success of any project she sought to promote.

Lady Rebecca's ability to draw people together was remarkable, a fact I remembered being expressed on many occasions. It was that part of her personality that held the key to her success. I was both friendly and outgoing, so it was natural for me to model my efforts in a like manner. Experience was the best teacher, and I had witnessed milady's every move, her every plan and decision. I had served in one fashion or another at all of Lady Rebecca's affairs. Mary and I stood by her side. We ran her errands. We saw to the details. We staved off the many small disasters. All in all, I understood the business of charity better than anyone else my age.

Even when knowing well what experience I possessed, I took time to search my heart and determine which aspirations would be mine in life. I viewed my future from every angle, and after much thought, concluded I was making the right decisions. I hardly underestimated the challenge in taking Lady Rebecca's place, but I was gaining confidence and moving closer to trying on her shoes for size.

Privately, my only apprehension was a fear of failing to reach Lady Rebecca's standards, not before the community, not before Mary and Allen, but in the eyes of Mr. Claussen. I was frightened by the faith he placed in me. I was afraid of the comparisons he would surely make. I wrote him of these fears. I would go into great detail about my insecurities. He never seemed to tire of my ramblings or whining and worked hard to convince me how capable I was in my own right. He encouraged me in every manner to press forward, to give my all.

He instructed me to use the 'account' whenever I saw the opportunity to be charitable. He said it would guarantee my forgiveness for many small mistakes I might make along the way.

I had come to understand that Mr. Claussen needed trustworthy people to oversee his money for the poor. He was pushing me, preparing me to become one of those people. He wanted me to spend generously, albeit wisely for those in need.

I began to accept Mr. Claussen as more than merely a father figure. He was attentive to my interests, supportive, and quick to encourage. He was directing my life by pressing me into pursuing my interests and realizing my dreams. I would seek his advice with every stroke of my quill. He was my soul mate, my confidant, and I wrote to him of the most personal matters without shame. His letters in return raised my hopes and sent my spirit soaring.

18-10-13

Darling Elizabeth,

I have recently received your letters. Who can know my joy? I have read them so frequent; I fear they split at the folds. How comes yet my agony returning to remind me of the losses in my life. Then, as if from heaven, as the albatross alights upon my deck, comes your letters to save me from my remorse. Such is your medicine for my weary heart.

If there were to be a thermometer so able to measure the warmth given my cabin by stove, bottle, or pen during the cold damp nights at sea, I can only say it would reveal that nothing might further warm my self than words flowing from your heart and hand.

I read with great interest your accomplishments in school and community, and also the goings on of family and friends about Boston. I must say I am pleased and continually inspired by your unselfish devotion to Caroline, one so wronged in life. Thoughts of her situation pain me, but what prevails in my mind above all else is your attention to her cause, your determination to remain strong in her behalf.

How I wish you might have known the strength of my Rebecca. What I would give to hear Rebecca voice her admiration for the mature young woman you are today. She would have been aglow with pride, as am I. She would have beamed in your presence, as would I. She would have showered you with her praise; of all these things I am certain. I have every confidence that although she is unable to convey her compliments to you, trust she has seen all, and the good Lord has gotten an ear full. Stay the course, Elizabeth, stay the course.

As for myself, I show my pride by asking you to be my hand, to move funds in my behalf. In this case, to oversee a transfer of money from the account for the benefit of young Caroline and the family taking her into their care. Also, present whatever you deem necessary to make joyous the families of the orphans through gifts and merriment these Holy Days.

Also, if I may impose upon your good nature one last request—being that the children are in the custom of posting cards to one another during the season—might you present to them the list of names I have included herein. I ask they send my men a card or letter; it will do much to lift their spirits, they being so far from home during the Christmas. Your attention to this matter would mean a great deal to all aboard the REBECCA.

The sun now sets and soon I must close. Let me be quick and say that I marvel at how time has transformed you into a person of esteem. I applaud Dr. Sawyer on his request to be on a first name basis, and implore you extend this same privilege my way so I might no longer be approached in such formal and distant manner. I beg you know me as Christopher, or if you so prefer, 'Claus' as my close friends have nicknamed me. Please, honor me thus.

Again, for your inquisitive mind, I am presently lat. N 15 & lg W 150 deg. making way for Hawaii. The weather this evening is fair and the wind fresh with a following sea. It rises well on our stem. The mates are fine as always, not an 'old sailor' among the lot. They ask often of you and the orphans, and will be eager to hear news of your activities and well-being.

I must retire, for my eyes grow weary in the dim light of the lamp. If fortune is with us, we will sound an eastbound vessel, and I shall convey this letter to you with speed. Post next to Valparaiso, I should be there, moored in three months time. May God be with you, my child.

Love, Christopher N. Claussen (Claus)

P.S. Please, remember the Holy Day cards, and know my Christmas gifts and wishes for you are soon to follow. Expect your birthday present to arrive in Boston any day now. Use your account, Elizabeth, or my work to profit is for naught.

* * *

Mr. Claussen was the whole of my private world. He was mine, and mine only, as were my invisible friends when a child. I hardly attached a face to the man anymore, for I came to know and love him through his words. They made him almost omnipotent, a sovereign being living within the letters to satisfy my soul of every need. He was my heart and conscience, too far away when I wished to see him, and too near when I read his reprimands.

In order to understand how private a part of my life he was, one had to know that from the day he sailed for China aboard his REBECCA, even though we wrote each other the best we were able, I next saw him four years after his departure. It was on my sixteenth birthday in December of eighteen-thirteen.

Mary and Allen, in cahoots with our close friends, made a big deal of that day. It was a combination of things they wished to celebrate, my age now being sixteen, my becoming an adult, and among other things, praise for my going to the aid and standing by Caroline, a fact that was still being greatly touted much to my embarrassment.

Christopher had kept up with my affairs through his letters, but he never made mention of coming to Boston to share in my day. In fact, he had said only that he expected to be in Valparaiso. In spite of what he said, I dared to believe he would be present out of foolishness. Enough so that when he appeared I was speechless, but not nearly as surprised as one might have expected. In spite of my common sense, since my days as a small child, I always believed Mr. Claussen was able to read my mind. I believed he felt my needs.

At his request, I spent the night seated directly across the table from him so he might *'fill his eyes with the sight of me'*. I sat blushing, while he sat tan and swarthy looking. He sported a beard and no longer looked empty and lost as he had following Lady Rebecca's death. He looked every bit as I remembered him during those heady days of past. He was a powerful man, a man of great stature, and as I studied him I wondered why he paid me any mind at all. I was spellbound by his presence.

It was an awkward reunion, for we were both changed enough as to appear strangers before each other's eyes, but my heart knew him at once, and he produced within me a fountain of emotion. He looked upon me with eyes that displayed dedication, love, and affection. I could hear his heart in his voice, and feel its warmth in the touch of his hand.

These sensations were to become my new memories, for the dinner lasted but only a few hours whereupon he departed as quickly as he had arrived, leaving me alone with his gifts to pine for a second time. I never concluded whether seeing him for so short a time after so many years longing, served to raise my spirits or destroy them. It was a numbing event filled with insufferable self-awareness made all the worse by a tongue bent on twisting itself into one irreversible knot after another.

So self-conscious. I remembered little of his words although my evening was spent no farther than an arm's length away. I was embarrassed beyond measure by my behavior and immaturity, and I welcomed a return to the safety of letters. Sadly, the return was to last for many, many years.

8-8-17

Dear Claus,

How I wish you were with me. Forgive me if the ink is smeared for my tears are in my way. I have broken off my affair with Michael and I think dying would be easier.

I am not certain if I suffer more from a broken heart or embarrassment. He came by last night to call on me, and as often is the case, Lydia Pennington was visiting. I introduced them, and the evening went on as might be expected until it came respectable for Michael to take his leave.

After his departure, Lydia and Mary called out to me to come and sit. They looked concerned and voiced a need to discuss a certain issue of delicacy. It turns out that Lydia knows for fact that Michael is betrothed to another. I have no reason to doubt her words, as she is a close friend and knows virtually every person to have ever set foot in Boston. I can only assume Michael was courting me and weighing his best financial future or hoping to fulfill a final sexual conquest prior to his marriage.

I will say in honesty that no such union took place. For that matter, I barely even kissed the man, though my heart yearned for him most positively. I was crushed by the news, for I have lost either way. I felt every bit the fool.

The ruse only strengthened my belief that I am destined to endure ill-fortune with men. I fear I have no understanding of them whatsoever. What possesses them to wreak such havoc upon a woman's heart? If it isn't sad enough I lack the lure to

124

draw a man to my side, I suffer to know that my appeal attracts only the worst of the gender. If only I had your shoulder to cry upon. Why are men not more like you? Why are you not here? Why must I be a nineteen-year-old spinster?

Forgive me my selfish rambling, I shall write you a proper letter soon, one free of complaint. For now I am pressed to confide in your spirit, to seek solace while sorting out my troubled heart. My thoughts of you settle me, as does nothing else. I know you understand.

I beg you take care.

Love, Elizabeth.

* * *

I turned my attention entirely to community work and most of what we discussed in our correspondence centered on charitable activities. I followed his direction and made the best of his advice, which came free-flowing and filled with insight. We worked together planning strategies and placing financial assistance. Of course this is what I would have expected, for as *'his hand'* I was spending *'his money'* most liberally.

Aside from issues of charity, Mr. Claussen leaned hard on me to keep at my studies, not only assuring me I would earn my credentials as a teacher, but also fully expecting it. He made my education a priority—even above the work I did for others. He always said, *"education missed at an early age costs one years of meaningful life; and like time lost, that can never be retrieved."*

The thought of my becoming a teacher pleased him very much, and he was never short on words to express it. His pleasure was in stark contrast to the common men who suffocated me and disapproved of women *'ruined by knowledge'*.

TWELVE

When autumn of eighteen hundred and nineteen came to pass, I was twenty-one years of age, soon to be twenty-two. It was frightful the way time sped by, but this was a memorable season because much to the joy of everyone close to me, I had finally finished all of the requirements needed to become a certified teacher.

On top of this, there had been a good deal of talk about town regarding the opening of a public free-school. We were vocal in our support for such an institution, as it would be the first in the nation. However, the idea of a woman teaching in such a facility was still heavily frowned upon by both church and community, a frame of mind seemingly impossible to change. Yet, I was not to be dissuaded. For one thing, only *'unmarried'* women were allowed to teach and that was certainly my situation.

Christopher was Christopher. He had sent numerous graduation gifts from the Orient including bolts of silk, handiwork in mother-of-pearl, and promises of pieces of jade. Mary and Allen were making a big deal of the issue in the same way they made a big deal of my every accomplishment. They spoiled me as rotten as might any parent. To honor my graduation, they threatened to hold a grand celebration and invite half the town to participate. I knew better, but would be quieted only after they agreed to a private affair, where all attending were genuinely happy for my achievements and for me.

The night was joyful, our dinner was delicious, and other than the suffocation of embarrassment for all the attention paid, I should have had a good time. It was interesting, though, how one little flaw magnified itself into my only thought for the evening. It might have been likened to the unraveling of a fine formal gown, whereby only one thread was pulled. At first it seemed nothing, but soon the beauty of the garment began to disappear, until eventually because of the one thread, the dress and its splendor vanished entirely.

So it was with the splendor of my party. About midway through the festivities, I found myself mildly disenchanted. At first I was hardly aware of anything amiss, but as the evening progressed, I came to realize how disheartened and wanting I had become. Later that night, after an hour or two of lying in my bed restless and unable to sleep, I realized I was fully depressed. At that point, I needn't a doctor to tell me what it was that ailed me. I only had to reflect on the evening, and the way I kept looking out the corner of my eyes for a sign of Christopher.

I watched for him the whole of the night and behind my smiles a growing sadness lurked within. He never made an appearance to share in my success, and there was something of the whole affair left tarnished by his absence. I chastised myself for being so selfish. I knew that he came back to Boston to be at my sixteenth birthday. I believed he could read my mind then and I believed he could read it now, but I also knew it was a trip half way around the world, and I couldn't expect him to perform such feats every time I enjoyed some success in life.

Nevertheless, it was a notable day in my life and one that Christopher had missed. I understood I was taking it too personally, and I actually felt guilty for dwelling on it so, but I couldn't escape the fact that it hurt. I hoped the day would have been reason enough to see his face after so many years. I drifted off too sleep with an emptiness inside that no late night fare could fill.

* * *

It may have been that living on my own was accentuating a sense of loneliness or abandonment, for Boston was still my home, but I was no longer residing with Mary and Allen. I had taken an apartment some years prior, in the spring of 'seventeen' to be more precise. I was financially secure, and I felt it time to give back to Mary and Allen some of the privacy I had stolen over the years. With each passing season Mary and I only grew closer as the difference in our ages disappeared.

It may have been because we were so equal that I began to feel as though I were intruding upon their relationship. I was quite naive and knew very little of the intimacies between a man and woman, but on more than one occasion, I definitely sensed something awkward about my presence in their home. Much to their objections, I knew enough to understand it was time for me to take my own place. Mary thought me foolish and cried as though I was her last child and moving to the moon.

And so it was, a couple of days after the graduation party, I should be at my apartment browsing over teaching positions when I was suddenly interrupted by a knock at the door. I opened it, and nearly collapsed from the surprise. I can't describe the emotion that poured out as I took in the sight of him.

"Hello, Elizabeth."

Christopher stood proud as ever upon my porch. His size always amazed me. He towered over me, grinning like a devil and carrying the aroma of fresh leather. He wore more years on his face than last I saw him, but what he had lost in youth he had gained in character. He appeared robust, rugged and healthy; he was attractive. Lord, was he attractive.

"May I come in?" he asked with some concern, jolting me back to my senses.

"Oh! My word, yes! What a dolt I am, come in! Come in! I can't believe my eyes! I knew—I just knew you would come." I went to him. We embraced affectionately; I squeezing him with all my strength as he lifted me off my feet to twirl me like a paper doll. What a fabulous feeling. I was filled with genuine happiness, unbelievable happiness, teary-eyed little girl happiness.

"I don't know what to say! Why didn't you tell me? You didn't write to forewarn me, to say anything. I would have prepared—*something*. I would have at least—I don't know—at least washed my hair!" I felt suddenly very self-conscious. Christopher roared with delight.

"Elizabeth, Elizabeth, let me look at you! You are ab-so-lute-ly beautiful—stunning! You were irresistible as a child, gorgeous at sixteen, but god almighty what a lady you've become! All of twenty-one and as tempting as Eden's apple."

"Oh, please don't say such things. You make me blush. I'm a mess and you know it." I wiped tears of joy across my face. "What are you doing here? Come in, come in, and sit, sit! Let me make you some tea." I took his arm and pulled him force-fully. I led him to the sitting room. "I am so happy to see you." I began to cry. "Oh, my. Can you believe the way I am gushing?" I let out a long breath and settled myself down. "Oh, Mr. Claussen, it's so good to see you—and you look so good to see. You look healthy, healthy as a horse, and I like that."

"Mr. Claussen!" He looked hurt. "Mr. Claussen? Since when, am I Mr. Claussen? I thought we had an agreement. I thought we dispensed with those formalities years ago. I thought you elected to call me Claus because you said only Rebecca called me Christopher and for you that was impossible." He was teasing me half-hearted.

"I'm sorry, I'm sorry. Truly, I am. It's easy to say Claus in letters, but standing before you—that's entirely different. I am not accustomed to addressing you so informally to your face. For me it's always been Mr. Claussen in person."

"I hope it was for the last time, Elizabeth."

"For the last time, Claus. Claus! Claus! There, Claus it is, if that will make you happy."

"That will make me very happy, thank you."

"I promise I'll do my best. Now stop teasing me and tell me why you are here. I mean it's been what—five, six years this time, at least that many I am sure."

"Five."

"Five, then, but it seems more like ten. This is such a surprise. And so suddenly, you show up at my door out of thin air like a ghost from my past. I can't believe it! I mean, what is this about? I'm so happy to see you. I cannot believe you are actually here. And the gifts—thank-you for the wonderful gifts. Why are you here? You're supposed to be in China. I don't know what to say." I went on babbling nervously, incoherently. I was giddy with emotion.

"Ha! As if you didn't know, your certification as a teacher, of course! Did you believe I would forget such a thing? Have I not followed the course of your life through every turn, through every bump in the road? Have I not been witness to your every accomplishment and achievement? You have always made me proud, and how many would know your merits better than I?

"Moreover, you have kept me in your confidence, and now I bask in your glory. You are special, Elizabeth, not only in your studies, but also in your heart. I can truthfully say that you deserve all the praise bestowed. I hoped very much to give my congratulations to you in person. So, I used your letters to adjust my schedule and bring me home as close to your party as possible, and regrettably—I missed it—but I am here."

I shook my head in disbelief. "I should have known you would come. I'm so sorry I doubted you. When I didn't see you at the party I felt just terrible. Events aren't events without you, and I kept looking and watching and hoping. You never showed up, and I was honestly depressed. I went to bed that night and I couldn't sleep. I laid there the whole of the night wondering about what became of you. And now, here you are, and I am happy to see you, very happy to see you. I guess I should know by now that you never forget, do you?"

"No, my darling, I never forget."

I began to wipe away my tears a second time, as he followed me into the kitchen and sat at my table.

"Take your coat off." Sniffling through my stuffy nose, I poured two cups of tea and sat down next to him.

"Well, the party wasn't really about my being certified as a teacher anyway. I only completed my courses and took the examination. But, I did pass the tests. I am waiting for word—and you know how *men* can be. They are funny about those things. A female instructor, a head mistress if you will, is a very touchy issue. You know, I might be an immoral woman."

"Well, you are that!"

"What?" I looked at him somewhat taken aback.

"Certified!?" He was grinning and obviously flaunting a secret.

I studied him for a moment. "Claus, I haven't been told—."

"You will be soon enough. You proved yourself in your studies over the years. You proved yourself in your determination to achieve your goals. You have proved yourself by a thousand efforts to help others about you. I have no intention of allowing some pompous ass with a head full of personally demented moral persuasions redirect your future at this point. You, my darling, are a teacher—fully capable and fully certified."

"Are you saying that you addressed the board? Is that not cheating?"

"You bet it is. Cheating for the good, my child, and I am sure it would have been cheating in a different direction if they'd had their way. Persuaded is probably a better word. Those men think too highly of themselves. The moral quickly become immoral when it comes to filling their coffers. Remember what you wrote about the tutors? Besides, their view of women dates back to the

131

Stone Age, and when a man looks out at a woman from inside a cave, he suffers tunnel vision."

"You are shameless in your shining armor, Mr. Cla—*Claus*. I pray you didn't come all the way back to Boston to do this for me. Please, tell me different."

There was a twinkle in his eye. "Such a foolish question, Elizabeth. I came back for business of course—but as long as I was in town, if I might offer a hand in your behalf then...."

"I came back to see you were in a good way before I—ahh—told you that I am leaving so to speak—and—well, I wanted to be sure all was in order before I—you know, left, you know what I mean, peace of mind. However, I assure you, I did nothing for you that you had not already earned on your own."

I wouldn't have doubted that Christopher was in Boston *only* for my sake, but for an unexpected slip of his thoughts while speaking. He was quick to refocus on the subject, still a glimpse of something had been revealed. I studied him for a moment.

"I think we need to skip over the part about what I did on my own, and focus on whatever it was that you just said about your leaving. I just know I am going to hear something less than joyful. You have already said the 'leaving' word and your coat still hangs upon your shoulders. It isn't that I should be surprised, but why are you stumbling over your words? You are always leaving. Is this somehow different? You already broke my heart once, and even though it was years ago, I promise, you may rest assured it will not happen again." I was only kidding, but I felt uneasy. Christopher was not one to stumble. Warily, I waited for his response.

"When standing in a hell of guilt and remorse, I believe before God there is always a chance for forgiveness, but before a woman, I don't know. —Different?" He looked out the window into the distance. "Yes, this time the leaving is different."

"Oh, Lord, Claus, it isn't your health is it?"

"Absolutely not. No, no nothing like that. Nothing of the kind."

"Oh, thank god."

"It's ahh—, let's not go into all of that right now."

"But—."

"No buts."

"But—."

"No buts. Let us just enjoy our time together while we are able. Do me the honor of joining me for dinner tonight. Please." He offered a broad smile.

"Dinner! Tonight! Well—well—why not. All right, I'll ask nothing more—for now. Dinner it is. Lucky for you, I haven't been to dinner on the arm of a man since the birth of Christ, and for that reason, I'll hold my tongue and questions for later, but later I will expect some answers."

"I'll agree to that."

"You must give me time to bathe myself and prepare. I scarcely remember how."

Christopher looked at me in astonishment. He tilted his head and spoke hesitantly.

"There is something seriously wrong with the men in this town. Is it possible they are all eunuchs? Are they all light on their feet or blind? I would do nothing less than chase the likes of you to the ends of the earth."

"Move back." I teased. He laughed and then spoke seriously.

"I would think you should prefer I left you to your business and returned later, yes?"

"Not on your life! *I should prefer* you lie back on my bed and rest yourself. I am certain that once you walk out that door, my dinner will vanish as will you for another five years to be certain."

"I wouldn't do that."

"Oh yes you would! Your record proves it! Now take off those boots. They stay with me in the bathroom."

"In the bathroom! Surely, you jest."

"Surely, I do not. Surely, they will not leave my sight. Now, give me that coat and come along." Christopher did as I asked and I led him into my bedroom. I made sure he was relaxed and comfortable. I leaned over to kiss him on his forehead. "Would you like to be tucked in?" I teased.

"Ha! That would be motherly."

I turned to leave, boots assuredly in hand. "Where are you taking me for this glorious dinner?"

"The Barrington of course."

I stopped dead in my tracks. Slowly, I turned back to face him.

"The Barrington Hotel?" I couldn't believe what I heard. I couldn't believe he said it. Any lingering thoughts about our earlier conversation regarding his leaving were suddenly wiped away. I was stunned.

"It should be interesting don't you think?" he asked.

"I never went back. I haven't been back since Lady Rebecca's death."

"Nor I. All the more interesting."

"Claus, I am serious. Through all the years, I have never been back. I do a lot of social work and I pass on every event that is held at the Barrington. Is there a reason it must be the Barrington?"

"I believe what you say, and I understand, for I too am still trying to put old memories and feelings into their proper perspective. The Barrington is one of the few that remain to be sorted away, and it's time to put it to rest. It is just a hotel, and for a decade I have paid for half of the third floor. I always thought if I were ever to go back, I would wish to go back with you. Will this be a problem? Is it more than you can handle?" He waited for my answer as I thought it out.

"No—no, not anymore. Not if I go back with you, if we go together. At least I won't feel a need to explain my emotions. You are right about one thing; it will definitely be interesting. Fortunately, I've had my years of youth to erase away the memories that troubled me most. I'm concerned it will be more of a problem for you."

Christopher placed his hands behind his head upon the pillow. He stared up at the ceiling. "Oh, I'll be fine. Don't worry about me. It was hard, Elizabeth, hard as a sailor's knuckles, hard as a belaying pin, but for the most part, I survived it." He looked at me. "I think tonight, instead of letters, tonight we talk. We talk, and talk, and we talk. We talk about all these things. Some will be funny, some will be tearful, but all will be faced, and done so face to face. Now, go and get yourself ready. I promise we will have a wonderful time, in spite of old memories that are all too often sad."

It took awhile for me to feel myself presentable. Needless to say, I fussed over every detail of my appearance ten times more than necessary. I wanted to look my best because I knew that Christopher and I would draw Boston's undivided attention the moment we passed through the front doors of the Barrington Hotel for the first time in ten years. Our appearance in the lobby would not only be the talk of the town, but most likely the front-page story of tomorrow's Boston Journal, for our absence from the Barrington Hotel had been legendary.

To be entirely honest, there was also a personal reason I fussed over myself. I wanted to look ravishing. For the first time in my life, I would stand at Christopher's side as more than just his ward. I wanted him to know I had grown up. What I couldn't keep secret from myself was the embarrassing fact that I wanted Christopher to feel jealous of other men's stares.

135

Our relationship was markedly changed, just as it had been the last time we met. I was now relating to him as an adult and our conversation moved words and thoughts between us that reflected my maturity. We laughed and conversed lightheartedly while I dressed until his responses tapered off and eventually stopped. I wasn't surprised, in light of the way in which I was rambling on mindlessly for the sake of entertaining.

I returned to my bedroom with boots in hand and was amused to find him sleeping. It was a good thing, for it gave me a moment to settle down and relax. To see him so comfortable in my home warmed my heart, and I moved to the side of my bed, where I gazed upon him for the longest time. I watched while he snored ever so gently. It was a sound almost completely alien to me. It was a sound that all married women knew like the cry of their babies, a sound that some cursed while others found comforting and reassuring.

It occurred to me that in all my years knowing Mr. Claussen, I couldn't ever recall seeing him sleep. I had seen him lying on his bed aboard the REBECCA on many occasions, but he was always reading, never asleep. I felt as though he had let down his guard, and for the first time ever, I was standing on the inside of the walls that protected him.

I reentered the bedroom every few minutes to reassure myself that he was really sleeping in my bed. Each time I left the room, it seemed as though I was too long away. Each time I returned, I studied him and tried to make logical sense of the enormous pull he had on me. I was dressed and now ready for dinner, but instead of waking him, I stood again leaning closely over him, watching him with fascination and a measure of shame. I studied the details of his face, his color, the lines of wear across his brow. He was older than I by some years, but he was incredibly handsome. He kept his beard short, but is was thick and chiseled. It accentuated his strength. I wondered what it would be like to be held in his massive arms, to lay alongside him as his lover.

I leaned closer to feel his breath. I was deep within my curious thoughts, wondering what it would be like to kiss him when suddenly he opened his blue eyes and pinned me in place. I flushed profusely. I smiled awkwardly, too embarrassed to move away, feeling it would only emphasize how closely I hovered over him. I was convinced that my radish-colored face revealed every thought of my amorous fantasies. He grinned at me. I countered.

"I was about to wake you. I am now ready."

"My word, so you are. Tell me I am not dreaming. Tell me you are real, for if you are not I must never awake. Only angels and mermaids look so beautiful."

"I am no angel. I am as real as real can be, and hungry *(and utterly embarrassed to death)*."

"If you are real as real can be, then I am lucky as lucky can be, and I too am hungry. It looks to be a good night for us both."

Desperate to hide my face, I focused on his arm and pulled him up from the bed. He was stiff and a little groggy. I led him by the hand back into my kitchen where he put on his boots and retrieved his coat.

"I must say you have always looked your best in red. I must also say that I believe the last time we ate together in public at the Barrington was the night of your twelfth birthday. You wore red that night as well. Whenever I think of you, in my mind you are always dressed in red. I suppose that is why I mention it. It is how I know you in my heart."

"Your memory serves you well. Lady Rebecca and I both wore red that night. Our dresses were matched. I wear red often. It suits me."

"It does indeed. Sit." He pulled back a chair.

"Pardon, me?"

137

"Sit. *Please*." He took my shoulders firmly into his large hands and sat me down. He reached around me from behind and placed a gift upon the table in front of me.

"Go on, open it. I've carried it a long time, waiting so I might see the look on your face."

"Oh, Claus, no, no, no. You shouldn't have, really, you shouldn't have." I knew at once that it would be priceless. Christopher was very generous with me.

"Nonsense, I wouldn't have it any other way. Go on open it. I will carry the look in my heart for the next ten years."

"Ten years! Wha—."

"I'm just kidding, a figure of speech." He turned my head back toward the table. "Go on now, open it for me."

"Oh! I know I shouldn't do this." I covered my face. I was most uncomfortable.

"I beg you open it, Elizabeth. I have waited so very long a time, and I swear I will have a tantrum if you don't oblige me."

"Ohhhhh." I let out a breath of exasperation. "We mus'n't have that, I hate brats."

I removed the wrappings carefully and opened the worked leather box.

"Oh—my—word. Claus!" I gasped. "I can't accept this."

"Oh yes you can. Go on now; take it out. Go on. Don't be so shy. I swear before God Almighty, I have never heard you say that you could accept a gift."

To please him, I lifted out a wide gold necklace sprinkled with hundreds of small diamonds. It reminded me of a field of frost in the morning sun.

Christopher smiled and reached around me with both his arms to take the necklace from my hands. "Allow me." He stepped behind my chair and lowered the necklace past my face much the same as Lady Rebecca had done once many years before. He leaned down and whispered in my ear. "You now own Boston." I spun around to look up at him.

"You remember!" I was shocked.

"I never forget," he insisted. "I remember Rebecca's words as though it were yesterday. I thought it was one of the most fitting truths she ever uttered."

"Oh, Claus, it is so nice to have good memories walk through that door. I have missed you so."

I stood up from my chair. I turned and moved into his arms. I kissed him. It was a simple kiss, not meant to be on the lips, but forced there by his thick beard. It was a kiss of gratitude. It was a kiss of joy and meant to be nothing more, but it lasted a second or two longer than I might have expected. It lasted just long enough to rock me to my foundations. It overwhelmed me, changed me. It was the first time in my life that my feelings felt strung about me in a hopeless tangle. The kiss completely altered my perception of this man. It stirred everything within me—moved me, choked me.

I had always felt Christopher to be a father, a protector, a teacher, a soul mate, yet this sensation was much, much different than that. I suddenly felt him physically. I found myself especially aware of him, his movements, his fragrance, the texture of the man. He had changed so much. He exuded a rugged confidence and strength. He was no longer the polished, conservative, discreet man I remembered as a child. His years at sea had salted his blood and changed him for the better. In my eyes he was everything, absolutely everything a man should be.

I was fully taken in by his presence. I was at once aware of how desperately I wanted him close to me, how much I wanted to press myself against his chest, and so I pushed away. I forced myself back from his embrace. I was shaken and feeling more than a little disoriented. I studied him briefly at arm's length as feelings of guilt welled up within. I was confused. I felt light-headed, faint.

"Are you all right, Elizabeth?" He watched me with concern as I widened the embrace.

"Yes, yes of course." I tried to collect my thoughts amid the swirl of sensations. It was as if his inner spirit captured my heart and soul, as if I had been instantly drugged. "Too much excitement I'm afraid, too splendid a gift. I love it, Claus. How could I not? But I would be embarrassed to wear it. It is just too rich. I really wish you wouldn't have. To see you again is enough for me." I struggled to refocus. My legs felt weak, my heart raced, and my insides were all a jitter—but not from the gift.

"I carried it a long time in waiting, and whenever my thoughts would turn to you, I would remove the necklace from its box and hold it up to catch the light. The more it sparkled; the clearer became my memory. I could see the way your eyes sparkled as a child on board REBECCA as we stood together looking off her bows. You must allow me a small boldness by saying, I can see that sparkle hasn't left, but instead has become flashes of fire."

I said nothing. His words squeezed from my heart every drop of emotion I possessed. I could only return his gaze, only look back into his remarkably blue eyes as a second and more profound wave of unfamiliar and overwhelming urges rushed through me. What was happening?

How could he reach into me so? There was no longer any doubt about the extent to which he was capable of moving me emotionally. He was proving to have a formidable grip on my feelings, an ability to manipulate my heart whether by intention or not. I had only barely kissed him, but in some inexplicable and mysterious way it was transformed into an act of unexpected passion.

I was horrified. The rush of feeling frightened me out of my wits. Was I being incestuous? Was I out of my mind? Had I no control of such base desires? My guilt ran rampant beneath this unmistakable attraction for him. I was being propelled into a place I did not understand. I needed to slow things down, to stop the world. I averted my eyes and escaped from his arms to slink back slowly into my chair. For the first time ever, I prayed that Christopher truly did not have the ability to read minds. I prayed he could not read my thoughts or sense my confusion. I prayed he could not feel the pounding of my heart.

"Forgive me for asking again, are you all right?"

I couldn't face him. "I am fine, Claus, the gift took my breath away. I am speechless."

"In that case, I am overjoyed to hear nothing. Now, if you would allow me to show off the only woman beautiful enough to do this necklace justice."

THIRTEEN

"To sparkling eyes and contagious laughter."

"Oh, thank-you".

"May your beauty—your wit—and your determination bring to bounty the fruit of your labor. May you realize every dream. May you hold the respect of friend and foe—and may love caress you for all your days. I salute you."

Our glasses clinked. We drank to each other with arms entwined. His eyes never left mine, and as I looked at the world through my glass of wine, it glowed; I glowed. I was euphoric. I put aside my earlier feelings of guilt, dismissed my reservations, and immersed myself in the unrestrained lavishness Christopher chose to bestow upon me. His attention was mine, all mine, and

I satiated myself with sinfully expensive wine and the glory of his affection.

We ate, we drank, and we danced before the whispering crowds. The owners of the Barrington were most pleased to see us, for many a profitable event was lost but for my reluctance to enter the hotel. Christopher and I discussed all of our memories both good and bad. We talked face to face, and faced our fears as he had promised. We were engaged without distraction, and before I realized, the night was growing late. It had passed much too quickly for my liking, and I realized it was time for me to again ask about the secret he yet had not revealed.

"Now, tell me, Claus, being that we seem to have covered most everything else, what were you stumbling about earlier this evening. What was it you wished not to reveal. I know it was about leaving so don't deny it. Is this another of your wonderful adventures? I'm going to be jealous, aren't I? It's going to be exciting, isn't it? You can tell me, I can withstand the pain.

"Are you certain I won't dishearten you with such talk?"

"No, no. At this point nothing could make me feel bad. I have enjoyed just the right amount of wine, just the right amount of dance, just the right amount of you. Please, tell me what you are up to. I want to know."

"Very well, then." He looked over my head as if searching for a place to begin. His eyes then dropped to meet mine. "I have swallowed the anchor as the old salts say—given up the sea. I am about to embark on a journey out west. Exactly where, I am not sure. For how long, I cannot say. I am merely passing through Boston long enough to see Mary, to take care of business, to gaze upon you—to see that you are comfortable and want for nothing, and then I am gone, the sooner the better for my sake."

"I can't believe my ears. You? Giving up the sea? Never."

"It's true. True as truth can be."

"I don't believe it."

"You must."

"Why would you be possessed to do such a thing? It's your life."

"Ah, well. It is, yes and no. To understand the hows and whys of my ambitions, I must remind you of those days when you first came to my home in Sweden. Back when I was young and very excited to discover what adventure was in store for those willing enough to pit their wits against the challenges of the New World.

"Remember, I was born to a fortune that was built on trees, not the sea. My ancestors owned timber in Sweden that was coveted by all, but none more so than the British, for whenever they saw a tree that scraped the clouds, they saw a ship's mast. Whenever they saw a stand of mature forest, they could see only a fleet of ships. Their visions, or might I say shortsightedness, stripped England bare of her woodlands, and once done, they had little choice but to turn to land owners the likes of my father and I for the lumber needed to support their navy and merchant fleets.

"Obviously, my family possessed plenty of those resources, but just as important, we also had the means to mill and move it. We had architects that designed and built ships specifically to transport wood, unlike the British ships that were often a combination of merchant and war vessel. Our ships were much more efficient and thereby more profitable.

"Now, don't misunderstand me, my family has been in this business for centuries. However, when there is a conflict between nations, such as there was when you came into my home, back when Napoleon struck out across the Continent, the demand for our wood and transports soared. Profits were often obscene, and I am first to admit as much.

"What you probably don't know is how I used to spend a great deal of time in and out of ports about northern Europe on my father's behalf, learning the business of our shipping and trade. I had many an opportunity to listen to stories and see

143

examples of the lumber that grew wild on unclaimed lands in the New World, and so my ambition—my blind ambition, was to go to America. The stories about timber were so unbelievable, so fantastic; I had to go see for myself.

"Yet, as fate is my master, instead of pursuing my expertise in forestry, I ended up engaged in a thriving shipping adventure between America, Europe, and China. I had never planned such an adventure, and it came about unexpectedly for two reasons.

"First, a combination of Captain Stowington's letter of nonintervention, which I received at the onset of the English blockades, and the passing of the Embargo Act by Congress. I trust you remember the day I received that article."

"Who could forget, I thought we would all wind up dead."

"We very nearly did, my love. Anyway, that letter not only opened every port for the REBECCA as he originally granted, but eventually for nearly all of my fleet. It became a guaranteed safe passage to the most handsome profits you could possibly imagine. Captain Stowington, I am certain has no idea to what extent I profited from his gratitude.

"The second reason, also completely unforeseen, was Rebecca's involvement with the charities. What began as passage for a few orphans, turned into her life's commitment. Not in my wildest dream would I have anticipated anything of the like, and I came to realize that she would have been heartbroken to leave her work behind and head off into the interior or the West Coast wilds trudging along at my heels in search for stands of lumber. I dare say by the time she passed on, Rebecca left her mark in virtually every port touched by the Atlantic.

"At least that is the way it felt to me, and that was the reason I so desperately needed to leave. There was no escaping her presence."

Christopher's expression changed.

"Let me take a moment to say something, Elizabeth. I know that we have written of this many times, and I know that years have passed to clear the air, but being that we are sitting together for only the second time since Rebecca's death, I wish you hear me out.

"I want you to look into my eyes and know the truth when I say that I was painfully guilt-ridden about leaving you. It was the worst year of my life—losing Rebecca and leaving you. You must understand that I had to free myself of my grief, and it could never have been done so long as I remained in Boston or anywhere along this coast. Had I remained, I fear I would have ended my life in order to escape my memories and misery."

"I understand, Claus."

"When I looked into your eyes, Elizabeth, it hurt. I saw your pain. I saw my own pain. I saw Rebecca and the young girl who always stood at her side. She adored you so. I adored you. I just couldn't bring myself to face you knowing how you thought me a god in those days, and how I had nothing to offer you but my weakness and more pain by my leaving. I wish there had been a way I might have acted differently, but emotions override sensibilities.

"My thoughts back then were selfish and even hateful. I wished only to be as far removed from this place as possible. I wanted nothing to do with love and the pain it brought to my life. I wanted another life, something different, something totally remote. I wanted to find a place where the only emotions that mattered were those of excitement and fear, and the REBECCA was my means of getting there. Do you understand, Elizabeth? Do you understand what it is I am saying now that you are older? These issues still trouble me, and to this day even with the passing of years, I worry that you may still harbor resentment toward me."

He looked at me with a sense of sorrow that moved me, for I could see that even now the pains of his past were barely healed and still tender to touch upon. The passing years that had been long for me as a child were but a blink of the eye for Christopher.

"Don't think on it so, Claus. Mary and Allen were there to help me, and the day came when I finally understood your motives and the fickle hand of fate. You must understand, that you were closer to me in your letters than you would ever have been had I been in your home. As you saw for yourself, it is difficult for me to address you as Claus in person, yet in our letters we were as one and the same. We shared things far too personal to be presented face to face. Our hearts were open. Know that my life worked out well for me, and you had much to do with that.

"Mine was a life you didn't have to bother with, but you did. You were far away—untouchable, unreachable. You could have forgotten me in the winds of wanderlust and never looked back, but you chose not to. Truly, you always showed great interest in everything about me, and I believed in my heart that you cared very much. I cherished your letters, and I gained much strength from your years of encouragement. Any other father would have taken my presence for granted and been hard pressed to put up with me. It wasn't that way for us. Now, I say to you, put your conscience at ease. The past has passed, it has worked out well in spite of all, and the future is bright and ours to behold."

"Bless you, Elizabeth. I wonder if it's because our paths cross so rarely that I love you as I do. You can't imagine how much I need to hear those words, even now." He thanked me and then somewhat awkwardly changed the subject back to his upcoming adventure.

"I didn't mean to get—to get so far off track. No, that is not true. I did mean to. I just never have an opportunity to express myself about these issues the way I would like. In the privacy of my cabin aboard REBECCA, I have had this conversation a thousand times. I hope for the last thousand times." We laughed.

"Anyway, back to what I was saying. Let me see—I was about to say that after Rebecca's passing, upon the high sea I discovered a niche in the furring trade that looked promising for profit. You see, the fur traders were catching, trapping or trading for pelts with the Indians of Columbia and northern California, and after filling their holds, they would set sail for China.

"The problem with that strategy is in the cost of keeping sailors during those months at sea. Much time passes as you sail back and forth from hunting ground to market and vice versa. Time can eat away profits to the point where it just isn't worth the effort, especially after accounting for the risks presented while undertaking such a long-term voyage.

"Seeing this as an opportunity, I assembled a fleet of ships outfitted with everything imaginable, even ladies of pleasure." He winked at me. "With holds chocked full and brimming, I traded all I had for pelts right there on the open sea. The masters and owners were nearly overcome with gratitude. They were then able to keep their men in the strict process of gathering pelts, which was where their profits were made. And so it went for many years, I overseeing a fleet of about twenty vessels employed in such business.

"During this time I had ample opportunity to assess the potential for profits all along the California coast. We did a good trade in those areas, most of it being hides, but my eyes were always drawn to the land. More and more I found myself step- ping off REBECCA's quarterdeck and heading into the interior of that wilderness. I managed to see with my own eyes the vast stretches of forest that were every bit as real as the stories I had heard years before on the docks of Copenhagen and Stockholm. Those western lands were carpeted with mature forests, trees of a height and girth beyond one's wildest imaginings.

"I decided it was time to get back into the business that made the Claussen name famous, and so I set forth surveying large tracts of these forests. Next, I went on to construct mills for the processing of the lumber. I helped the shipmasters even further by employing their trappers during the off-seasons to work the mills.

"It was the transporting of this lumber that presented me challenge. And it was a formidable challenge in every way. Most of this wood I shipped to China, where the market kept it in high demand and I fetched a good price. Yet, I believed truly lofty profits could best be realized by getting it to the East Coast in quantities larger than shiploads, and without having to face the perilous southern voyages. It kept my mind focused on a finding a route across land, to the point where this became my obsession.

"This country devours raw lumber with an appetite that is staggering, Elizabeth. Next to food, building materials for shelter and growth are the greatest needs of this nation, and will become more so as our western borders reach out toward the Stony Mountains.

"There exists, in the most basic terms, nothing between the Mississippi and those mountains but sky, sand, and grass. As far as I am able to discern, taking into account the records of Lewis and Clark and others, the west is a great desert with nary a tree to be seen. If you choose to believe it, some say the land crawls with prehistoric monsters.

"Still, there are people brave enough to move into those areas, people who need everything from powder to plows, goods of all sorts—and lumber—lumber, which doesn't exist anywhere in quantities worth their while. On the plains folks build their homes out of mud and grass. At this point, they have little choice but to truck goods by wagon. It is as long and arduous a journey as nature could invent and it stops as soon as one reaches the mountains from whatever direction.

"I am convinced there must be a viable route across that desert, especially a passage to and from the West Coast through those mountains; a route that could eventually support a reasonable amount of safe and inexpensive trafficking of goods between the east and west. By this route, raw lumber and hides will find their way to the eastern markets and manufactured goods will find their way to western settlements.

"Change is in the air, Elizabeth, and the key will be railroads. This will happen soon and make distance a thing of the past. On this fact, I will stake my life. It hasn't happened yet, which simply means I have every opportunity of being there when it does. There is a great deal of wealth to be made and opportunity to be had. There is also danger and much to consider while employed in the business of making it happen. Railroads and mountain passes, that's the whole of it. That's the business that brings me back to Boston and to you.

"Coincidently, I have just finished meeting with a number of gentlemen who are looking hard at the possibility of constructing a railroad right here between Boston and Providence."

"Is that a fact?"

"Yes, very much so. It would be a number of years before completion, but we have already provided some reconnaissance, which is to say we have surveyed many of the properties by eye. We started along the South Boston Turnpike, and then eastward through Milton, Sharon, and Attleborough, crossing the Wading and Ten Mile Rivers over where Lydia Pennington once lived, and lastly the India Bridge at Providence.

"Second to my desire to see you, my interest in this railroad required that I return to Boston in person, for the investments involved are respectable to say the least. I also wished to inspect these steam engines to determine how suitable they might be for use in the mountains."

"Sounds like you have been busy, busy, busy. So what happens now? I mean, thousands and thousands of miles of nothing but wilderness with so much ground to travel and all of it unknown, how will you know where to go? How will you ever find your way back? Oh, lord, Claus, what about all the Indians? Don't you fear the savages?" Christopher's undertakings were always thrilling to hear, but thoughts of his leaving stripped my evening of much of its dream-like quality.

"Yes, no, yes, no, yes, no, and I don't know, if you must know the truth of it. Do I fear the savages? Mmm—no, not really. Will I find my way back? Mmm—who says I want to come back? How will I know where to go? Well—on that count I am thinking of traveling up along the Hudson and into the Great Lakes region, maybe into the Michigan territories. Then possibly south onto the Ohio River, rafting along it to the Mississippi and then hiking westward along the Platt, or as of late, I have been leaning more to heading north along the upper Missouri and following it northwestward into the district of Montana.

"I may even venture as far as the Columbia River in the Oregon Territories. I have already ventured up that river from the Pacific Coast. It is beautiful country, wild and untamed, magnificent in every way. In any event, from those regions I plan to keep up my search for a pass through the mountains. If I don't succeed in that objective, then I shall concentrate all my efforts on establishing a route for lumber and furs from those mountains to markets here in the east by means of a railroad across the desert. That is all I can honestly say at this point." He stopped briefly to look at me, maybe to wonder what was on my mind. "Besides, at this very moment what does it matter? What's important is I wished to see you again, to be here with you on the day that you became certified. I want to know in my heart you are well and in need of nothing."

"I'm fine."

"Wonderful. I guess aside from that.—Oh, yes! god forbid, I should forget! I wished to thank you for the letters. You will never know how I enjoyed reading them. On nights I couldn't sleep, late at night, I would read them over and over, sometimes twenty or thirty times until I received your next posting. Being so far away, so long gone, those letters meant everything to me—more than you could possibly know."

"I'm happy you enjoyed them."

"Enjoyed them! Oh, girl, I kept them always at hand. I kept them in the top drawer of the nightstand close to my bed. I always thought of that drawer as home. You do realize that without my father or Rebecca, I cherish you and Mary as the only family I have, and I will miss those letters."

"I don't want you to go."

"Oh, ho, ho! You are an angel, but I must. There is much to be done."

"So, I am to face years of letters, once again."

Christopher winced.

"Well, that is something else we must discuss." Christopher reached for my hands. He took them firmly into his. "This is the hard part. You see, Elizabeth, this isn't the same as the time I spent sailing the seas. Even though I was half way around the world, the lines of communication were in place and we were able to write freely for the most part. This will be different. There are no places to post letters or to receive them. If someone wants a letter to find its way back east, they nail it to a tree and hope someone will come along heading in the opposite direction and take it with them before a squirrel eats it.

"Elizabeth, I will be entering into the deepest wilderness known to man. Who knows—maybe dinosaurs do still roam the earth. Can you imagine that? I must say honestly that our correspondence will not be nearly what it was, not at all as frequent and timely. I may even disappear from your life for long stretches at a time, maybe a year or more at a time. Do you understand?"

"I understand that I am not very happy right now." Christopher looked at me; unsure of what to say next that might console me.

"Will you ever settle down?" I asked.

"I have no place to call home, Elizabeth. I have no desire to go back to Sweden and its old ways. I have no father. I have no desire to live here in Boston in the shadow of Rebecca's love, besides Boston isn't what it used to be. It's a beacon for my heart only because of you and Mary, and Mary is now happily married and leading her own life. I can't imagine either of you giving up all you have here for the hardships of the trail.

"For me, to be settled down, means to watch the sun set across a snow-covered valley without another living soul in sight, without a single distraction to disrupt my thoughts or the memory of you and Mary in my heart. This is what I know of home." He slapped his hand upon his chest. "I don't know if I can explain it any better than that."

"But what about the REBECCA? How can you leave her, she was so much your pride and joy? I remember how you beamed whenever you were near her, the way your eyes would sparkle, the way your face would light up at the mention of her name. What about all of that?" I was unable to believe he could do such a thing.

"She is now under the command of Master Brig Rings, and I feel good about it as I know she will get nothing but the best of care. I have allotted funds just for that purpose. She will always be a magnificent ship. The logbooks are all I command now, mine to read when I am old and decrepit."

"Brig Rings." I repeated slowly searching my past. "I remember you mentioning her in your letters, but I cannot place her."

"Do you remember the young girl who saved Marion McCurry from the shark? You should, you were there in the hold. It was when we battled the pirates. She was the stow-a-way."

"Oh, yes, yes, I do remember—the blonde-headed girl. Britany, that was it, Britany Allison. She was a few years older than I. So—that is Brig Rings." I now remembered the girl, but over the years, the terror of the shark was pressed so profoundly in my memory that it overshadowed all else. I remembered Lady Rebecca and Darin O'Kurk being near me, and until this moment, that was about it.

"Britany Allison Coombes. She is now master of REBECCA, and a hell of a master she is. Her reputation precedes her across all seven seas."

"What about Mr. Beckwith and Marion McCurry, how can you leave them? Are they not family as well?"

"Oh, they are good friends, but they haven't been on the ship for some time. They are still with me. They work as administrators of my fleets. Marion lives in New York with his wife, Katriina—."

"Oh, Claus, you must tell me about Darin. Darin O'Kurk. Oh, how I have missed his songs. I enjoyed him so. On that day you summoned me to your quarters, I asked him to pray for me. Darin was the last person with whom I spoke before stepping off the REBECCA for the final time. My word, how often I have thought of him. How is he? Still singing his heart out?"

Christopher paused a moment.

"Ahhh, my love—Darin is no longer with us, I am afraid. He's now numbered among those in heaven. It was quick and merciful. He fell from the yardarm trying to get our sail reefed before a storm. It has been just a year since his passing, and even as much as Rebecca's death affected the crew, hers was nothing compared to the heavy hearts and sorrow at the loss of such a long time mate. The men loved him, as did I. He was a dear friend to me from the very beginning. He assisted me in catching Rebecca's attentions. There has been little singing since his passing, and I will always long for his company and good nature."

The news cut deep into my heart. I sat and stared at the face that conveyed this unwanted news. Feelings for Darin moved through me. I closed my eyes and saw him waving good-bye, saw him giving the Morning Prayer in London. I remembered his words at Lady Rebecca's grave, *"Bow your heads me bonnie ladies...."* I could blame it on the wine, but at that moment I wished only to cry.

Christopher went on to breathe new life into many of the characters from my past. We spent the remainder of our night in conversation until leaving the Barrington Hotel out of consideration for the service. Christopher came back to my apartment and spent the night, but only after a great deal of insistence on my part. I had a spare room and was determined to keep him near.

We spent the following days recounting years gone by, and how time changed our lives for better or worse. It was a heart-warming experience that filled in many of the blanks and reinforced those unspoken feelings we felt for each other. During our time together, our hearts sifted and sorted the emotional ties we still held dear and strengthened bonds secure enough to weather the upcoming storm. Never had I felt so at ease in the presence of a man.

To the general public, Christopher was mostly forgotten and now appeared to be an anonymous suitor, whereas I was readily recognized, and many would pass our way just to say hello to me. A good number of people were lost for words when I introduced them to the Mr. Christopher Claussen of Claussen fame. It came as quite a surprise if not shock.

However, it was Christopher who got the first real surprise the night we dined at the Barrington. We arrived inconspicuous and without notice, yet it was just a matter of time before someone recognized me and addressed me as Elizabeth Claussen. The look upon Christopher's face was hilarious.

"What? You don't think I would make a good Claussen?" I looked at him wondering what he was thinking.

"Elizabeth Claussen?"

"Now you know very well that is how I am known in Boston. I have mentioned it a million times in my letters."

"I think you mentioned it a million times, once years ago. It either slipped my mind or I completely forgot. That was a strange thing to hear. Elizabeth Claussen. For a minute there, I felt like I was married again."

"So go the twists of fate." My answer was too quick, and I regretted it. But, his comment about feeling as though we were married unnerved me. It made me feel uncomfortable and self-conscious. I felt as though I had tread on sacred ground, a place beholden to another.

Christopher had one last surprise for me as well. He threw his own party in celebration of my becoming certified to teach. As always, it was like having a god or a great warrior in your midst. He held everybody in awe, for his stories went unsurpassed. His tales of distant places brimmed with color and intrigue and guests gathered to surround him, huddling close so as not to miss a word. Christopher commanded attention without effort, and he kept me tight at his side, never failing to show me off before his audience.

The event was a heady affair that left me swimming in ecstasy. I felt like a queen. The emotions of the night were intensified even more by the fact he was leaving within hours. He showered me with hugs, kisses, and gifts, but couldn't give me an answer as to when I might see him again. As the night drew to a close, I accepted how his departure was near at hand, and it burdened my heart with much sadness. I prayed each passing moment would last forever.

Just as he did once before, he cupped my face within his strong hands. He kissed me on my forehead and looked into my soul.

"I enjoy the sight of your tears as much as the sound of your laughter. I am overjoyed to know someone loves me so. If I should travel so far across no-man's land that I might find myself upon the moon, I promise you that when day is done and I lie down to rest, I will watch the sun set and think of you. I love you very much, Elizabeth."

It was time for me to leave, for I was crying openly upon hearing his words. He drew me in tight to his chest where I sobbed like a child. I only wished now to go to my bed and prolong these feelings for him in my dreams. Arm in arm, he walked me outside to where my coach and escort were waiting. He opened the cabin door and we stood a moment as he again wiped tears from my face.

"You break my heart Elizabeth. Don't cry so."

"I'll be all right. I am terrible at good-byes, especially when it comes to you."

I reached up and pulled him down so I might wrap myself with him one last time. He placed one arm around me and securing me within his embrace, he stood up, bringing me up to his height. We said our final good-bye. My feet never touched the ground. He placed me onto the step of the coach. After assisting me to my seat, he closed the door behind me. The coach moved away, but my eyes remained fixed upon his massive frame. He was dignified in every manner, not only in appearance, but also in action. He remained at the curb unwilling to take his leave until I was completely out of view.

FOURTEEN

Although I attempted to write as promised, the difficulties of our pledge were soon to become evident. At best, an exchange of letters was rare, the occurrences coming few and far between. His letters came regularly at first, but my only successful postings were to an address in Cincinnati, Ohio that eventually failed the test of time.

My disheartenment deepened with each letter returned as undeliverable. I feared greatly that he believed I was failing to write when the truth lie in my inability to catch up with him.

156

To make matters worse I would only realize my failure months after the fact when I believed at last I would surely be receiving word in return. It was as Christopher had said, *"a different kind of leaving."* It was hopeless at best, but unwilling to accept his loss; I continued to write anyway.

Not that I could speak for Christopher, but I am sure he would have agreed that more and more time squeezed itself into the spaces between our attempts to connect. Not only that, but the older I became, the more I was locked into a lifestyle that consumed my every minute. Having never married, my work was my life, and the pressing issues of the poor were relentless. Work was my focus, and most likely an intentional means of leaving myself no extra time to think of those personal aspects of life I had failed to realize.

Boston had become a city in twenty-two, and word of its new status and the promises of a better life attracted many impoverished from the countryside. There was a sudden increase in the numbers of needy and homeless. Children six and seven years of age were forced to work for sixty or seventy cents a week. The hours of laboring for them were long, ten to twelve a day and the work brutal.

Their misery broke my heart. It was one more of the many things to suffer my conscious and increase the demands upon what free time I had left over after teaching. Between the balls and banquets, the food tents and collections, I was barely able to separate one day from the next. The weeks and months blurred into one another until I found myself always playing catch-up, wearing winter boots in spring and summer shoes in the snow.

I had no doubt that aside from the obvious difficulties of distance, it was for reasons simple as these that our correspondence faltered to the point of ending. No harm was meant, quite the opposite in fact, but the damage was done and for the first time ever, we completely lost one another.

Long delays in sending and receiving word meant that more than two years passed before I understood the truth of it. I came to realize my loss one day while on summer break from teaching. I had been sitting restless and thinking about far away places. I was actually bored, if one could possibly believe such a thing, or maybe I was just tired.

Either way, my thoughts turned to Christopher, and once I gave him the benefit of my un-distracted consideration, the realization of how much time had passed since I last received word came swift and punishing. How long had it been? I went to my letters and looked at the dates.

"Nearly five years! No, that can't be." I said to myself, refusing to accept the fact. "That can't be right, certainly not five years."

I went back through the letters again to assure myself they weren't stacked out of order. I looked through my desk to be certain none were missing. I read the letter dated last and knew with all certainty that nothing had come since. Even the customary cards for Christmas were missing.

In fact it was just over four years, and the truth of it left me reeling. I felt as though my insides had been scraped out. I felt hollow, painfully empty. I sat down on the edge of my bed with a heavy heart as I held onto his letters and stared through my bedroom window, looking beyond the city and out to sea. I spoke to him aloud.

"How could this happen, Christopher? Where are you? Why have you not written me? Not even a card for Christmas. You know I have no possible way of finding you. Are you alive or what? How long must I wait to find out? How long must I suffer to know?"

I then went to my desk, took up my pen and pleaded.

11 August 1823

Dearest Claus

Please, please, please answer if you receive my letter. I am beside myself with sadness and worry at the realization it approaches five years since I heard from you last. I have no idea where I might send this letter other than an address in Cincinnati.

I have asked the bankers. I have asked the agents. I have asked all about the docks and warehouses and am unable to find anyone who knows of your whereabouts. Some say St. Louis; some say Michigan Territories or the Missouri; others say the Stony Mountains. I suffer to accept knowing that even as I write this letter, my endeavor is in vain. It will never find its way to you, and yet I have no choice. My heart demands I make the effort.

I pray to God Almighty that you are safe and not lost among the dead, buried in some faraway wilderness never to be heard from again. I have little desire to wait forever and never know, for I am now burdened with disillusionment and emptiness that only your words can fill. I am dreadfully upset. Please, Claus, find your way back to me.

Love, Elizabeth.

* * *

I was left with what I desired the least—time. I waited forever for his response. Month after month passed, and I watched, hoped, but there was nothing. It was then another year, and another, and as they coursed on one after the next, and in the end, I lost all hope of ever hearing from Christopher Claussen again.

I had considered many times that Christopher might have died, and yet something inside always told me it wasn't so. I was certain that if he had passed on, somehow I would know in

159

my heart. Nevertheless, I was given no choice, but to cherish him as a memory, one that brought me peace, but also much sorrow as it moved deeper into the shadows of my past.

My life moved on to take a turn in direction. To the astonishment of many, I retired from teaching. In spite of my ambitions and determination, I caved in to the lack of appreciation paid me as a headmistress in a world of male instructors. The harder I tried to make inroads to the profession, the more I was despised. The better my students performed, the more I was resented.

In the last couple of years other women were beginning to follow my *lead and suffering*—some more successful, some less. Emma Willard was doing quite well with her classes for women on religion and morals, literacy, domestics, and decoration. On the other hand, schoolmarms were paid barely two dollars a week plus room and board, little more than mill girls. Not to mention that when school was out nobody got paid, and this fact alone forced me to earn my keep in other areas.

Maybe it was fate's intent from the start that I should be kept uncomfortable at teaching. It was for certain my efforts in other areas drew an entirely different reaction. In social work, people thrilled to have me take up their cause. Requests for my appearance came in daily. I had stacks of invitations to every event in Boston both big and small. It was a hectic business and there seemed no end in sight, but whatever hand I offered, my labors felt worthwhile and most appreciated.

Still, it was only possible for me to pursue this calling because I was supported by Christopher's generosity through the account that remained available to me. I often wondered if I would have earned his approval or disdain for giving up the teaching in behalf of charity. I wondered about many other things, which in years past I would most certainly have asked.

I went on to live modestly, never abusing his generosity, but had I, I doubt he would have noticed. I often wished it wasn't so, for as cold and unfulfilled as the account was, it remained my last and only connection to this man from where I stood.

FIFTEEN

December sixteenth, eighteen thirty proved to be a Thursday morning just like any other Thursday morning. That was a problem. I mean to say, it was *exactly* the same as any other Thursday morning. I knew this because for the better part of an hour, I sat up perfectly still on the edge of my bed and waited, and waited, *and waited* for something special to happen.

Nothing did.

I was emotionally dead. I looked out over Boston's streets through a frost-covered window that filtered the snow and sleet from blustery winter winds, but failed to stop drafts from entering my room. Chills moved up my legs as cold air washed across the floor in waves that rolled over my ankles and splashed up to my knees. The cold worked hard to invade my blankets and caused me to draw my feet up onto the bed.

The rooftops beyond my window were covered in old snow. It was the dirty, soot-blackened snow of a city's winter day. It made funny streaks and swirls, unpleasant patterns to an eye searching for things bright and fresh. It was the worst type of coal-smudged snow, having too long collected the droppings of a dismally overcast sky. Gray on gray, the view beyond the panes matched perfectly my depressed state of mind. It was cold and bleak outside, cold and bleak inside, and cold and bleak within my heart.

Today was my birthday. The measure of its insignificance was amplified by the stillness that surrounded me. All the world was hiding, hibernating, sleeping sound beneath the snow, and except for the occasional creak or ping of sleet upon the pane,

161

there was nothing to fracture the silence that engulfed me. There was certainly no hint of birthday cheer in the air, not so much as a singular 'happy birthday' let alone a rousing unrehearsed song.

As of this morning, I was officially thirty-three years old, and aside from my dearest friend Mary and her Allen, there was no one special in my life. *No man*—if I were to be more specific. *No man*—who might bring a birthday cake to my bed along with a special surprise gift handpicked just for me, something carefully wrapped in ribbons and bows. *No man*—to sing me happy birthday or read me a poem, words from his heart to mine. No special someone to stand beside me as my friends teased me about old age and offered up a toast in my honor on this my day. Love and all the wonderment it brings had not only escaped me, but thoroughly failed to notice that I was ever born with a heart that needed to belong to someone.

So successfully had I failed in this one area of my life, even I was genuinely amazed. I spent most all my adult years searching the streets, peering around corners, looking through doorways and down hallways for the one man who was looking back, the one man promised every woman. I never saw him, not a sign, not a glimpse, nothing from that gender giving any show of interest in swaying my attentions. I saw only years of loneliness, which led to discouragement and finally despair.

I wish I could have called them years of indifference, but I couldn't. I wished I could have been blind to all things male, but I wasn't. I noticed it all, and it all made me lonely, unbearably lonely. At night, while in bed, I fantasized. I sang songs of the heart to my invisible lover. I sang aloud in the darkness. I professed my adoration and listened to the conviction that strengthened my voice as it resonated between the walls of my room.

Alone at night, I often considered how every house on every street had a bed with a man in it. I heard all the stories of how they snored and sweated, how they passed gas without refrain, and how they came to bed unwashed and stinking filthy.

I heard about what little regard they had for freshly laundered sheets and towels, and how not so much as a hint of gratitude would be heard for a well-cooked meal. I was told how they started out as husbands, kind and generous then turned foul, preoccupied in the end with only one thing—*sex*.

I heard how fortunate I was for not having to endure such unpleasantness every single night of my life. I tried to imagine how terrible were all of these manly traits. I tried to convince myself it was all true, and I was much better off on my own, but I never could lie, at least not to myself for my heart would have no part of it.

'Terrible' to me, was going to bed and having no reason to undress or climb under the covers, or maybe falling asleep in a chair next to a spent candle and a mountain of books. 'Terrible' was shopping for a new nightgown and buying only a dull no-frills garment because it stood up to a washboard and lye, knowing no one would ever see enough of it to laugh. 'Terrible' was staring into a mirror at a newfound wrinkle while struggling to save a once youthful body so a lover might still find something to cherish. 'Terrible' was laying stock still in the dead of night, hiding under blankets in fear, wringing wet with sweat, but for some silly noise, and praying mightily for God's protection because there was no one else to save me. Terrible was most simply possessing a heart that was utterly alone, a heart starved for affection, a heart dying a slow mournful death.

My views of terrible were not the same, and so I poured every ounce of my imagination into bedroom romances. I tried to imagine the strength of a man, the feel of his passion, his sweat. I imagined his arms wrapped tightly around me, and the anticipation of surrendering all to his determined advances. I imagined myself enticing him, seducing him, driving him crazy with desire. Sometimes I was demanding, sometimes demure. Mostly though, I glossed over the details, for I had no idea what really went on behind closed doors.

I tried to recall in the most precise detail those tangled feelings of emotion that engulfed me when I once kissed Christopher. I fought to keep alive that feeling that so overwhelmed me, the sensation that shot instantly through my body. That momentous event opened my eyes and colored my every dream. Whereas I had nothing but scant memory and disdain for Michael, Christopher was a perfect model for all my make-believe.

At least I was attracted to Christopher, and so he made a wonderful dream-world lover. I often dreamt of romance and love in his arms, and I stretched my dreams to the limits of what I knew of passion, amplifying the feelings I craved. I stretched the feelings as well, through the night, through my dreams, and into the dawn until I was forced to awake and face my mirror with all its depressing realities. I talked to my reflection and explained how I had to accept my life, *"for better or for worse till death do I depart"*, a life that plodded along in a most predictable fashion and possessed little chance for change.

I had reached a point where I was terrified of an intimate relationship, a point where I was too humiliated to admit I was a retired schoolteacher spinster who had no concept of the intimacies of married life. I spoke proudly of my accomplishments and my activities, which I assured everyone hardly left me a moment's time for socializing. I camouflaged my depression and the fact that, aside from my nighttime fantasies, I had become wary of men. I shunned them more and more every passing year. These truths fueled my deepest disillusionment, but there were others.

My work with the orphanages and poor houses had become less fulfilling. People no longer sought me out with a rush of anticipation and a look of hope in their eyes, for I had become distant. I had lost much of my drive. Often my work felt more a chore. It may have been due to the fact that my work grew to be meaningless without someone with whom I might share my successes. I managed to cope, managed to get by, but I found myself longing more and more for something I couldn't identify.

I had lost my sense of pride, the joy of seeing young children smile, the appreciation of the many small things—those tangible rewards I used to thrive on. They had become impossible to see beyond the piles of paperwork that stood tall and demanding, but which governed the flow of money and the direction of money-making events.

In comparison, I felt short, shallow—boring. Somewhere behind those stacks of records, I disappeared. I was no longer centered in the arena of the active and involved. I had reduced my movements to that of the comatose. What had happened to me? I began to wonder if there was any point in anything that I did. I wondered if it was worth living this drudgery anymore.

I was exaggerating, blowing my situation totally out of proportion. I couldn't deny my state of depression, but I had no desire to end my life. Nonetheless, I was glad to be saved by a knock at the front door, which returned me from the oppressive gloom that was blinding me this morning.

"Mary?" I wasn't expecting her this early.

"Liz! What's going on? Are you all right?"

"Oh, I am fine. Burrrr. Come in. Hurry, it's freezing out there." I shivered beneath the blanket that had been draped over me for the last couple of days. Mary closed the door behind her and cut off the flood of icy air that pooled about my bare feet.

"Happy Birthday," said Mary with a look of concern.

"Thank-you."

"Is everything all right?"

"Shouldn't it be?"

"You tell me. Marguerite called on me to say that you have not been to your office for three days, and that you missed the Walker street dinner last Saturday. What's with that? Since when do you miss an engagement? I told her you must be painfully sick. She was quite worried, and so was I. I told her I would come by at once. Look at you. You look awful. What's the matter? Are you sick, are you not feeling well or what?"

"I haven't been sleeping."

"Liz, darling, it's going on noon, and you're not even dressed. This isn't you. I know something is wrong. How come you didn't come by this weekend? You know how I worry about you."

"I know, I know." I sat down in the kitchen, while Mary went straight to the cupboard to make tea.

"So, talk to me. Something's up, I know it. You are depressed because it's your birthday, right? Hey! Wait a minute. Is there a man? Is that it? Is this because of a man? It there something you haven't been telling me?"

"Oh, please! If things aren't bad enough, must you bring that up?"

"Aha! Just as I thought, things are bad."

I have no idea what happened next other than to say I was suddenly overrun with an urge to cry. I laid my head down upon the table. Atop my folded arms, and without making a sound, I closed my eyes and squeezed out a torrent of tears.

"You're sure it's not a man. Liz?" Mary turned to look at me and saw at once something was very wrong.

"Elizabeth? Oh, for heaven's sake, girl. What on earth is the matter?" She walked over to me and began stroking my hair. She pressed her cheek to my head and kissed me. To this day, even at my age, her affection could ease every pain that came my way.

"Elizabeth, what is it, honey? What's the matter?"

"*I don't know* what's the matter. I've been trying to figure it out for weeks. I cry for no reason. I feel frustrated. I feel lonely. I feel—feel—I feel like I wish I were dead." I began to cry afresh.

"Now, now, now, baby. We can't have talk like that. No, ma'am. I'll tell you what the matter is. You have spent way too much time alone in this apartment. You don't get out, you don't see anyone, you don't talk. You don't come visiting. It's not good, Liz. It's not healthy. You've got cabin fever, girl. You've got the winter blues."

I sat up and tried to regain my composure. "I think too much, Mary. I think about life. I think about my life, my future. I wonder why I am not in love? Why in thirty-three years haven't I found a man who wants me? What's wrong with me, Mary? Why can't you just tell me what it is about me that repels men? Do I look funny? Do I walk funny? Do I smell funny? I mean, what is it about me? God! I have tried to think of everything, but I can't figure it out. I just want a man. I just want to be happy. I just want to have babies. Why can't I have those things?"

"Ohhh, angel." Mary sighed. "I can't explain the ways of love, but I assure you there is absolutely nothing wrong with you, nothing at all. You are as beautiful a woman as any I have known. Maybe you are just too beautiful, too influential, too—too—I don't know—too Miss Claussen."

"*Too Miss Claussen*? What ever does *that* mean?"

"Oh, Liz. I don't know. I mean you are so public, so in control, so—you know."

"No, I don't. I don't know. That's the problem, I don't know. You tell me, Mary. Tell me what I don't know."

"I think you probably scare the daylights out of men, Elizabeth. You're so strong and willful. You are a natural leader. It's in your blood, and it probably scares the wits out of ordinary men. I mean what don't you know, what can't you do. I mean what is there in the world that could ever hold Elizabeth Dennison down?" She looked to me for an answer.

"Oh, please, Mary. Is this a way of saying I've been ruined by knowledge? Because I was a schoolteacher, I can't be a wife. I'm too smart for my own good. You can't have a brain and a heart; books ruin a mother's instincts. My god, this sounds like the public outrage last year when that girl mastered geometry. How many times do I have to hear all of that nonsense. For one thing, it's pathetic dribble, for another; I don't teach anymore."

"Oh, forget I said anything. Besides, today is your birthday and look at you. This isn't how birthdays are supposed to work. I thought we were getting together tonight to celebrate. How on earth did you ever come to be so depressed?"

"I don't know. My whole life is making me depressed. It really hit me after something I saw the other day."

"Something you saw? It must have been pretty unsightly judging by the dreadful way you look."

"Oh, thank-you, Mary. I needed that. I especially needed that now."

"Should I lie?"

"That might be kind. I know I would have considered it."

"Medicine is bitter, Elizabeth, now swallow it and tell me what it was you saw?"

I took a deep breath. "Ohhh, it's a long story and probably pointless."

"Liz, honey, we have tea and we have time. It's too cold to go outside, and I'm all ears. Let me get a blanket, then tell me what you saw."

Mary returned with a blanket, sat down across the table and poured tea. I dried my tears and went on to speak. "You know how the League always erects the Christmas dinner tent down by the docks?"

"Mm hmm."

"Well, I don't know if you recall, but last year I told you about the storm that came through and how the wind nearly blew the tent, tables and all into the drink. You remember that?"

"Mm hmm."

"Well, we all knew the tent was pretty badly torn and we would need to look it over before we could use it again this year. So, I sent word to Charlie Gestus, down at Claussen's wharf, and asked him if there was any space available in one of the warehouses that we might use to lay out the tent for inspection and repairs, so as not to freeze to death doing it in an open field. He said in about two weeks he was sending a fleet to England and that one of the bays in the East Building would be emptied.

"Thursday before last, Charlie sent word back that the fleet had weighed anchor as scheduled, and that he had cleaned the building, paying special attention to giving the floors a thorough sweeping just for us. He said he borrowed a couple of stoves from the sailmakers for heat and wanted me to come down and see it for myself. I was more than happy to do so, and so rode down to look everything over and see how much room we had available and so on, so on, so on.

"Anyhow, right from the start, the visit was peculiar because when I arrived I was greeted by a sizable mob of children milling about the warehouse looking for handouts—you know, street children, and so I made a comment about their number.

'What is this, Charlie? Are you throwing a party for the children or something?'

'Hardly. What I'd give to be rid of their lot. They never leave. I mean the faces change, but the kids never leave. It's gone on this way for years, ever since Claussen left Boston. What was that, a decade ago? I keep chasing them out so they don't get hurt, but they keep coming back. They must like something about you. I usually don't see this many about. They pass stories down from one to another about how someday

169

Claussen is going to return to Boston and if you are a kid and lucky enough to be on the dock when his ship arrives, he will shower you with more gifts than you can carry. Wagonloads! They call him Santa Claus of the sea.'"

I looked at Mary. "Charlie threw his arms out in a great arc signifying an enormous heap of gifts. He said those kids come from miles around just to talk about it, just to sit about and wait. *'Santa Claus of the sea'*, doesn't that beat all." I looked for Mary's response.

"Maybe it isn't so bizarre. I was just thinking that I recall Mr. Claussen always bringing gifts for the street orphans when he anchored," said she.

"As well do I, but now it seems as though his toy giving ways have grown legendary with the children. It's been going on for years, but there's a whole lot more to it than just this."

"What do you mean?"

"Well, Charlie escorted me inside, and while we stood there talking, a yardman entered and called him away to address some small emergency. He excused himself from my side and left me to inspect the remainder of the premises as I pleased. Everything was in order, and while I awaited Charlie's return, I meandered about until I reached the opposite end of the bay. At the far wall, I noticed an entry door that lead into an adjoining bay, and being nosey as I am, I opened it to take a peek inside.

"At first glance, I didn't see anything unusual. It appeared typical of a warehouse, packed full of crates and what not, mountains of odd and ends pushed here and there. But upon closer look, I noticed at the very back of the bay, beyond the crates, there were stacks covered with tarps and buried under dirt and dust. Much of it looked as though it had been stored since the beginning of time. Needless to say, I was intrigued and please don't ask me what was going through my head, but I stepped through the door and began wandering around the aisles poking about everything and pawing through the various

170

piles of rummage. You know how it is; you always think you're going to be the one that discovers some incredible treasure unbelievably missed by the rest of the world."

"Yup."

"Most of the crates near the door looked the same and were clean so I knew they had just arrived or were in transit. They had no specific markings that spelled out what they contained and so I was forced to peek into cracks between the planks in order to make something of what was inside. I must have circled around twenty crates before I figured it out, and then it only happened because one had been damaged and a couple of planks were missing. Do you know what was inside those crates, Mary?"

"What?"

"Toys!"

"Toys?"

"Thousands of them, crates and crates of them. I have never seen so many toys in my life. No wonder the kids are milling about. You can bet he'd be called Santa Claus if they had an inkling what was inside that warehouse. It reminded me of that time when we were on the REBECCA. Remember? Remember when we fetched Lady Rebecca her Chambois and stumbled into all those crates of toys down in the bilge?"

"Gosh, I forgot all about that. My word that was a day wasn't it? Remember how sick we were?"

"How could I forget? I thought for sure you poisoned me."

"That's right. My word, some friend you were. I *should* have poisoned you."

"I was young."

"And foolish."

171

"Yes, yes, well, anyway, it was just like that only many, many more crates—tons of toys. I found it especially ironic after having spent so many years working with children and charity. I had always heard those rumors amongst the kids about toys, but paid it little mind. I never dreamed in a million years there might be thousands of them left sitting or forgotten in a warehouse right under my nose in the middle of Boston. I can't believe Claus never made mention of it."

"Well, Liz, Mr. Claussen is in the business of shipping. He must have tons of everything lying about in warehouses. I mean, how could he possibly know what even half of it is? Especially when you're talking about one bay in one warehouse, and knowing he hasn't been around here for years. How would he have any idea what might be packed inside those crates?"

"I can understand why you might feel that way, but I sensed there was more to it than that. This seemed to be more personal. Call it intuition or whatever. Anyway, it didn't end there. When I reached the back wall of this bay, I noticed at once what appeared to be an enormous crate tarped over, but it was roped off and nothing whatsoever had been placed inside this roped perimeter.

"You have to imagine in this bay, where everything else is packed in like penned pigs and sardines, there stands alone this one heavily draped crate removed from everything else for a reason that could be nothing other than protection. The light was so dim back there that I couldn't make anything of it, but I figured it must have been something pretty valuable if covered with canvas and separated in such a manner."

"And it would be utterly out of your nature to have a look an' see."

"Utterly. I was beside myself to know what on earth it could be. So, I made my way over to the corner and slipped beneath the ropes. I could tell by the amount of filth covering the tarps that it had been setting undisturbed for who knows how many years. Anyway, I started peeling away the tarps to have a look, and I swear, Mary, you'll never guess what I found."

"What!" Mary was engrossed.

"You aren't going to believe this."

"What was it?"

"It wasn't a crate, I'll tell you that."

"Well, what was it? What! What!"

"Lady Rebecca's coach." I said solemnly.

"No!" Mary sat upright in her chair and took a deep breath. Her chin dropped. "You are kidding!" The words blew out as if a sneeze.

"I swear. I swear to God above. I nearly collapsed from shock. How long has it been, Mary? Twenty years, maybe, who knows? When I saw her name on the door, it sent the chills straight up my spine. I had goose flesh so bad I started shaking right there in my shoes."

"Oh, that is spooky. He kept it all these years in the back of that old warehouse." Mary's amber eyes were big as saucers.

"I was just thinking. I am thirty-three today and I just turned twelve when she died. Twenty-one years, birthday to birthday, it's been sitting there waiting twenty-one years for who knows what."

"*Twenty-one years!* He kept it for twenty-one years and never sold it. Isn't that something? I think it's sad in a way. Can you imagine how he must have loved her?"

"Honestly, I can't. I can tell you how many hundreds of times I wondered whatever became of that coach, but who would you ask? I wonder if Charlie even knows it's there."

"Mmmm. That's something indeed."

"There's more."

"More? There's more!"

"Oh, yes." I nodded my assurances. "I tried to move the tarp far enough away from the coach so I could see it, but it was so dirty all I could do is see myself ruining my clothes, so I thought enough of that and gave it up. However! I did manage to get the tarp back far enough to get a good look at the cabin. It was absolutely flawless. Not a scuff, not a scratch anywhere that I could see. I kept thinking about how those sailors aboard the REBECCA were so suspicious of it. Remember how badly it scared them?"

"Oh, my word. I forgot all about that. We went through that battle and there wasn't a mark on it anywhere. I remember. You know, now that I think about it, that really is pretty spooky."

"Let me tell you, Mary, everything about it was spooky, but even so, I opened up the door and climbed inside."

"You didn't!" Mary placed her hand to her mouth.

"I most certainly did, and it was dark in that building, really dark, and dead quiet. Once the cabin door closed, it felt like I was in a coffin. It was an unnerving sensation, and yet I was drawn by the smell of Lavender, and guess what?"

"Oh, my Lord. What?" Mary rolled her eyes.

"You won't believe it."

"Liz, you're killing me. What?" Mary was riveted to my every word.

"My old ship's blanket was folded up on the seat."

"Impossible! You can't be serious." Mary sat up and slapped her hand upon her lap. "You have got to be kidding!"

"Dead serious. Wait, I'll show you." I arose from the chair and went to my room as I talked.

174

"You might know, that miserable tarp slipped free and covered the coach back up with me inside. It about scared the everloving daylights out of me. Talk about pitch black!"

I removed the old blanket from my dresser and returned with it so Mary might see.

"I can't believe it. How many years did we spend looking for that?" She fingered the frayed edges.

"I know. I sat there inside the cabin thinking the very same thing. I was holding it up to my face and remembering how I was holding it just that same way when I left the cemetery. The smell of it brought back so many memories."

Mary and I sat looking at each other without saying a word. We were both momentarily lost in memories of another time, a world of children. At last I broke the silence.

"The problem now is that I can't escape those memories. It's like I have been drugged. It's as if that cabin door opened up to something more, something inexplicable that now haunts me to no end. I feel like I'm standing in the company of ghosts. I just sit here and think back on my life, remembering things that would seem impossible to recall, thoughts of Sweden and England. Do you remember London, Mary, the good time we had there, the mudlarks? Do you remember the mudlarks?"

"How could I forget? It was one of Lady Rebecca's many lessons." It was a snide remark Mary made, and that brought forth an instant laugh from me.

"Yes, yes, that's right. Eating rats. That was it."

"Mind you, I am a good deal older, and I still say I would die before I would eat one of those disgusting rodents." She succeeded in making me laugh good and hard for the first time in days.

"I believe you; I do. Anyhow, I've been thinking about all of that, the voyage, the REBECCA, Darin and the mates, the pirates. Remember the fire and the shark? I remembered the first time I

175

saw America and the way it smelled. Remember the excitement, the thrill of the adventure and the feeling of discovery?

"I was thinking about the way it was when we were younger. How the future held so much promise in those days. I thought of all the activity that surrounded us when Lady Rebecca began the foundation for the orphanages. The clear purpose of it, you know? I remember waking up in the morning and bouncing out of bed, eager to see what the new day would bring. I had reasons to wake up, reasons to live. Goals seemed so well defined back then. All those memories were like chapters of my life that I could look back upon with a sense of having lived to the fullest. I know it wasn't just my memories as a young child. Those were times when life was indeed rich."

"Don't forget, Liz, that we nurture the good memories and forget the bad. There were lots of good times, many more than bad, but there were bad times as well. It wasn't any different back then than now, Liz, you just see it that way because you are depressed. The good ol' days, you know?"

"Ohhh!" I felt exasperated. I clutched my hair. "I don't know, Mary. I just know I have to do something. I have to—. I'm going crazy! Can you see that? I am going plain stark raving mad! Ahhhh!"

I clenched my fists. My insides writhed, twisting to be free. I squirmed with nervous tension. God help me, but I felt trapped, boxed in, shut in a cellar with just a window to watch the world pass me by. I couldn't bring myself to go out on the town, even to socialize once in a while. I wanted to be part of my old world again; even after knowing the pain I had endured. I wanted once again to live and breathe air that was saturated with life and emotion.

My frustration kept me from sitting any longer and I sprang to my feet. I left Mary in the kitchen and stormed through the apartment, ending up back in my bedroom. I was beset with anxiety, brimming with nervous energy. I wanted to bust out of my shell, to burst forth into a run, anything to relieve this pent-up restlessness, to escape this dogged depression.

So within the closed confines of my apartment, facing the city from behind those panes of glass that kept me safe from the cold air and dirty Boston snow—and now kept Boston safe from my sudden impulse, I screamed as loud and long as my lungs would allow. I did it again, and again until dropping backward onto the bed. Mary came running into the room. She was dumbfounded.

"My god, Liz! What are you doing? The neighbors are going to think I am in here clubbing you to death or something. Are you crazy or what?"

"Very."

"Are you all right?"

"Better now, thank-you."

"I do hope that helped."

"It did somewhat." I sat up on the edge of my bed and again looked out the window. Mary came close and sat by my side. I shared my blanket with her as we stared outside together.

"Mary, you've got to believe me, it isn't just cabin fever brought on by winter doldrums and loneliness. I know it's not. It's more than that. There was something about that coach. The smell of that lavender, something is telling me that there is more to my life than this. A door has been opened. I feel like a change must take place. Some force, something bigger than me is pushing me, prodding me to move in a different direction. Just saying the word 'change' brings me relief. It makes me feel good. It makes me smile. It is almost as if Lady Rebecca's spirit was there waiting for me all these years. She's pushing me just like she used to, saying 'go do—go do—', I don't know, go do something!"

Mary didn't respond, and so we sat in the silence of our private thoughts. Maybe this kind of talk frightened her. I gazed

177

through the gloom of my room and out across the city, above the rooftops, past all the smoking chimneys, toward the place where the Boston Community Church once stood. Its burnt hulk had long since been cleared away in the name of progress. Instead of the tall white stately twin bell towers, a reddish brown brick office building of no consequence or character now occupied the space.

As always, my thoughts of Lady Rebecca brought me again to Christopher. I hadn't received a single word from him in eight or nine years, maybe more. It disheartened me to think of it. Space and time separated us. Did he marry? Did he die? I had no idea. My trust fund was probably set up for life, and he might very well be dead. Who would think to tell me as much? These thoughts made me feel lonelier and even more depressed.

If only he had written me. Even now, just a short letter, nothing special, just *'Hello, Elizabeth, Happy Birthday, I love you, I am well, how are you?'* I could respond; I am miserable—trapped—lonely. If only I could see you, if only I could see you wherever you might be, see the way you stir up the world. If only I could feel you put your arms around me, for the sake of a hug, if only—if only—if only. I squinted my eyes. If he was alive and hadn't written in all these years, I swear I would kill him. These thoughts swirled about me, around and around until they condensed into one last question.

Why couldn't I go see Christopher?

Why—couldn't—I—go—see—...Christopher.

Now there was a thought. A thought indeed! The last time I did see Christopher, he dropped in on me out of the clear blue sky, very ungentlemanly, but very thrilling nonetheless. So why couldn't I go and see him? It was only a matter of finding him out west, difficult yes, impossible, no. There just weren't that many places out west to call home. It wasn't as though he would be lost in the crowd. *And*—wherever Christopher set foot, he left his print, usually a big one. Try as he might to go unnoticed, Christopher never failed to make an impression and in short time it was known by all that he was in the area. Surely there must be a well-marked trail.

There was recently a lot of talk in Boston about a newly published work by a local schoolteacher named Hall Jackson Kelly. I had the opportunity to talk to him on occasion when we met at social functions for the school. He was now quite the celebrity and an interesting and well-read individual to boot. His piece was called 'Geographical Sketches of Oregon' and was based on the findings of Lewis and Clark and his many interviews with other trappers, Indians, and guides. He was in demand because people were in fact looking west. I saw no reason why I couldn't be one of those people.

"You know what I would like to do, Mary?"

"What's that?"

"See Christopher."

"Christopher who?"

I turned around and looked at her with contempt. "Christopher Claussen. Who did you think? *Christopher, who,*" I said with disgust.

"Now, how would I have guessed that?" She was serious.

"My word, I have so many, many, men in my life, especially 'Christophers'."

"Are you telling me that you have heard from—!"

"No, no, no. I didn't say anything of the sort. I haven't heard from him in—I don't know, eight or nine years. Well, you remember when we got his letter. I think he might have been in Cincinnati."

"Barely. It's been at least that many years, if not more."

"I would give anything to see him again."

Mary looked at me oddly. "I am not sure what I am supposed to say, Liz. You, and this thing you have for Mr. Claussen. I worry about you some times. I often fear he is the reason you don't find a man."

"Oh please, Mary. What are you saying, that I am in love with Mr. Claussen? I hope not."

"I don't know, Liz. He holds something over you. I often wonder—."

"Mary! Stop. For the sake of god, *I am not in love with Christopher Claussen.* I can't even believe you dare utter such nonsense."

"Fine. Nonsense it is. Whatever you say, Elizabeth."

"I am not in love with Christopher Claussen, Mary! My god, that's like incest or something. What are you thinking? How can you even insinuate such a preposterous notion?"

"All right, all right, I apologize. I understand you would just like to see him, as would we all. It's been a long time."

"That's all I'm saying."

"I believe you. We all wonder what kind of life he leads, what he's been up to. I can't imagine the stories. But, he is bound to be a long, long way from Boston, and nowhere you'll ever find him."

"I could find him."

"You and the British army, maybe."

"No, I could find him. I know I could. I can feel it. I could find him, Mary. I am certain of it."

"Elizabeth, I don't even want to get into this discussion."

"I could find him, Mary. I know I could."

"Forgive me, Liz. I keep forgetting about your mysterious powers." Mary wiggled her fingers at me as if casting a spell. "You see—I don't possess the ability to locate *one* man standing on *two* square feet of earth in the middle of *three* million square miles of hopelessly desolate wilderness! Small thing, you can understand, I am sure." Mary was scolding me.

"Don't take it to heart, my love. Not your fault you ended up a mortal. Remember what that old fortune teller said when we were kids; *I was the chosen one*. Oooooooooooo." Mockingly, I wiggled my fingers back in her direction.

SIXTEEN

Looking back, it seemed from the moment I sat in Lady Rebecca's coach on that wintry December afternoon, my fate suddenly became significant. I preferred to believe that it was I who determined my destiny, that it was I who directed the changes in my life and set the course, but I found myself dogged by a sense of some greater force playing out my hand.

I felt positive that buried deep within me was some special purpose, some special calling. More than ever before, I recalled how the old fortune-teller had made her pronouncement, and how she had frightened me as a child. Having grown up, I put little stock into such unworldly revelations, which made things all the worse, for I found myself feeling supremely stupid each time I considered some sign that might have singled me out to be her so-called chosen one. One thing for sure, at my age, giving birth to a savior was out of the question.

After weeks of serious soul searching—time spent dwelling on these thoughts and many more that caused me to question the purpose of my seemingly out-lived and stalled existence, I came to a decision. Whether by predestination or personal choice, for better or for worse, I would change my life.

I remained resolute in my intention, and my frame of mind was markedly improved the moment I decided to quit my old life and start afresh. My new life began first thing on Monday morning when I walked into the office and resigned my position as head of the Boston Charity League, this to the utter shock of Mary and all my working companions of many years.

"Surely, you can't be serious, Elizabeth!" Marguerite's hands bordered her wide-open mouth.

"Marguerite, I haven't been this serious about anything in the last seven or eight years. Believe me, I am teetering on the toe-hanging edge of a dismal drop into oblivion, and I need to do something right now. I need to end this unbearably pathetic life of mine."

"Pathetic! Yoo-hoo, are we awake or what? Am I not speaking to the Elizabeth Dennison Claussen, well heeled and connected—?"

"You see. Even you call me a Claussen. I am not a Claussen. My last name is Dennison. Do you understand, it is *Dennison!*"

"Dennison, Claussen, who cares? All I know is that you are the same Elizabeth I knew last week who is my friend, and whom I have watched accumulate a life long list of accomplishments that are recognized by everyone in Boston. *Pathetic?* My word, Elizabeth, these are prideful things, achievements the rest of us can only dream about. I wish somebody would just one time notice something I did."

"Enough, enough, Marguerite! I can see you don't understand; nobody understands. You don't know what I am going through. I mean, you think it's all about work. You all have your husbands and children; you have your families that keep your lives filled with surprise and a sense of worth and fulfillment. You share your successes with each other.

"I don't do any of that. Recognition doesn't mean anything to me. It doesn't mean anything when it comes from crowds of people I meet time and time again at balls and banquets. They all have smiling faces; they all mean well, but I don't know any one of them from Adam. I go home to an apartment of walls and awards, plaques and porcelain pets that have never once said, *I love you mama or good job honey; I'm so proud of what you've done.*

"Besides which, I feel as though I haven't done anything worthwhile in years. My life feels meaningless, insipid, boring. I need a change, Marguerite. I need a change of magnitude. And I need it now, not tomorrow, not next week, but right this very minute."

"Elizabeth, listen to me! A change is a holiday on the sea, or a stay in the mountains, a week in the summer sun, or maybe a weekend ice-skating on the bay during December. You're not talking about change; you're talking about suicide—this notion about—*going out west?* Have you lost your mind? I thinnnnk soooo."

"Oh, no!" Jennifer popped up out of nowhere to join in the conversation. "Out west? Out west! Is she talking about that again? Lord help me, Elizabeth! No woman in her right mind would travel in that direction. The place is nothing more than a bone-dry wasteland that attracts Indians and snakes, nothing but endless deserts where you die after being scalped or bitten by spiders the size of dogs. I was told they wrap their web around you then hang you in trees where they slowly suck you dry. Oh! I get the chills just thinking about it. Yuck! You better think twice, Elizabeth, or you may really come to regret any hastily made plans. I have heard far too many stories about what goes on out there, and one thing is for sure; it's no place for a woman."

"She's right, Elizabeth," said Anne. "I think you should look around you—look hard. This is where you belong. We need you here. Can you not see that? We're your friends and family. We toil as one. We appreciate all the things you have done. We recognize those things. We're a part of you; you're a part of us.

You're wanted here. What are we supposed to do without you bossing us around?" She teased.

"I shudder at the thought," continued Marguerite. "I mean—I just don't get it, Elizabeth. What's out there?

"Mr. Claussen," said Jennifer.

"I beg your pardon!" I exclaimed.

"Is this all because of that Mr. Claussen you keep talking about? Are you in love with the man?" asked Anne.

"Oh, my god! Why does everybody keep asking me that! I'm not at all in love with *the man*. My word, *the man* could be my father! Do you understand? He could be my father! Where do you people come up with these outrageous ideas? I can't believe you even utter such— I don't know—such—such nonsense."

"So you're not going out west to see him?" asked Jennifer.

"Of course not!" I glared at Jennifer.

The girls stood silently watching me. It made me wonder if I looked as though I had a tantrum. "Well, not entirely. Well, maybe a little bit. What am I saying? Yes, I am going out west to see him. I aim to find him. But, I certainly am not going out west because I love him."

"I don't believe what you are saying," said Marguerite. "You haven't seen him in years, Elizabeth. What makes you think he wants you out there? I wouldn't be one to bet on your visit making him very happy. It's like Jennifer says, it's no place for a woman, and it might be a real burden on your Mr. Claussen having to worry all the time over your safety. Besides, if he's married, he may only be protecting you from his wife or—*vice versa*."

Marguerite's last point bore deep into my heart. I was wounded. I tried not to let her sense my insecurity, or know how I had asked myself these same questions many times during restless nights while wondering about the sanity or insanity of my intentions.

Even now, I drifted away from the voices of Marguerite, Jennifer, and Anne to ask myself again the same questions. Assuming I did find Christopher, then what? Would I just turn around and come home? What if he was furious upon seeing me, and took to scolding me and insisting I turn around and go home at once? No, no, no, that would never happen. I knew in my heart even if he was upset he would be a gentleman. But what if I discovered that after all these years he actually was married?

The thought sent my heart crashing to the floor. It was difficult for me to imagine sharing his affections, or even worse, seeing them directed entirely to another. It was unholy, and I found the thought appalling. Yet, it was a risk I was willing to take. My attention returned to Marguerite. I interrupted her blathering.

"Do you want to know what my greatest fear is, Marguerite?"

Marguerite halted her lecture.

"Tell me."

"It is the thought that whether I see Christopher or not, the trip will probably be exciting beyond my wildest dreams. I fear I will return charged and full of life—with little option, but to face the same old mundane routine that has been my life every-day for the last ten years. The only thing left for me at that point is to drop dead and wonder if anybody will notice.

"That is why I have no plans to return here to work in the office, but instead, when and if I return to Boston, I plan to go back to working on the street where I can look people in the face and know right then and there that I am doing something worth my while, something good. I want to see the results of my effort in their eyes."

"I know how you feel, Elizabeth. I sympathize, really, I do. But try and remember you can't do any better job on the street

185

than any one of us here. One thing we all possess is a lung full of kind words. But, there isn't anybody we know who can achieve the things you accomplish with your connections through this office. This is where you are needed and where you do the most good even if it seems personally unrewarding. I know without a doubt that you have no idea what your efforts produce. Remember there are a few of us that were here before you came. It's different now. There is no comparison. It's so much better, we do so much more, and it's all because of you. It used to be Lady Rebecca, but now the Rebecca Foundation is you."

"I'll second that!" Jennifer yelled from across the room.

"I choose you!" said Anne.

"Thank-you, thank-you, thank-you, I will try very hard to remember all of this. For the three of you, I will try very hard."

I stood fast against the unrelenting barrage of protest both in the office and out, none more uncomfortable than those words from Mary herself. She was mortified at just the mentioning of such crazed notions. It scared Mary, and frankly, it scared me. Nevertheless, I was resolved to go through with my plans, for I was compelled like never before to find Christopher and a new life.

Weeks went by, falling away as months, afterwhich everyone finally accepted the fact I truly intended to leave. I had spent the remainder of my winter reading articles and attending any lecture at the local lyceum that focused on issues of the far west. Even spring with its tempestuous and fickle weather was now behind me, leaving only the comfort of summer well at hand. I was booked to board a packet from Boston Harbor to New York on Friday the first of July.

SEVENTEEN

I willingly consented to spend my last remaining week in Boston with Mary. And so, I stood watch at my window in the cool quiet of early morn waiting for the sound of Allen's horse and buggy to come clacking its way up the street. As soon as he arrived at the curb, I left the window and went straightaway to greet him at the front door, thereupon waving him to come inside. I left the door open and saw to it that my bags and trunk were in order, a neat row for the taking.

I felt anxious in my final moments as I looked around my home and greedily stuffed my head full of memorable things that were close to my heart, things that would just have to sit tight until I returned to cherish them with renewed vigor. I reached out to console my porcelain cat. It would never purr, but I picked it up anyway, held it to my cheek and kissed it.

"Bye, kitty."

"Morning, Liz!"

"Good morning, Allen!" I turned to acknowledge him.

"Is this everything, here at the door?"

"That's it." I answered as I moved into the front entranceway. He lifted one end of the trunk.

"Good lord, Elizabeth, you load this up with rocks or what?"

"Books."

"Same thing. I should have known." He carried the baggage out to the buggy. I offered to help with the trunk, but he would have none of it, so I stood by embarrassed while he struggled.

"Why would you bring books on a vacation?"

"For something to read."

Allen stared at me incredulously before moving through the apartment to inspect the window locks, and check whatever else

187

he felt necessary to assure himself that all was secure before closing the place.

"Everything looks to be in order, Liz, windows locked, drapes pulled; shouldn't be any problems." He walked around taking one final look through the rooms. "Couple o' months you'll be back. In the meantime, I'll see to it that Mary or I look in on the place a time or two while you're away just to be safe."

"I am grateful, Allen. God knows where I would be without you and Mary?"

"You'd be fine, trust me."

"You know, it feels like I'm leaving forever even though I know in the blink of an eye I will be right back here sitting in this chair reading myself to sleep at night. I think that's the part that scares me the most."

"Hey, be careful now. Traveling has never been for the weak. You know what they say, it never goes as planned. You might end up on your knees praying to get back to the solace of an overstuffed chair and a thick book before the warmth of a fire."

"Wouldn't that be nice."

"As soon as you're ready, Liz—. I'll be down at the buggy waiting. Take your time. Holler if you need something else."

"Thank you. I'll be quick, I promise."

I walked quietly through my rooms, now darkened by drawn curtains. I slid my hand across the backs of my covered chairs and said good-bye to my curios and precious mementos. I encouraged them to wait for me in the sleepy stillness that I could feel filling corners and seeping into spaces. I returned to the front door and looked back one last time into the shadows and stillness now swallowing up those material things that represented my life. I whispered my final farewell.

"Good bye."

I then pulled the front door shut, feeling as though it were a great seal, a door to a safe or a tomb. I turned the key, and with it went my stomach, 'round and 'round. *This is it,* I thought to myself as I trod down the front porch steps.

"This is it."

* * *

Mary and Allen lived atop Fort Hill overlooking the bay. It was a place high over the water. There, yards were scented with the smell of the sea, honeysuckle, and all variety of flowers that overflowed the many well tended gardens in a profusion of bloom. Their home was an older but delightful English two-story cottage of split stone and cedar. It was smaller in size when compared to the neighboring mansions, but it shared the same stately old oaks, and was certainly second to none in terms of charm.

Being an older home, the original owners had selected one of the finest plots of land to be found, one that boasted a clear-water spring. The house was designed with a 'spring room', which added great value to the home. It offered fresh running water in the dead of winter for drinking, bathing, and most important, filling of the icehouse. During the spring and summer, the runoff fed Mary's garden. The spring was the envy of all who viewed the property.

The design of the house focused not only on the spring, but also on a large dining room papered in the best wall covering that Boston could import. The room could be opened to the kitchen by folding back a partition made up of eight large and impressive wooden door-like panels.

This disappearing wall of wood was a most unusual feature and spawned a good deal of conversation. When completely folded away during large informal gatherings, the exposed kitchen activity added a cozy atmosphere to the open area. Only on those occasions were the menfolk allowed to mill about the private realm of the kitchen with its fireplace and coal-fired stove to enjoy first hand the aroma of baked breads or watch over the shoulders of their womenfolk working meals in the making.

The area was enormous when opened, some twenty by forty feet. It was usually closed in the summer so as to keep the rest of the house cool and protected from the heat of hearth. In the winter the reverse was true, the panels being kept partially opened to warm the rest of the house.

A handsomely crafted oak table occupied the center of this spacious room. It came fitted with six additional leaves that extended its length to all of sixteen feet when necessary. As a rule, the table was kept small with an armchair at either end, reserved for Mary and Allen, and four side chairs to be used by the boys and me. For the longest time, Mary kept a high chair to her left, while the unused side chairs were backed to the walls. The table was always covered with fresh fruit and flowers.

A splendid sideboard competed with the grand table for attention. Its backboard was generously carved by Dutch cabinetmakers and served to inspire every male known to tote a pocketknife. It contained four drawers for the silverware and linens, cupboards below, and it was topped with a long white marble surface. This surface was perfectly matched by another that topped the serving table on the opposite wall. A permanent feature atop the marble slabs was either a large round tin of fresh sugar cookies during the spring and summer, or a wrapped basket of warm donuts during winter.

I was still living under Mary's care when they purchased the old English home, and I was given a room upstairs at the front of the house, a room that was never given to another. After my moving out, my room was left undisturbed, and so quite often, especially if I felt lonely, I would return to spend a week-end, or even stay weeks on end during the summer months.

It seemed that all the worries of my world disappeared during those Saturday and Sunday afternoons when Mary and

I were stooped over shoulder-to-shoulder, chatting endlessly, while working our fingers through the moist earth of her spring-fed garden.

By example, she taught me from an early age the art of fussing over flowers. I helped weed row upon row of her treasured annuals and perennials, her numerous urns dripping with brilliant blossoms and the many minor plantings of box or whatever else enhanced the groups of rocks that bordered the road or surrounded the trunks of those majestic oaks. I tended the thorny but fragrant roses so heavy with perfume they seemed to drag down their vines. They were strategically placed upon trellises about the yard mostly upwind of the house so that every room might be aired with their sweet summer scent.

Mary and I would wind down those days by wiping clean the wrought iron chairs and sitting in the warmth of the sun to enjoy iced tea and biscuits upon a freshly cut lawn. There we would talk while looking out to sea and take pleasure in the sight of those magnificent ships under full sail making way for far-away places.

At one time, anything said regarding ships always brought Christopher into our conversations, but as years passed, Mary and I became content to leave talk of sailing to sailors, choosing instead to lose ourselves in slothfulness, small talk, and sleepy afternoon naps. We sat about lazily enjoying our years-old habits of combing for nits, needed or not, reading to each other, and consuming chocolate.

Except for those few months when Mary was distracted by Allen's courting to marry, she and I remained very close. I was one of the midwives at the birth of her boys and cried with her joy in my arms. We were inseparable even during our rare spats, choosing to speak freely of our injury and working out the differences between us. Anything less only served to leave us miserable.

It had been a difficult adjustment for both of us when I finally worked up the courage to move out of her home and into my own apartment. Even then, we lunched at least two or three times a week and spent most of the weekend hours in each other's company. I generally went to her, because Mary had her boys to watch, and there was always plenty of activity in her home to entertain me. I loved the feeling of family that surrounded her. The cottage was never distant from heart or horse.

* * *

"Hi, hon!" Mary hollered out across the yard. She stood in the doorway, waving. Her cloth apron was dusted with flour.

"Hi!" I yelled up the walkway as I slipped down from the buggy seat and reached for my bags.

"Go on up, Liz. I'll take care of these, unless you wish to carry the trunk," Allen asked sarcastically as his eyes bored through me.

"Well—give me one side."

"Oh, I am sure, *I am sure*. Get!" he scolded. "I'll just take my time. There's no rush. I mean I have all day to get it to your room, right? If I'm late, eat without me and rest assured should I get tired, I'll just open it up, browse through your library, and have a good read until I'm rested enough to continue."

I had no choice but to laugh. I couldn't stop. I was splitting my sides. "I'll take an end—."

"Get! Get!"

"Fine, then I'll take a couple of bags." I reached for the bags and left Allen at the buggy mumbling under his breath. As I walked up the stone path toward the back porch, I saw him climb back into the buggy and start off across the yard. I climbed the steps to the back door.

"Hi!" I said to Mary.

192

"Hi to you!" She leaned over, to save me brushing up against her soiled apron. We kissed. "Got all your belongings, huh?" Mary looked past me somewhat confused as Allen drove their buggy across the yard toward the house.

"What on earth is he doing?"

"I don't think Allen appreciates the books I've packed for Julia."

"Julia?"

"Julia Tonnazo. She was one of the orphans. We keep in touch. Doesn't look as though he wants to carry the trunk, does it."

"Books! Ha! I'll bet that'll do him in. Men deserve to suffer a little now and then. They can never *not* do something, especially if it has to do with strength. It just affects their manly pride to no end. I just think that is so funny. Look at him, I swear. He would rather die than have one of us help him."

"Well, I grabbed my bags, that was my part."

"And you did goooood. Now, take 'em upstairs, your room is ready. I aired it out this morning, the bedding is fresh, and I even tightened the bedropes for you."

"As always, Mary, you are such a sweetheart. Why should I expect less? Mmm. Whatever is that wonderful smell? Apples?" I asked, filling my senses.

"Applesauce pie. I dug out our favorite American Orphan Chef."

"Amilia Simmons," we chimed together.

"None other."

"How long do I have to wait?"

"Almost done. It should be cooled enough for a topping. Hey, we haven't been starving ourselves all week for nothing. It's time to start doing some serious eating!"

193

"Whipped cream with a little cinnamon sprinkled on top?"

"Soon as you get back down."

"Yes!" I whispered with a thrill. "I can't wait."

"Go upstairs and unpack. It'll be on the table when you return—tea's already on." She returned to her stove.

"Hi, Aunt Liz!"

I turned to see Mary's sons, Josh and Juny standing at the back door.

"Hello, boys. You two staying out of trouble?"

"Yes, ma'am." They answered in accord.

"In school?" Their faces scrunched.

"Umm hmm! That's just what I thought. Better be careful or the girls will make fools out of the both of you."

"Aw, girls don't know nothin'."

"Anything!" Mary corrected.

"You better be careful, Allen junior, or one may just steal your heart away."

"Not likely!" said Juny in protest.

"C'mon Juny," said Joshua. "Let's get going. Bye Aunt Liz, we gotta go."

"We're going for rabbit—maybe for dinner. We'll see ya later, Aunt Liz."

"Take care not to shoot yourselves!"

Amid a flurry of objection to my insult, the boys started off across the back yard with muskets in hand. I watched until their britches passed from view, thinking how fast they had grown up, and how much I wished I had boys of my own.

"Better hurry, Liz. Tea's almost ready."

194

"I'm going."

I started up the stairs with my bags and carried them into my old bedroom. As soon as I entered, I felt a wave of peace wash over me. This was my room; it belonged to no other but me. It had always been mine. Here was a place that brought me contentment. I knew the smells from the kitchen. I knew the smells from the garden. I knew every blossom that patterned the carpet, every squeak in the floor. I felt more secure here than in my own apartment. It was the last bastion, the last haven, the last retreat when my world grew too far out of control or unbearably lonely.

This was the only place that held so much comfort for my soul, it could dissuade me from seeking out Christopher or ever think to wander westward. After removing clothes from my bags and spreading them across the bed, I closed my eyes and inhaled deeply an air thick with the taste of applesause pie. My mouth watered. I exhaled the aroma with a long low moan and with it went any hint of anxiety or apprehension. As expected, there appeared a certain ages old smile that spread across my face to prove how perfect was now my mood.

Once unpacked, I went downstairs to relax and sit with Mary. We conversed endlessly over a stream of hot tea, and it seemed as though when I stood back up from the table, sixteen pots of tea, six pies, and worst of all, six full days had passed. The days slipped by in the blink of an eye, time going by unnoticed as it does during a sound night's sleep. At least, like sleep, my time spent with Mary did much to settle my nerves and rest me up for the trip.

Dawn to dusk, Mary doted on me hand and foot until I finally had my fill and was forced to scold her. I knew it pleased her to pamper me, but I wanted to enjoy her company, not her service. I understood the basis of such attention, for it had much to do with habits drilled into our heads as youths; serving was second nature to both of us. In any event, it seemed as though I had just kissed her in that flour-covered apron, and here the week was drawing to a close.

It was now Thursday evening, the thirtieth of June, the last day of the month, and my last day to enjoy time with Mary, Allen, and their boys. Tomorrow, I would be leaving. To see me off in style, they made arrangements to host a farewell dinner in my honor. My closest friends and co-workers at the Boston Charity League, Marguerite, Jennifer, and Anne, had been invited along with their husbands and escorts.

Lydia Pennington, her husband, Earl, and Mary's close friends, Bonnie Lane and Patricia Borden, along with their men were also invited. These three women were old hats in the business of charity and knew the work second to none. Mary had earned their friendship years ago after having met them through Lady Rebecca and suffering with them through the period of her death.

The three ladies were older than both of us, and I didn't know them in the same social sense, as did Mary, for reasons of age and circumstance. I was more familiar with their husbands who were all successful businessmen, and who often stopped by the infirmary to debate or play cards with Allen.

Allen had made arrangements with a nearby inn to provide cooks and servants to prepare and assist with our dinner. It wasn't that Mary lacked the ability or desire to prepare the meal; rather it was I who refused to spend my last day watching her slave over stove and hearth in my behalf.

Mary didn't employ a full time maiden servant, but instead kept three or four on call. Her disadvantage in being exceptionally well trained in the art of service was the way in which she was now utterly incapable of finding help that met her high standards and expectations. She lived with the frustration of knowing what perfection should be. Even in the sweeping of a floor, Mary had to supervise everything and could drive a person insane if they didn't know her ways.

This day Allen directed the servants, the cooks did their cooking, and I kept Mary as far away from the kitchen as possible. For an entire afternoon, we walked leisurely through

196

the streets of the city, shopping and visiting old friends as we wished. I coveted whatever precious little time remained for me in Mary's company, and as we walked arm in arm, I was all the more aware of my deep affection for her. Impulsively, I drew her in to me and kissed her long and lovingly on her temple. She started to laugh.

"What are you up to?"

"I wonder if you truly know who deeply I love you."

"I think I do." Mary was flushed and smiling broadly.

"Do you?" I asked as looked directly into her eyes.

"Look into my heart, Liz. You'll find the same love. Been there since you were that high." She held out her hand waist high.

"Your love is what gives me strength, Mary. I often wonder where I might have ended up had it not been for you."

"You would have probably been our first president." Mary shook her head with a sense of relief. "Honestly, I am certain the only thing I ever did was hold you back, speaking of which; we should probably get back home. Dinnertime is certain to be near."

We remained arm in arm upon the carriage seat and returned to see a number of buggies lined up in the yard. Folks invited to dinner were now milling about the gardens. Mary, who had been fussing about dinner even before the horse halted, left my company and waved to everyone she passed by en route to the kitchen. She was bent on putting her fears to rest. In spite of my need to freshen up and sit for a spell, I crossed the yard to greet our guests.

Mary never reappeared, but shortly thereafter the servants stepped outside to ring the small dinner bells that beckoned us to the table. Inside, we moved to the chairs and sorted ourselves out. I was given the seat of honor at Allen's immediate right. Once situated, he asked us to be seated and officially started the feast. We were all in great spirits and immediately lost ourselves in the abundance of food and drink placed before us. It came in courses.

The meal was purposely extravagant and wasteful; meant to satisfy all tastes by offering a choice of baked ham, bundled veal, roast beef and chicken, smoked pheasant, fried fish and gravies for all. There were boiled vegetables, baked mushrooms, buttered cobs of corn, rice, a large casserole dish of sweet potato pudding, cornbread, cranberries and side dishes of every description.

Under pressure of all present, I stuffed myself sick. This was believed by everyone to be my *last supper*, my last meal guaranteed good and healthy, and I ate until I simply could no longer stand the sight of food. I pushed my plate away, leaving my fork where I stabbed it last to stand upright like a miniature flagpole. I sat there staring at it as my jaw stopped midway through a final unwanted mouthful of sweet potato pudding. I felt sick to my stomach. Only now were my complaints finally taken seriously and passed on as a compliment to the remarkable skill of the chefs. The meal was ended.

Mary's boys were quick to excuse themselves from the table and went off to busy themselves with a trap-building project. I was grateful to get on my feet and move about with the rest, who were also longing to stretch legs and seek relief by walking the food through their bloated bellies.

We women wrapped ourselves in shawls and migrated toward the gardens for fresh air while the men remained on the porch igniting their pipes in the last remnants of blue-gray light. The sun had long since dropped behind the wooded hills west of the cottage. Mists now encroached upon the bay, and moving past us women, threatened to overrun the tenuous wisps of smoldering tobacco that floated lazily across the porch.

The conversations that followed us outside from the dinner table were sufficiently entertaining to keep us engaged and unwilling to wander far from the glow of the porch lanterns. In time, Mary drew us back from the gardens and the invading mists to the cozier atmosphere of the porch. There we breezed through a myriad of topics with the men until we women complained of being chilled by the damp and were escorted back inside.

To our astonishment, inside we discovered the kitchen table to be covered once again. This time with liquors, brandies, juices, coffee, tea, and an assortment of sweets. We were soon back to our seats and steeped in late night conversation interrupted only by our guests concern for my need to rest.

"Are you sure we shouldn't call it a night so you might get some sleep?"

"I assure you, Lydia, there is no way I am going to sleep this night."

"She's too excited," said Earl "As if anyone should be surprised."

"Yes, I am. I am very, very, very excited and a little bit drunk."

"Keep drinking that spiced rum, and you'll be sleeping soon enough," said Paul, husband to Patricia.

"I keep thinking about what Jennifer said about Indians and snakes. Have you no fear?" Marguerite gasped, a little tipsy herself. "I'd be worried to death. You might be sleeping on the ground, you know. Just the thought of something slithering or crawling over me makes me feel faint. Ugh!"

"You must be talking about Harold", said Anne feigning disgust.

"I beg your pardon! I have *never* slithered. Stumbled often, but *never ever* slithered over anybody." Harold was humorously defensive.

Anne dismissed him and the laughter as she reached across the table, sliding her hand in a serpentine fashion and making hissing noises. Her eyes looked devilishly sly and threatening.

"Sssssss sssssssss ssssssssss."

"Oh, stop it Anne," said Mary while brushing away the imaginary snake. She then turned to me. "Aren't you just a little nervous? I would be out of my mind at this point. It's like I've always said; you possess all the courage in this family."

"She's thrilled!" Jennifer jumped in. "Can't you tell? I can't believe the change I've seen in her over the last couple of months. You've changed, honey!"

"She's gone completely crazy over the last few months if you ask me," said Marguerite.

I laughed. It was true. "Oh, I suppose I have, but shouldn't that be expected? After all, I don't know entirely what I am getting myself into. I will say this; make no mistake about it, I already feel my life has improved for the better. I mean what a night this has been, and it is only the first of many to come. I haven't had this much fun in ages, and all I've experienced of the trip thus far is the anticipation."

"Let's hope that the rest of the trip is as safe as the anticipation," said Marguerite.

"Marguerite, you live your life and that is fine. You all live your lives and you all have your happiness, and I am happy for all of you, but for me, I am at wits end with my life as of late, and I won't deny it. I need something new. I want something fresh. *You* understand, don't you, Mary? You know what I mean. I want something to make my life seem worth living again like it used to be when we were young. I want to feel those rushes of excitement we knew back then. I want to feel alive."

"That rush of excitement is called a man, Elizabeth!" Bonnie hollered. Everyone roared at my expense, save for Mary. She smiled at the humor, but she knew of my loneliness and how easily this matter pained me.

"The odds are definitely in your favor out west. I've seen plenty of advertisements for women," Paul added with encouragement.

"Yes! I have too! They take them out in groups of fifty! Wagonloads, all at once like cattle! *Can you imagine?*" Jennifer's distaste was evident in her voice.

Allen turned to Paul. "It's true then, the west really is wild." His delivery was purposely deadpan and everyone exploded into laughter.

"Stop!" cried Mary. "You're embarrassing Elizabeth. Stop all of you!" She scolded, but it was too late for they were engaged.

I *was* embarrassed. I was so sensitive about these matters that I sat flushed in the face with a silly smile and stared at them. I was at once severed from the party, for unlike them I alone was unmarried. Long ago, I had walked away from the world of lovers, and so to this day, even at my age, I remained ignorant about the intimacies between couples. I had little chance of appreciating their humor or sharing their jokes. It was much like sharing stories about children; they were always amusing, but you really needed to live it in order to laugh from the heart.

Those few times I had kissed Michael, I had gained a sense of it. The time I had kissed Christopher, the earth shook. I remembered that. It seemed the whole of my life had been wasted holding on to that feeling. I imagined being kissed without care, kissed passionately, and wondering how exhilarating the feeling must be when done without guilt or restraint. But imagine was the extent of it and nothing more, certainly nothing more would have been proper.

I was again the outsider and here was a conversation in which I did not belong. I had nothing to contribute. I discovered in horrible ways that speaking on this subject without firsthand experience made one look like a supreme dolt. In order to be a member of the club, you had to know the rules. I learned most of what little I knew the hard way—through brutal embarrassment.

I discovered that in order to survive these conversations, it was best to sit politely on the side with ears open and mouth shut, giving the faintest of 'knowing smiles' and working hard not to draw attention so as to be called upon for an opinion.

The rest of the party continued to banter in a stream of innuendoes. Even Lydia and Earl, at their age, laughed and teased with an insightful air. It didn't surprise me in the least, for the world was well versed in matters of relationships, marriage and sex, even those people who never made mention of it for life was nothing if not a story about relationships. And relationships were the reminders of my life's failure and the enormity of what I had missed. I had developed an aversion to the entire subject and even now I was looking for an unobtrusive way to excuse myself from the table. I felt as though everybody was looking at me, as though everybody was screaming, *"Look at Liz, she's a spinster! She doesn't have a clue as to what we are laughing about."*

I was almost in a daze as I watched my guests laughing louder and louder at the table. I assumed that a minister would have blushed at much of what was being said. I let it go. I put on my faint, 'knowing smile' and mentally removed myself from their conversation.

Mary being ever so kind and sensitive to my regrets in this matter offered what she might in regards to sex and relationships over the years. There was no place in my circle of friends to learn about these things and my limited understanding came mostly from her. Even then, it often came in difficult and unclear fashion during my inquisitive youth. She was only a few years my elder, but held a lifetime of experience in those particulars I entirely lacked; those *'things'* not easily discussed. I recalled one especially painful memory from my innocent and awkward years.

"Mary," I complained. "I did as you said. I watched all the animals, and I saw the same thing I have always seen, the stud climbs on back of the mare, the boar climbs on back of the sow,

202

the sire mounts the bitch...." I scratched my head, trying hard to think this mystery through. "So are you telling me that if you want babies you get down on all four and Dr. Sawyer climbs on your back and then...." My words stuck in my mouth. I continued no further for Mary was looking at me positively aghast. Her amber eyes opened like full suns in the glow of her crimson freckled face. She was speechless, totally speechless; she stared at me utterly shocked beyond words.

"Elizabeth!"

"I said something wrong?" I looked up at her, unknowingly.

"Elizabeth!"

I was called back to reality. I looked about the room. Everybody was staring at me. Whether by guest or by memory, I was bright red with embarrassment.

"Are you still with us, honey?" Mary asked. "Are you all right? You look flushed."

"I'm sorry, just embarrassed at having missed the question. I was lost in my thoughts."

"I was asking what comes next?" Mary had arrived to rescue me from both my humiliating memories and the subject at hand.

"Yes! What will be your itinerary? Is it worked out?" asked William. My Marguerite tells me you plan to venture far into the west."

I cleared my throat and swept my head clean of old disasters.

"All I can say for sure is that tomorrow I board the packet BLUEWATER, for New York. It's been awhile since I've sailed the coast or seen New York, and I enjoy both. New York is fun even if only passing through. There's so much to see there, the place never looks the same. It's never boring. Once in port, I will transfer to the Albany Steamboat Line on the Hudson River, and that is what I most look forward to."

203

"I don't know how you can do that," said Bonnie. "Water scares me to death, especially going out on the ocean. No thank-you. I would much rather travel through the towns and see more of the countryside. I like the trees and wildflowers, the cottages. Leave water to the whales is what I say."

"I gave thought to doing that, you know, taking the Old Post Road south to New York and passing through Providence, Mystic and the rest, but I kept thinking of how much I missed my days aboard the REBECCA. I haven't stood beneath billowing courses in such a long time. Besides it's a hundred and seventy-five miles cross country and a good two weeks instead of a few days."

"I'm with you," said Bonnie's husband, Joseph. "It's actually must faster than two weeks! But, I mean to tell you—even two days travel on the lower road will drive every tooth out of your head, shorten your spine, and spread your bottom a foot or two on the best of roads. Take a ship and be well rested for the Hudson. You won't regret it."

"I hope not. I've never been one to get seasick so it seems the most sensible way. They say there lies along the Hudson five hundred miles of the most beautiful scenery to be seen in the country. I should be taking in about a hundred and fifty of those miles by boat whilst traveling from New York to Albany."

"Oh, lucky you! The Catskills and the Palisades, can you imagine?" said Lydia.

"You know the Hudson?" I asked Lydia with surprise.

"No, no, just what I've heard. I mean who hasn't heard about the Hudson. Everyone says it is absolutely majestic."

"Stay clear of the boiler room!" Harold warned sternly. "Stay up near the bow or better yet near the stern should the vessel run into a rock, but stay clear of the middle. They have the unhealthy habit of blowing up!"

"Truer words never spoken, Elizabeth. If mention is made of racing captains, avoid them as the plague," Earl added with conviction. "There's no way to gage the pressure in them boilers, and the hasty captain stands the best chance of blowing his boat to smithereens. Pride and arrogance does 'em in every time."

"Agreed!" The vote was unanimous among the men.

"Use your better judgment, Liz and you'll do fine. Those steamers have been running up and down that river for a decade now." Allen reassured me, but I decided to make a mental note of the advice just to be safe.

"So, as you were saying, Liz." Mary asked further.

"I was only saying that I am especially looking forward to that part of my trip along the Hudson, for I have heard the banks are the most beautiful in the country. Like Lydia said, majestic. I'm told some of the finest mansions ever built will be visible from the water as we steam upriver. I am bound to see a great number of interesting sights."

"Then what?" asked Jennifer.

"After Albany, I am not so sure. I will either take the pike westward through the Mohawk River Valley and across upper New York, or boat along the new Erie Canal to Buffalo. That's at the westernmost part of the state on the shore of Lake Erie. I hear tell a railroad is under construction, but unfortunately I am a year or so too soon to take advantage of it. It's too bad, I would have rather enjoyed the thrill of it."

"Actually, a railroad has been proposed from Boston to Albany," said Henry, who was Jennifer's intimate friend and escort.

"Oh! Don't say it," fretted Bonnie. "One would have to be daft to board such a dangerous contraption. I heard they go fifteen or twenty miles in an hour. Lunacy! Good for a bunch of crazy Indians and nothing more. I say take your time and enjoy the Hudson and the canal."

"You're growing timid in your old age, Bonnie," said Joseph.

"I'll show you timid!" Bonnie stood up from her chair to stare down upon her husband in a threatening stance. "It wasn't me that broke an arm in that stupid racing cart of yours!"

"Oh, please!" Joseph protested. "That was twenty years ago and you're still goin' on about it." We all laughed.

Allen then spoke up. "Speaking of Indians, you might chance upon them in the Hudson valley. There are still quite a few of them living along the river trying to eke out a living. Mohegan, Delaware, Wappinger, Iroquois, there must be remnants of a dozen or more tribes in the state of New York without having to travel any farther west. I don't doubt you'll see something by the time you reach Albany."

"I'm in no rush. Indians make me nervous."

"They scare me to death," said Marguerite.

"Me too," said Bonnie.

"You waste your time worrying about Indians around these parts," said Joseph. "They've been wiped out. They might be scavengers and thieves, headaches, but little more. However, let me say, you were speaking of the Erie Canal, and that is something I would very much like to see. The railroad would be fun, but that canal—that, Elizabeth, is a marvel of technology. Who could imagine anyone might connect the Great Lakes with the Atlantic, and yet, here it is a fact. Before you know it we will be on the moon." Joseph shook his head in amazement.

"Then what?" someone asked.

"Mars or Montana, what's the difference?" quipped Joseph without hesitation and everyone roared.

"She could always *read*," said Allen thinking about the trunk. The room grew silent as all looked at him with question.

"I heard that." I gave him a hard disapproving stare.

"Books," he whispered across the table.

206

I spoke over him and the giggles. "If I ever make it as far as Buffalo with my trunk of *books*—then I promised to look up Jennifer Laketon who lives up that way with her family. Her husband is a trapper and they're always on the go, but I made a promise to look for her. Of course, I laugh because I haven't seen her since we were ten. I don't have a clue as to what she looks like, but we have written back and forth many times over the years. She is one of the original fifty and it would be nice to see her now.

"Then there's Julia Tonazzo in Detroit, another one of the fifty, who has agreed to put me up for a stay should I make it her way. She has lived in Michigan for a couple of years now and seems thrilled that I might pay her a visit. She lives just outside of Detroit and claims to be the only white woman for miles around. Everybody else is Indian. The books are for her, *Allen*. She begged me to bring her something to read.

"I've packed books as promised, but honestly, I don't see myself going beyond New York. I hope she'll come east and meet me in Buffalo because I can't foresee myself in Detroit. I'm more apt to see me heading south toward Cincinnati. Michigan is too remote and not at all a simple trek from New York. One must board a ship.

"I'm quite content to focus on New York and once there it's mostly a matter of what takes my fancy. I wouldn't mind seeing the falls of Niagara, but wherever I go, I'll be asking and looking for signs of Christopher. My last address for him was in Cincinnati, but my letters were always returned." I glanced over at Mary who was standing behind Lydia's chair and noticed her to actually be teary eyed.

"Mary?" I teased. She laughed and quickly wiped her eyes.

"I just feel terrible that you are leaving me, Liz. It breaks my heart. I truly wish you wouldn't go. I know it's what you want, but I wish you wouldn't. I am already worried sick about you and you're still at my table." Mary reached for a napkin to dry her eyes.

"I'll be fine, don't worry about me. I'll write everyday. I promise."

"If you don't, I swear I'll never forgive you." She sniffed.

"I will! I promise, I promise, you have my word. It will only be a month or two at the most, just long enough to enjoy the Hudson. I'll spend some time looking for Christopher, and if I don't find him then I'll be right back here eating Amilia Simmon's applesauce pie."

Mary nodded in understanding, but held a towel to her face. She was truly upset and I felt the wound in my heart.

"What good are husband's anyway, when women only have need for each other and applesauce pie?" Allen piped up playing the role of a rejected husband for the amusement of all and to ease the pressure of attention upon his wife. Mary regained her composure and flashed him a look of mock sympathy. Her reaction invited a badly needed laugh.

Mary's sudden show of feelings brought an unexpected moment of silence whereby someone yawned and caused all to follow suit. Earl stood up and stretched. He looked to Lydia. The rest shifted in their chairs. It was clear that the night's energy was spent. Bonnie made note of the time and whispered to Joseph. This time it was late and all were ready to succumb to the effects of a night of food, drink, and laughter. My friends arose to take their leave and forced me into a promise that I would keep them posted.

"Better yet, keep a diary, so we can read it later. I want to know everything." Marguerite demanded.

"I will for you and Mary both. I promise. Now go home, get some sleep. I'm the one who is going on vacation not you."

"Good-bye, Elizabeth. Please be careful."

"Good-bye, Marguerite. I will, I promise. Good-bye, William."

After a great deal of embracing and kissing, wishes of good fortune and prayers, I also bid Lydia, Earl, Bonnie, Joseph, and the remaining guests good-bye. Slowly, I closed the door behind the last guest. I placed my head upon the door, closed my eyes and captured the sight of them for memory. I then turned to face Mary and Allen, and let out a sigh of relief.

"What a night." I looked at the kitchen.

"Leave the mess." Mary insisted.

"I'll agree only if you go to bed as well."

"Sounds good to me, I'll need something to do tomorrow to keep my mind off of you anyway."

"Stop. You're bent on breaking my heart."

"You don't need to go."

"Yes, I do."

"No, you don't."

"Yes, I do."

"No, you don't."

"Yes, I do, I do, I do."

Mary and I wrestled within an embrace as we followed Allen up the stairs to the bedrooms at which point we kissed and parted company for the night. I fell fast asleep, no doubt, from an overindulgence of brandy and spiced rum. Yet, after a deep sleep of about four hours, I found myself lying in bed wide awake, and suffering from quickly building anxieties and the nervous antici-pation of the departure day now arrived.

Unable to remain still any longer, I arose and quietly began to wash and dress myself. I packed my belongings, all except the few essentials I would use before our departure. All this time my stomach churned. Quietly, I made my bed and picked up about my room as the pale gray light of dawn started to work its way into my room.

I was sitting on the edge of my bed when I heard a stirring down in the kitchen. I listened carefully and understood no mouse could make those noises, so I went downstairs expecting to find Mary fussing about. Any sane person would have been in bed, but Mary was up suffering the same fate as I, and had commenced to clean up the mess from the night before.

The servants would return to clean up, but we were both grateful for company and a task to occupy ourselves, and so after putting on a kettle, together we attacked the clutter. We enjoyed the break of dawn while conversing quietly, except for those times when we struggled to hold back our laughter for Allen's sake. We giggled the most while reconstructing memories of our days as table maidens.

We tried hard to slow each passing moment, to savor what remained of our time together, but there came that realization when we stopped all talk and simply stared at each other.

"Well...." I whispered.

"You better go up and get dressed," said Mary.

"I can't believe how fast this week has passed." I stood up from the table. "At least I can say that if a week flies by this quickly, a month certainly cannot be that much longer."

"Agreed"

I left Mary at the table and found myself once again standing at my bed. It was an exact reversal of my arrival. Now, I removed my folded clothes from the bed and placed them into my bags. Now, there was no aroma of applesauce pie. And when I inhaled deeply, I seemed to take in all the anxiety and apprehension I had exhaled the week before.

At least the day presented itself with beautiful blue skies and a brilliant morning sun to invigorate the spirit. My time of departure was now upon me, and Mary was visibly upset. I insisted she ride to the wharf with Allen and me, but she preferred to remain home due to her continued weeping out of worry. I refused to take no for an answer, and she and Allen accompanied me to the docks.

* * *

The BLUEWATER appeared ready to depart; her rigging stretched tight, her hatches sealed and decks cleared. She was a ship of Christopher's merchant fleet. We strolled about the wharf, back and forth before her bow, staying within earshot while awaiting the captain's final call to board. It was soon to come and we made our way to the boarding plank.

"Well, I guess it's time. My stomach is in a terrible knot." I kissed Allen. "Thank you for everything, Allen."

"No problem, Elizabeth, couple of days my back will be good as new."

"Allen!" Mary hit him on the arm.

"No, seriously, I'll listen for word of your return and hopefully I'll be here to meet you. Until then, I will leave you and Mary your privacy for what time remains. Good luck, safe journey, and may God speed."

"Thank-you, Allen. Thank you for everything."

"Your welcome, Liz. And remember, should the ship sink, don't swim for the trunk." He laughed as he turned away.

"Allen!" cried Mary.

"Oh, he's fine, Mary. Besides, I need to laugh. You are the hardest part. I will miss you terrible."

"And I you, Elizabeth." She forced out the words as the tears filled her eyes. We embraced.

"You know this is so stupid," I said as I wiped my own eyes. "Anybody watching us would think I am moving away forever.

My word, I am only leaving for a month or so to enjoy a trip I have longed to take in the worst of ways. That's the long and short of it, and then I'm back in good ol' boring Boston with you for the rest of my life." We laughed.

"I know," she responded. "I tell myself the same, but traveling is so dangerous and anything can happen. Don't forget the one and only time we have ever been apart was when Allen and I went on our honeymoon, and you know how that went."

"My word, Mary! That was nearly twenty years ago. You worry too much. Besides, maybe this will prove to be a trick of fate. I leave to go on my honeymoon, and I come back married. Wouldn't that be special? I might find some dashing ol' lumberjack or riverman who takes my fancy. I would like that."

"So would I, Liz. One never knows." Mary shrugged her shoulders. "Anyway, good luck and God bless. I pray He brings you back soon—with or without a man, I don't care, just safe."

"I love you, Mary." We kissed. My eyes blurred with emotion as the dockhands reached for the boarding plank.

"Hurry, hurry, you must board," she urged.

"Good-bye."

"Good-bye," she answered. I turned away and climbed the plank. I started up and paused momentarily halfway to the ship, where I looked down into the brackish water. It brought back memories of childhood fears. I could almost feel my grip on Lady Rebecca's hand.

I boarded and then walked aft along the gangway to the aftdeck. I climbed upon it and moved over to the rail closest to where Mary and Allen stood upon the dock and waited.

"Take care of yourselves. I love you!"

"God be with you, Liz."

The mooring lines where soon cast off, and I raised my hand in a final wave.

"I'll be back soon. I promise."

"Be careful, Elizabeth," Mary cried out.

They waved, Mary blowing me her kisses. I glanced up as the tops'ls unfurled overhead to block out much of the afternoon sun. A certain pang of anxiety moved through me as we began to drift away from my beloved Boston. I stood in place watching Mary and Allen until they passed from view.

I continued to gaze toward land. We were well across the bay when I looked above the shoreline and noted the park where Mary and I spent many a summer past picnicking. I reached for my diary and entered a recollection of a little girl named Caroline, who came to mind.

The BLUEWATER took to the wind smartly. She stood out of harbor to bear south and stayed her course. The day held fine, bright blue skies dotted with clouds that might have passed for small floating balls of cotton. The breeze remained fresh and agreeable. I turned and looked out to sea.

EIGHTEEN

I would safely say that entering the sound and harbor of New York wouldn't be anything if not thrilling. No place on earth expressed an appetite for growth, as did the city that pressed against this shore. It was a flood of expansion, and before me it spread out in every direction like milk spilt from heaven.

By every measure, New York was the undisputed champion of the New World, an irresistible magnet, a beacon that beckoned all; a placename that rested permanently on the lips of every European who longed for a better life. All across the globe, in the hearts of the oppressed and impoverished, its name sounded a song of hope and promise. And because of this, New York now boasted a population of nearly one hundred and fifty thousand people.

In contrast, my hometown of Boston had waned, never fully recovering from the damage done by years of blockades and the Embargo Act. Secretly, I complained little about this failing, for truth be known, I found its slower pace endearing. It made for a more compassionate community, a place indebted to those who chose to remain behind in the struggle to shore up Boston's foundering fame.

Ironically, it was the failing, the lack of change that gave Boston a peculiar sense of permanence, a strength and stability revealed only after being stripped of all glitter and glory during its battle to survive. To be sure, what remained was a core as solid as bedrock, and foundations now ages-old and proven after having stood the wear of time and war. It was these institutions that gave Boston its backbone and afforded me, as many others, certain peace and solace.

I don't mean to say that Boston had become a relic of the Stone Age; there was plenty of life and hope for a brighter future. One might cite the new and glamorous Tremont House, which replaced the old Boston Exchange coffeehouse after it burned. The Tremont boasted locks on all doors, a reading room, separate tables in the dining room, and most impressive, eight toilets on the ground floor that flushed.

The point I make is that unlike the Tremont, we had many more places such as the Boston Commons, our oldest square, where cows still roamed the streets freely and forced one to step with care. Because of cows, I understood that when I should return, everything in Boston would be just as I left it—no unexpected surprises, no change. Unlike New York, its welcome home would be warm, familiar, and sincere.

However, to be honest, Boston's ailing atmosphere was reason enough for my impatience to enjoy the utter craziness of New York. In New York, I expected—no, I demanded—that surprises be laid out before me. I wanted to be amazed.

New York Seaport

I wanted to extend my hand at every corner, to point this way and that while gasping in wonderment. I delighted in standing beneath newly erected structures that reached up three and four stories and made one dizzy when looking out across the city. I loved standing before the impossible span of a bridge with its girders dressed in fresh paint and gleaming with pride.

New York with its bustling harbors, ferries, and traffic was anything but dull. It was pushy and obnoxious, bursting at its seams, flexing its muscle and changing its face day to day as might any actress, but its part played remained the same, growth, growth, and more growth.

During the past few years, New York's rate of expansion was staggering to say the least—a fact that went sorely noted by Boston's editorialists. They cried out in despair as they pointed out each story of success with jealousy and disbelief. Surrounding their columns and complaints, reporters routinely gave accounts of how New York City planners were daunted by the tasks of meeting demands made by their burgeoning population.

News articles highlighted the construction of new streets, new housing, new public works projects, new parks, and countless other small necessities not thought of until presented as a do-or-die dilemma. Understandably, the most notable story was never put to print; yet, the suffering poor read its invisible headlines loud and clear. New York needed laborers, and many of the best in Boston were leaving their poverty and woes behind to head south.

They flocked to New York City in droves, answering the beck and call of industry both public and private. Not only did the workers arrive from far away places overseas, but like giant musical chairs, New York caused pockets of population up and down the eastern seaboard to shift and shuffle, but always settling closer to her borders.

On occasion, the well heeled would turn up in great style with their fortunes and flamboyancy, but for the most part, the immigrants were common folk. They came by the boatloads, arriving sick and weary after their voyage, often dropping from fatigue or to kiss the compacted soil of the famed city now resting firm beneath their feet.

These were hopeful souls, eager and ambitious, starry-eyed seekers of fortune looking to find work, thankful to escape disease, oppression, persecution, or poor land. At the riverbanks and forests where once a white man was seldom seen, there now stood vast laboring crowds.

Much of this was illustrated in a meeting of happenstance aboard the BLUEWATER with one Marybeth Cradle, an elderly woman who was part of a large family and troupe of neighbors from Vermont. I recalled much of our conversation as we passed the hours sailing south along the coast between Boston and New York—.

"Oh yes, we're a bunch aren't we? Mercy, me. An' I'm blest t' see as many as I do. Too many 'ave fallen by the way. Does my heart good t' know the family is together an' leavin' Vermont once an' fer all. I seen too many people laid t' rest in that country, too many wasted lives for my liking. If it weren't pox or consumption, it was the cold and hunger."

She had a private thought, and then broke into a chuckle as she turned to share it with me.

"Mercy, me! They were so worried 'bout me makin' the trip an' all. Nonsense, I sez; you just stop your constant jawin' an' get on with it. So we sold off all our land an' packed up. We were hardly alone as you can see by our number. Only a handful's fam'ly, the rest is neighbors an' friends. Takes but one to make that first step, to make the first move an' you know what they say, *where goes goose goes gander*. I was the first to walk out the door, an' the whole lot followed. It weren't goin' to be me that held up the line, no ma'am. I ain't looked back, not once." She collected more of her thoughts then continued.

"Did ya ever hear 'bout the winter of sixteen?"

"It was cold, I remember that." I replied.

"Cold! Oh, mercy, me! Cold!" She laughed. "Up where I lived we called it 'Eighteen hun'erd an' froze ta death'. Lots of people called it the 'Famine Year'. I lost my man just after that. He was tough an' full o' grit, but the place killed him off, ground him thin fer just tryin' t' survive.

"They say it was the worst year ever, an' I agree. Not only was it the worst weather I'd ever seen; it was the worst weather I'd ever heard spoke of. Nobody'n those parts ever saw nothin' the likes of it before or since.

"I don't know 'bout your summer in Boston, honey, but on June eighth, smack in the middle of what we call summer in Vermont, we got twelve inches of snow. The wind howled for two days an' we had drifts three feet high an' more. The whole countryside was snowed in. In some places we had snow up to our waist. Couldn't get to the animals or crops. We were trapped in our cabins, wrapped in blankets an' strugglin' to keep warm.

"More snow fell in July an' August, an' that was followed by terrible frosts in September. There was hardly a crop to be found come harvestin' time. Most o' the livestock either froze ta death or died o' hunger. So did lots a folks—got weak from not eatin', got sick an' passed on. We had all we could do just scroungin' for the sturdiest of those plants that managed to survive; you know, like nettles an' wild turnips—hedgehogs now an' then, anything we could eat. Slim pick'ns it was, honey. I was lucky to have kids that could look after me." She made a great sigh.

"Yes, ma'am, we were miserable. Mercy me, were we miserable—an' ya know it jus' wouldn't let up. It got so bad up that-a-way, it finally drove half the folks in Vermont to head south. Friends, family, those we had known for a lifetime, all up't an' left—gone, quit the land. But, my husband was as stubborn as a mule, an' refused to give up that rocky godforsaken slab o' granite he called a farm. He planted everything imaginable, includin' his own corpse. He worked himself t' an early death the followin' spring after years spent fightin' Vermont. I saw it

219

comin'. So did my boys. In the end, there was nothin' left of 'im, and even so, we couldn't find soil deep enough t' bury the man.

"I will say this, at least he taught my boys well. I have t' give 'im that, an' they were a whole lot less willin' t' make the same mistakes. They had no axe t' grind or points t' prove, an' bein' they knew more o' the country beyond Vermont, they made a brotherly decision t' pick up an' head out. One day they walks in to me an' says; 'Momma, we're goin' for the rich soil o' upper New York's Gen'see valley'. I was all ears, 'cuz' what they were a sayin' sounded like the garden o' Eden. That was good 'nough for me.

"Far as I can tell, Vermont's only good for huntin' an' trappin', an' not much else—'specially not for raisin' a family or building a town. I gave my boys my blessin' an' a hallelujah, an' now only hope t' live long 'nough t' see 'em all settled anew, safe an' prosperous. As hard as they are, an' bein' 'customed to fighting for a livin', I don' doubt they'll do jus' fine in a gentler land."

NINETEEN

Marybeth was only one of many people that had migrated south from the upper east coast, and although I had the benefit of hearing her story first hand; it was not unusual. Many like her had passed through Boston, leaving in their wake numerous accounts of the hardships in those states above Massachusetts. Her experience was typical of most of those who gathered up family and migrated toward New York, swelling the population of the city, the state, and increasing the activity up the Hudson River to Albany and west along the Erie Canal.

The lure of the Hudson and Erie was nearly that of New York proper, and probably a good deal more appealing for the many unaccustomed to city life. The Hudson was renowned as a place of serene beauty, its attraction being international and irresistible to both artist and aristocrat. It drew many famous names to its spectacular shores, and I was most impatient to travel its course so I might experience personally all that I had read regarding that wondrous valley.

The BLUEWATER slipped through Long Island Sound, sailing past Fisher's Island and New London. We moored for the night at New Haven. The following morning we sailed east past Stratford Point at starboard, and into Hell Gate. There, we awaited a harbor pilot. Taking charge of the helm, the pilot plunged us into the confused flotilla of East River traffic. We fell in with a fleet sailing downriver and sifted through those fleets heading opposite for the sound. We eased past Burnt Mill Point and the shipyards, sailing around Corlear's Hook close enough in to watch the traffic on Front and South streets. I watched as ships untangled themselves from the web of rigging, masts, and spars that stretched like a fisherman's net across a shore long since hidden by hulls, wharves, and unending rows of evenly spaced docks.

We sailed slowly past Rutgers, Pike, and Market slips. We passed the James slip and then moored just east of Peck's slip, where we landed upriver of the New Haven and Providence Steamboat docks on South Street, a stone's throw north of Fulton Market where the activity of New York slammed into us immediately.

Filling the market and surrounding streets for as far as the eye could see was a maze of crowds, crates and casks, hogsheads, stevedores, animals, carts and wagons. Horses burdened with tackle worked their way through the restless mobs, guided by masters who sounded warnings to keep clear of the lines.

The teams went on repetitiously loading and unloading the holds, while dockmen hollered across the calls of wharfingers, who were collecting fees and also yelling out directions to hordes of roustabouts engaged in the placement of stores. There were merchants yelling as they chased thieves zigzagging through the crowded square. The place was noisy, busy, and riotous to say the least. Simply put, the place was perfectly New York.

Once ashore, I stood upon the wharf beneath a canopy of uncovered wooden frames. For sprouting from ship's stems sometimes bare or sometimes graced with splendid sculpted maidens and more, were bowsprits that projected high over our heads to point ashore like a row of canted pikes positioned to challenge the city. They nearly touched those brick buildings that bordered the street to face the water, each tip a threat to the unprotected windowpanes that dotted New York's own 'China Wall' of four story warehouses stretching as far as one could see into the distance.

These buildings housed some of the most successful merchants of the eastern seaboard or anywhere in the world. They were heavily plastered with signs and plaques advertising goods. Here, from all four corners of the earth, merchandise of every description could be found piled high in stacks both inside and outside of street-front doors opened wide for business.

Occupying what little remained of open pavement were crowds of bargain hunters who scrambled through the assorted piles of rummage and unclaimed freight like sharks in a frenzy of feeding. To the newcomer it could only be an overwhelming state of confusion, a conflict of the masses compressed into an arena of claustrophobic congestion. It was anything but a place for the faint-hearted.

Amid the melee, my baggage found its way onto a private coach owned by a driver whom I employed to take me to the renowned Astor Hotel on Broadway. I stepped inside the cabin and upon closing the door, clearly felt a sense of security from all the sound and insanity that surrounded me. We were immediately on our way.

Leaving the market and East River behind, we followed Fulton Street past Holts Hotel and the Dutch Reformed Church, then to Broadway where we turned right heading north past St. Paul's Episcopal Church. The next block was occupied entirely by the Astor Hotel where it sat directly across the street from the central park.

At the Astor, I reserved a room for the night. I followed my baggage up to the room and was pleased to see I had been given a spectacular view of the park, the theatre, and the museum from my window. My room was agreeable, and having no reason to call it a day, I proceeded at once to find the Albany Steamboat Line for my own peace of mind.

I returned to the lobby and stepped outside to wave down a second coach for transport across town to the Hudson River. The driver returned us to Fulton Street and continued on from where I left until it dead-ended into West Street at water's edge and Washington's Market. We turned right on West, and it appeared in every respect a mirror of the East River. Across the street, to my left was now the Hudson River docks and piers packed tightly with steamers, ships, sloops, and packets. One difference, here there were more barges, most going to and from the upper reaches of New York and the Erie Canal.

At the Albany Steamboat establishment, we were rushed by a collection of criers who seemed just short of brawling with one another. While distributing handbills and denouncing the inadequacies and dangers of their competitors, they bellowed at the tops of their lungs, cajoling, mocking, and persuading us to listen to the sensible reasons for boarding their particular steamboats. The criers were brazen and unabashed about stealing away customers from Albany Steamboat or any other line.

I brushed the boys away and began strolling down West Street passing the innumerable slips and ships in order to see for myself how the Albany Steamboat Line measured up when compared to the others and determine if I felt it to be the safest and most reliable.

As I did so, I allowed myself to be distracted by the colorful assortment of people walking with and against me. The street felt entirely transient, flowing like the river itself. I flowed with its current, ebb and tide, back and forth, up and down the pavement until I found myself 'moored' once and for all back at my start point, the Albany Docks ticket office. There, I stopped to rest my feet.

One thing was for certain, I saw firsthand how the steamboats were a loud and smoky lot, and I felt especially nervous about stepping aboard such creations. It seemed small consolation knowing that the Albany establishment came highly recommended by my contacts in Boston.

At least the Albany line appeared most used by the public, if judged by the number of notes and messages matted upon its office walls. This seemed to me a better testimony to its popularity, and hopefully a sign of sensible captains who put safety before speed. I prayed this to be so.

The notes and messages were quite an attraction, something of an acceptable form of eavesdropping. I was fully drawn to them, and disappeared within a group of people already amusing themselves at the board for purpose of passing time.

We stood shoulder to shoulder sharing quips and comments as we looked at the hundreds of postings pinned and plastered to the front of the building. Most of those in our group were illiterate and delighted in listening to those few of us who could read as we deciphered the scribbled code. We made a game out of trying to find the one note connected to the farthest point west. It wasn't the posters or placards that held our attention most, but rather the snippets of information written on scraps of paper by unseen hands or scratched into the wood and mortar.

There were postings of every type. Layered like shingles, these bits of paper called out to the general public, to families, or specific people, offering news, advice, warnings of thieves and robbers, or pleas of assistance in the search for lost loved ones. There were directions to distant places that touched all four points of the compass. There were notices about kidnappings that both saddened and unsettled me, giving rise to feelings of insecurity that I was quick to snuff.

There were public notices for property, government grants, and tracts of cheap land being offered for sale to settlers and would-be buyers in great number. There were all varieties of advertisements from wagoneers, stagecoach firms, riverboat lines, blacksmiths, gunsmiths, livery stables and wainwrights, all promoting their trades and craft.

We laughed and marveled as we stood reading through the countless clips of paper, some fresh and some so faded that only by group effort did we take up the challenge to pick out what few letters were discernable and thereby construct words and sentences to revive the meaning.

Privately, I imagined how each note was like a tiny bell competing with the rest to ring out and say that someone, somewhere, was hoping not to be forgotten. That bitty piece of paper was the only connection to one distant person who I assumed was far removed from the civilized world. The sight of so many messages stirred up within me a swirl of excitement and wander-lust, an anticipation that passed through me in a great shudder.

NORTHWEST TERRITORIES

JAMES R. PEPPER

Owner

PEPPER STEAMERS

BUFFALO to DETROIT

Proven Vessels • Boiler-Safe

Passenger and Cargo

Weekly Schedules-Reasonable Rates

Inquire at Albany NY

RACHEL

I AM WAITING

IN ALBANY

CALEB

GODFREY PARKER

WAINSWRIGHT

Finest Woods

Spring Wagons

Conestoga Our Specialty

Our Seasoning Process

Best for the West

TWO YARDS to SERVE YOU

ALBANY & CUMBERLAND

Located at the Eastern Terminus

Of the Great Roads West

New York Turnpike & Cumberland National Road

Need a nail, a pail, something fail?

No need to fret or wail

Out there, on the dusty trail,

I got it all and it's all for sale!

DUSTY PEDDLER

MISING

Margrit Lin Frost

9 yrs old blu iz drk bron hare

takun 8/9/29

Form Buflo doks at Erie

Are only child

Pleze tel ofise if yu seas her

God bless yer help

TWENTY

I watched with apprehension time and again as numbers of
our group were called away by captains and ticketmasters, who
would step out of their offices and sound the call to board.
Stragglers were hustled across the planks, which were then
pulled back to shore in the nick of time before the steamers broke
away beneath thick clouds of black smoke, steam, and falling ash.

I was amazed that the vessels didn't vibrate completely apart
even before moving to face the current, for they trembled terribly
the whole of their length. I could only imagine how these boats
tried fearfully to contain the pressure in their boilers while
powering the paddles under such strain. I suffered a disconcert-
ing wariness, which grew increasingly unbearable with every
subsequent departure.

It brought clearly to mind William's stern warning at Mary
and Allen's table about boiler explosions, and I found myself
flinching with each horrific blast that erupted from the escape-
ments at the turning of the great wheels. I was beset with pause

and questioned why I, or anyone for that matter, would choose to travel in such fear.

In the end, thoughts of fighting the river current while standing beside a floating bomb commonly known to let loose without warning was more than I could bear. And so, falling prey to my fears, I elected to give up the modern Albany Steamer for one of the older and quieter historic sloops that were as much a part of the Hudson as the water, *even* if it meant spending an additional week on the water and an extra night or two in New York, *even* if it meant rising before sun-up in order to cast off with the flooding tide. Sail was something I understood and enjoyed.

Being outfitted with mast well forward, a jib, and occasionally a topsail, the river sloops held a certain charm. They sported high quarterdecks much like poop decks of old. I found them a welcome alternative, beautiful, peaceful—a far cry from the shuddering steamers that were determined to replace them.

As day neared end, the lamplighters appeared with torches in hand and dailys tucked under arm. Hollering *"wuxtra, wuxtra, read al' o' 'bout it!"* they moved from lamp to lamp igniting pine knots and selling papers. I bought one then returned to the Astor to retire and enter the day's events into my diary.

I spent the following two days traveling about New York City searching for signs of Christopher while waiting for the next sloop to depart. The signs were everywhere. Unfortunately, there were too many to sort out, and after much investigation, deemed too distant and impersonal. Summed up and simply put, word had it that Christopher was out in the far west.

There was no point in pursuing him further in New York, and so I had my baggage collected and transported to the Albany docks where I confirmed my passage aboard the ANNIE DEE, the next sloop casting off for Albany. She was about seventy feet long, made of red cedar, but painted up the likes of which I have never seen. Gaudy was hardly the word to describe her. She was a floating kaleidoscope of color, blending in perfectly with the rest of the outlandish sloops in her fleet, all competing for attention and passengers.

I soon realized that nothing less than a vessel of such multi-colored gaiety would suffice in the eyes of the sort of passengers looking to board them. Unbeknownst to me, these sloops were customarily used for great parties and dances as they sailed slowly up and down the valley. The festivities began long before they departed the landings, as crowds about the boats and banks beside them filled the air with laughter and jollity.

I watched a good number of the male travelers seek out certain captains who sponsored the rowdiest of carousers so as to join in their league. Nonetheless, regardless of captains or crew, the patrons started early into their drinking and diversions while on shore and kept hard at it until the wee hours of the morning. It was my misfortune they should pay so little mind to a good night's sleep, for I had paid handsomely for a private room—a waste of money to be sure. I tossed and turned all night, sleeping poorly, but for the rumpus outside and the tramping back and forth on deck. If not for time taken to sit up and pen Mary and Allen, the night would have been a complete loss.

When I arose the next morning and stepped out, I was imme-diately greeted by the hooligans, most of who were lying about from stem to stern on the damp dew-covered deck in complete disgrace. Somehow, they had managed to collect themselves aboard ship, safe from roaming robbers and thieves, but were now at my feet fully unconscious in pools of their own trash and vomit.

It was a scene I could have done without. A few of the women were wrapped in blankets, but the men lay beneath an open sky sleeping off the drink and damage done during night hours past. Only after pushing the lifeless bodies out of harm's way did the captain cast off on the slack, using the incoming winds to his advantage. The breeze not only swept us into the wide-open waters of the Hudson, but it also tore loose the stench seemingly impaled upon the masts of the ANNIE DEE and freshened me in spite of my present company.

At least we were off, and almost at once I sensed the difference between the crowded East River and the expanse of the Hudson. The Hudson offered relief from the congestion of the city. It tempted one to leave for a reprieve. It was soothing. It hinted of other places, peaceful places in the wilderness of upper New York State where life was said to be good and untainted.

TWENTY-ONE

My decision to board a sloop was soon found out to be seriously misguided, for instead of sailing peacefully upriver free of boilers and worry; I found myself aboard a boat standing dead still in the water merely four hours after setting sail. We had barely sailed our first reach, the Great Chip Rock still far in the distance, and there were thirteen yet to go. At first becalmed, the captain anchored against the current a scant few miles upstream from our place of departure. The morning wind had not only fallen off, but worse, turned against us.

The splash of ANNIE DEE's anchor may have been disheartening to me, but it was a sound instantly recognized by all drunkards on deck as the call to return from the dead. In a feat I would have thought impossible, they rose upon stiff and shaky limbs and again began drinking and dancing, high stepping with renewed vigor and ready to waste away another day. To add to an atmosphere already thick with alcohol and immorality, there were a number of other sloops surrounding us, all suffering the same fate and engaged in a similar state of riot.

I was caught up in a crowd of a different kind, and I cannot begin to express the outrageous activity that was taking place before my eyes other than to recount that which was conveyed to me by another nervous female passenger.

She had told me how the elders of the Houses of Congregation in New York were in an absolute uproar over the lack of attendance on the Sabbath due, in their belief, to the temptation of Satan's will aboard these sloops of sin. I truly believed her every word.

Apparently, people flocked to the sloops for Sunday excursions. It also appeared that Satan knew how to have a good time, no matter what day of the week. In my naivety, I first accepted the flirtatious invitations to partake in the festivities, but discovered in short time they were designed to get out of hand, especially for an unescorted woman such as myself. There was nothing flattering about the uninvited advances and groping hands I had to ward off at every turn.

By early evening, the passengers were thoroughly possessed by the devil. The only reason I didn't call the experience an all out orgy was because some of the women still had fragments of their clothes about them. In the space of a day, I saw more than an average life's' worth of drinking, vomiting, dancing, molesting, and fighting. After the second and third time I witnessed another terrified, half-drowned wench plead to be hauled back on board, I removed myself to my cabin, blocked the door, and elected straight away to take leave of the ANNIE DEE.

* * *

The following morning, while still surprisingly in possession of my life and virginity, I waited impatiently to confront the lesser risks of exploding boilers on a steamer. I could hear the steamer's approach some two or three miles off, and recalled

231

when young to having seen a small tugboat in the London docks persuade the REBECCA into the flow of the Thames—my, how things had progressed. I remembered Christopher's predictions about the future of steamboats while I stood at the gunwales and watched a large 'side-wheeler', as folks now called them, chug along hastily up the Hudson toward us.

Steamers were completely changing life on the water. Before, if a luckless person took up passage on an old Hudson sloop and met with disagreeable wind or weather, a trip upriver could cost that person the better part of a month. As I discovered, two or three days at a time could be spent at anchor holding on to whatever gains were made while awaiting rescue by a wind fresh enough to overcome the force of the current.

Christian passengers often milled about the riverbanks picking berries or whatnot until such a breeze happened upon them. Needless to say, I hadn't booked passage on a Christian sloop, and so rather than pick berries, the men aboard only spoke of squeezing melons. In any event, a steamer easily completed the same journey in as little as two days.

I gave thanks for that moment when the captain cast off his dory for those of us who chose to flee the hullabaloo aboard his vessel. He sent us merrily on our way across the river to meet up with the mammoth side-wheeler BARREL ROLL. The steamer barely slowed as we came alongside.

The deckhands manning our dory strained to keep pace. Pulling heartily at the oars, they swore a blue streak at the riverboat captain with each and every stroke. They were a fine lot, young, strong rivermen that made a pleasant sight for youthful girls, not to mention someone a little older. I couldn't help but to laugh at their plight, for I was convinced the riverboat Captain was teasing them by remaining just ahead of our bows.

TWENTY-TWO

It may have been my imagination, but I think more so the Captain's mercy that allowed us to catch the side-wheeler and stand safely upon her aftdeck. Other than the time it took to attract a small curious crowd who watched the men attempt to haul my trunk up from the dory, we were underway beneath the telltale haze of smoke and ash. I waved good-bye to those handsome dorymen as they floated away with the current, happy to rest their weary arms.

They were replaced by a school of dolphins that joined us as we steamed up the Tappan Zee headed next for Haverstraw Bay and World's End. In their playful company, we headed upriver watching the west bank rise in a spectacular display of vertical cliffs reaching straight upward from water's edge five hundred feet and more.

The formation continued on for the better part of twenty-five miles, it being known as the Palisades of which Lydia had spoke. The fortress-like walls of rock then fell away, retreating so the banks might separate, giving the river space enough to settle down and spread into an expanse of water resembling a very large lake. This was Haverstraw Bay. Edging up to its distant east shore, between Croton-on-Hudson and Peeksville, where lived the legends of sunken treasure and Captain Kidd, was the grand estate of Boscobel, eminent amid its thousand acres of privacy.

By the time we passed the massive estate, we were in the waters of World's End where the Hudson current entered the bay from the north. It ran frightfully turbulent at this point, for the river was forced to churn edgily through the narrows and around a sharp bend. This it did twice daily under influence of ebb and tide.

Steaming along at a brisk pace, we put Palisades, Haverstraw, and those turbulent waters of World's End quickly astern to disappear beyond our wake. Now, we passed by the foot of Bear Mountain to arrive abeam of the nationally celebrated West Point Academy. It was situated strategically upon a high ridge that jutted into the flow of water from the western shore between two bends in the river. The academy's cannon enjoyed a commanding view and stood poised within striking distance of anything afloat below. During the Revolution, our patriots had strung chains across the river in this area to stop Bristish ships from sailing upriver.

The marvelous overhanging cliffs of stepped rock that supported the academy kept pace with us until giving way to the entirely new vistas of the Highlands. For fifteen miles we gazed upward until we at last set eyes upon the Highland's northern marker, that being the prominent Storm King Mountain, the last notable feature before arriving at Newburgh.

If ever a steamer was to be safer than a sloop, it was here, a place called Mother Cronk's Cove. It had a well-earned reputation for being an especially nasty stretch of river where winds were cursed and came roaring unexpectedly through the gap between Storm King and Crow's Nest mountains fully bent on swamping boats.

Stories flourished afresh to recount the recent tragedy of the sloop Neptune and the way in which it was blown over causing the death of thirty-five people. The accounts added significance to the Dutch name for this place, which when translated meant 'Martyr's reach'. Its reputation gave one plenty of reason for pause while staring into the murky and rippled wind-swept waters.

Putting fears aside, I went on to observe all I hoped to see of the spectacular Hudson River Valley. I made note after note in my diary of the marvelous landscape that Hudson River painters and artists from abroad came to capture for posterity. I had absorbed the richness of nature's colors and sighted a world of wildlife long since extinct in Boston.

I surveyed the blue-grays that saturated the lower forests of hickory, chestnut and oak, and looked upward to higher elevations where tints of green marked the northern hardwoods, beech, sugar maple, birch and hemlock, and higher yet to see the spruce and balsam fir brushed by red-tailed hawks on wing.

I applauded the occasional bald eagle seen gliding effortlessly upon winds that rushed down through this forested valley adding to an already lasting impression.

Across the water, beyond the banks and gaggles of geese, deep within woods teased by the flicker of titmouse, the flash of crimson cardinals, and blur of a streaking bluebird, came the riveting tat-tat-tat of unseen woodpeckers that penetrated even the hoarse chugging of our boat.

I being one of the unfortunate few, missed within that place a black bear as it rambled through the undergrowth foraging for berries, but did glimpse high above, the sight of a sandy colored catamount lying upon a sun-warmed precipice. I marveled at the number of white tailed deer moving deftly through the forest clearings beneath the cat's wanton stare, then bolting away in leaps and bounds, frightened not by the clawed hunter, but by the boisterous intrusion of our vessel into nature's unspoiled reaches.

This rugged untouched terrain amplified sharp contrasts between the domain of man and beast. Much to my benefit, there were fewer signs of man because when they appeared, they came as terrible scars. Increasingly, along the water's edge, the wounds became visible.

Trees by the thousands were being clear-cut for purpose of feeding the insatiable boilers aboard the ever-larger river steamers. Thousands more stood as markers, killed for want of their bark. They were the stands of hemlock, tall and ghostly, stripped alive of their skin by unconscionable profiteers for the purpose of tanning hides.

This was the most unconscionable act. After the war of eighteen-twelve, shiploads of hides were hove up the Hudson from South America to be trucked by the wagon into the mountains where stood the large groves of Hemlock. At the edge of every stand stood a tannery. The forests were alive with the sound of men at work for it took a full cord of wood to tan ten hides. Tanbark peeling, as it was called paid handsomely and a good peeler could produce two cords of wood a day. The result was thousands upon thousands of dead trees left to rot as fuel for the forest fires which destroyed what little remained.

The damage cut deep into the valley and made soulful and sensible people sick with remorse by the nonsense of it. Those visions could not be erased from memory, for the scars remained. They could only be put out of mind, blurred into the background as one fought instead to focus on the still pure thrill of a blue heron beating wingtip to water or a kingfisher making his swoop.

Fishermen floated with the river between these natural havens, tending their nets and spilling out the overflow of slippery striped bass, sturgeon, codfish, and the aquatic delicacies of both fresh and brackish waters. They kept a wary eye on our approach, we being one of a growing number of behemoths that required constant consideration.

We passed many such fishermen plying their trade late into the day before disappearing into the creeping valley shadows as the sun sank low in the west; its warmth being forced out by the cool evening breezes that chilled those close to the water. I stepped back from the rail, retreating begrudgingly from the rapture and rugged beauty of the highlands, as might a reader closing the cover of a fine novel.

Although my work in charity had offered me occasion to visit New York, I had never laid eyes upon the upper reaches of the Hudson and had always felt cheated. Hardly a soul in the land might be found deaf to stories about the magnificence of this region. The personality of the Hudson was as magnetic as that of New York City, drawing into its valley the artists, the poets, and the prosperous—*especially the prosperous.*

From the earliest days of our nation, the well heeled took up residence in this valley to enjoy its beauty and commerce. The same river that conveyed furriers to and from Canada through unbroken wilderness, now allowed lessers to observe the splendors of success and imagine the lifestyles of the wealthy, as timeless currents flowed past prehistoric shores now made ostentatious by the mansions of the Middle Hudson.

Montgomery Place with its impressive Federal architecture was positioned on the East shore at Annandale-on-Hudson opposite the panoramic Catskills. With its gardens and grounds, scenes stolen from paintings, its patios were placed strategically for the benefit of all who approached by way of water.

Farther north, there was Clermont, the second largest private holding in New York. Fully one third of the county of Columbia, the estate originally covered thirteen thousand acres of land. The home I observed was actually the second one built, the British having burned the original structure to the ground during the war.

There was Springwood in Hyde Park and Bard Estate built in seventeen and ninety-five. All these homes were inspiring, but not more so than the families that owned them. Names synonymous with the nation's blood and soul, names rooted in the earliest settlements; the Lewis's, the Livingstons, the Schuylers, Montgomerys, and Ten Broecks, the Van Cortlands and Crawfords, to name but a few.

These sizable estates brought back to me recollections of the expansive Claussen estate in Sweden. Awe-inspiring indeed were these homes along the Hudson, but for me they paled by comparison. It may be that memories from my childhood distorted the truth, but I recalled the way in which the wings of the Claussen mansion disappeared into the snowy distance.

I recalled castle-sized doors that marked the main entrance. They stood side-by-side as if solid wooden walls rising up from the back of an immense circular bed of granite. This was the porch, its dark gray stone ringed by pillars and steps, highlighted by bright swirling streaks of inlaid Italian marble that flowed ribbon-like to connect exquisite patterns spaced geometrically across its surface with degreed precision.

I remembered how impossible it was for my young arms to reach around the diameter of the great granite columns. I remembered standing at their base and looking up, my eyes following the stone shafts as they soared above me. I remembered birds fluttering about as they sought to catch tidbits in the nightlight of lanterns that formed haloes around the chiseled granite crowns.

I recalled the vistas visible between the pillars, the views of the gardens, the valley, and mountains beyond, the curvaceous craftsmanship hammered into the wrought iron gates that separated us from the wilds. I remembered the mills, the workshops, the fine furniture, the wooden horses and all the toys.

The toys?

My thoughts froze. I had completely forgotten about the toys. A sudden revelation was upon me. Had I just realized the origin of those mysterious crates of children's joy that popped up on ships and in warehouses, those many gifts given upon the docks from none other than my lost—*Santa Claus of the sea?*

How incredible I had never made this connection. How could I have forgotten the toyshops? For whatever reason it came to me now, I could hardly imagine. Maybe, it wasn't so much that it was coming back to me, but more a matter of my being older, and only now realizing what activity went on in those days.

Now, as I thought back, it was obvious. They were making toys in those shops—a perfectly sensible activity during the dead of winter. In fact, it occurred to me, there must have been literally tons upon tons of scrap wood produced in the Claussen lumber mills. What better source for making toys. An endless supply of raw material and a sensational means of leaving nothing to waste. Toys, it was perfect—*thousands upon thousands of toys!*

I was consumed by my insight. It was as if a cord had been pulled that released a flurry of sensibilities inside my thick skull. It was certain that the staff employed by the Claussen estate was enormous, and it would have been entirely practical to have business opportunities for the husbands and wives of those who served the Claussens.

I knew Christopher's heart, and he would have thought it inconceivable that a maiden servant might finish her day's chores and face the hardship of traveling many miles in the cold to be with her family at night. Better to have her family living at the estate; she to do her chores, and her loved ones to work nearby in the shops if at all possible. For that matter, maybe the shops were the first to exist and the estate was enlarged to house the workers. Maybe that was why it was so large. I had no idea.

I shook my head in disbelief while remembering all those crates I happened upon at the warehouse in Boston. I laughed at myself for having never pieced all of this together. It was so simple a puzzle, to think of it left me embarrassed. My only consolation was gained in the knowledge that I was but nine years in age when I left the estate and understood little of anything that went on about me. In any event, the toyshops, the mills, the grounds—Claussen's estate was enormous and as of yet, for me, unequaled by anything so far to be found in this valley.

* * *

We steamed past Poughkeepsie, Kingston, Saugerties, and spied those secret havens of sleepy hollows before arriving at the port of Hudson on the east shore, where we landed for an exchange of freight.

Hudson was reputed to be the first chartered city in our nation, and I observed it to be a busy place with a sizable shipyard, a large distillery, a sperm whale works, and a number of rope and sail making facilities. I spied as least thirty or forty ships moored in its port.

By the time we reached the town, many of the passengers aboard the BARREL ROLL were preparing to turn in for the night.

239

A few newly made friends and I were in too high a spirit to sleep, and so decided to venture from the boat with a mind to seek out a reputable little inn that came highly recommended by a smartly dressed young man in our company.

Following his lead, we went ashore and commenced to stroll down Warren Street through the center of town. I could see even in the darkness of night that the community was graced with many fine houses bordering the water's edge. The young man pointed out one such fabulous home, which according to him was built by Mayor Jenkins of New York City at the turn of the century. This was only one of many attractions that added interest and ambiance to the place.

Apparently, the city was founded by a group of prominent Nantucket whaling families who feared the British were about to reclaim the colonies. The community felt especially vulnerable living fifty miles off the mainland coast and so in seventeen eighty-three an affluent few went in search of a safer place to do business and call home. They settled upon this tract of land a hundred miles upriver, which at that time was called Claverack Landing. Soon thereafter families from Nantucket, Martha's Vineyard, Newport and Provident followed their lead. I was amused to hear how many dismantled their houses and brought the pieces with them, in order to rebuild anew. Our walk was informative and most pleasant and nothing of Hudson's history or charm was wasted on me.

The inn, which our young leader, one Mr. Cotter, and the regulars called the Reindeer Cove, catered especially to the river traffic and often stayed open all night to serve. The stopover would allow us time enough to sup leisurely at the establishment.

Banks of river fog wafted about the shores to bring a chill to the bone, but Mr. Cotter assured us the inn would soon be found nestled in the woods a short ways south of the landing. We were to watch for its oil lamps aglow in the dark of night beckoning passersby to step in from the damp river air for an ale or better yet, a hot meal.

And so the place stood as promised alongside a peacefully still pond. The inn exemplified the rich Dutch heritage of this area, a cozy story-and-a-half structure with ducks and chickens waddling about the yard and water. It was a red-bricked building of sturdy construction with a steep roof and parapet gables. Each room set aside for boarders had a private entrance and was well furnished with sturdy beds and handsome furniture.

From the cool air of the street, we entered a dining hall that was large and conveyed the feeling of security with its massive post and beam construction. Solid tables were placed close to a daunting fireplace so patrons might enjoy the warmth of the hearth. Numerous pieces of Dutch porcelain, tiles, pictures, and engravings were displayed with prominence and added much to the atmosphere.

If not a pleasure for the eyes, or place of rest for the weary traveler, the inn certainly was a call to the hungry. The aroma was unforgiving as it escaped up the chimney, reaching for us in the lane and pulling us inside to the fire where it swirled about the skewers, pots, and pans to assure all of the tasty pleasures to be had. The meats roasted, the soups boiled, and the potatoes, pies, and cobblers baked. We left nothing to imagination, but discovered for ourselves how well one could feast.

As we dined and conversed, I learned a good deal about this young man who introduced us to the inn. He was about twenty-five in years, notably informal and most likable. He insisted on being called 'Billy', 'Silly Billy', he said, after a few mugs of ale. He was a cargo agent and often called a scalper. He was a buyer and seller, a mover of goods, and it sounded as though he moved as often and distant as the merchandise in which he dealt. There was a notable trait of Dutch country in his voice albeit softened by his travels.

'Billy' had spent his life traveling the rivers and all of New York country. It was soon obvious that he was anything but silly.

He was wise for his young years and remarkably well versed. Not only could he give a full account of Hudson River Valley history, having been born on its banks in eighteen and five and having lived within view of its waters ever since, but also that of the Mohawk River Valley, the Great Western and Mohawk turnpikes, all means of travel, and of course the Erie Canal.

"Da canal's used mostly voor freight. Het's slow but ya don't hafta worry about low water. We got turnpikes if your impatient, but da canal's what drives dis area. 'Sides, slow can be good. 'Vore dey built it, we had only one route voor freight, a white-knuckled trip down da Mohawk wit' little more dan a prayer en a kiss of luck. Many a time I prayed *'God watch o're me'* while in doze gorges. Rapids run pretty much da whole of hets lengt', en dey get real nasty in places."

"Ik don't know how jou do het. I would be utterly terrified," spoke a young woman, who seemed to have taken a fancy to our Dutch host.

Billy laughed. "Jou don't want t' be dere if ya can't swim. Actually, jou don't want to be dere even if ya can swim. Het's no river voor da timid, no ma'am. I've rode it out more times dan I care t' count. Het's notting like dis sleepy Hudson.

"On da Mohawk, dere's a gorge at Little Falls some sixty miles west o' Schenectady where da river plunges trew da cliffs en drops a good vour hundred feet as it makes hets run eastward. At hets mout', where it empties into da Hudson, da rapids are totally impassible voor any boat, en before ya even get dere, jou must first face da rapids at German Flats en anutter especially bad set at Oswego. Da Mohawk makes da Hudson look like a wading pool."

"My word!" The young woman exclaimed; her face lightly flushed.

"In da old days, we'd go downriver until we reached a stretch o' rapids, where we had no choice but t' unload our boats, haul 'em out da river, carry 'em overland along da most miserable, rocky, ankle-breaking trails jou can imagine voor a mile or more, den put 'em back in en re-load da cargo. Het was backbreaking work dat rubbed a man raw. Took voorever, I know, en I say good riddin's t' rapids en days past. Dat canal is a blessing."

"Het sounds en looks as if de canal might even be making jou rich, yah?" said another in our party, who was most certainly alluding to Mr. Cotter's fine clothes.

"Oh, I don't know if I'd go so var as to say dat, but I'm not complaining. Voor me, hets been one of da greatest projects ever built, notting but opportunity. I've reaped da benefits, jou can be sure. Voor otters, het's been different. Da wagoneers are taking het plenty hard. Same wit' many of da old inn-keepers. Da turnpikes are fading away to some extent. Hardly anyone uses dem voor freight anymore, not like dey used to. Da canal is much easier on cargo. Jou can float a ton of goods wit' hardly any effort; no more getting bogged down in da mud, no more broken wheels en axles, no more corduroy roads, just smoot' easy travel—long as da banks aren't breached."

"I'm looking forward to seeing it." I said with sincerity.

"Jou'll love it, Miss Claussen. Jou'll love all of it. Jou'll love Albany as well."

"Yah, Albany is nice," concurred another in our group.

"Mmm, Yah," came murmurs and echoes.

"Het's a busy place, growing, interesting," said Mr. Cotter. "Be het da Hudson, da Mohawk, da turnpikes, or da canal, hets still all about moving goods east en west trew Albany.

"I do a lotta business in New York, en dat's da only place I know dat maybe outdoes Albany in growt'. But, we know well around here dat New York is only gaining hets glory en surpassing da otter Atlantic ports because of da trade het gets from us."

"Yah, yah, dis is true." Again, the group agreed with Mr. Cotter.

"You can take my word for het, Miss Claussen, I know. Buying en selling between here en New York is my business, en I make a good living packing grain, hides, coal, flour, or whatever else I can fit into dose boats. Het all turns a profit. En dere's a lot of profit. Has it made me rich? I don't know, but comfortable, absolutely, en I'm still young. I guess time will tell."

I for one was mesmerized by young Mr. Cotter's commentary on the construction and progress of the canal. He was full of interesting facts, a youthful mustached encyclopedia of sorts. For this reason among others, I sat quietly taking note of his comments, often answers to my many un-asked questions. I listened to his stories with great interest during our dinner.

"Seven hundred thousand acres! You can't be serious." One at the table voiced my disbelief. He too must have been new to the area.

"Indeed, I am. All o' Albany is but a mere speck of space on da grounds of an enormous estate owned by da Van Rensselaer family. Jou can imagine his is a well known name in dese parts."

My jaw dropped. I sat speechless in my chair. America was supposed to be the land of freedom and equality. However, while growing up with the Claussens, I learned that beneath the surface, in America, wealth and power was held firmly within the hands of a few, thanks to old world land grants, patents, and favoritism, but this story was unbelievable even to me. The enormity of such a manor was beyond comprehension.

I suddenly felt uncomfortable knowing I too was connected to such wealth. Guilt greased my insides for I was one of *those* people who lived a life filled with the trappings of comfort and opportunity. For most others, a connection to great wealth was one of horrible memories, terror, and oppression. Other than the old Loyalists, most Americans eagerly severed ties with the Old World. I wondered if any of these New World American aristocrats were as generous with their fortunes as was my old-world Christopher. It was certain he hob-knobbed with their kind, and I hoped his generosity rubbed off.

Beyond Billy's stories and all our cares, those employed upon the BARREL ROLL and the other side-wheelers in port continued to labor long after dark. The steamers had no reservations about traveling the river at night and so a messenger was sent to summon our return near two in the morning. We were lazily sitting about chatting away the wee hours over warm chicory, coffee, and tea, and feeling much disturbed by the interruption. Our every attempt to persuade the roustabout to join us for a spell was for naught. Instead, he persisted in prodding us until we were at last on our feet and the lane so the boat might get underway.

Aboard ship, our number was forced to call it a night and quickly broke ranks. Now subdued, all headed for the cabins. I did likewise, but after seeing to it that my sleeping arrangements were in order, I stepped back outside one last time before retiring. The oil lamps burned silently along the deck as the large paddle wheels began to blend the night air above with the black water below. The misty mixture reached me at the rail and prompted me to draw tight my wrap. From where I stood, I tried to pick out the lanterns of the Reindeer Cove amid the lingering lights of Hudson, which were now receding into the distance.

The chugging of the engines and sound of water cascading off the paddles worked to drug me by drowning out the distractions of my day. The vibrations soothed me, making me ever so sleepy. I began to sway back and forth until gaining enough sense to return to my cabin. After having spent a night filling myself with food and drink, I was most relaxed and all but asleep on my feet. Overcome with drowsiness, I undressed with eyes already closed and felt my way under the covers. Maybe for a moment, maybe for two, I relived one of the day's more memorable pleasures. I fell fast asleep with a smile light upon my face.

TWENTY-THREE

I slept barely three hours, but I slept hard and woke well rested at the break of dawn. I was eager to get back on deck so I could enjoy the views sure to surprise me at day's first light. Determined to miss nothing, I gathered my wrap tightly around me and stepped outside to meet the chilly river air.

I wasn't the only brave soul to confront the damp morning mists. I found myself in the company of many other early risers now leaning over the rail trying to peer beyond the wisps of fog. Only the deck hands who darted from post to post snuffing lamps, and their mates, who were serving fresh steeped tea, appeared oblivious to the quiet beauty we now disturbed.

The mists were thick directly upon the water and quite effectively obstructed our view. There was little choice but to observe the heights, yet one could hardly have been disappointed. As the sun rose upward in the east, a rich orange wash spread across the peaks above the western bank and bled downward to illuminate the fog that blanketed us below.

The river coursed unconcerned through these heights, and the higher rose the sun, the lower fell my attention from the mountain tops to moving pockets of mists that were now dissipating to reveal the shoreline drawing near. At first I paid the shore no mind, but soon realized the passenger cabins were emptying out, and my fellow travelers were gathering up their belongings as though preparing to disembark.

In no time, I went from being confused to disagreeably anxious. To my surprise and relief, I spotted our dinner host, young Billy Cotter, standing among the many early-risers gathered against the portside railing to watch the shore draw near. I intended to press him immediately for some answers as to our whereabouts and reasons for all the commotion.

"Good morning, Mr. Cotter."

"Goed Morning, Miss Claussen. Did jou sleep well?"

246

"Yes, thank you for asking. Are we going in? Are we about to land? This boat does go to Albany, does it not? I am wondering because I see nothing that approximates a city." My questions shot out rapidly one after the other with a voice that revealed something of my nervousness. I was searching the riverbanks and beyond as I approached. He knew I had jumped ships, and probably assumed I knew right where I was headed.

Nothing could have been further from the truth. I noted the shore drawing near, I observed the landings up ahead and the long rows of firewood in waiting. I also observed the general movement of the passengers, especially the women, who continued readying themselves to disembark and this worried me because women wouldn't be readying themselves to go ashore during a stop for firewood. The boat was a good place to be; the bank was not—unless one liked bugs and snakes. Women only left the boat when they were becalmed on a sloop and fighting to protect their *'melons'*, or when arrived at their destination. Yet, everybody was gathering up belongings.

There were other riverboats at the landing to be sure. However, this place was in the middle of nowhere and still there was nothing to be seen of a city. Had I made a mistake? Billy could see my confused expression. Surely, he could sort it out for me.

"Is this Albany?" I forwarded my final question, seeing nothing of the city and feeling stupid.

"Yes en no," he answered with a smile. "Yes, we are about t' land, but no, dis is not Albany. We aren't far, dough. When jou jumped ships, jou should haaf picked one of da more expensive charters out o' New York en den jou would haaf sailed straight into Albany.

"Jou chose da BARREL ROLL, a boat dat's owned by da captain. He charges less en lands downstream because dis is da closest he can get to Albany en still pick up firewood cheap. He passes da savings on to us. Trucking firewood into Albany is expensive, so a number of da captains stop short, en we pay voor a stage to take us da last few miles."

"Oh! I was starting to worry." I let out an air of relief and studied the bank as we drew near to shore. Sure enough, there were a number of stagecoaches lined up behind the rows of firewood. Mr. Cotter continued to speak.

"Going into Albany nowadays can be a real test o' nerves. Every boat, barge or barrel dat floats outta da Erie empties into Albany's basin en in my opinion only idiots choose to face da mess. Hets notting to see a hundred or more sloops en schooners movin' about in dat cramped space fightin' da current en each otter at any given time.

"I've seen too many boats nearly get sunk in dat confusion. Da canal caters to barges dat come trew het end-to-end in lines of ten or more wit' an ambition to run you over. You get in deir way en you lose. No captain in his right mind wants to deal wit' all dat when he can stop short, get in, get his firewood, en get out in an hour's time."

"I didn't know."

"Don't fret. Only da one-time passengers complain about not goin' all da way. Hets only a couple of hours to Albany from here by stage, en dat's as fast as da boats can do itt after working deir way to a landing. Jou'll be dere 'fore ya know it. So, tell me, did jou enjoy your trip upriver? Was het all ya hoped for?"

Feeling relieved, I willingly accepted his attempt to converse because Billy saved me the trouble of small talk. He spoke freely and informatively. "Oh heavens, yes. It was magnificent, more than magnificent. I must admit it met my every expectation. The scenery was sensational; the mansions were spectacular, huge! Marvelous, all of it."

"Excellent, I'm pleased t' hear it. Het's sad t'say, but having spent my whole life travelin' da river, I forget to notice. I forget how splendid it really is. Het's good dat someone like you reminds me on occasion.

"I recall last night at dinner jou mentioned jour plans are to search Albany voor Mr. Claussen an' continue on westward if need be."

"You remember well. Knowing Christopher, most likely I'll need be heading west." I answered.

"Jou may be right, but at least jou'll have plenty o' company. I would wager dat a quarter of da people in Albany are going jour way. Da city has become da new gateway to da West."

"I am surprised. By all I have heard from you and the others, I can't imagine why anyone would care to leave. It sounds a perfect place to stay and settle."

"Het very nearly is perfect, an' you're correct, a good many do haaf a change o' heart an' stay. Da place is growing by leaps an' bounds. I'd wager het's doubled in size as we stand here talking."

"That's a boisterous bet, sir, a bit of a brag I would say."

"Not really. Albany offers more dan most people can turn away. Het's a great place t' do business. Het's perfectly situated near da confluence o' da Mohawk an' Hudson Rivers, da only two natural passageways dat traverse dese mountains. You're about t' land at da only junction o' practical routes dat stretch from da Atlantic Ocean in da east t' Canada an' da waters o' da Great Norttern Lakes, an' over t' da Ohio and Michigan Territories to da west. Dat's why I say, ya'd be amazed t' know how many people pass trew here."

"Do most people take the canal?"

"More en more as time goes on. I imagine jour Mr. Claussen would haaf. To appreciate it's potential, he would haaf to see da canal voor himself. I suspect jou'll find much o' jour Mr. Claussen about Albany. I've seen his name about en heard talk of him. Dis is his kind of place. Let me jus' give jou an idea o' what Albany means to a man like Mr. Claussen. Jou said he's in da logging business among otter dings.

"Well, you may or may not know dat transportation is probably da toughest part o' logging. Logs are heavy, en b'fore da canal, ya could only move dem on sledges during da winter when roads were frozen solid. Transportation is da primary obstacle to profit in dis country. Dat's da long en short of it. People are spread out all over, bot' sides o' da mountains, bot' sides o' da lakes, bot' sides o' da river. Dey all haaf eitter a stack of logs, or a field, or warehouse full o' grain, or goods t' sell, but no way to move het t' market. Same wit' people dat wanna buy, dey haaf plenty o' money, but no way t' get deir hands on da materials dey need.

"Before da canal, in order to ship somet'ing from da eastern shore o' Lake Erie across upper state New York en down da Mohawk, or along da turnpike, en den down da Hudson to Manhattan, used t' take every bit o' twenty days or more. Het could be a mont' if luck was against jou. Now het can be done in eight days often enough t' bet on it.

"Not only can het be done nearly tree times faster, het can be done at a cost o' only five dollars a ton whereas het used t' be a hundred or more. Each en every one o' dose five-dollar tons passes trew Albany. I guarantee dat would peak Mr. Claussen's interest. If I were jou I'd check da boat yards. Seems I remember somet'ing of him having a connection wit' boats."

Boats indeed! Nearly everything that came out of Silly Billy's mouth was a pertinent fact or point of interest. He might have been young, but his mind worked like Christopher's, and his advice was every bit as sensible. I made a mental note to check out the boatyards first, but even though Mr. Cotter suspected I would find *'much of Mr. Claussen in Albany'*, I suspected I would find nothing of the man whatsoever. It would have been too easy for him to write me from Albany over the years. No, in my heart I feared he would be a long ways away from the likes of Albany.

After seeing to my baggage, I accepted Mr. Cotter's arm and was escorted ashore. I was in good health, good humor and good company. We climbed the bank and followed a well-worn trail that passed between towering piles of chopped firewood, some already on its way into BARREL ROLL's furnace. It was good-bye to the water, and hello to the dusty road as we prepared to embark on a jaunt that would take us into the heart of this unseen city.

TWENTY-FOUR

The stagecoach yards at the landing were permanently manned and presently in the process of hitching up teams. The captains were joking with one another as they parked their coaches in a row, each named after a famous ship. They were ready to whisk away newly arrived passengers as soon as they stepped ashore.

"Go, go, quick, Miss Claussen," urged Billy. "Take dat coach, da one wit' da flat top! THE BLUE SEAS; het's a good one."

"Which one?" I asked.

BLUE SEAS! 'ALBANY OVERLAND STAGE'. Right dere, straight ahead, dat's a good coach. Hurry up, madam." Billy pushed our party promptly toward the open door of a cabin where a ticketmaster stood with one hand on the opened door handle and the other waving tickets as if to scoop us up. He was sporting an inviting smile and beckoned us to be quick.

I, being the only lady in our group, was quickly escorted forward and allowed first to board. The broadside stated that ticket prices were based on weight, and the ticketmaster looked over my frame with two lecherous eyes void of shame or decency until coming to an unblinking stop and stare at my bosom.

"Well, now. What to we 'ave 'ere? A 'andsome woman if ever I saw. I am undecided. I am un-de-ci-ded. Do you weigh more—or—less than a cheerful canary, my good lady?"

"Oh, spare me, good sir! What kind of talk is that?" barked out Thomas Carrington, one of my dinner companions who was appalled by such an indiscretion. Feigning shock, the ticketmaster turned to face Thomas.

"I beg your pardon, sir. Is this 'andsome woman your wife?"

"Uh, n-no."

"No? Nooooo? What are you saying then; the lady resembles a whale? I pray not!" The ticketmaster glanced at me with the same eyes, now opened wide with humorous horror. I couldn't help but to chuckle. At once, I understood this man to be a character for sure.

"Of course not. I insinuated no such thing!" Thomas was at once defensive before the man's glare.

"Do you think she is less than the most beautiful creature man ever laid eyes upon?" He turned to face me. "Maybe he would prefer I looked upon *him* with such affection." He winked an eye knowingly.

"Oh, for the sake of heaven! I cannot stand one moment more of your boldness and incivility." Mr. Carrington, crushed by the embarrassment of discussing such a thought went silent and turned to look away.

I returned the stare of the ticketmaster's dark devilish eyes. He was an older man, rather overfed, unshaven, unkempt, and he did nothing for the nose, but he had a way about him, a certain smile and another look in his eyes that spoke of a big heart beneath his boisterous character. It made up for his shortcomings. In short time, I found nothing about him offensive. I smiled, held my tongue, and let him dream as he might. It was obvious he favored me, and in the end having no desire to insult me; he flattered me with a lesser charge—*much less*.

"You may ride for free, my sunshine. I thank you for lighting up my dark and dreary heart. I shall cherish your beauty this day and many more I am certain."

"Ohhhh, for the love of god—." Thomas moaned behind me.

I inhaled guardedly to escape the ticketmaster's odor as he leaned over me to whisper loud enough for all to hear. "I assure you, madam, I shall make up for your fare twofold when I charge that blind overfed oaf of a gentleman behind you."

"What!" Thomas protested, he being a lean man.

We all broke into laughter. My male companions rolled their eyes and howled. In good fun they chastised me for being a temptress and chided the ticketmaster mercilessly for being so openly lecherous. He laughed heartily, obviously being a man used to giving and taking taunts from his customers. The jabs and laughter continued for some time, for we were enough to fill his cabin, leaving him unhurried. His joviality was thoroughly contagious.

It was not so much the ticketmaster, but the reaction of my friends and the fuss they made that embarrassed me the most. I couldn't recall the last time anyone paid such mind to my appearance, and I flushed terrible. With my fair complexion, this was something I was unable to hide and so attempted to put a timely stop to the malarkey.

"Enough, enough, you're either too kind or too cunning. I must pay."

"I would never accept it." He raised his hand to ward off my offer.

"Seriously, I must pay. It is unfair to the others." I insisted.

"The others 'ave done nothing for my eyes as 'ave you. The others 'ave done nothing for my 'eart as 'ave you. The others are but mere passengers, collectors of dust, whereas you, my lady, are nothing if not exquisite."

"Good night, sir!" howled, Mr. Carrington. "Are you in the employ of transportation or theatre. Is Shakespeare to be next? Where are thou, my Romeo. Hast thou forsaken me? No, no, my Juliet! I stand in line—*still*. I wait, I wait, and yet I wait further to board the BLUE SEAS coach ." No one escaped the hidden message or the hilarity of Mr. Carrington's impersonation.

"As you wish." I relented. "Have it your way. I can take no more of this attention."

I felt the heat of self-consciousness rise off my brow. The ticketmaster could see my state plain enough, and felt pleased. He offered me his hand, a mischievous grin, and a window seat at the back of the coach that faced forward much to my satisfaction—*all for free*.

"I pray you enjoy your ride, my sunshine, and should you need a brave knight during the night, or any other service while in Albany, I beg you summon Orval Baker." He bowed as he stepped back.

"Thank-you, Mr. Baker, you're much too kind."

"Much too cunning," said Mr. Carrington.

"Maybe so, sir. Your driver is Captain Van Camp, an experienced man, born to the box. You can do no better. Good luck and God speed you all."

Once inside, things settled down. Mr. Carrington was indeed charged more and advised to diet, but bit his lip in good sport and took a seat. I listened to the ticketmaster as he returned to his obligations and the business of barking out orders at young stableboys chasing down baggage. This followed by the 'thump, thump, and THUMP' of our belongings being tossed overhead onto the cabin roof. The coach suddenly tilted a little to one side.

"What on earth was that," said Mr. Carrington.

"Who among us is hauling rocks," asked another.

I said nothing, but evaded their inquisitive stares by feigning interest in the appointments of the coach. In fact, I noted the coach was well constructed with plush fabrics and overstuffed seat cushions to help deaden the vibration and noise. I found it inviting, even cozy of a fashion after having spent so much time outside in the open air upon the decks of boats.

"You were right. This is a good coach. Well appointed, and a good ride I should imagine." I complimented Mr. Cotter on his choice.

"Da best part is what jou can't see. Can ya feel da way da cabin seems t' float about?"

"No."

"It might have something to do with that trunk, Mr. Cotter," said Mr. Carrington.

"I beg your pardon, sir," said I, unable to keep a straight face. The others laughed.

"Yah, indeed," continued Mr. Cotter. "However, in spite o' da trunk, I do believe jou will notice a difference. Dis is one of da new Concord coaches. Instead o' being fastened hard to da frame, het's attached by two t'ick leatter straps—."

"Very thick, we hope."

"All right, enough is enough. I have only brought a few books, nothing more." I protested amid the teasing.

"Most certainly, we understand. A learned woman on the road," said one Mr. Cragar.

"Why ever have I bothered with lightweight clothing, I can't imagine. Books on the other hand...."

"You gentlemen are cruel, all of you. Now, as you were saying, Mr. Cotter—thick straps—."

"Yes, t'ick straps. Dey call 'em t'oroughbraces an' dey greatly reduce da objections o' da road. Dat's why I urged jou t'seize het at da landing. Dose in da know, travelers like dese gentlemen, seek 'em out en snap 'em up quick. If ya know da term 'Gut Shake Line', I promise jou'll appreciate da wonder of a Concord."

Having done a fair amount of traveling in the past, I knew the term well, but for the last few years, my excursions seldom left the paved streets within city limits. The thought of traveling across country by coach entered my mind more than once. It was true that upon the water there were no bumps or bruised rumps, but I often wondered whether I was drifting fore or aft while at the mercy of the wind with its trickeries.

My plan was pretty much to continue westward via packet boats that traveled the canal at a leisurely pace. I envisioned the vessels offering me ample time to take in the sights, to sketch, converse, or write and make notes. I expected it to be a wonderful experience, but that is not to say the stagecoach didn't offer certain temptation.

For one thing, some of my fondest memories were of times spent in the comfort of Lady Rebecca's vermilion coach. When we traveled about, as a child I liked the sounds when entering towns, especially the 'clop clop' of horse hooves hammering streets and echoing back and forth between the buildings.

I remembered climbing into the shade of the cabin to escape the scorching sun. I remembered staring out the window to watch the passing countryside as our horses trotted along stirring up cool breezes that buffeted my face and hair.

I remembered being wrapped up in cozy comfort, secure within Lady Rebecca's silent embrace beneath thick woolen blankets in the dead cold of a winter's night while my feet thawed over a footwarmer filled with hot embers. I could still hear the sound of Christmas bells ringing in step with the great white horses, and see crowds of stick people I scratched into frost formed by my breath upon the glass.

One never saw glass panes in coaches, especially in those days. Even now it was rare. As nicely appointed as was this Concord, it could never compare to what I had known. Leather blinds on Lady Rebecca's coach were used only for decoration and shade, not as a hopeful means of keeping out the cold, wind, and rain as were the ones rolled up before me now.

Lady Rebecca's coach with its glass panes, flawless vermilion finish, and fancy trim was suited for city pavement and well groomed roads, and by no means meant to withstand the hardships of western travel with its teeth shattering stretches of corduroy, intruding tree trunks, potholes, washouts and muddy ruts.

It was nothing like a stagecoach built to take a beating on the open road. I imagined these coaches journeying at breakneck speeds along the western turnpikes that headed out from Albany to the frontiers. I imagined an exhilarating rough and tumble ride, flying through the countryside making five or six miles in an hour. A daring dash indeed, as we kicked up stones, dirt and dust, sending debris a-churning in our wake.

On a stagecoach I would have no fear of yawning or dozing, as I might aboard a boat while waiting for the next puff of wind to fill the sail, or the next port to pass. And unlike the sedate attitude of the eastern driver, here the captains snapped their whips and gave orders with an equal measure of impatience and impudence, and God be with the drovers or whoever else stepped into their path. I was impatient to make my way west, and the idea of such swiftness come rain or shine was appealing. It would certainly move me to the frontier and return me back to Boston and my beloved Mary all the sooner.

"Tell me Mr. Cotter, where are the other coaches headed. I see a good many of them haven't followed our lead to Albany."

"Dose would be headed nort'west voor da Great Western Turnpike, or Cherry Valley. Lots of dose folks are probably heading Ohio way."

"I see."

"For dat matter, many of dose who are following us aren't headed voor Albany eitter. Remember I told jou Albany is a gateway to da west. Most of da coaches now going voor Albany will only pass trew. Dey'll be heading nort' on da King's highway voor Schenectady, en some fart'er along da Schenectady-

257

Utica turnpike dat follows da sout' shore o' da Mohawk toward Lake Erie. Lot of 'em heading Michigan way."

"I thought the canal went from Albany to Schenectady."

"Het does. En if ya were a piece of furniture or freight, dat's da way jou'd go. As a passenger, dat's da one way jou wouldn't go if ya knew better. Putting aside all da boat traffic, da confusion en congestion I mentioned earlier, jou haaf t'imagine da Albany area as somet'ing like da territory o' Michigan. Da fastest way from one side to da otter isn't sailing all da way 'roun' da territory, but riding straight across overland. Da fastest way to Schenectady is by stagecoach 'long da King's highway in a straight line. Jou save a full day's travel at da least.

"Don' misunderstand me; a good many people today are boarding packets dat depart vrom Albany t' be sure. En dey book passage voor da entire lengt', all da way to Buffalo. Da stretch o' turnpike dat runs between Albany en Cherry Valley isn't nearly da busy route as in days past. I traveled het many times over da years en I assure you, het was once overburdened wit' traffic.

"Da migration into Ohio en Michigan was, en I should say, still is felt most certain upon dat stretch o' road. Het's true da canal has taken up much of da business, but imagine dis; at one time voor a distance of some sixty miles, dere was a tavern t' be found at every mile mark, en all doing a brisk trade. Dere were nine or ten stagecoach lines en upwards of a hundred stage horses employed in Cherry Valley alone. Da rush of people en dust along dat turnpike could be positively suffocating."

Rush was a good word. I felt as though it applied to everything about me. My, how fast things changed. First there were foot trails, then horse trails. Then came the land roads from village to village. Next came the 'through land roads' which passed through many villages.

Usually, villages sprang up along rivers and so these roads seemed to always follow watercourses. They were born out of necessity, for going upstream was difficult at best and as terrible as land travel proved to be, it was still better than poling upstream.

Now, we had our famous National Cumberland Road. Now, we had highways and turnpikes going this way and that, and to help pay for such roads, to no one's surprise every five miles we came upon a toll station. Like all else, they were busy places and added to the confusion and impatience.

I was told by Mr. Cragar that the Albany to Schenectady turnpike was built back in eighteen and two, and made claim to being the first toll road built in the country. It now stretched all the way to Lake Erie. Private concerns paid for the construction of turnpike and afterward the public was charged a fee to use them. I kept reaching for my purse, but to my surprise we never stopped. Mr. Cotter noticed this and enlightened me, as was his way.

"Jou may hold jour money, Miss Claussen. Da toll was paid bevorehand en was included in jour vare. Well, maybe not jour vare, but in Mr. Carrington's vare vor certain." The comment brought a fresh round of laughter to all in the cabin. "Unlike da general public, stagecoaches are vree to continue on so as not t' waste time voor da payment o' tolls. Da only otter travelers who might pay little if anyt'ing at all are eitter beautiful women or dose traveling in da Conestogas," he kidded me. "En dat's because da wheels on dose wagons are so wide dey flatten en repair da ruts in da road. Dey often go voor vree."

We were fortunate that summer was dry, and although we choked on the dust, we were free of the muddy quagmires that often made up the entire length of country roads. The roads were rock-hard, but scarred by fallbacks, which were ruts cut across the road to drain off excess rainwater. Hitting them at any speed made for a terrible jarring even for a Concord. It caused everyone to pitch forward and back. The men were all looking at me, and so with a devilish grin, Mr. Cotter commented.

"As voor beautiful women, a good bouncy ride can hold a man's attention voor hours on end, making da worst road seem like a highway t' heaven. Dat's why we call dese fallbacks 'tank-you ma'ams.'" The men laughed and prolonged the memory of the ticketmaster. I crossed my arms to firm myself up, and shook my head with much embarrassment.

On those occasions when we did stop, if one could call it a 'stop', it was only briefly for a change of teams. While still rolling, the captain tossed his reins to a waiting groom who unhitched the spent team, and having another at the ready, immediately hitched the fresh horses and threw the reins back up to the captain. With only seconds passing, while we were still rocking to a halt, we were jerked aback again at the same hurried speed, having scarce enough time to take in a breath of dust free air.

"At da next stop we shall eat," said Mr. Cotter. "Da otter reason I selected dis coach is dat da line is dependable en as a rule stops up ahead voor dinner every noon. Da food at deir stations is better dan most, but if we don't make het by noon, we don't eat."

The news came as an appealing thought not only to me, but also to the rest of the passengers, all of whom rose early aboard the riverboat and had nothing more that coffee or tea.

True to Mr. Cotter's prediction, at the next station the captain pulled off the road and stopped alongside a number of other coaches. There were two buildings at the station. One was little more than a roof atop standing timbers with no walls, and filled with people who appeared to have brought their own fixings. They were busy stoking small fires and feeding children in the same fashion as one might at a picnic.

The second structure, the one we were directed to enter, was totally enclosed and well built with a sizeable porch. It was a grocery-tavern-grogshop. The front door was propped wide open for fresh air. We stood on the porch crowded among other groups also waiting to eat until our party was called inside for what was known as 'having a public dinner'.

I was immediately caught up in a race for the washbasins followed by a second sprint to secure a table. We then took up our seats at a long table that was being hurriedly set, but no move whatsoever was made to serve or even acknowledge us. We sat waiting like a schoolhouse full of children with nothing to do but watch crocks of molasses being overrun by a crawling carpet of ants and black flies.

As if doing us a favor, our captain appeared and seated himself. At that point everything went into motion, and from the get go, it became an experience I was not about to forget. The food was practically thrown at us and why not? This was no place to stand on manners. The captain ate like a pig. He certainly was not alone for even members of our own party, although dressed like gentlemen, presented themselves to be no more refined at a table than was the captain—my friend 'Billy' included.

The men had one habit in particular that I found most revolting. They would eat of everything with a single knife that they were in the habit of licking clean with their tongues before sticking it into the serving bowls from which we all took our food.

To gaze upon the encrusted globs of food, snot, and saliva that fell off the unshaven chops of a dust covered driver, half-man, half-animal, and see him drag his knife across a mush covered tongue and through dripping wet gravy-coated strands of gnarled beard hair and then stick it into the communal butter dish was enough to make me vomit. If ever I was happy to be a woman it was at this sitting because at least some effort was made to offer me my servings first before the pigs touched anything or slobbered into the bowls.

Still, the effort was inadequate, for I was next immersed deep into the distasteful sounds of mouths opening and closing, the

261

sucking slurps of toothless gums and tongues rolling food this way and that. I was unable to escape the belching, the sniffing, and the stench of the un-bathed, all of which when combined in one crowded room made it perfectly impossible to enjoy an appetite in the same county.

The moment the captain stopped knifing down his food, he rose to his feet unconcerned about whether anyone else had eaten or not and stated flatly that the coach was leaving in two minutes and those not aboard would be left behind. Some had barely finished their mealtime prayer. I was hungry, having hardly touched my food, but was grateful nonetheless. I promptly arose from the table and left the remaining pigs with their two minutes to gorge themselves sick in the sty.

Exactly as announced, without regard to our still starving passengers, the captain cracked his whip and we bolted on toward the city in haste. I was only able to settle my stomach and erase the memories of my companion's table manners by taking in a view to my left of Shuyler's mansion and his estate known as the Pastures.

I entered into Albany hungry, but none the worse for wear. We were being drawn by six horses and traveling by way of a well-constructed road, which farther down the line was macadamized, that is to say covered in crushed rock and of the highest quality. Even so, I was given a sound reminder that a stagecoach, Concord or not, no matter how well appointed, was still a bone-breaking, jaw-jarring ride, and nothing to be dismissed lightly even on a well-constructed road.

I was left to consider that an overland journey into the wilds would certainly be hard on one's health, and to be well rested was as important to one's countenance as was eating and drinking. Probably more important if one was forced to eat in a way station. Pure and simple, the choice was speed versus comfort, and although I was impatient to go west, it was obvious that making a rash decision might prove woefully regrettable in the long run.

THE STAGE DRIVER

TWENTY-FIVE

Our group arrived in Albany with neither complaint nor reason for concern. I watched the profile of the city take shape and found myself intrigued by the contrast between the populous areas of Albany and New York with all their hustle and bustle, and the seemingly unpopulated areas of wilderness that separated them along the banks of the Hudson.

The contrast was so pronounced, it gave one the sensation of hop-scotching from one civilization to another, one planet to another, one place of security to another, all the while praying not to end up stranded in the broader wilds between.

Fortunately, I was never lost to the wilds, and aside from one outrageous experience aboard the ANNIE DEE, the river trip proved restful in every way. Even so, I looked forward to spending time in Albany relaxing and enjoying the sights while searching for some signs of Christopher's whereabouts.

Our driver entered the grid of city streets and traveled north along the waterfront. I was observing the Hudson from my window, and as we came upon Albany's basin and the canal, I saw it to be thick with ships and barges true to Billy's word.

"My lord, look at all those boats." I was amazed. "You were right about the congestion. Look at all those ships, there must be at least a hundred."

"Quite a sight, is het not? Since dey opened da canal, het gets worse by da week. As dey say, a picture's wort' a t'ousand words, en now jou know why only first time travelers sail into Albany. We woult probably still be out on da river hungry voor dinner en waiting t' dock, or dropping anchor en contemplating a long swim t' shore."

Near the canal entrance at the north end of the basin, we approached our final stop, and I could see the ticketmaster and his stableboys standing at the stageyard ready to meet us. Our coach began to slow and the ticketmaster reached up as if

265

preparing to catch us by the door handle. The coach came to a halt, the captain set the brake, and our cabin door swung open without the ticketmaster taking a step.

"Welkom in Albany...."

The ticketmaster suddenly choked on a thick cloud of passing dust that overtook us from behind. He swept the air with his hand, turned to face the stableboys, and coughed out a command. "Kom jon boys, skeet op daar—*cough, cough*, en breeng down some blasted rain met dose bags!"

He then turned to me and offered his hand, but spoke to all in a recovered voice. "Ik hoop jouw trip was goed! If anyone needs booking voor Schenectady, Utica, Rome, Syracuse, Sherry Valley, Tonawanda, Buffalo of points between, niet te worry, yust stap in my office. Udderwise, enjoy jouw stay in Albany en de boys will haaf youw coffers down nowu."

As the stableboys scrambled atop the coach for our baggage, I accepted the ticketmaster's hand and stepped off the coach to be followed by the rest in my company. I waited to wish my fellow passengers farewell and the best of health. I thanked Mr. Carrington for maintaining his sense of humor, and then turned to offer Mr. Cotter my gratitude for his generous assistance, which he was still giving freely.

"Now remember, should jou choose t' take da canal west, don' start here in Albany. Take da King's highway overland to Schenectady en go aboard dere. Het's by far da best way, en da stage leaves early."

My attention was drawn to the ticketmaster who was nodding in support of Billy's advice, and who was compelled to offer his own two bits.

"Furst coach voor Buffalo via Schenectady en Utica at precise seven uur. Jou save un day travel."

"Dere ya go. Stage leaves first t'ing in da morning. I must go. Hets been a pleasure knowing ya Miss Claussen, en I hope

266

jou enjoy your stay in Albany. Het's a great town." He was stepping away backwards leaving a broad smile in his wake.

"Thank-you, for all you've done."

"We may meet again, one never knows," he yelled as he turned about and waved back over his shoulder.

"I'll look forward to that day."

I watched Mr. Cotter head across the lot and disappear into the crowd. The ticketmaster had been dragging his feet in my behalf. He noticed I was unescorted, and I believe he waited nearby in case I was in need of directions. Now, with an inquisitive look about him, he walked to where I stood with my bags. I addressed him.

"Very well then. It seems as though I'll be taking your stage to Schenectady to save a day's time."

"Most wice, dame."

"In the meantime, may I ask what has Albany to offer in the way of an agreeable meal and a clean bed? Something fit for a lady, I pray."

"Yah. Yah. Van Meriden's. Beste eten plaats in de town. Niet sheik, but goed in cheap, en de volks know het voor de beste keuken in deeze place. No gruel slappen at jou daar, no dame. Goed eten, goed cheap. Sixpence um te eten, sixpence um te slep. Er rooms are added te de boarding huis many times so te keep dose volks who wish te stay voor de eten. Het's a goed place, a goed en safe place voor a dame te slapen widout worry."

"Do you suppose they'll have rooms free to let?"

"Yah. Niet te worry, dame. We keep rooms yust voor volks like jou. Dis is a service te coach company has voor gasts who don't like slapen in de stall."

"In the stall! Oh, well, barns aren't for me, I assure you. I must tell you before I accept one of your reserved rooms that at this moment I have no idea if I will remain in Albany a day or a week. Will that be an imposition?"

"Impo-si-shun?" The ticketmaster questioned me.

"A problem?."

"Oh!. Nah. Nah. No problem. Niet voor me, Ik slapen at home." The man laughed. "Niet te worry. Ik wil niet say a ding as long as jou take our stage to Schenectady like de man say. De coaches are booked vull en we keep dem rooms cheap t'rough de company. De company pay voor dem, neit me. Nowu, Ik do haaf een open seat voor tomorrow if jou interesses."

"Tomorrow is impossible. Forgive me, I wish I could offer you more. Honestly, I do, but I am unable. I must first complete my business in town. How would it be if I stopped by tomorrow evening or the following morning? I will better know then."

"Yah. Niet te worry, dame. We'll be hier."

"Wonderful. In that case, if you would point the way to Van Meriden's."

The ticketmaster turned about, "Jonah!" he hollered across the lot.

"Yah, Mr. Kuiper."

"Kom hier, boy." He turned back to me. "I'll haaf Jonah fetch jouw stof en help jou go daar. Voor a small fee, he fill jouw bath met heet water en give jou help voor de day if jou need help of whatever. De boy werks hart voor his keep. He goed boy, he makt jou happy, yah."

"Thank-you, sir. That is most thoughtful."

Jonah lifted one end of my trunk and then looked up to the ticketmaster.

"What's de problem, boy? Er jou niet man enough?" Mr. Kuiper reached for the handles and after a yank, he looked at me in shock.

"Woult jou take dis trunk op te jouw room, of wouw jou yust like me te keep het hier in de office tot jou go."

"That's fine. You may keep it here. You will keep an eye on it, I trust."

"Yah, yah. Niet te worry, dame. I don't dink anybody will be runnen off met dat trunk anytime soon. If dey did, I don't dink dey go very var."

I left the station with Jonah and bags in tow as Mr. Kuiper struggled to drag my trunk across the yard. It was but a short walk to the boardinghouse from the station, and the aroma met me almost as soon as I sighted the inn. After a word with the innkeeper, I led Jonah through the dining hall and upstairs.

"Come along, Jonah."

"Yes, dame."

The food smelled second to none, but I had only to open the door of my room to know it proved less accommodating than I had hoped.

"Oh, Jonah. What a sty."

"Yes, dame."

I shook my head in dismay as I looked through the door. I spoke aloud to the boy.

"Dare I step inside? Nope. No, this will never do, Jonah. I would hardly consider this a room to my liking. It may be fine for a horse thief, a drunk or a dead man, but it is most unfit for a refined soul with any sense of cleanliness."

"Yes, dame."

I didn't think myself unreasonably fussy, and I hoped that unlike Mary, my standards hadn't become impractical due to my years spent cleaning rooms. I simply held little desire to sleep in unknown filth, because I could only envision a plague of bugs and infestations. I turned to the boy.

269

"Hear me out, Jonah."

"Yes, dame."

"Run downstairs and tell the head mistress I would like to bathe. Let me know as soon as she is ready for me. Do you understand?"

"Yes, dame."

"Good. Then, while I wash, I wish you to clean this room. Give the floors a good sweep and mopping. Air the room. Go to the head mistress and see to it that you are given a proper set of freshly cleaned sheets. Tell her I will pay extra for the washing. Tighten up the bed ropes. Be sure to get the corners of the room swept and scrubbed down good. If I see anything crawling, I'll be none too happy. Later, I'll be back to size up your handiwork, and if you have done me a good service, I promise, I will pay you handsomely."

"Yes, dame!" His eyes lit up.

* * *

Once summoned, I went down the hall to bathe and left Jonah to his duties. I turned over my soiled clothing for washing and sank into a hot pool of soapy water that did wonders for my minor aches and pains. After a respectable soak, feeling again dust free and revived, I dressed in fresh attire and prepared myself to go out.

I asked the chambermaid to return my belongings to my room and see to it that Jonah was working and that he was fed. I asked her to inform him that I would return later in the afternoon to settle his wage, or I would look for him at the station.

Having said my piece and settled accounts, I stepped onto the street for want of a walk along the new canal. It was still early afternoon and a superb day to be outside. I was past being hungry and free of obligations, and so set out to take my time, enjoy the day, and investigate whatever opportunity might arise regarding Christopher's whereabouts.

As I walked, I noticed right off that Albany was indeed different. Its unique character was not to be hidden. It was definitely Dutch in feel with its gables and front porches all facing the street. Everything about the town appeared healthy, clean, and affluent.

It was a busy place, full of activity and attraction. The shoreline, the streets, the merchants and their establishments, all reflected the frenzied activity one would expect only in New York City. There was however, a twist. In New York, everyone seemed to go about in circles, going around and around city blocks big or small, slow or fast, but around in circles nonetheless.

Here, the crowds mostly went in one direction. It wasn't just my imagination, for there were numerous stagecoach yards, wagon yards and keelboat landings that all had at least one thing in common. They advertised movement west to regions of Ohio, Indiana and the Michigan Territories.

Rarely did I see a placard or poster that said go east or go south. A few made reference to New York City, but the feeling for the most part was very much one-way—*west*. Albany did appear to be a jumping off point, a gateway just as Mr. Cotter said, and the one thing that added more than anything else to this impression was the local tongue.

Albany's citizens mostly spoke Dutch. Here was an entire city that spoke a different language. English was not their nature, and that aspect alone made the place odd enough to seem at once a foreign land to a newly arrived easterner such as myself. It was a place of fascination, and although I kept one eye open at all times for signs of Christopher, my other eye was glued to every distraction that surrounded me. I was certainly lost in my curiosity about these people and the charm of their town.

271

To be sure, the most prominent feature in Albany or anywhere in upstate New York for that matter was this newly constructed Erie Canal. *'Leave it to the Dutch to build a canal'* was my only thought. They had completed it in eighteen twenty-six, just four years before, at least according to the plaques that were all about. The markers described in detail how three thousand men with picks and shovels, five hundred horses and two hundred yoke of oxen constructed the long awaited and much-heralded waterway.

It had been touted with great pomp and ceremony. The historic announcement of its completion was made before the nation with a symbolic pouring of Great Lakes water into the Atlantic Ocean. What I never found written on the plaques was anything about the great stink that arose over the less than decorous pouring of alcohol down the throats of the dignitaries in attendance. They spent days stumbling about blind drunk aboard a celebration barge that floated down the canal from town to town.

I heard all about it during one of Mr. Cotter's dinner stories. His version was hilarious. According to him, by the time the boat reached Albany the passengers were in such a state of disgrace, being ill mannered, immoral, and vomiting over the rails and such, that the townsfolk were left standing at the shore in near shock. Dumbfounded, the citizens hastily shooed away their children and sent them to safer ground. Listening to his account, however bloated it may have been, was enough to drive us to tears; we laughed until we cried.

Everything I saw appeared exactly as Mr. Cotter had described. The Great Lakes region and nearly all the western reaches of upper New York used the canal as a conduit for annual migrations. As soon as the ice broke, barges ferrying lumber and furniture, grain and flour, stone and hides, passengers and parcel, all began their voyages to and fro. Heading eastward, I saw a number of boats filled with coal and ore pass through Albany making for the basin and then heading south down the Hudson bound for Kingston.

Since the completion of the Delaware and Hudson Canals, Kingston was now a major shipping port. We had passed it on our way up the Hudson, and I noted the activity about the place. It was in Kingston that the boats and barges transferred their cargoes to the larger Hudson riverboats, or waited to be towed by steamboats to the markets of New York City.

Lined up stem to stern and heading westward or "locks up", as they said in these parts, merchants shipped manufactured goods. There were all variety of items sorely needed on the frontier including clothes and sundries, logging and mining equipment, and especially farm implements. Also to be going west were a great number of settlers. Most of whom I understood to be families headed for Michigan. I didn't envy the way the were crammed into the packets.

From where I stood, the boats and barges stretched as far as I could see in both directions. They passed by me in what should have been an unworkable tangle of tow ropes. The boats moved along slowly and silently, drawn by teams of mules, or on occasion, horses. Prodded by drivers, the teams towed the boats easily as they moved with the current toward the basin. It was a different story when they headed locks-up against the current.

Hooves clopped methodically up and down the towpaths that were cut into rock walls or laid down atop the embankments. The towpath followed the canal the whole of its length through the numerous locks and levels. The mules, the boats, the people, the new stores; all of it was hectic, yet peaceful. In spite of the crowds, I could appreciate the safety and tranquility of the canal in contrast to the days of danger facing fear, drowning, and rapids, while braving the Mohawk.

The activity about the canal took some getting used to. It was so choked with keelboats that only by miracle might anybody make headway in one direction or the other. It may be that the near dead crawl was for the best, for I noticed many of these boats had families living on board.

273

There were children of all ages scampering about the decks both above and below the drip of drying laundry, either evading a mother's cane or putting fear into her heart should they fall into the water and drown. When viewed as a whole, they represented as much a floating community as a commercial enterprise. They were a world akin to floating gypsies, and I wondered about schooling for the children.

Wherever I walked, I could hear the laughter and conversations typical of family and friends. They all appeared to know one another and for good reason, much of their private lives were made public by the way in which they hollered news back and forth from boat to boat up and down the canal.

I must have passed a hundred boats, listening to these conversations before satisfying my curiosity about the people living in them. Finally, after strolling a good measure, I doubled back and returned to the stagecoach yard, that being where I arrived in Albany, and also the place from where I began my walk.

It was there in front of the station that I spied a free space upon a seat where sat a youthful and attractive woman. She appeared some ten years my younger, and busied herself on the far end of the bench darning socks or something of the kind. She glanced my way long enough to assure herself that I meant no harm, and at the same time offered me that type of friendly smile that invites one to sit and join.

I took my place opposite the woman and straightened out my legs to ease the complaint of my feet. Between the loading and unloading of the canal boats and wagons lined up along water's edge, and the stagecoaches filled with passengers coming and going in a whirlwind of dust, I was offered plenty of entertainment while resting up.

I was content to sit and write in my diary until my attention was at last lost to a simple game of tag being played by a bunch of half crazy boys running about the stageyard. The whole gang of youngsters was laughing so hard that I started to laugh as well just from hearing them and watching their antics. There was no

274

end to the amusement, and apparently my laughter pleased the woman on the bench, for without ever looking up from her work, she began to speak.

"They are fun to watch are they not? So full of life and laughter—not a care in the world at that age."

I turned to face the woman, but her eyes remained focused on her work. "You speak English," I said somewhat surprised after having given little thought to the children hollering words I understood. "I don't speak a word of Dutch. That is certainly to one's disadvantage in these parts."

"Nor do I for the most part. I've learned a little. Mostly, I've leaned to understand the local's manner of speaking English. My husband and I were originally from the east. After being married we spent some time in New York before doing what many did, that is to say, took advantage of the opportunities here in Albany that came with the opening of the canal."

"I can only assume these boys must be your sons. They are a handsome lot. Boys to be proud of."

She then looked up at her sons and smiled. "Yes, very much so. Thank-you. Do you have boys of your own?"

"Oh, no, not me. I would have been thrilled to have just one let alone three. I assume all three are yours."

"All three, trouble, trouble and trouble."

"Oh, no. I refuse to believe it. How fortunate you are. I'm afraid for me, it wasn't meant to be. No family, no children." I shrugged as I watched the youths. "They sure carry on, do they not?"

"If you could only know. They'll drive a sane person mad as a coot. It's good for them to get out and run. It's good for me when they get out and run," she laughed effortlessly. "There's little opportunity to do so on the boat. I worry they spend too much time cooped up in the cabin. Normally, they don't get on shore until later in the evening. Albany and Medina are the only exceptions because as a rule we have to wait a couple of days for loading and unloading. For the boys it's like time spent in heaven. Me too, it gets them out from under my feet."

"Don't you worry about them falling into the canal?"

"Never really have. All three swim like fish, and there are cutouts along the canal where the animals and men can climb out. Kids usually know better than anyone where the cutouts are; no doubt they use them enough. I suppose any mother worries about her toddlers, but my boys are now older and getting taller so it isn't quite the worry it used to be. The canal rarely gets deeper than four feet or so.

"I feel for the settlers. Those immigrant mothers are constantly in a state of nerves worrying about their young-uns falling in even if they are goin' on twenty-some. They're afraid of the canal. I listen to them all the time hollering at their babes to be careful."

She returned to her needlework, and I sat silent for a moment as my mind drifted. I wondered about what these boys learned of life. I wondered how these children would fare after surviving the perils of growing up on the canal only to face a future where they had to find meaningful work in the industries of the east, industries that were reaching farther into these regions and replacing farmwork.

School and teaching had been a big part of my life, and schools were almost unheard of in these parts. Children, especially the likes of these who were always on the go following their families from place to place, stood little chance of ever learning to read or write. They would be good only for the hard labor of moving stone that now took place before me. The boat was crowded with men unloading squared stones from the hold and stacking them into waiting wains alongside us. I closed my diary.

"My name is Elizabeth." I held out my hand.

"Dorrie. Dorrie Anne."

"It's a pleasure, Dorrie. Is this your boat, then?" I asked.

"Yes."

"You haul stone I see. Hard work I dare say."

"As of late. Quarry stone from Medina for street work here in Albany. It's in big demand. Albany is growing the likes of nothing I've ever seen. Every time we return, I swear it looks different. They pay good for stone, but you are right, it takes a lot of work.

"It's dangerous, not like hides or grain, but my husband prefers it because he says you don't have to worry yourself sick all the time about it getting wet. It takes strong teams and a different type of boat. Ours is built heavy, double hulled to take the abuse. It cost a lot to build, but no one said floating stone was cheap. We make good money, because stone can't be moved by wagon in any practical manner. Teamsters hate us for it.

"I worry about them more than the canal. Of course, they probably wouldn't if they had to live with the smashed fingers and all the noise in the holds, you know, the pounding, slamming and such. *'It's not cotton'*, is what we always say in the business. When it's time to load and unload, I get off the boat and go ashore. I wait it out. Besides, after scrubbing clothes in hot water, cooking over a stove and working inside with the sun beating down and all, I'm plenty ready to feel fresh air. This bench suits me just fine."

Dorrie wasn't the least bit shy, and made no excuses to converse with me as she watched over her boys, the boat, and the workers while her men were off on business. She wasn't the least bit put off by the obvious difference in our dress and backgrounds.

I sat with her for some time and thoroughly enjoyed her stories of canal life and the accounts she gave of experiences as a mother with three boys on a boat. Her descriptions were vivid, varied, some sad, some wonderfully funny, and all most colorful and entertaining. I was held to her every word. Her life seemed

277

so much more interesting than mine, and so much harder as well. Despite her youth, I sensed she was also wise for her years, and in many ways tough as old leather. She was the kind of person that in my mind would make the very best of friends, someone who was bright and strong and loyal. At least that's how I wanted to imagine her.

I was too entertained to hurry off, but the last of afternoon was now upon us, and at about the time I was feeling hungry enough to be on my way, she looked up over my shoulder and came to attention. Her eyes lit up.

"Here comes my husband Robert, now. He's the one with the staff. The man with the bag over his shoulder is 'Gardy' our steersman, and the one behind leading the mules is 'Whither' our driver."

I turned around to see the three men approaching, followed by two teams of mules back from pasture. The boys ran out at once hollering for their father's attention. Her husband acknowledged me by a nod of his head and proceeded to inform his wife that she could rest easy, for he had been by the broker and secured a profitable contract for their return cargo.

Except for expressing his relief for not having to be delayed a week waiting for a return contract, he said nothing further. It was Dorrie who told me that return cargoes were preferred light because the teams had to pull the boat west against the current, and because anything was light when compared to the stone they brought locks down. More than likely, they would be loading stone cutting equipment and supplies for the quarry.

She placed her darning back into her bag and stood up. I did as well, and seeing that she was now preoccupied with attending to her husband's needs, I bid her farewell, bowed out gracefully and left her to her man.

As for myself, my feet felt much improved. I had spent a good four or more hours walking the canal and city streets that were in part the busiest area of Albany. I had even stumbled upon a significant find that surely would have been all the bait needed to attract Christopher—*a railroad.*

It was to be the first in the country. The tracks were being laid between Albany and Schenectady and scheduled for completion in about a year's time. In spite of such powerful attraction, there was nothing to indicate that Christopher had been in Albany anytime recent. And so, I figured as long as I was at the stage yard, I might as well book passage on the morning coach for Schenectady and see if anything turned up at that end of the tracks. Either way I had already planned to pass through Schenectady and now only needed a seat on the coach.

From the bench upon which Dorrie and I sat, I could see the ticketmaster was anything but busy as he hollered back and forth to a couple of gentlemen crossing his yard. This was as good a time as any to make arrangements so I started in his direction.

"Hello! Mr. Kuiper!" I cried out to the man. He was about to re-enter his office when he heard my call. He turned about, broke into a smile and came to meet me.

"Hier so soon. Was het de room of de food dat upset jou?"

"I have yet to taste the food, and short of a good sweeping, the room will be fine, thank-you." I lied. "I enlisted young Jonah's services as you suggested. He's cleaning it up a bit."

"Goed. Is dere somet'ing more Ik can help voor jow?"

"I'd like to go ahead and book passage on tomorrow's stage for Schenectady. Seven sharp, do you still have an open seat?"

"Oh!" he said with disappointment as he swung his fist in a low arc. "Ik yust sold de last two seats te dose two." He pointed to the men I had seen crossing the yard. "Mmm. Niet te worry. Let me dink—I got seats voor Dursday morgen—. Wait! Jou know—Ik haaf a private coach reserved voor two older couples dat goes at de break of dawn, six, six-dirty, even bevoor my normale departure. Ik coult get jou a seat w'th dem, en Ik dink

279

jou wil be comfortable in deir company. No offense, but like jou, dey're niet what Ik dink to be plain folk."

I frowned upon hearing his words.

"Sir, they may not be common folk, but if they have reserved the coach, it stands to reason that they may wish their privacy and not take kindly to a complete stranger in their midst, especially in such close quarters. I'm not sure I would feel comfortable."

"I assure jou dame dat gentlemen, married or niet, zou never say net to een lady of jouw rank speciaal when dere is een empty seat. Also, jou woult do me pleasure by taking my offer. Voor Ik haaf taken a lower fare to let out de coach voor dis trip. If Ik hat taken passengers along de way Ik woult haaf maak more money, yah."

"Why then did you allow them to reserve the coach?"

"De fare may be lower per persoon, but het is still a goed sum, en het's voor sure paid." He led me inside, afterwhich he attempted to hand me a ticket. "Ik wil tell de gentlemen of deir goed deed. Take de ticket, en niet te worry. Dings wil be fine, Ik promise."

I hesitated. "It seems as I have little choice but to trust your good judgment. May I see the coach?"

"Niet possible because Ik sent het over to de wheelwright deze morgen voor een inspection. Jou go yust to Schenectady, but de odder volks go far to Buffalo. Ik want no wheels falling off in de middle of de pines.

"Jou trust me. Jou haaf niet to fear, dame. Deze haaf taken my beste coach. Het's een Concord, en dat is as goed as het gets. Het is been cleaned en scented voor de odder volks. Jou wil find niet better on wheels. Het is wel built, comfortable, drawn by six, en is better on de road den all de odder coaches. When jou arrive in Schenectady, jou wil be intact en feel goed. Ik give jou my word. Niet te worry, dame. I promise."

280

"I am familiar with your Concord, sir. It is indeed a fine coach and I believe all you say. What then will be my fare?"

"T'ree quarters."

Feeling as though I have been fretting over nothing, I gave the man a dollar and watched as he carefully folded it into quarters and then ripped off one quarter and handed it back along with my receipt.

I was now confronting the pangs of hunger and craving a well-cooked dinner with a good glass of wine. I thanked the ticketmaster and returned straight away to Van Meriden's with peace of mind and a voracious appetite.

I entered the inn and for some unknown reason the atmosphere inside the boarding house brought back a recollection of a time when I was a child at the Barrington Hotel. Maybe it was because Van Meriden's was a place where many of the people knew each other as regulars. I could give no other explanation.

One thing was for certain, the patronage at Van Meriden's added an air of familiarity and joviality to the room during the dinner hour that was distinctly missing from the atmosphere of the way station. You could sense the feeling of extended family and at least a semblance of courtesy and manners.

There were a few small tables in the room for purpose of making the best of space and offering privacy of sorts if needed, but for the most part, seating was at long tables shared by all. Conversations often crossed parties and privacy generally lost out to performance. Talk was as much gossip as anything, and there was always a conversation filled with shock and disbelief, the words *"sudden death"* frequently being heard.

Regardless of whether or not the stories were true, the term emphasized a fact of frontier life. At every stop, at every board-inghouse, at every town eatery there would be at least one story of some unfortunate soul who was taken from family and loved ones at the drop of a hat by disease or drowning, injury or arrow.

It was no wonder that the closer one moved toward the frontier, the holier one became.

A person's first step westward was to place one foot in the grave. Common knowledge would argue that the surest way to encounter misfortune or sudden death was to leave the security of home and take up travel. Being that travelers accounted for a quarter of the people in Albany, myself included, it was no wonder the town was thick with spiritual gatherings and churches.

During dinner, I overheard stories both horrible and heart-warming. The conversations were unending and entertaining at worst. In comparison to the weigh station, Van Meriden's dinner fare was far more inviting, and to my utter joy the food arrived on it's own plate. What choice did I have but to over eat. And so, in spite of engaging dinner talk and a fine cup of tea, between my stuffed belly and hours spent walking in fresh air; I succumbed to drowsiness and a need to retire.

Upstairs, I opened the door and found Jonah sitting in the corner half asleep. He sprung clumsily to his feet with eyes stuck half shut.

"Dame."

"I see you grew tired of waiting for me."

"Yust a little," he worried.

"Well, let me have a look and then you're free to go."

I checked the corners as promised, and sat upon the bed to test the ropes. I was pleased with what he had done. The bedding smelled fresh and the room was clean and presentable.

"You've done me a good service, Jonah. Here, I hope this will do. There's a little extra for your wait."

I handed him the quarter bill, and his face showed all the thanks I needed. I wished him a good night, followed him to the door and latched it behind him. I undressed, pounded some softness into my pillow and then fell back comfortably upon the bed. My back was in its glory. Everything seemed in order; my belly was full, my day eventful, and I no longer feared falling asleep in a room full of creepy crawly spidery things.

TWENTY-SIX

After a rewarding night of rest, I arose well before dawn feeling refreshed and in good spirit. The smell of coffee and bacon was thick in the air and taunted me into leaving the warmth of my blankets. I easily made use of the washbasin ahead of the other boarders, then dressed and descended to the dining room eager to breakfast. At this hour there were but a few individuals to be seen at the tables, businessmen, merchants, settlers en route, folks like myself with plans to get off to a good early start.

Having nourished myself, I sipped my morning tea as my thoughts drifted away into daydreams of adventures bound to come my way. I thought of raging rivers, of wilderness; I thought of Indian savages and imagined them riding spotted ponies across the shadowed plains beneath the Stony Mountains. Not that I was heading for the Stony Mountains, or even thinking of Michigan at this point in time, but daydreams were meant to be more than mundane.

My thoughts were torturing my insides, for butterflies of anticipation were all but doubling me over and sending me repeatedly to the outhouse to relieve myself. Finding it near impossible to remain seated any longer in order to while away time, I arose from my table and made good on my debt. I was anxious to leave the inn, and so with bags in hand, I made my way to the stageyard in hopes of speeding up the clock and therefore my departure. The morning was cool but agreeable. To my surprise, I discovered that my traveling companions had already arrived.

"Goed morgen, Dame Claussen."

"Good Morning, Mr. Kuiper."

"Op bevore de sun, dats goed. Jou must be een early bird, yah?" The ticketmaster greeted me with a cheery disposition. "Please, Ik taak jouw coffers. Ik help jou to de coach en introduce jou to de odders. Everyding is in order, niet te worry. De odders haaf said dat dey like voor jouw to go, en dat dey woult like to meet jou."

"I appreciate your telling me. I feel much better in knowing, thank-you." I stood by as the ticketmaster instructed Jonah and one of the other stableboys to retrieve my trunk from his office and bring it to the coach. With his help, they muscled it onto the coach. The ticketmaster was grunting aloud as he stood on the driver's bench and hefted my trunk up over the luggage rail and onto the cabin roof. I watched to be sure he secured it adequately. He looked down at me.

"Deze trunk is small, but heavy. What's in het, rocks?"

"Books."

"Ahh, same ding. Nowu, Ik know. Er jou een skol teacher of someding?"

"I was at one time."

"Ahhh." He studied the trunk and pulled on the tie-downs. "Mmm, dat should werk. Het'll be fine, so long as het don' fall on de kaptain's head." He jumped down off of the coach. "Er jou ready to board, dame?"

"As ready as ever."

"Goed. When de kaptain is done met breakfast, jou'll go. De kaptain is Harold McGregor, yah. He don' talk en he don' listen to a ding jou say, but he is very goed on de box. Kom nowu, Ik introduce jou to de Schuellers en Gunninks." I followed Mr. Kuiper around to the opposite side of the coach. There at the cabin door stood two well-dressed men. If appearances mattered, then they mattered.

"Dame Claussen—Mr. Schueller en Mr. Gunnink. Gentlemen, Dame Claussen. She wil travel only to Schenectady, but niet te worry, she maakt goed company. Ik promise."

"Good Morning, Miss Claussen." The gentlemen greeted me in unison.

"Any connection to the financier, Christopher Claussen?" asked Mr. Schueller.

"Yes, as a matter of fact. Do you know him?" I was assaulted by the offhand question, totally blindsided.

"No, ma'am, only of him. His name is known in these parts, especially in the Buffalo-Tonawanda area where we live."

"I see," I said, feeling the sudden rush and fall of excitement.

"Is he there often?"

The men looked at each other then nodded their heads. "Don't believe I have ever seen him," said Mr. Gunnink. "We'd be about the first to know if he were in town unless his aims were secretive."

"It's mostly business concerns we see. Lot of lumber concerns if I am not mistaken," said Mr. Schueller.

"Yes, that sounds very much like him." I agreed.

Both men were polished in appearance, elderly and dignified, obviously men of refinement. They were enjoying a last minute smoke outside so as not to offend their wives in the scented cabin.

The ticketmaster opened the door to reveal a warm and cozy cabin lit softly by the light of a lamp. The ladies, who had heard my approach, leaned forward from their seats and urged me inside with open arms. They broke off any further opportunity for questions I might have asked the gentlemen outside. They were chattering away, gushing with pleasure at having my company. Not only were they gracious, but also utterly likable, affectionate from the get-go, and seeing to it at once that I was comfortable and feeling welcome. We wasted no time in getting through introductions, while their husbands remained outside the closed door to enjoy their cigars for whatever little time remained.

It hadn't yet struck six-thirty, and with one or two exceptions, there were few people to be seen about. Earlier, a wagon crammed full of supplies had rolled past me in the yard to a stop at the canal's edge while I was headed to meet the ticketmaster. Its driver and helper were talking to a couple of canalers, and now untying the canvas cover and folding it back in preparation to unload.

At the back of the yard, I noticed a suspicious group of Indians gathered along the fence and looking up to no good. They had emerged from the shadows as the morning light began making its way across the sky. I made their number to be a good dozen or more. They were a scruffy looking bunch that served to unsettle me.

I was most suspicious of Indians and considering there was a wagon full of supplies nearby, I was somewhat surprised that the men about seemed to be little bothered by their presence. In my mind, knowing what I did about Indians, I questioned myself as to whether or not they could be trusted, and so kept a wary eye out for dubious intentions. Other than this, most folks were just now beginning to stir.

Having finished with names, and feeling comfortable, the ladies and I started out with a safe conversation about the weather and goings on in Albany. As would be with any proper hostess, the ladies were full of questions and showing a respectable interest in my person.

Soon I was lost in the retelling of a humorous story I over-heard at Van Meriden's during dinner, when suddenly in mid-sentence the whole inside of the cabin was bleached white by a blinding flash of light. Instantly, we were hammered by the brutal concussion of a tremendous explosion that literally drove our coach into the back of the team.

Because I had been sitting next to the window, and its leather curtain offered scant defense against the force of the blast, I was knocked momentarily senseless. Whether by concussion or from striking my head against the widow post, I couldn't say at first, but what I did know was that I had been left with my wits scrambled and unable to hear a thing.

Unable as well was I to comprehend what was taking place, for all hell was breaking loose about us. Flying shrapnel and debris had slammed into our coach and pelted the horses so severely, that the startled team immediately bolted ahead in a dead run, their speed surpassed only by the race of my heart and tangled thoughts.

I looked to my left, glancing first at the frightened ladies beside me, and then to my right, ripping away the blind for a second's glimpse through the windows toward the canal. As we stampeded across the lot, my only coherent thought was of the two gentlemen who had been smoking outside, and must have been knocked to the ground, for they were now nowhere to be seen.

I was thrown back into my seat by the lurching coach as I observed everything along the canal disappearing behind a wall of flame that stretched the whole of the stage yard. Frantic, I struggled, pulling myself back up to further witness the mayhem behind us, but quickly changed my focus. With both hands gripping the window post, I watched fearfully in the opposite direction as the frightened horses stampeded straight for the fence at the rear of the yard. In the light of the fire, I again noted the Indians that I had previously been eyeing with suspicion. Many of their number had been knocked to the ground and were still trying to get back onto their feet, confused and mindless of our situation.

I braced myself, as the team headed for the fence, when suddenly the animals turned sharply to the right, followed the fence line, and plowed directly into the baffled collection of Indians at full speed with our coach rumbling madly behind. I knew for certain that at least one little girl, frozen with fear, was unable to move clear of the stomping hooves.

Through the painful ringing in my ears I heard the agony of her mother's screams. I perceived little more than the blur of her contorted face, eyes wide and wild with fear as she passed by my window, dropping to her knees and reaching for a child I now feared below me within the whirling wheels.

My head spun about, eyes fixed upon the mother until my attention was drawn beyond her by the two cigar smoking gentlemen, suddenly reappeared, and running diagonally across the lot in a hopeless attempt to head us off. I could see the tiny explosion of sparks as they tossed their cigars aside before falling away into the distance. At the same time, I saw in their company the ticketmaster, and a vision of another man running hard with a large hat and flailing coat; a black silhouette against a wall of white smoke, and bound to be the worst vision of all—*Harold McGregor!*

We were on the road to ruin without a captain, but that was only the half of it. The front seat of the coach had suddenly become an issue of its own sending up thick smoke to press against the draped windows. Frantic to understand what was taking place, I realized that either the blast or a piece of shrapnel had shattered our lantern and dislodged it from its holder. It was lying across the front seat amid the glitter of broken glass and leaking the contents of its reservoir. The exposed wick had ignited the oil now soaking into the seat cloth.

My memories of the Boston Community Church and Lady Rebecca's fiery death were immediate. My irrational fear of fire surfaced instantly causing me to shrink away terrified. I was trapped in the coach and wanted out at once, but that was impossible as I watched everything outside speed by in a blur.

I sat back cowering and unable to breathe, suffocating in the smoke for what was hardly more than seconds, but for what seemed like eternity to me. I was facing my worst nightmare. I managed to take my eyes off the dull orange cast long enough to look over toward Mrs. Schueller and Mrs. Gunnink, whom I prayed where about to rescue me. Unfortunately, as their expressions flickered in and out of a smoky darkness broken by the creeping wisps of fire, I realized how badly traumatized they were and how serious was our situation.

Breaking out in a sweat of terror, I watched horrified as the smoke rising from the forward seat transformed itself into a small inferno. All the while, our coach pitched and swayed wildly out of control being dragged helter-skelter behind horses half crazed. If we didn't burn up this moment in a blaze of glory while trying to get to our feet, we were certain to wreck and meet with injury or death of another kind.

We needed to act in some fashion, and we needed to act now before the moment was wasted. In every way our situation appeared hopeless, and the three of us entirely helpless. I wasn't a young girl or even a young lady for that matter, but my companions had no connection with the word 'young' in any manner, and so it was up to me to make a move if there should be any hope of survival. I determined that if my death was to be inevitable, I might just as well die making an attempt to avoid it.

I pulled away the blanket that covered the laps of my elderly companions, and in spite of my cumbersome dress, I dove over the middle row of seats, dragging it behind me. I was being thrown about the cabin in every manner and direction, coughing uncontrollably, and struggling to keep my balance. I suffered to untie the leather straps of the blind with eyes watering too severely to see. Working mostly by feel, as soon as I succeeded, I risked burn by snatching up the leaking lantern and heaving it outside before a trail of flame.

I threw the blanket atop the fire that was now feeding itself and growing with intensity. As the flames spread before me, I chased them with the heavy fabric, pushing the blanket around and rubbing the seat vigorously. I pounded the blanket with my fists, hitting it with a vengeance that reflected my subconscious hatred of the deep-rooted enemy that lurked beneath. The smoke billowed but, by the grace of God, I managed to sop up the spilled oil and suffocate the flames.

Aside from the released blind, and the one at my seat, which had been partially raised so the women might speak with their men, the remainder had been drawn down tight to keep out the morning chill. Because of this fact, not only were we trapped inside with the smoke and darkness, but worse, we were running blind down the road in fear of knowing at any second we might collide with some unseen object and smash ourselves to smithereens. The women were working the blinds with all speed.

I had yet to save us, and the bulk of my dress only served to fight my every move as I was bounced back and forth between the seats.

"Quick, Get this dress off me! Hurry, hurry, the skirt, the bustle! Hurry!" I screamed as I fumbled clumsily at my clothes. The women had been blessed with good sense and sharp wit, and wasted nary a second in tearing away at the leather blinds with one hand and my cumbersome apparel with the other. Whether by button or bow, shredded or whole, both were removed in a matter of seconds; the windows were stripped of their blinds, and I was stripped of my restrictive clothing, petticoats and all, until I was left wearing only my whites. I was too preoccupied with saving our lives to give any thought to saving my respect as I reached for the cabin door and flung it open.

As detestable luck would have it, the horses charged down a narrowing lane and because we were still swinging recklessly from side to side; we smashed directly into a coach parked at the shoulder to our left. At least we saw it coming. We attempted to brace ourselves, but were nonetheless thrown violently to that side of the cabin, and our door, now opposite us, slammed shut hard.

The collision sprung our left rear wheel and caused the coach to wobble madly. Shaking and shuddering most severely, it skidded back across the road, sliding to the right and scaring the daylights out of a troupe of bystanders who leapt for their very lives.

In the next instant our right side careened into the wall of a building, striking it with full force. The collision threw us back across the cabin, piling one into the other, and all against the door with impact enough to bust the latch. The door broke free and swung out against the building. We pushed ourselves back in the nick of time, as the door scraped along the wall then suddenly snagged and shattered with an explosive force as it was ripped off its hinges and turned into a spinning disk of wooden splinters.

I was lucky not to have had my face ripped off with the door, but before I might even think to faint from such a close call, the right rear wheel, which protruded out as far as the lost door also engaged the wall, and was subsequently sheered clean off its axle. If not for the coach leaning into the building and being pressed hard to scrape along its front, we surely would have flipped over on the spot. Instead, we slid off the wall, and the coach rolled severely to the wheelless side, but remained upright and hell bent to kill us yet.

The floor dropped out from under my feet, causing me to fall backwards toward the doorless opening that was now mostly below me. I reached out to grab anything solid as my head and shoulders passed through to the outside. It was only by the grace of God, the quickness of my companions in their reach for my clothing, and their tenacious grip that saved me from fully spilling out onto the passing road. By all accounts, I should have met my demise there and then.

Instead, they pulled me back into the cabin, but not before I glimpsed what lie ahead. A half a mile down the road stood a small and narrow bridge that we simply would not be able to cross in one piece due to our swaying back and forth from one side of the road to the other.

The end was in sight, but my fear was suddenly gone; that feeling now buried far beneath my will to take control of the situation and live.

"Hold on to me! Hold on to me! I've got to get on the roof. I have to do it now!" I screamed. I didn't wait for an answer, but reached outside the door opening and felt along the roof for a hold until I grasped the luggage rail atop the cabin. With the ladies holding on to me like 'Concord's' leather straps, they secured me against the seesawing motion of the coach. With their help, I pulled myself up atop the cabin, dragging my swinging legs behind.

I found my way through the luggage as I had crawled across the steeply pitched surface. Staying low on my stomach, I slid forward until I could steady myself with a grip on the front luggage rail above the back of the driver's bench.

I thanked the Lord out loud with relief as I spotted the reins still looped about the hand brake within reach of the bench. I looked down the road. I had only seconds before the bridge would be upon us. I swung my legs over the front luggage rail and dropped daringly onto the driver's bench.

My weight now being farther forward forced the left front wheel down closer to the road and the coach struggled to assume a more level position. As if uncertain how best to straighten itself out, it teetered back and forth undecided between two of the three wheels.

I reached for the reins and then with all my might I pulled hard upon them. I screamed for the horses to stop, but all to no avail. They were six and running mad.

"Move to the front of the coach fast and hold on! Hurry! Hurry! Do it now and hold on!" I screamed to the women below. "Hurry!"

The bridge was merely a stone's throw ahead. Frantic, I grabbed the hand brake and pulled with the strength of a man, but it was an effort wasted, for it did absolutely nothing to slow the horses. Yet, because of the women repositioning themselves, the coach righted itself onto its two front wheels as we made our approach.

With the wind in my ears, and hooves kicking up dirt and dust across the dashboard, we attacked the bridge square on in the best possible manner. The front wheels struck the ramp, left the ground, and came crashing down hard upon the deck. The remaining rear wheel, damaged as it was, did likewise, but went on to explode into a swarm of flying spokes. Its steel rim went bounding off to the side making a whooping noise that was lost in the crash of the coach as its bed dropped out from underneath us to break apart upon the bridge.

The newfangled leather straps that made a Concord a "Concord" were the only things keeping us connected to the front axle. The roof top baggage was left hanging high in the air with little choice, but to fall upon the road behind us.

We slid along the railing, breaking it loose in the process, but cleared the bridge, and between the drag of our wrecked coach and my efforts with the reins I finally brought the horses to a halt.

* * *

Nobody moved. Nobody breathed. Nobody dared utter a sound let alone question who might be dead or who might be alive. All that remained was fear of spooking the horses anew.

I tried mightily hard not to faint. I sat still with palms bloodied by my own nails, the reins fused tightly within my grip, for I expected at any second to be off again on a run. My heart pounded as if it possessed hooves of its own. Only after a full moment of passing in which to study the condition of the horses, now heaving for air, was I convinced that the animals were spent. Only then did I have the freedom to become frantic. My eyes filled with tears and I began to shake uncontrollably, but I understood that we would all live to tell this story to others.

"Thank you dear Lord, thank-you, thank-you, thank-you." I closed my eyes and tried to catch my breath.

293

The cautious sounds of relief coming nervously from the women inside distracted me from my prayer.

"Are you all right, Elizabeth?"

"Yes, I'm fine, how about yourselves?"

"Well, we're still in one piece, hard as that is to believe. We sure clobbered that bridge," hollered Mrs. Schueller.

"The back seat and half the bed are gone. We can see the road plain as day from in here," said Mrs. Gunnink from below.

"Good thing you said to move forward, the whole back of the coach is gone," yelled Mrs. Schueller.

"Actually, there ain't much left keeping us from seeing anything plain as day," said Mrs. Gunnink. Then in an undertone to her friend, "I haven't had this much excitement since the day I lost my virginity." The women began to howl.

I didn't believe my ears. They were most certainly in shock. We were all in shock. I sat yet stunned and listened to the two friends, who unbelievably, were now rolling with laughter.

"Sixty-seven and still not ready to meet my maker."

"You got a lot of sinnin' to make up for, Opal."

"Yes, indeed, I have."

"I'm tellin' Charles."

"You ain't telling nobody nothing lessin' you want me to bring up that little incident with the captain last —."

"Opal! You shush your...."

Their voices dropped off into a whisper and suppressed giggles. What a pair! I dismissed them both, believing they had temporarily lost their minds. I turned around to look back along the road. Without rear wheels the coach dropped off steeply, and the roof was also partially collapsed at the back for lack of supporting sides. It made for an open view of the road behind.

What I saw was an unending trail of busted spokes and broken boards mingled with luggage that was rolled, ripped apart, and emptied. My bags were battered and scattered like scared rabbits, clothes and belongings on both sides of a road scarred long and deep by the scrape of the Concord's underbelly. This was the scene clear back to the bridge.

Oddly enough, my eyes dropped to see my burdensome book filled trunk still bound firmly to the front luggage rail of the roof. I chuckled with disbelief to think that its added weight over the front wheels may have made the difference between life and death.

Beyond the bridge and this trail of litter were a number of horsemen galloping toward us with speed. They were quick to cross the creek and within a moment were upon us. At first, they said nothing, only staring at what remained of the coach as their horses danced about snorting and gasping for air.

The men circled us a time or two with the look of astonishment smeared across their faces. They sat in their saddles staring and shaking their heads, studying how badly wrecked was the coach. They were trying to make sense of what happened, and I imagine were unsure of what gruesome sight might next greet them. A ruggedly handsome man at the forefront finally spoke up.

"Ladies." He tipped his hat to Mrs. Schueller and Mrs. Gunnink. He then looked at me. "We din' pass any bodies on the road, an' I mus' say that has to be a mir'cle in itself. Are you ladies all right?" I could tell by his voice that he hardly dared to ask.

"We're fine." I let out a breath of gratitude. I tied off the reins and slid over to the edge of the driver's bench.

Mrs. Schueller and Mrs. Gunnink poked their heads through the tangle of splintered wood frame. They were sitting side by side upon the blackened cushions of the burned out front seat, which was about the only thing left of the coach. Their feet rested upon the remaining floorboards that now angled steeply downward and rested on the dirt of the road. Still, they greeted the horsemen with a rush of encouraging chatter and assurances.

"She saved our lives, pure and simple! You should have seen her climb out of the coach! No man could have done better. Hauled herself right on up to the roof and took the reins. That little girl has nerves of steel." The two ladies were babbling away, giddy with adrenaline. I was embarrassed and immediately dismissed such nonsense.

"Little girl? Oh, my word! What a thing to say. If only there were some truth to it. You can see for yourself there's nothing 'little girl' about me."

It was as though I stuffed both feet fully into my mouth. No sooner had the words escaped me than I remembered I had no clothes on. I could only imagine how it must have sounded, and how I must of appeared sitting on the driver's bench half naked in only my whites before these five men.

"Yes, ma'am. We can see that shore 'nough. Maybe you would care to dress."

They were no longer staring at the remains of the coach, but rather at the remains of me. I nearly died with discomfiture, and all thoughts of the near death experience just passed evaporated into thin air. Their eyes were riveted upon me, and my flushed face made it clear that I realized it. Instinctively, my arms crossed my chest as if that would somehow block their stares or conceal my near nakedness. I shrank to make myself small.

"Maybe you would care to turn around!" I retorted with disdain.

"Beggin' your pardon, ma'am."

The men proved civil enough to show me some mercy by turning their horses about and allowing me the privacy to climb off the coach. I went to retrieve my clothes and discovered to my dismay that anything unsecured inside the coach was somewhere back on the road.

Mrs. Schueller and Mrs. Gunnink raised themselves from the seat and pulled out the oil soaked blanket from beneath them.

They handed me the sooty blanket and encouraged me to wrap up with it.

* * *

Amid unending praise and gratitude from the two elderly ladies for having saved their lives, I wished only to leave the whole of this debacle as soon as possible and find a quiet place to bathe and settle myself down. Another coach would certainly be dispatched to fetch us, claim the wreck, and return the team, but rather than wait for it and collect my trunk and baggage; I asked the ladies if they would mind instructing the stableboys to gather up my belongings along with theirs and drop them off at Van Meriden's.

I decidedly had my fill of travel by coach for the day. It had been fast and furious and all within only a couple of miles at most. The women were more than happy to oblige me, and I removed myself from the confusion of the wreckage only to return to even greater confusion and wreckage at the canal.

TWENTY-SEVEN

At the canal everything was in a state of hysteria. Van Meriden's along with most other establishments must have been nearly emptied of their employees and patrons, for people were appearing out of nowhere. They were flocking to the canal in droves after being summoned by the blast and attracted to the smoke and commotion.

Whereas the streets had been virtually empty only moments before, now they were crowded. Firemen were forming lines, scooping up canal water into leather buckets and passing them

297

hand to hand as they doused blazes big and small. The flow of water was only interrupted for those rescuers arriving with stretchers to aid the injured, and the line was angrily defended against curiosity-seekers searching for the damage, the wounded, or god forbid—the dead.

Three of the five riders that came to our rescue remained to stay with the elderly ladies at the wrecked coach. The three had stepped out into the street after hearing the explosion, and belonged to that group of bystanders who leapt for their lives rather than be run over by our stampeding horses. Seeing no captain and thinking fast, they mounted up and rode out to give chase having never seen anything of the tragedy behind them at the canal.

The other two horsemen, Jack and Gerald, escorted me back to the stageyard. They had grabbed saddled horses from the station livery and witnessed the explosion first hand. While riding, we observed a huge cloud of white smoke hanging overhead in the sky and drifting slowly to the east. I listened to the men's remarks as they studied it, and realized that they were as mystified by the cause of the blast, as was I.

Both of these men were stagecoach captains and gave priority to catching the runaway coach instead of running away to catch the fire. They were familiar faces about the yard and were immediately approached upon our return. An acquaintance yelled at my escort as we crossed the lot.

"Hey, Jack!"

"Lewis," he nodded.

"Did ya catch yer coach?"

"More or less—wasn't my coach. Was McGregor's, an' there wasn't much left t' cetch ceptin' a heap o' splinters on the end o'va harness. Hell o'va mess—Kuiper'll be happy. If it hadn't been for this here lady, I suspect we might a been doin' some buryin' today."

"Looks like we'll be doin' some even so."

"How's that?"

"Word has it a three or four are missin' and feared lost."

"Anybody we know?"

"Don't believe it."

"Anyone figure out what happened?"

"Wagonload of powder went up. Ain't heard much more than that. Nothin' left o' the wagon, an' looks to be a coupla' boats got sunk. Bunch o' people hurt. I hear yer stage busted up some Indians."

"Don't know." Jack shrugged his shoulders. "Like I said—wasn't my stage. I'll talk t'ya later—gotta get the lady inside an' dressed proper. B'sides, I see Kuiper comin' an' I don't wanna be the one t' tell him he's out a Concord." The stranger nodded and fell back into a crowd that was gathering to gawk at me.

Jack prodded his horse to move on, ignoring Kuiper's call in the distance. I could plainly hear the ticketmaster's voice above the crowd, but what echoed in my ears the loudest were the words of Lewis. They filled my head with a vision of the little Indian girl being trampled to death. I recalled the look upon her mother's face, and was suffering through the recollection when our horse came to a halt at the livery.

"Where wou'ja like me t' take ya, ma'am?" Jack turned his ear in my direction.

"Van Meriden's, if you don't mind. It would save me the embarrassment of walking through the crowd looking like this."

"Don't mind at all. Giddup."

"Tell me, Jack, when you rode out across the lot did you see anything of the young Indian girl who was struck by the stage? She was back there by the fence." I pointed for the benefit of no one. "I am certain she was one of the Indians that your friend

299

Lewis spoke of. I know she must have been badly injured if not killed outright."

Jack looked off to his right, and then leaned over in the saddle in order to twist around and look back at the fence and at me. "No, Miss Claussen; can't say I did." He looked back ahead and continued. "I do remember seein' the Injuns. They were pretty worked up an' mostly getting' outta my way, but I don't recall seein' any girl in partic'ler. By the time I got t' the fence, I was ridin' hard, an' only payin' 'tention t' cetchin' you."

Jack barely finished his sentence when his partner rode into earshot of our conversation and spoke up. He was by far the younger of the two, barely into his twenties.

"I saw 'er ma'am!" he hollered. "Yeah, she was all but dead. Wasn't movin' none. I'd say the brat got trampled good, but you shou'nt be frettin' 'bout her. You be wastin' yer time. Them Indians take care of their own. 'Sides, if she don' make it, she's better off than livin' a life o' beggin'. Blessin' of sorts. Blessin' for them an' us both. One less of the cussed breed t' grow up bein' a thief or whore, or whatever for the worse."

I acknowledged the man, but was too appalled to respond. I held no love for Indians to be sure, in fact I was mortified of them, but I could hardly imagine anybody openly displaying such disdain for another without a hint of conscience. A good many folks harbored similar sentiments—feelings kept inside regarding Indians and Negroes, but to hear this man's outburst so odiously voiced in public and with such cold-heartedness was sobering.

I don't believe a soul lived who didn't grow up hearing stories of Indian butchery. And, I understood how the fear of Indians drove many faint of heart into endless rounds of nightmares. But this was here and now, and we were discussing the life of a child that was guilty of nothing more than standing in a stageyard in the middle of Albany, New York.

Such disregard for a young life, Indian or otherwise, fostered only my utmost contempt for this stranger who I knew only as Gerald. I could hardly take my eyes off the man, yet I was unable to face him, fearing he would see my own prejudice *toward* him. He disgusted me, and although he sought my attention, I asked nothing further. Instead, I turned away and looked over Jack's opposite shoulder at the growing crowd along the canal until we reached Van Meriden's, where I dismounted.

"Thank-you for your assistance, gentlemen."

"Think nothin' of it ma'am." Jack spoke for both. "We're just happy t' be bringin' ya back sittin' on the back o'va horse instead o' lyin' on the bed of a wagon waitin' t' be buried. I think you're special, chosen one or sump'in—can feel it in m' bones. Good Lord's watchin' for ya, Miss Claussen, or ya'd surely been dead today."

The comment entirely disrupted my thoughts. I stared blankly at Jack being momentarily lost for a response. His eyebrows lifted his weathered skin into an expression of anticipation.

"Is there sumpthin' else yer wantin' t' ask?"

"No." My thoughts returned. "No, just something you said, something that reminded me of ahh—nothing. No, I'm fine, thank-you. I may still have a room here. You have done me a good deed today, and I am most appreciative. If God was watching over me as you say, he surely was riding your horse. I thank-you again."

"Our pleasure. Good-day then."

"Good-day."

The men tipped their hats and rode off. Dismissing his comment and the strange sensation that befell me, I stood still barely long enough to see them turn about and leave, for I was scantily dressed and attracting much too much attention from the men spilling out of the boardinghouse to have a look at me.

"Miss Claussen?" The headmistress appeared as well, already at the front door to have a look and see herself. Her mouth was open, her face expressing both surprise and shock as she stood taking in the sight of me.

"Mrs. Van Meriden." I responded coolly. "I trust you understand, I don't make a habit of walking about outside in my whites. As you might imagine, it has been a trying morning indeed. Fortunately, I am alive. Unfortunately, I would rather be dead than be seen by one more man. I pray my room has not yet been let, for I had it cleaned to my liking yesterday and wish it back in the worst of ways."

"No, it is free. For heaven's sake, go up immediately. Jacklyn! Accompany Miss Claussen to her room and see to her needs at once!"

"Yes, ma'am."

We wasted little time escaping the wanton stares and secretive remarks that were being whispered all about me. I brushed the men aside, stepped quickly up the stairs and hastened down the hall to my room. As soon as the door sealed me in safely from the men outside, I shed my smelly oil soaked blanket and collapsed upon the bed.

"Oh, god help me. What a morning."

While I stared at the ceiling and collected my thoughts, Jacklyn fetched warmed water for my basin. I was amused with myself for having remained calm while in my whites amid the crowd of men. Only last week, I would have collapsed from embarrassment. Last week, I would have left the boarding-house by the back door and been loathe to show my face for a month afterward. I would like to have believed I was somehow changing, but I knew better; no one changed in two weeks.

With Jacklyn's help, I stripped off my soiled whites and washed myself free the foul odors of burnt hair, smoke, and sweat. At the same time, my clothes were retrieved from the road and brought back to me in great wads stuffed inside my bags. The trunk was none the worse in appearance.

It was almost hopeless trying to find something suitable to wear but for all the dust and dirt. Dabbing here and there with soap and water, we worked to clean what I needed, and I was able to produce fresh undergarments and an acceptable outfit. The rest was sent down with Jacklyn for scrubbing.

After an hour or so, I was relaxed, presentable, and debating how best to make good of the day remaining. I decided to first seek out a seamstress that might fit me for a simple dress, something without bustles or petticoats, something that would stand up to the rigors of travel and allow me the freedom to move without restraint. I now fully appreciated the plain dress of the frontier woman, and had no plan of ever again being restricted by the silliness of fashion in the face of an emergency.

At least Albany was a city well supplied, and in no time I found a reputable seamtress and a fine selection of soft and durable corduroy fabrics. I also found it near impossible to hold her attention to the task at hand, for she could plainly see all the commotion about the canal from her shop. Only when, to her horror, I requested to be fitted for two pair of men's trousers did I capture her undivided attention.

By the time my fitting was complete, it was noon and apparent I would not be departing on any journey this day. For one thing, it would be at least another day or more before my new clothes would be ready. Nonetheless, I wasn't to be bothered, for I couldn't fight fate, and there was no point in my becoming impatient.

I decided to avoid as much of the commotion outside as possible and rest my nerves for the sake of health. I would go back to Van Meriden's for tea and later contract passage aboard a packet going up the canal. At this point, if my journey took a day longer on water, so be it. The tranquility would be welcome.

Apparently, while I had been busy at the seamstress, the Schuellers and Gunninks had paid visit to Van Meriden's and left strict instructions that I should be well fed and kept without concern for cost. The news came as an unexpected surprise.

"They were most adamant that you were not to be bothered with expenses during your stay in town."

"I appreciate what you say, Mrs. Van Meriden, and please thank them for me, but I assure you I am fully capable of covering my own costs."

"Of course, and I meant nothing other. They only wish to show their appreciation. It means a great deal."

"I accept their gratitude, madam, but covering my room and board isn't necessary. It only embarrasses me to receive payment for something that any Christian would have done with equal enthusiasm."

"Miss Claussen…." Mrs. Van Meriden dropped her gaze in a manner of resignation. "Please understand that the Schuellers and Gunninks are well known in these parts and long-standing patrons of our boardinghouse. I have no desire to press this issue and risk your anger, yet, I feel most obligated to do them this service.

"If I fail, rest assured they will not hold it against me, but I will be most disheartened for not having realized a wish that means so much to two very deserving couples. I will promise that should you deny them this gesture, they will return with another, and another until you surrender. It will be a matter of conscience with them."

Witnessing the despair of Mrs. Van Meriden and appreciating her looming disappointment, I was given reason to pause, after which I relented much to her relief. I withheld any further objection other than to state a final time that the fuss was completely unnecessary and made me feel uncomfortable. My words fell upon deaf ears as she gushed with thanks, dismissed my feeling, and escorted me to the dining room as if I were royalty to be pampered and served.

I begged to be seated as far removed from the other patrons as possible, and was happily led by Mrs. Van Meriden to one of the small tables tucked in an out-of-way corner. I ordered tea, and discovered immediately that my preference for privacy was well placed. A wise move indeed, for I found myself driven to hide my face from the moment I sat down. The inn was awash with stories and laughter about the *'lady in whites'* who rescued the Schueller and Gunnink wives.

While sipping my beverage, I was deeply disheartened to overhear plenty of talk about my doings, and much about rewards and gratitude, but nothing at all about the Indians and the little girl who was overrun by the horses. The majority of conversations centered on the explosion itself, and each minute that passed brought more details in from the street until everyone knew most of what had happened.

The first rumor deemed indisputable stated that three boats had been sunk. On this everyone now agreed. The second more sobering rumor-turned-fact came shortly thereafter, when it was confirmed that the explosion was due to a cargo of black powder being loaded aboard a boat headed locks-up for the new Ryan Sandstone Quarry, and that the wagonmaster and an apprentice where killed outright.

From there on, the stories remained to be only rumor and often outrageous. And yet, certain stories persisted in putting forth for fact, that there would be more counted among the dead. At least two boat owners, a steersman and possibly a driver were said to have been killed. Another claimed that two deckhands had been killed and two or three bystanders had likewise been seriously injured or killed. The numbers changed by the minute, but the theme was persistent.

The rumor most upsetting of all, the one that caught me completely off guard, was the story of a mother and her sons aboard one of the boats. It was said they had survived the blast,

305

but hearing the word *mother* turned my blood cold, for I immediately thought of the woman whom I had met. I set my teacup down at once. I turned my head, closed my eyes, and listened intently to what was being said.

For all purpose and intent, I didn't know the woman, and so amid the confusion and misfortune of my morning, I hadn't given her the first thought. Only after hearing about a mother being in the vicinity of the blast, did I stop to think about how the place where we had sat together on the bench was very near to where I had seen the wagon being uncovered.

Mentally, I raced to retrace the course of my walk along the canal, and was quick to figure out that if the woman's boat had not been the one that blew up, it was certainly dangerously close to the explosion. It might very well have been one of those that sunk. Worst of all, I remembered her saying she was headed lock's up with supplies for a quarry in Medina. And, she did have three sons. I opened my eyes. I pushed my cup and saucer away.

My thoughts filled me with dread, and I suffered at once to know of her situation. I left my table and the boardinghouse, setting out in haste to follow my footsteps from the day before. I headed in the direction of the station with a sharp eye in search for her, the boys, or at least the bench, which I knew was at the edge of the yard.

Impatient and upset, I started to run toward the lot and soon met up with the crowd. It was very large by this time and packed in tightly around the bank watchmen, officials, and inspectors gathered along the towpath to survey the damage. I didn't want to face the possibility, but as I worked my way through the throng, in the pit of my stomach I sensed I would find her at the center of this tragedy.

As I had feared, the officials were precisely at the place across the yard, from the stage office, where we had sat and conversed. I worked my way to the front of the crowd and observed a pile of rubble where the bench once stood. It was a sizable heap of wood and junk, bits and pieces blown across the yard, and personal belongings collected in the clean-up. Much of it was still smoldering.

True to gossip at Van Meriden's, three boats were sunk. The boat I came upon first was badly wrecked at its stern and was resting on the bottom of the canal. The far boat appeared whole and undamaged, but only in appearance, for it was resting on the bottom of the canal as well. Between the two sunken vessels was the woman's boat just as I had feared, and like the others it was also swamped with water high on the hull. The cabin and hold were all but submerged. The forward hold covers, deck and bowstable were blown to oblivion and nowhere to be seen, but even so I recognized the boat as the woman's.

Chunks of mule carcass were floating about inside the wreckage amid clumps of blood stained straw. Schools of frenzied fish were busy devouring the fleshy remains. It was a sickening sight, and it held many of the bystanders spellbound while they most certainly contemplated the similarity between corpses of animals and men.

All the litter of family life, keepsakes, clothing and the like floated above or hung suspended just below the surface of the reddened water. The many varied items drew children from other boats to jump in and out of the canal, all the while laughing and carrying on as they snatched up whatever treasure took their fancy. They ducked the hands and threats of irate canal workers who were distracted from drawing up plans to clear the wreckage.

It was an unwanted piece of fabric that suffered me most to see. Mingled within a small float of hay, impaled by the splinters of fractured timbers that held it fast to wave in the current of the canal was a pattern I recognized instantly from the day before. The woman had been darning it one row at a time as she told me about her life.

It saddened me to recall how proud the woman was of her boat, how it was used to transport stone, and how it had been built extra heavy with an second inner hull to protect the outer

307

hull from the bashing of rock. It was a strong vessel just as she had told me, and for the most part it appeared as though it had withstood the explosion fairly well.

This fact was confirmed in conversations I overheard between the Division Boss and the repair crews. They found the outer hull to be solid and intact enough to salvage. They hoped to refloat the boat and also the one beyond instead of blowing them into pieces, and in that way preventing further littering of the canal or damage to the embankment. The remaining boat was too weak structurally, having lost its stern, and would therefore be broken down and dragged out.

The death count at the site was said to be seven. And by all accounts given, it was rumored that a woman had lost both a husband and son. I had little doubt that they spoke of the woman I had met, and although I was happy to hear she was alive, my heart swelled with sorrow knowing how she must be suffering her loss. I wanted to go to her in the worst of ways.

I searched the crowd for any sign of her and the boys, but saw nothing. I began asking bystanders if anybody knew the whereabouts of a woman named Dorrie, who with her husband Robert owned the sunken boat. Following one direction after another, I eventually found myself standing outside the door of a small chapel. I wasn't alone.

There were others who were approaching the door, some to offer a prayer, some just to look, but not one of these people did I see make move to enter. A few stood awhile with heads bowed then turned away after leaving flowers or lighted candles at the doorstep. I assumed them to be people who also lived aboard the canal boats, maybe friends or acquaintances that felt for the woman. They had built relationships over the passing of many trips up and down the canal, but not close enough to actually enter the privacy of the chapel.

For me it was different. I didn't know her at all, and so I stood before the chapel door for some time before summoning up enough courage to enter. It wasn't easy. From where I stood on the street, I could hear the woman's anguish. Her cries made it almost impossible for me to take those last few steps. I felt as though I were intruding into the most private of worlds. I felt as though I were interfering with the deepest of emotions. I was torn between my fear of intruding and my need to go to her.

I reached for the door handle. I pulled slowly upon it and slipped inside as quietly as I was able. I looked about a small room lit dimly by parchment windows. It appeared crowded with its six simple benches. There were no backrests, they being little more than planks across sawed tree trunk sections. There was a miniature altar, little more than a podium at the back with a wooden crucifix and a number of burning candles.

Collapsed upon the floor and leaning against the altar was the woman with whom I had previously laughed and admired for being tough as old leather. Now she appeared small and insignificant, crouched from the weight of her loss. She was weeping over a son, who only one day before was running carefree, playing tag with his brothers and calling out to a father who no longer answered him in this world.

Dorrie's tears fell upon the forehead of the boy she embraced. Her own head rolled about as she drifted in a place of utter misery. She was wringing wet with sweat. She violated the silence of the chapel with high-pitched squeals that dropped into low gurgling murmurs. These were indecipherable words that her soul spoke aloud to spirits surrounding her, spirits that could be touched and were real in her world. She struggled to hold on to the light of fading life. She refused to let go. She was fighting a losing battle to shore up every vestige of her love and reason to exist.

Dorrie held close her boy, stroking his hair and face where he lay across her lap eternally asleep. Her husband Robert laid next to them beneath a blood soaked blanket that even she dared not remove. Across the floor, another bloodied blanket covered the remains of two others recognizable as men only by the scorched boots on their feet.

I felt the dread of death in this place and was so overwhelmed by Dorrie's misery that I myself began to cry. I drove my teeth into my tongue in order to replace the emotional pain with the physical. It was impossible. I sat on the last bench as a witness, watching her while trying to imagine how it must feel to be so deeply in love. I wondered what it must be like to make another, a man to be more specific, the center of your universe, the sole partner in your life. I wondered what it meant to carry his child.

I thought of Mary and Allen. I thought about the strength of their bond, and the way Mary came to rely upon Allen as the source of her love and reason for being. I tried to imagine having it suddenly taken away from her forever. I tried to imagine the death of their boys, Joshua or Juny. I never experienced the motherly bond or devotion before me now, and although I felt guilty, believing I had no right to empathize with Dorrie, I cried with her nonetheless.

My memories of fear and emptiness returned me to another church that many years ago crushed me with this same heartbreak. I thought of how Christopher had suffered. I also thought of how in my younger years I imagined having this bond with him, wanting him to be the center of my world. Mary said I was devoted to Christopher, but I disagreed. Those were childish dreams, fantasies, and as a grown woman I would only admit to having devotion to Mary. To see the misery in this chapel made me wonder if maybe my life of loneliness wasn't for the better after all.

I put aside my mental wanderings and dared to approach her. She was weak with exhaustion, and so I sat down upon the floor and took her into my embrace. The harder she cried, the harder I cried, for in this small place there was no escaping the emotion. My tears fell upon hers. The sight of the young boy was more than I could bear. I drifted between this vision, and that of a mother reaching for a young Indian girl.

"Let me help you," I begged. She opened her swollen eyes and tried to look at me. She stopped sobbing for a brief moment, maybe to wonder why a stranger would beg to help her, or maybe why a stranger would invade her privacy in this her time of mourning. Yet, she spoke to me, or maybe she only spoke her own thoughts aloud and I was there to hear them.

"What am I ever to do? I have nothing left. Nothing," she whispered. "No husband, no home. I have lost my son. Nothing, I have lost most everything, most everything." She dropped her head and again she wept. I put my arm around her and she accepted my closeness.

"No, no," I whispered. "What has happened is terrible beyond doubt, but you still have two wonderful healthy sons that need you. Come with me, Dorrie. You must come with me." I rose to my feet and reached down for her, but she refused to take my hand.

"I can't leave them. I can't. I can't," she protested.

"They know how you feel, your love, your grief, but they are in God's hands now. You must think of your other sons, and your health. You need rest. Please, Dorrie come with me, come with me now."

"No, no, I can't. I can't leave them, not now, not for a while. They're still here. I can feel them."

I pleaded with her gently, but steadfastly she refused to leave, and so I again sat down alongside the altar and remained with her through the rest of the day. I sat in silence and watched over her until she finally succumbed to exhaustion and swooned away.

She leaned up against me in a deep sleep undisturbed by the chapel door, which opened now and then with an inpouring of light, mostly due to her two remaining sons popping in and out of sight. The townspeople also poked their heads inside in order to assess the goings on, and it was in this way I was informed that the other bodies were thought to be those of the steersman and the driver. This was told to me by a group of ladies who entered to offer their services in preparing the deceased for burial. I thanked them sincerely, informing them of my intention to remove Dorrie from the chapel and put her up at Van Meriden's. I gave my promise to contact them when time was best.

Eventually, Dorrie stirred and returned to the world of hardship. This time I was able to strike up a conversation, something that had been much easier to do the day before.

"For the briefest moment everything was fine just now," she said. "You know those few seconds after waking when you have yet to remember your troubles."

"Yes, I know."

I reminded Dorrie again of her two boys, they being concerned for her well-being and in need of her attention after having been without her the whole of the day. Her initial impulse was to resist, but she came to reconsider. I watched her eyes sweep the room searching for the boys' presence. Certainly, it was only the thought of her two living sons and her instincts for their safety that changed her mind.

"Are they all right?"

"I believe so. Folks are watching over them. The younger doesn't fully understand what has happened."

"That's Jack."

"How is Kenneth? Is he all right?"

"I think Kenneth is having a harder time of it. He wants his mother."

Dorrie rose to the occasion. For the sake of her boys, she was able to accept leaving her lost ones with God in the sacred space of the chapel. With the greatest of tenderness, she rose to her knees while lifting her boy off her lap and lay him down alongside his father. She drew the blanket up over his face and then spread it out neatly, removing all creases. Without a word, she turned and looked up at me as if to say it's time.

We let those come in who wished to help by making the necessary arrangements. Dorrie rose slowly to her feet and was visibly shaking from fatigue. I took her by the arm and guided her toward the door. I could feel her trembling and I knew she was in a state of shock. I had witnessed the condition many times at Allen's infirmary.

I persuaded Dorrie to accept my hand, and after a moment's hesitation before a door still closed to the outside, Dorrie collected herself and allowed me to lead her away from so much love departed. As if by a spiritual connection, her two boys emerged from the crowd and approached us the moment we stepped into view. She pulled them into her embrace, kissing them on their heads and reassuring herself.

During our time in the chapel, I introduced myself once again and learned in return that this woman's full name was Dorrie Anne Whipsman. Her boys were Kenneth and Jack, nine and five years of age. Dorrie and both her boys were covered with numerous small flecks of dried blood caused by the flying sand and splinters. All three had been bleeding from the ears.

The sight of them made me realize that luck was a matter of perspective. I thought I was lucky to have lived through the ordeal of a run-away coach, but I was talking to a woman and two boys who were practically sleeping atop a mountain of black powder kegs that brought so much death and destruction, and yet they managed to survive the blast. They were indeed very lucky to be alive. Chosen ones, I thought to myself. *They* were the chosen ones.

As if repeating Jack's message to me, I pointed out to Dorrie that God had a special plan for her or else she surely would have died in the explosion. I said many other things as well in an attempt to keep her talking as much as possible. I wanted to bring her out of shock. Bit-by-bit she opened up, telling me this and that until in the end she gave me her account of what had happened.

"I had been up on deck with Robert and Whither to tell them that I was about to start breakfast, and I wanted to know if it was a good time to do so or not. They were loading cargo, and I wasn't sure when they would be ready to eat. Whither was in the hold with one of the deliverymen and Robert was on deck. He was just starting down the horse plank to have a word with the wagon master who was on shore directing an apprentice from his seat.

"I went down into the galley," she paused. "I stoked up the fire and that was when it happened. It wasn't but a moment after that I was knocked to the deck. At first I was stunned from the concussion and didn't know what had happened or where I was, or anything else for that matter. I just remember crawling around. I remember feeling prickly all over and a sense of firelight coming through the bulkhead. There was water coming in everywhere.

"Instantly, I thought of my boys. They had been playing hard all of the day before—well, you know. You saw them running around, remember?"

"I do remember. They were funny. I laughed just watching them carry on."

"They were tired. They were plum worn out and sleeping soundly. Anyhow, I realized they were now all three upon the floor, having been knocked out of their bunks. Jack and Kenneth were crawling around like myself, confused and badly fright-ened." She started to cry. "Jerry—Jerry, he—he just la-aid there on the floor. He didn't move. I knew—I knew—something was wrong. The bulkhead behind his bunk was stove in. It was there I had seen the light. I imagine a plank had been ripped loose by the blast. It must have struck him—with such force.

"I went to him. I lifted him out of the water and at the same time some men came down the companionway. The boat was sinking. I remember things floating about. I was scared to death at that point because the water was rising so fast. I had to get the boys out. The men grabbed Jack and Kenneth, and I carried Jerry. He never moved. I knew it wasn't good. The side of his face was turning dark.

"I looked out from the companionway, and there was fire everywhere. There was a big blaze just alongside the boat and many more little fires scattered about the area. I could see that the bowstable was completely gone and underwater. The wagon was gone. Whither was gone. It was then that I understood Robert.... I realized then...."

I was compelled to pull this suffering soul into my embrace, which I did. She shuddered with grief, but quickly calmed herself.

"Robert was gone. Even so, I called for him. I called for him because I didn't know what else to do—but I knew."

Dorrie stopped walking and pressed her fingers against her eyes as if to force the tears back inside. She wept afresh, and the sight of her suffering tore me in two. My eyes filled with tears as my heart went out to her.

"I am so sorry, Dorrie. I can't imagine your suffering. It's a wonder any of you survived."

"The boat was built heavy," she sobbed. "Remember, I said it was built heavy. It had to be strong—to take the pounding of the stone. I was at the back of the cabin, near the stern. If it had been any other boat, we would surely have been killed."

She was right. From all that I heard it was determined that the wagon exploded first and the boat took the brunt of the blast before its own cargo was ignited. A number of kegs had been placed into the holds, but the bulwarks contained most of the blast and its force went skyward. Those boats either side of Dorrie had been demolished.

According to witnesses, Dorrie's husband and the wagon master had been seen standing at the wagon overseeing the transfer of the powder kegs. Remains of their bodies were found badly mangled in the station lot some hundred feet from where the wagon had been parked alongside the canal. Nothing was found of Whither the driver, or the apprentice who had been

315

loading kegs into the forward hold. Maybe it wasn't mule carcass in the canal after all.

The wagon master's horses had been dismembered, but the chunks of their remains had been removed before I arrived. It was fortunate for the rest of the community that many of the kegs had been placed down into the boat's hold by the time of the mishap or else a good number of buildings may well have been flattened by flying powder kegs. It was the shower of splintered wood from the wagon and boat that pelted our coach and crazed the team. This was the return cargo Dorrie's husband had made mention of the day before. It was indeed a light load to take locks up, but it came with a heavy toll.

I led Dorrie and her boys back to Van Meriden's, and as we walked along the canal the bystanders pointed, whispered, and closed in upon us. Before long, a procession formed that followed us to the boardinghouse. I led mother and sons inside and upstairs to my room.

I tucked Dorrie into bed, and after convincing her I would care for her boys, I persuaded her to take a stiff drink of spirits, which put her back to sleep due to her fatigue. When I felt she was sleeping peacefully, I led the boys back downstairs and made yet another appearance in the dining room, where I was quickly becoming a regular.

Beyond the windows of the inn, I could see the crowd lingering outside busily discussing the days' events. I paid them little mind and focused my attentions on the boys, getting to know them, caring for their ears, and seeing to it that they were fed to satisfaction. The realization of what happened was now starting to sink in and they were becoming withdrawn. The two boys sat in their chairs seemingly void of emotion, seeming to wait for a second tragedy to strike at any second. While I was making every effort to keep them talking, a gentleman approached me at the table.

"I pray you will excuse me my interruption, my name is Gregory Boswell, and I was hoping I might have word with you." He bowed in our direction. "I have been asked to speak for most of the folks you see outside who wish to express their sympathy for the widowed Mrs. Whipsman and her sons."

"Please, sir, sit down."

I asked the man to join us, not because I was concerned about courtesy, but because I knew that Dorrie needed all the help she could get. He accepted my offer and got to the point.

"I have no desire to be forward, nor do I wish to be nosey. I have only come to say that our number have taken up a collection of useful gifts and cash to help Mrs. Whipsman through her hardship. I trust she is free of injury in the physical sense."

"Yes, yes, she is. She is exhausted, tired from grieving and suffering from shock as you might imagine. It is certain she will need a day or two to regain her composure before presenting herself. She is sleeping soundly in my room, and so I am taking this opportunity to feed the boys. She is a fine woman; Mr. Boswell, and you may rest assured that she appreciates your concerns and generosity. I know for a fact that she has lost much if not all of her possessions and will be in need of any charity that may come her way, however small."

The gentleman was very compassionate and he went on to ask of any additional gesture that might be done in Dorrie's behalf. We discussed a number of things until I elected to change the subject.

"Tell me, Mr. Boswell, have you heard anything of a young Indian girl, who I am certain was badly injured in the mishap. I believe she was overrun by our coach, and am told she was seen to be covered in blood. Forgive me my indelicacy, but I am unable to rest easy over this matter. I am most concerned for her well being and have been powerless to find out more regarding her condition." Mr. Boswell looked at me strangely as though I had asked something improper.

"There has been mention of such a child, but no one has paid it much mind. The Indians will care for her, as is their custom.

317

They don't mingle with whites as a rule. I suspect she has been brought back to the Indian camp a day's ride south of here. That is where most of them live. It's a place of Mohawk, half-breeds, Huron, run-aways, and god only knows. They come from all over and collect there to find work along the canal or beg along the basin when all else fails. The matter of the girl really isn't our concern and I wouldn't fret over her. The Indians have their ways."

Mr. Boswell threw up his hands as if to say *'what's the point'*. I was baffled to understand how this man could be so full of compassion toward Dorrie's plight on the one hand, and completely indifferent to the suffering of an Indian child on the other. I gave no outward sign of my bewilderment.

"Thank you, Mr. Boswell, for your compassion and the information."

"It was my pleasure to be of help, ma'am."

Nothing more was said between us. Mr. Boswell excused himself from our company, and I returned my attention to the boys and what action was next needed.

The morning was nearly spent, and so having finished our breakfasting, I set out to let another room, this with two beds, one for Dorrie and one for her sons. In the meantime, Dorrie had awakened and was in a markedly better way. I saw to it that the three were settled in comfortably in their room and then returned to my own so I might lie down awhile and think out my short-term plans. It was given, I would remain in Albany a while longer, as I was squarely committed to the welfare of this now destitute family.

The townspeople were very generous and soon filled both Dorrie's room and mine to the ceiling with donated goods for the family. After a couple of day's worth of rest, she regained her strength and composure, but grew understandably more anxious over her future and that of the boys.

I could hardly blame her, for the days to come looked far from bright. The repair of the boat was an expensive proposition and one she could not afford. Her husband Robert had a substantial investment in the vessel, but improper insurance, and the insurer balked when told Robert had been hauling explosives instead of stone and merchandise per his contract. Rightfully, they claimed he had not acted in good faith, and they were not obligated to cover any of the damages although they made a sympathetic concession. Repaired, the boat was worth a great deal, enough to sell and buy a small home. In its current state, it had little value.

Over the course of the next few days, I pondered many possibilities that might work to ease Dorrie's plight. I considered her strong points and her frailties; her likes and dislikes. I noted the things in life that held attraction for her. Summed up, in spite of knowing her only a few days, I was convinced that Dorrie was a woman of strong character and morals.

I even came to one particularly promising idea that could lead her out of the hardship she faced. It came to me with such speed, I questioned whether the idea was my own, or if God put it in my head. I didn't know. Maybe it was Christopher's sense of business and Lady Rebecca's nature combining to rub off on me, but that night at the dinner table I offered Dorrie a bold proposal.

"You would pay for the repairs?" She looked at me incredulously.

"Not exactly. I would do it in behalf of Mr. Claussen. I have mentioned him to you before."

"He would pay for the work?" She studied my face, unable to believe what I was saying, maybe even fearful of a swindle in the works.

"Mm-hmm." I nodded it so. "He is a very generous man, Dorrie. He does many things for others. He will do this for you. I know it as sure as I am sitting here at this table."

319

"I don't understand, for what gain? What am I to him? Nothing is for free, Elizabeth, nothing. I have spent too many years working, and I know that above all else."

I could see Dorrie felt out of control. She appeared nervous and full of suspicion. I did my best to reassure her.

"You are correct. I agree, and if I gave you the impression it would be for free, then I erred. Nothing is for free and you will have to do your part as well. It will require a commitment from you to have a go at an experiment of sorts." Dorrie grew silent. She had little room to maneuver and so listened cautiously to what I had to say.

"What kind of experiment?"

"A floating school." I offered. Dorrie stared at me dumbfounded. She was totally lost. I went on to explain.

"Remember when we first met, I sat down next to you on the bench to give my feet a rest. Well, I had been walking for hours up and down the canal taking in the sights of Albany. And what interested me most was the people who worked and lived on board the boats, the *canawlers* as you say. I've never seen anything like that before. I tried to imagine what it was to live that kind of life, like nomads always on the move. When I spoke with you, I was captivated by your every word. I saw so many children including yours, and I wondered how they came by their education. I wondered how they would fare in a society that puts more and more emphasis on books instead of brawn.

"As I stilled along, I happened to stop by one of the local inns to have a drink and watch these children amidst the loading and unloading, and all the other goings on. Meanwhile, at the table next to me were three gentlemen having coffee, local business owners I suspect, who were having a discussion about property taxes.

"One of the issues they were absolutely livid about, was the fact that all these children I was watching attended their schools, and yet they paid no taxes. I listened for quite awhile and wondered why, if this was such an issue, didn't the boaters have their own school? It's clear there are a lot of hard feelings between the residents and the boaters about who should be paying for the schools and also the jails that apparently house boaters all winter. All this turmoil can't be good for children caught in the middle. You tell me, Dorrie. Is schooling an issue?"

"Schooling is always an issue. Landsmen think of us only as gypsies, as owlers. They think we are all thieves that pass secretly through their lives at night and take with us whatever isn't nailed down. They think we are a bad influence and lure their children away with wanderlust. What they never bother to see is that every shop, every inn, every store and town along the canal is only there because of the business we bring. We don't own property so we don't pay taxes, but we do bring them their wealth."

"I'm inclined to agree. But, still you prove my point about the children. Dorrie, let us not pretend to the contrary. Taking your settlement into consideration, you may or may not have the means to repair the boat. Even a generous offer will do you little good, as you still owe for that part, which was not paid to the builder. I needn't remind you that Robert's decision has left something to be desired." Dorrie understood this fact painfully perfect and so I continued.

"I am proposing to you that we set our minds to rebuilding the boat and converting it to a floating school for the children of the canalers. Judging by what little I have seen, there is no shortage of children in these parts and their numbers must increase by the day. I have plenty of experience in this area and I can see there is need here for a school. It would serve to care for and educate this nomadic collection of youngsters that spend their lives floating up and down this state."

Dorrie looked at me with disbelief. "I don't know what I'm supposed to say, Elizabeth. I'm no schoolteacher. To me the

321

idea seems insane, especially if you think;—I mean, I can't even read. I am a mother and—."

"Dorrie, you are perfect for this. You possess a wealth of experience, more than you realize. I love to listen to all you reveal about life on the canal and in upper New York, and about the people you meet passing through here on their way westward. You have a rich collection of stories to share with others. You know 'matter of factly' more about this western life than any of the best-learned scholars back east have learned from their shelves of books and hear tell.

"Don't worry so much. Everything will be fine, believe me. I will see to it there are proper instructors for the formal classes. Imagine not only a venue for the local children to learn, but also the chance for children from far away to visit and experience life in one of the most exciting places in the nation, truly the gateway to the west, to the Great Lakes, to Niagara. I see them coming in the company of instructors from Boston, Providence and New York to enjoy field trips up and down the canal. Your sons will have the opportunity to earn a formal education, and so will you if you should so desire. I believe it could work, Dorrie. I believe this with all my heart. What do you think? What do you say to such a proposition?"

"Elizabeth. You are asking the impossible of me. I know nothing of books and learning. I can't read or write—." I broke her off mid-sentence.

"Don't bother yourself with such concerns, Dorrie. There are plenty of people who can teach one to read and write. You know the history of this region. The instructors will hang on your every word. They will take notes. They will chronicle all of what you say. Your worth is in the knowledge of this country and the workings of the boat. You know the canal and the children of the families. They trust you. You will do fine, better than fine. You will be perfect for the job, Dorrie. I know this in my heart, I promise."

"Oh, Elizabeth." Her head swayed back and forth until she stopped and looked at me straight on. "You promise my boys would be educated. They would learn to read and write."

"Yes, I promise."

She took a deep breath as she sat up and rubbed her hands back and forth nervously atop her thighs. "Very well, then. I'll do as you say for their sake, but if all goes wrong remember I told you the idea is sheer lunacy. I go along with this because I trust you and because I have nothing before me but certain poverty." She let out another deep breath.

"Great! That is all that I ask. We now have a plan. You won't regret it. Trust me, and I'll prove all your fears baseless."

I felt wonderful about giving Dorrie Anne something to look forward to in this her time of need. I knew I had raised her spirit above the misery of a bleak future certain to befall her, and yet, I remained further burdened by conscience.

Night after night, I suffered from troubling thoughts. In the dark of my room I relived the memory of another mother's face gripped in anguish. The blur of an Indian complexion, background to black eyes that seared my soul, the echo of screams that refused to be silenced reverberated within my head. I tossed and I turned, unable to escape the terrible accident. Even sleep failed to present relief. My dreams haunted me, and time and time again, I found myself searching a murky wilderness for a mother and daughter.

I felt I had to find them. I had to seek out this mother and child, and assure myself there was nothing I might do to ease the young girl's suffering should that be her state. I needed to do this unless I was prepared to spend the rest of my life wondering of her fate and what part I might have played in its course.

I had asked about town until feeling confident I knew the whereabouts of the Indian camp. Now I was determined to go there without further delay. Having come to a firm decision, I fell soundly asleep and was left untroubled by my dreams.

TWENTY-EIGHT

I set out early the next morning on my crusade armed with purpose, trousers, and determination enough to face my objective and a long day's ride. I left Van Meriden's for the stage office in search of Mr. Kuiper, whereafter I informed him of my intentions and needs. He was not at all helpful.

"Dame Claussen, please! Ik wish to hear no more of deze nonsense. Jou put me in een bat place. Ik haaf no objection to providing jou met een horse, but to do so in order dat jou might ride to de Indian camp is no goed. Ik woult niet slaap at night knowing Ik help met such een bat plan. Jou understand me, yah?"

"I understand, Mr. Kuiper."

"Het is niet safe, dame, niet safe. Bat enough jou er een woman en all. Dere is no man in his right mind woult go near dat camp alone, day of night, unless he wish to die. You understand me, yah? Niets dere but mob of dieves, en whores, en worse, hidin' like animals in de woot. Only een fool met een gun or een crazy man woult dink to go voor such een visit. Ik trust jou haaf een gun of een knife to fight met, yah?" Mr. Kuiper looked at me hard with a hope for reassurance that somewhat annoyed me.

"I am neither a gun totin' fool nor insane, sir; and I don't carry a knife. But, make no mistake about it, Mr. Kuiper; I am determined. I have every intention of traveling to that camp without guns or knives, with or without your blessing, and with or without your horse. I have worked all my life among the poor. I have waded through their filth, witnessed the worst of their miserable downtrodden lot, their dread, and their dead. I have never felt the need to be armed, and I surely can handle this." I leveled my stare directly at him.

"Ik bite my lip, Dame Claussen. Ik bite my lip." Mr. Kuiper did as he said and turned his head upward with closed eyes as if praying to heaven. Carry on as he might, I was not to be dissuaded.

"I shouldn't imagine this place to be any more dangerous than the docks of Boston or New York. I have seen honest people steal, Mr. Kuiper, because they starve. I have seen honest people hide because of ridicule, and I have seen them run mostly out of fear, not guilt. I am a woman of good sense, Mr. Kuiper; not a fool, not easily frightened, and above all else committed to assist that child. Do you understand? I *am* going to that camp." I brought any further discussion of the matter to a halt. Mr. Kuiper took a moment to size me up.

"Ik see dere is no talking sense to jou, Dame Claussen. Ik wil go deze minute en saddle my beste horse voor jou. Ik dink Ik wil never see deze horse again, but Ik wil do deze to maakt up voor how jou almost die in my coach de odder day. Ik feel bat because Ik dink deze time jou may wel get kilt. Als jou die, don't kom back en haunt me. Remember, Ik say jou niet to go. Jou understand me, yah? Deze is een bat plan, Dame Claussen." He shook his head with regret. "Wait here. Ik kom back met de horse."

Mr. Kuiper stomped off somewhat indignant, but returned soon after with a handsome horse, one able to stand the trip. The looks of the animal pleased me as I reached across its withers and ran a hand along a solid flank.

"Voor jou, Dame Claussen. Deze is my beste horse. Het haaf goed wind. Het was shoed last week en is goed as ever to maakt de trip. Jou wil like him, yah, he is neit mean, niet te worry."

"Thank you, Mr. Kuiper. He's a fine animal. And please, do not think me ungrateful of your concerns. You are a kind man to fear for my safety and that I shall not forget. All will go well, and I promise to bring back your horse none the worse for wear. Does he have a name?"

"Jou can call him, Catch-up. Heir, Ik give jou deze oil cloth shoult jou get caught in de rain."

325

"You're most thoughtful, sir. Catch-up. I promise to bring Catch-up back home. In your own words, Mr. Kuiper; *not to worry, not to worry.* Now, what do I owe you?"

"Don't even say het! Jou owe me nodding, Dame Claussen. Ik hate to dink what people woult say if Ik charged jou voor a horse en sent jou to doze Indians. Dey run me out of town. Ik zei my piece, en dat is all Ik ask. Ik haaf no wish to maak profit voor sending jou to een camp of snakes. Jou may keep de horse as long as jou wish, but Ik wil say again dat Ik dink het beste jou niet go. Als de animal comes back to my stable, dat wil be all de payment Ik want. Jou see, Dame Claussen, Ik fear dat Indians like horses as much as dey like whiskey en women."

I accepted Mr. Kuiper's comments without comeback, for his heart was in the right place. I also accepted his hand in mounting Catch-up, in spite of his less than favorable opinion regarding women in trousers. Once, safely in the saddle, I looked down and thanked sincerely for all his concerns. Giving him a last wave and farewell, I started my way westerly along the Old Dam Road in search of the Indian camp. I soon lost sight of the stageyard, the businesses bordering the canal and basin, and eventually all the outlying dwellings of Albany.

* * *

It wasn't long before I felt loneliness creeping about me, and so worked to strengthen my resolve by thinking of the young injured girl and her suffering. I also began forging a strong bond with Catch-up, who I talked to almost non-stop.

Together we rode mile after mile passing one farmhouse after another, all seemingly cozy not because of foul weather, but rather due to the distance between the homes and the slim chance of seeing someone out and about. I never missed a chance to call upon a person in passing, who might be repairing the road or working a field within ear's shot, this to reassure myself of headings.

I continued journeying in a westerly direction as morning changed to afternoon, time marked by a sun that crossed overhead to cast its blinding light into my face. In contrast, ever longer spindly shadows were being cast by the evenly spaced cornrows now dwindling behind me. Their growth had appeared stunted in the dusty earth of farms now seen less frequently.

The open fields looked fresher and healthier as they flowed around random stands of trees that increasingly replaced the farmer's orderly plantings. To my dismay, the day was growing late, and the Indian camp was proving to be much farther away than I had anticipated.

Eventually, the terrain became hilly, forested, and a good deal less traveled. There was hardly reason or need for the road, and so it abandoned me, leaving little more than a trail to draw me into the barely broken thickets of brush. At least I traveled a well-established path, dry, hard packed, and suitable for my horse.

I had now been a good hour into the trees, and only half that time spent in the subdued light of the forest would have given the strongest of character reason to pause. Only a liar would have claimed having never looked back across her shoulder or suppressing anxieties about shadows that seemed to move alongside her from tree to tree. If I could have leaned forward and rode comfortably with my arms wrapped tightly about Catch-up's neck, I would have done so at once.

It was some time after being swallowed up by the forest that I encountered the first signs of an Indian camp; broken branches, marked trees, a piece of scrap cloth now and then indicating which fork to follow along the trail. I actually felt more at ease along the way knowing there were living people about who might chase away the spirits and shadows that haunted me.

At last, to my relief, there came the scent of smoke and roasted meat, and later the sound of distant voices. Floating

327

through the air, it was all easily lost in the dying breezes of day and branches of rustling leaves overhead. I was forced to pay close attention in my effort to track them. Quietly, and with caution, I moved forward following my ears until at last I came upon a creek beyond which there was a spacious but secluded clearing.

At water's edge I stopped to allow my horse a drink, while I spied within this clearing a number of large huts or lodges now dissolving into the obscurity of twilight. I felt a rush of uneasiness as I glimpsed two or three Negroes, certain to be run-away slaves, spring to their feet and sprint off for the safety of the brush. Aside from the horses and animals, the three were the only signs of life even though I heard many voices before I made my appearance.

I found myself caught between two evils. I had spent my last uneasy hours traveling alone in the shadow of trees at the onset of nightfall and was glad to be done with it. Yet, now that I found the camp and faced the prospect of entering alone with only questionable courage and a head packed full of dire warnings, I was equally uncomfortable.

I was clearly too far into the forest to consider going back this night, and so there was little choice in the matter. However, I held no doubt in knowing that aside from the sake of a little girl and the lingering smells of roasted food, there was no compelling reason for any outsider to take another step toward this suspicious place. Mustering up whatever courage I could find, I snapped the reins and moved to cross the creek.

A bluish haze of smoke rose lazily from thatched roofs that encircled a large campfire to hang thick and undisturbed in the cool evening air. It remained trapped within the clearing by the surrounding wall of trees and gave one the impression of a soft cottony blanket about to tuck this large family in for a good night's sleep. It might have been a perfect setting, if not for a pack of disturbed dogs that fractured the peace by protesting my approach.

Nervously, I entered the clearing and halted near the warmth of a campfire. With similar apprehension, the Indians also begin to emerge; some from within their lodges, some from behind the trees, some only partially revealed themselves, others preferred to remain hidden under cover of the shadows. The men were first to appear, followed by a few women and finally an eruption of curious and energetic children.

I was plenty worried before entering the camp, and now as I sat upon my horse amid such scrutiny and suspicion, I began to question the merit of my decision to call upon these people for any reason. Aside from the children, the Indians made no attempt to greet me nor did they offer the least sign of welcome or friendliness. Their outwardly appearance was distinctly distant and challenging, even more so than the dogs.

As far back as I could remember, I had heard stories about Indians as strong, fearless, ruthless heathens, who gave no value to life, limb or god—savages by every measure, a people whose hands were bloodied by atrocities; a people who were to be feared. My stomach sickened as I looked at the campfire and recalled tales of mothers forced to turn their babies on spits above the flames.

Every story ever told that put fear into my head was now fully resurrected from memory, but I refused to succumb to panic. Maybe Mr. Boswell, and Mr. Kuiper were right. Maybe I was the fool. Maybe I should have let the Indians *take care of their own*. And maybe a daddy would have whipped me for riding out here alone, but curiously, as I looked about, what I saw most spread out in this back corner of wilderness was a small collection of humanity drowning in poverty. This was something I understood.

Slowly the inhabitants began to appear and curiously go back about their business seemingly oblivious to my presence. I observed a number of women and children return to beating a fallen log stripped of its bark. They were separating the growth rings of the wood and then splitting the rings into long fibers that others were making into twine and materials for basket weaving.

They were an odd looking lot as they stood dressed in clothes fashioned from furs, leathers, and old discarded white man's rags. Yet, there was a look in their eyes that commanded my attention and warned me that there was a difference between these people and those I knew as poor. Their eyes spoke of an underlying strength. I studied their faces until my fear began to recede, it being overshadowed by a sense that in this camp I had discovered the remnants of a proud people who had long been forgotten by their gods.

I forced myself to dismount amid the indignant dogs, and the eyes that followed my every move as I stooped before the campfire to warm myself. Having no idea what to do next, I decided to sit down upon a log bench and wait for however long it took until one of the inhabitants elected to confront me. I was wary, indeed, but then I began to realize so too were they.

After fifteen or twenty uncomfortable minutes of feeling self-conscious and unwanted, of feeling like an intruder who barged into someone's home without invitation; a large male Indian made a move in my direction. He was not dressed so much in wools and fabric, but rather in the leathers and skins of Indian dress, which better supported my preconceived notions of proper Indian attire.

He wore a collection of beads on his vest, about his wrist and in his hair. He had a silver and gold broken heart medallion resting upon his massive chest. The piece of white man's jewelry was suspended from his neck by a leather lace and looked out of place on his person, most likely stolen. I would have expected to see a bear's tooth or claw. He did not sit down, but rather stood before me in a confident, almost threatening fashion to address me in a deep and resonant voice.

"What you're name?"

"Elizabeth," I answered

"Why Ezlbeth come here?" he bellowed.

"I am looking for a small girl who was hurt in Albany—at the stageyard." I held my hand low to emphasize my meaning of a small child.

"Girl, no here," he dismissed me.

"I mean her no harm."

"Girl, no here," he reiterated then began to turn away.

"I brought gift for her and chief."

This caught his full attention. He turned back in my direction and stepped closer.

"Show me gift"

I opened my purse, withdrew a few gold coins and revealed them on my opened palm. His eyes lit up at once and instinctively he reached for them. I snapped my hand back.

"You give me gift," he ordered.

"No."

I moved the clenched coins behind my back. I refused him in no uncertain terms. This was a risky move on my part. I understood that at any given moment, I could end up forever gone from the face of the earth never to be found again in this back woods country. Mr. Boswell and Gerald would laugh at my stupidity, Mr. Kuiper would be out a horse; I would be out my money and possibly my life.

Only an idiot would be carrying gold about this impoverished place, and I was certain that the man was at that moment devising a plan for my demise. Nevertheless, I stated my gift was for the chief, set the rule, and stood my ground.

"I speak to chief. I give gift to chief," I repeated.

The Indian arched his back stiffly and stared down at me as he contemplated our situation. I believe he decided there were too many others about, or maybe he didn't wish to provoke his elder, for instead of killing me on the spot, he rose without word and disappeared into the largest of the lodges.

About five minutes later, he reappeared in the doorway and stepped aside to allow a much older gray haired man to pass. There being a number of log seats surrounding the fire pit, he followed the old man past the log upon which I was seated, and they sat down together upon another.

I produced ten gold coins for all to see and placed them on the end of the bench nearest the frail elder. He leaned over and picked up one, holding it close to his eyes. I gathered he was nearly blind. He bit into it and rubbed its surface then spoke to me in his native tongue. The man with the half-heart medallion translated.

"Why you come?"

"To see hurt girl."

"Why see hurt girl."

"My heart sad." I clasped my heart and then made motions of falling tears with my fingers at my face. They studied me.

"Why heart sad?"

"I see horses hit girl. I feel bad. She small. I come to help."

"She *Indian!*" The large man suddenly snapped at me with disdain. This had not been a translation, and I sensed that the core of the issue was now at hand.

"Yes." I said. "She Indian."

I had little to offer in response. I responded firmly, but in a reserved tone of voice. The old man addressed the translator and they conversed, all the while darting glances in my direction. The two men finally rose to their feet. The translator looked down at me. His size and presence put the fear of God into me whenever he turned my way.

"Chief say gift good. You wait."

"I wait," said I, shaking my head in agreement.

I felt much better now that I had met with the chief and presented to him a gift that pleased. The crush of mistrust seemed to have been lifted, and having been told to wait; I understood the ball was rolling most certainly in my favor. I sat there upon the bench in better spirits watching the coals glow brighter as twilight gave way to moonlight, but when finally I saw the constellations clearly take shape overhead, I decided that the ball had rolled off into oblivion.

I now felt I was being played the fool, and my elation dwindled, after time passed went from moments to hours. It was now well into the dark of late night, and I was both famished and exhausted from my day's ride. I had no idea what the Indians were up to, but it was definitely out of the question that I might mount my horse and head back to Albany. At this late hour, if I didn't chance upon a bandit or rapist, there was always the danger of a stumbling horse or wild animal. Like it or not, I was here for the night, feeling again very uncomfortable and unwelcome.

At this point, I wanted nothing more than to lie down upon the ground and shut my eyes. I wanted to forget about this war of wills and waiting, but I was afraid the Indians would perceive any such move as a sign of weakness or a failing on my part. So, I remained seated upon the log and reduced myself to a show of spasms, jerks, and nods as I lost my battle to remain awake.

My last thoughts, half coherent, half dream, were based on my belief that I was being tested. This was undoubtedly their way to determine how badly I wanted to see the girl. I told myself it made perfectly good sense as I pinched myself hard and repositioned my weary bones.

Would I not also be wary of a complete stranger who requested to see a family member, a loved one, especially a child? Would it make a difference whether or not the stranger was bearing gifts? Of course not, anybody would understand that. I just had to wait.

333

TWENTY-NINE

Mary was frightened. She was calling to me.

"Hurry up, hurry up," she urged. The day was sunny and warm and the smell of food made my mouth water. Was something wrong? I looked over my shoulder. I was the last one left standing alone in an open field. The sky behind me was dark and threatening, the air chilly.

"I'm coming!" I yelled. "I'm coming!" I was running hard to catch the wagon that was heading toward Mary's cottage, a place of warmth and the smells of dinner. But that wagon was moving farther away. It was leaving without me. Mary was nervous; I could feel it.

"Wait!" I yelled. "Wait, Mary!"

I ran as hard as I could, but the field was freshly plowed, soft and muddy, and it sucked at my feet to slow me down.

"Wait, Mary! Wait for me. I'm coming. Wait!"

I pleaded fearfully. I had to get beyond the barrier of sludge that stuck to me like glue. Mary was moving slowly into the distance and calling out to me, telling me to jump for the wagon. Her arms reached for me in the distance. "Jump! Jump! Jump!" She cried.

It was now or never. I mustered every ounce of my strength and dove over the black gooey mess. My body shot out of the mud like a spring set free, but to my surprise, before my eyes the wagon suddenly vanished into thin air. My arms were outstretched, hands clenched into fists grasping not only nothing of the wagon, but nothing at all.

The scene was nonsensical. In confusion, I raised my head. I was utterly baffled. I found myself in a swirling crowd of fifteen or twenty people, all laughing uproariously. Laughing at what, I didn't understand. Who were these people, these strange faces?

The answers weren't long in coming once my head cleared. The Indians were standing over me, howling, laughing at my expense. I had fought hard to stay awake, but to no avail, and they had delighted in tip-toeing around my sleeping body, making breakfast and seeing how far they could carry the fun without waking me.

The tribe had built up the fire in the pit, had already roasted a number of rabbit and squirrel, and were busily eating a morning meal while I lay fast asleep in their midst yelling for Mary to wait up. I must have made a splendid sight lying there in the dirt leaping for wagons that rolled by in my dreams. I didn't move at first, but preferred to remain put while I collected my thoughts and sized up the morning's situation. I concluded that my embarrassment might have been worth the end results, which were the smiles on their faces.

The Indians were warm and friendly now and encouraged me to take some food. I pulled myself up out of the dirt and black ash spread about from the pit. I was a filthy mess. My mouth was full of sand, and I couldn't begin to imagine what all had crawled over me through the night. Repeatedly, I spit stuff out of my mouth, and each time I did so, the Indians found the act funnier than before. They understood the hazards of sleeping on the open ground and not only laughed at me, but went around mimicking my spitting and my expressions of disgust with great glee.

The large Indian sat down next to me and spoke.

"You speak with spirit, yah?" He made a sleeping gesture. He was referring to my dream, and possibly my talking while asleep. I would have agreed with anything at this point, but was immediately instilled with a revelation, and an unexpected quickness of wit, whereby I offered him the perfect answer.

"Yes, I speak with spirit. Great Spirit say, 'Go to little hurt girl and pray. Give gift.'" This gave the Indian a moment's pause. He nodded his head and smiled.

335

"Eat." He motioned to the skewered meat upon the fire. "Spirit talk to you is good. Good sign. You eat."

"Thank-you."

I answered him stiffly, not only because I wanted him to believe I understood the importance of spirit talk, but also because I *was* stiff; and I *was* cold, and I *was* wet and filthy. I imagined my hair to be full of nasty little crawling things, ticks, fleas and the like. The thought did not make me happy, as I pulled at my hair. This was not a good way to start out the day.

On top of everything else, as I reached for a piece of rabbit from the fire, I looked up about to express my thanks for the food, and spied another Indian holding onto a mirror with a blue painted handle. I turned to my horse and saw at once my saddlebags had been opened.

I set aside my food and walked over to the bags. I lifted the untied flap, and as I had surmised, it was empty. Everything had been stolen. It wasn't much to lose in terms of value, but it was the idea that the items belonged to me, I had brought them all the way from Albany and intended to give the majority of them to the young girl as gifts to raise her spirits.

Possessing a disposition formed by filth, exhaustion, hunger and irritability, my fuse was not only lit, but instantly burning fiercely. However, unlike my normal tendency to cast all care to the wind and vent my fury, this time I kept it bottled inside the best I could. Truth being known, these people made me plenty nervous—nervous enough to put a lid on my temper.

With a clenched jaw, I returned to the fire, sat down at my place and picked up my food. I had lost much of my appetite, but began to eat anyway. I chewed on the meat, and I chewed on the facts. I looked at the Indians about me; they were unable to meet my eyes. They knew. They wouldn't admit to stealing my things, but it was written all over their faces just as my anger was written on mine. It didn't take much nourishment to regain my strength and further fuel my temper. I looked up at the man with the half heart medallion and questioned him loudly so all might hear.

"What man take gifts from child?" He looked at me and pretended not to understand my question. I repeated myself.

"What man steal from small child—small man?"

"No man."

I shook my head back and forth in disagreement. "Small man!" I stressed. "Small man take gift from small child. Yes." I looked over to the thief and glared.

At that moment, it was as if someone drew back a curtain that had obscured my vision. For the first time I took note of something that had been occurring regularly about me. To be more precise, when I had accused the thief of being a small man, the women sitting about the fire all looked away, but snickered nonetheless. Their reaction and the timing of it were notable; for I had been struggling to get my feelings across in mannerisms they might comprehend. It was obvious they understood me much better than I would have imagined. Somehow, they knew.

I was drawn back to the matter at hand and the Indian who had been in possession of my mirror. In a show of supreme defiance, the thief strode up to stand before me. He literally leaned over me in a most intimidating show of arrogance and struck his chest.

"I Big Man! Small man, no!" He sliced the air sideways with his hand. "Big man!" He bellowed in an attempt to make me cower. He then produced the mirror and displayed it proudly before me, tempting me to try and take it back. Unfortunately for him, my fuse, short enough to start with, had now reached the keg. I was never one to be crossed before my breakfast. Explain it however you will, but know it is that time of day when I find myself very sensitive and irrational, and the sight of him holding my mirror was all it took to prove it. I jumped to my feet.

"Small man! Very small man!" I hollered into his surprised face and met his glare without a shred of fear. "Small, small man!" I yelled. The women now snickered louder than ever.

"Mugwump! (big man) Mugwump!" He protested angrily, throwing his arms out to increase his size, but I was not about to be subdued.

"Small man steal from girl! Small man! Small, small, small! Thief!" I emphasized my point by pinching my fingers together and spitting with great theatrics upon the ground. I must have been crazy. My gesture sent the women seated near me to pitching and rolling about, guffawing and snickering openly. Both the thief and I looked at them; I in surprise, he in anger, but instead of killing me on the spot, the enraged man threw the mirror down at my feet in disgust and stormed off into the forest.

I looked down to see the mirror unbroken. I sat back down and reached for it. Holding it up, I looked at my reflection and noted my involuntary expression of utter satisfaction. I smiled at myself then set it aside. Again, I chewed on my rabbit, only this time with better appetite. I ate with pleasure, and as I did so, the brush and comb appeared. So did a sachet of lavender and a number of ribbons. In time and without further outcry every missing item was returned. I looked at the women and smiled. They thought the whole affair was very funny and nodded their approval of my actions by smiling back and nodding vigorously. The chief had been standing before his lodge and sent word to me of his thoughts. They boiled down to this:

"It was honorable to be a thief, but a stupid honorable thief was still stupid."

The man with the medallion explained that the thief's grandfather was a white man and for this reason the Great Spirit did not give him a good brain. He said this was known by all. Hearing the chief's message and now this explanation, the women began to howl. They were all over themselves in laughter and saying other things that made them howl even harder.

I should have figured it out sooner. These people may have been Indians, but they had lived in this valley since the beginning of time. They were here when the white man first arrived and watched his progression across their lands. In other words, they had ample time to learn the white man's tongue and for the most part they did. These women understood much of what I said. I could see it on their faces. All of them, men, women and children, appeared entirely ignorant of the English language until the moment it suited them otherwise. Fact was in these parts, they probably knew not only their own language, but English, German, and Dutch to boot.

An older woman seated across from me arose to her feet and came to me with a warm smile. She reached out to take my arm.

"Come. Come, come."

Pulling me up from the log, she led me to one of the lodges across the clearing. I passed through the opening, while she held a wind blind to the side and out of my way. Inside, the air was warm and heavy with scent and smoke of firewood. Before me a warm fire still cast its glow even as the light of morning made its way inside the murky lodge. Upon the packed earth along the perimeter of the structure, there were a number of beds made up of wooden frames with furs draped over the rails; all raised a short ways off the ground. Above the beds were hung many personal items including spears, bows and arrows, leather garments, beads and various talismans.

To my left was the mother whose anguish filled my dreams. She looked up at me passively and then resumed praying at her daughter's side. The young girl appeared to me as any young child does, no matter what nationality or race, English or Indian. She was the picture of innocence, the face of an angel. Even the wounds inflicted upon her were unable to suppress her purity. My heart bled for her mother. It had been more than a week since the accident and the child had not regained consciousness. It was very distressing.

339

Another woman had entered behind me and brought with her my gifts. She placed them at the feet of the mother. The woman spoke to the mother briefly and then left us alone.

"Thank-you," said the mother.

"You're most welcome. Does your child get better?"

She rose to her feet and taking me by my shoulders she embraced me, first hugging me on one side then the other. She didn't answer my question. She only looked at me with the answers in her eyes, and then sat back down to resume her prayers. I too had prayed to see the child doing well, but that was not to be.

I picked up the blue handled brush and with my eyes, I asked the mother for permission. She nodded, and so with care and respect, I applied the brush, easing it through the young girl's hair. Over and over, I worked it through her thick black mane. The child was so adorable. How I wished to have just such a child to love and cherish. My eyes moistened, for it broke my heart to see so perfect a gift from God left hanging in the balance. I desperately wanted to ask the mother if I might send for a doctor, but somehow the whole concept of white man's medicine seemed sacrilegious in this place.

I stayed inside the lodge with mother and daughter for the better part of an hour, afterwhich I was forced to take my leave by the knowledge that I faced a long journey back to the station. Having finished an exchange of thanks for food and gifts, I mounted my horse and again crossed the creek.

It was with a heavy heart and a sense of frustration that I started back for Albany. A number of the younger boys mounted horses and accompanied me to the edge of the wood. I waved them a final good-bye and spent the remainder of the day riding home in low spirit.

THIRTY

Over the next four weeks, my concerns regarding the young Indian girl were forcibly repressed, for my every minute was committed to the restoration of both Dorrie's world and her boat. Neither was easy, nor inexpensive, and I wondered if the cost of my involvement passed by Christopher unnoticed.

I knew that unlike myself, he would never see Dorrie's mettle, her struggle to hold on in spite of the fact she had lost everything. Even her boat—for years the home to her family, was now all but lost to circumstance. It was about to become mine, or more rightfully put, about to become his although he would never know.

It was a sad affair, and seemingly unfair, but Dorrie was incapable of covering the costs before her. Like so many women, Dorrie had done nothing to justify being swept off the foundation of her life, nothing at all to warrant being stripped raw of everything but two sons. I knew this first hand. I knew because I had seen more than my fair share of women who suffered similar misfortune.

Over the years, I had learned how women were all too often widowed by husbands killed in war, killed by Indians, killed by disease, accidents, or a raging sea. Ironically, when men managed to survive the odds, then they just plain wore out and died of old age—*first*. Pray have mercy, I thought to myself, for those women without family to take them in, for the street was a cold and callous place to end one's life.

I suffered these truths, and it was but cheerless relief knowing that I for one would never be a *'Dorrie'* or destitute. How unlikely that I should be found left behind with a heart ripped to bleeding shreds by love lost, and scrambling in fear of the future with children at my feet. How unlikely I should find myself desperate to survive and defenseless in a world whereby I lived day to day on handouts without a moment's reprieve to ask *'why'* or reflect on the past and cry away my misery.

341

I was thirty-three in years, and my heart had never been given to another in such a way that the ravages of love might leave it so deeply wounded or unprepared. I was not a *'Dorrie'*, and yet, I wondered what was worse; to give oneself wholly over to love's rapture and suffer horrendously at its sudden loss, or never taste its sweetness and suffer the whole of one's life in sad remorse. I could only guess.

In spite of Dorrie's reluctance to give up something which so represented her husband, it was prudent that she sell the boat once repaired. In fact, it was by following her own advice that she did so. As she put it to me; *"for a good school boat, we need a packet and not a double-bottomed rock hauler"*. Even so, tears were shed as she faced up to the thought of parting with her home, which aside from her sons was the single greatest remnant of her life with Robert. I didn't rush or pressure her in any manner to reach a decision. Instead, choosing to put business sense aside, I gave Dorrie as much time as needed to accept what must be.

On the day of the auction, the two of us stood before her home a final time. That morning, Dorrie walked back and forth along the length of the hull, sliding her hand across its wooden planks as she stepped.

"It looks better than new. It needed a bottom coat. The varnish is wonderful is it not?"

"They did a fine job, Dorrie. One would never know the boat was ever damaged."

The two of us stood and studied the vessel as it sat on the blocks. Dorrie was quiet. I could imagine her mind to be moving through innumerable memories, and I knew when she walked around the stern beyond sight of the bidders and me, she did so to weep in private.

To her benefit, the boat fetched a handsome price, in good part due to kind hearts and sympathetic money. After the auction, whereupon all accounts were settled, a small sum was left aside to place into safe keeping for Dorrie's security. Her eyes were now red and swollen. I gave her a hug of reassurance and reminded her that we were only closing one chapter of her life in order to open another. I promised her a bright future if she stayed the course.

The following day, I urged Dorrie to use her expertise and find us the packet she felt would best serve our needs. I couldn't imagine what Christopher would say when he received the bill. If that didn't draw him out of the woods to have a word with me, I was certain nothing on earth would.

As was her nature, Dorrie took her task to heart. I did my best to keep her occupied, for as long as I was able to keep her attention focused on some goal, as long as I was able to keep her distracted from her loss, she fared much better in making it through her days.

* * *

In response to a flutter of activity, I arose to have a peek outside my room and was genuinely stunned to see the Gunninks and Schuellers grouped in the hallway. They were in a cheerful mood and grew most excited upon seeing me.

"Hello, Elizabeth!"

"Opal! Aggie! What are you doing back in Albany? Hello, Mr. Schueller, Mr. Gunnink. This is such a surprise. Why are you all here? Don't tell me you've come for another coach ride." I kidded as I stepped out into the hall to greet them.

"We're here because of you," said Opal laughing.

"Because of me?"

"We have brought you something special," said Aggie.

"Oh noooooo! Please, don't tell me that—." I began to protest.

"Now, now, ladies," interrupted Mr. Schueller. "Let us not cause Miss Claussen any undue stress just yet. Tell us, ma'am, how does Mrs. Whipsman fare?"

"So kind of you to ask, Mr. Schueller." I looked back toward the room and lowered my voice. "She is getting by, but it is every bit as painful as you might imagine. She will need time. My heart goes out to her."

"She is most fortunate to have someone such as you, Elizabeth. For that matter, aren't we all?"

"Oh, Opal! Please! You embarrass me, so." I blushed.

"Opal embarrasses us all," said Mr. Schueller.

"You shush your mouth, Charles, or I'll really embarrass you, and on that you have my word." We all laughed.

Mr. Schueller continued, "Miss. Claussen, we would like to ask—no plead, *beg* that you breakfast with us tomorrow. Let me say that we are most impatient to discuss the issue of the SCHOOLBOAT with you, and if you refuse us this request, we shall hound you forever without mercy."

"Glory be! How do you know about the SCHOOLBOAT?"

"There are no secrets along the canal," said Opal. "The best gossip ever—and fast."

"And surprisingly accurate," added Aggie.

"It's true! Lock to lock and town to town, word of the SCHOOLBOAT has made its way as far up as Buffalo. Everybody between has been watching for it. You've stirred up a good deal of excitement with your plans," said Opal.

"We're convinced it has to be one of the most remarkable and inventive ideas ever," said Aggie.

"It's so sensible—."

"Ladies, please. Never mind all that for now," Mr. Gunnink interrupted. "Let us leave you to your evening without further disruption and take up the matter tomorrow at the breakfast table. We have much to offer you in your venture, Miss Claussen. Will you join us?"

"Absolutely. I would be honored to say the least."

"Very well then, until breakfast."

"Thank-you. I don't know what to say. It's wonderful to see all of you again."

"And you. Until breakfast, then."

"Until breakfast." I answered.

"Good evening, Miss Claussen."

"Good evening."

We parted company and I went to Dorrie's room to sit and share my surprise. We were in the habit of leaving our doors open, and she had been watching from her room with curiosity while caring for her boys.

* * *

The next morning, Dorrie and I entered the dining room to discover the Schuellers and Gunninks already seated and awaiting our arrival.

"Good Morning, ladies." The men wore broad smiles as they rose from their chairs and came around to seat us.

"Good Morning, gentlemen." I returned. "You already know Mrs. Whipsman."

"Yes, yes, of course. Good Morning, Mrs. Whipsman."

"Good morning, all."

Dorrie was quite uncomfortable knowing it was the cargo aboard her vessel that nearly cost Mrs. Schueller and Mrs. Gunnink their lives. She was visibly nervous, but our hosts were kind, sensitive enough to notice, and quick to ease her remorse.

"My word, young lady, say nothing more, not a word. We are greatly saddened by your suffering and loss. With all there is to worry about, you having children and all, our mishap with the coach is nothing by comparison," said Aggie. "Besides, the Good Lord should have killed us off years ago."

"At our age, we have faced the grim reaper many a time and learned one only passes through the pearly gates when God wishes it. You can hardly be blamed," said Opal.

"Your words are both kind and comforting, but I can't help knowing what damage I have been party to," said Dorrie.

"You must put this behind you, Mrs. Whipsman," said Aggie. "Know that this is the work of God, for whatever his reason. It is not our place to question his ways. He has a divine plan of which we all are a part. As terrible as his hand might seem, it has purpose and righteous reason, even when appearing dastardly from every angle."

"That is the truth of it," said Mr. Schueller. "Let us take this SCHOOLBOAT for example. Who would have guessed that something as marvelous as a floating school might rise from your tragedy and lead the way to betterment for so many under-privileged children and their families?

"I assure you, Dorrie, the Lord has a design for your life in spite of the pain we all know you suffer," said Opal. "I am certain he believes you are strong enough to carry out his will. I suspect very soon you will see his reasoning in the results of these noble intentions. I mean to say—are we not four arrived from Buffalo with the sole purpose of supporting you in this venture? Is that not a sign in itself?"

"Understand, Dorrie, that the Lord has a purpose for us as well," said Mr. Gunnink. "These events most certainly have

346

occurred to provide us a way of doing his will. Consider that the Lord returned us to Buffalo a month ago disappointed and unsatisfied at being unable to show Mrs. Claussen our gratitude. And while steeped in complaint, word of your venture arrived in what clearly appeared to be a second chance to show our gratitude."

My ears perked up immediately. "Surely you aren't saying you have expended such energy solely to repay me for stopping the coach. This is really unnecessary, and by—." I was interrupted by Opal.

"It may have started out that way, dear, but put your mind to rest for that is far, far, behind us now. Actually, during our journey here to Albany, we had so much time to think on this undertaking, that we realized there is a great deal of satisfaction to be shared by all.

"Elizabeth, dear; listen to me. You are young and as beautiful a creature as I have ever seen. I, we, on the other hand, have long since seen those days pass us by—."

"Speak for yourself, Opal."

"Shush, Aggie," Opal retorted with a roll of her eyes. She looked back at me. "The four of us have been so far blessed with good health and we feel much younger in years than we look. Unfortunately, the rest of the world sees us only as a bunch of old busy-bodies, and never consider that we might yet have much to offer."

"We have a lifetime of connections," said Mr. Gunnink. "We have done more business up and down this valley than these young upstarts could ever imagine. We know how to get things done."

Mr. Schueller spoke up. "We so cherish the opportunity to do something constructive in the autumn years of our lives. I mean something really constructive. Something that will have an everlasting effect on the community, something that won't be taken away from us by young whippersnappers or politicians. Can you understand?"

"Of course, I understand. I find your enthusiasm wonderful."

"We're not going to be easily put off, Elizabeth," said Opal. "There's too much in this for us as well."

Dorrie and I sat listening to the four, and it was obvious that they had spent so much time discussing the prospects of the school between themselves while en route to Albany that they had formed ideas and visions far beyond anything we might have imagined. Their visions were spelled out in word and pencil at the table for our consideration, and in the space of three hours over hot coffee and eggs, months of expected work and preparation all but vanished.

At the conclusion of breakfast, it was decided foremost that Dorrie would never live in fear of poverty. Aside from what we already put away for her security, she would be given a stipend sufficient to care for herself and the boys, and the services of a financier to help invest her savings wisely. Furthermore, she would be allowed to keep any monies paid her for field trips by students that sought out her knowledge in the geography and history of the region.

Secondly, it was determined that qualified teachers and speakers would rotate tours of stay to best advantage for presenting their own lessons and lectures. They would offer classes to young and old alike, but always with a mind to help the transient canalers before all others, for this was to be a school for the large and overlooked boating community.

"Very well then," said Mr. Schueller with pencil in hand. "It's settled. We shall cover all shortages and the costs of Dorrie's stipend, the driver and steerman's wages, the upkeep of the teams, and all maintenance on the boat for the next three years. We will look at our situation again at that time, providing any of us are still alive." The four laughed. He looked at me. "You are certain that Mr. Claussen will agree to cover the cost of the boat and whatever expenses arise both expected and unforeseen?"

"I have no doubt whatsoever. I have placed funds in his behalf for many years in order to support all manner of charity. I can't begin to tell you the fortune that has passed through my hands alone in his name. This venture will be dear to his heart because Mr. Claussen is especially fond and sensitive to the needs of children."

"Does he have children of his own?" asked Aggie.

"No. I am certain he regrets the fact. I often think he is lonely because of it."

"Is he married?"

"No."

"You and he have a lot in common."

"Yes, I suppose."

"I trust there isn't a dreadful *Claussen curse.*"

I laughed. There was a moment of awkward silence. I imagined they wondered how people of obvious wealth could be so alone. I was merely a spinster, but they must have wondered if Christopher was unbearably eccentric or ugly and misshapen? It was too long a story to relate, and to utter a word about it only prompted more questions, and so I kept my thoughts to myself.

But it was there, deep within my thoughts, that I missed him. I missed those days when I pondered over his advice and followed his direction in these matters. I wished just once I might tell him how much suffering had been vanquished by his generosity. I wished that through my eyes he might have seen how over the years his invisible hand reached out to help so many in need, especially the children. He must have brought happiness to a thousand children, if any at all. He would approve of this school. Of this, I held no doubt. It was after all for the young, and the young remained forever close to his heart.

The conversation was rekindled, and I returned my thoughts to matters at hand. In hopes of seeing the school pay its own way, the four would initiate an effort to raise public awareness and contributions along the canal and organize the numerous volunteers already waiting within the communities that stood to benefit. They commented many times on their gratitude for having been given a project that felt so worth their while.

"I intend to have a plaque engraved and mounted on the SCHOOLBOAT that recognizes your efforts and contributions."

"What!" The four were horror-struck. "We would never stand for such a thing. It is gloating at its worst and we wish not to be braggarts."

"Indeed it is, but you have no choice. If you refuse my plaque, I shall refuse your assistance. I must tell you that I am well versed in the ways of successful charity. I had a wonderful teacher and learned much.

"Consider the plaque as a means of stirring up a little guilt in the conscience of onlookers as we travel town-to-town, lock-to lock. All they need is a little nudge to do their own part. If having their names mounted on the cabin of the SCHOOLBOAT becomes fashionable, you will see contributions enough to buy three boats. This I promise."

There was plenty of grumbling, but acceptance, and it was there that we called it a morning. It was now time for good-byes. Dorrie, for one, was growing anxious and feeling pressed to look in on her boys, and so we rose from the table as a group and parted in the best of moods.

Privately, I felt confident about this endeavor, believing that Christopher's account would back me, and that the school would most likely come into being whether we received help from others or not. That is not to say I didn't flinch at spending such large sums of money on the repair of Dorrie's boat, the price of a new one, and the start up costs incurred. I was relieved to see contributions from the community quickly grow in size and number.

If I wished to know the limits of my spending, this project would certainly be a good test, for I was unable to return money earned or refunded back to the account. For my own peace of mind, I decided that without knowing whether Christopher was dead or alive, I might as well spend his money without worry until something fell out of the sky to flatten me, or someone showed up to set me straight.

THIRTY-ONE

Dorrie proved she knew well the business of boats and canaling; I believed far more than even she realized. Her knowledge impressed me, for she handled every aspect of our operation without a hitch. She sought a strong and healthy team, hired a driver for ten dollars a month and a steersman for fifteen, both having dispositions agreeable toward children. She located a packet currently under construction in a reputable yard, and acquired it at just over two dollars a foot. She assumed control of the designs and build without hesitation.

"The yard has promised me we will have the boat in time to make Buffalo before the canal is drained at the end of the season."

"Excellent."

"I have worked out fitting all the lockers and storage bins for the blankets, tinware, and toiletries. And don't worry, I have put in plenty of shelf space for books and school supplies. Right now, I'm working on the berthing quarters for adults and children, and of course the galley, but I wish I knew how big that stove will be."

"Big, really big."

"I know, you keep saying that. Oh, that reminds me, I asked the carpenters to fashion a canvas awning for the deck. Robert and I never had one, but I have seen them on a number of packets for the benefit of the passengers. They're made to be raised

351

and lowered quickly at the bridges, and will allow the children to stay outside during the hot sun or rain. I promise you it will be well worth the money."

"That's fine, Dorrie. You do whatever you feel is best for everybody. Have you purchased the team yet?"

"Not yet. I wanted Buzzy to look the animals over. He's the one that will be driving them. I'm sure he will be happy with them. It isn't as though we are a commercial boat and need to keep a strict schedule of team shifts every six hours, twenty-four hours a day, seven days a week. As a matter of fact, I've decided there's no need for two teams and that will save us a lot of space normally needed for the bow stable.

"It's a good team. Three mules will allow us to rotate the animals and drive them nine or ten hours instead of six if need be, or to replace a sick or lame mule. I mean; I don't foresee that as a problem. Usually one worries about spavins or hocks disease, but we have no weight to haul, we're not in any kind of hurry, the team will rest well each night and I doubt they will ever suffer the ailments or abuse of hard driving. We don't have to buy a third mule, but the team has worked together, and I think best for the money."

"Go with your instincts, Dorrie. I won't question much."

Indeed, books would be the heaviest things we intended to haul. Auctioning books would be a big part of our fund raising activities. We would provide books and study aids to wanting families in upper New York, and those traveling in the direction of Ohio and the Michigan Territories. The books would be carried westward from these points with the movement of the *foo-foos* as Dorrie often called the foreigners going west.

I made no effort to slacken my expenditures. In fact, once started, I spent Christopher's money liberally while entertaining hopeful fantasies of driving him out into the open so I might find him. I passed a small fortune to be sure, but to my dismay, I heard not a word of question or objection.

Time passed by quickly in its attempt to keep up with our hectic schedule, and between Dorrie's responsibilities governing the boat and her two boys, she was spared precious little of that time to dwell on the painful absence of Robert.

I grew confident that Dorrie was now strong enough to stay alone, and so began leaving her in order to accompany the Schuellers and Gunninks on day long engagements. At every opportunity, I worked to teach them the ins and outs of community fund raising and the best methods of establishing a foundation for supporting the SCHOOLBOAT through social activities.

In return, they made good on their claims of having many connections and the ability to get things done. I was introduced to nearly every individual of influence in Albany and then some. Somewhere between Dorrie, the Schuellers, the Gunninks, the engagements and introductions, I made time to write Mary and Allen.

My dearest Mary and Allen,

Glory, glory, glory be! If I were at this moment speaking instead of writing, I would be entirely out of breath. Such is the pace of my existence. I cried for a change of pace, and I have gotten it. The richness of life has returned to me, and I cannot believe that September is already upon us. I was only to be gone for a few weeks, and already it has been more than two months. Impossible!

I am still with Dorrie and happy to say that her spirit improves with each passing week in spite of the heavy cross she bears. She has single-handedly purchased and outfitted the SCHOOLBOAT all the while keeping her boys in line. It is easy enough to see that she is every bit as shrewd as she is loving. You would admire her.

The Schuellers and Gunninks are still with us here in Albany, assisting in whatever way possible. There seems no limit to their generosity or determination. In fact, it seems Dorrie and I are

353

mostly assisting them in their endeavor. They are as energetic in character as any I know. They have taken me around Albany for introductions and the opportunity to see to it that every effort is made to further the cause.

We will be soon leaving Albany to make our way locks-up for Buffalo where I plan to winter. I know this must come as a surprise, and I hope not one that is hurtful. I pray not to upset you. I will have time to better explain once we are underway and left with little to do but sit and float westward.

My conscience and better judgement deem it both pointless and heartless to return home knowing Dorrie still requires a helping hand, the SCHOOLBOAT needs all the support it can muster, and that I have comfortable accommodations at hand for a trip to Buffalo in my search for Mr. Claussen.

Suffice it to say that I have been told there are many establishments in Buffalo owned and possibly visited by Christopher, whereas there seems to be nothing of him in Albany other than his concerns. I must have been mad to think different.

For now, I wish only to see this letter posted while in Albany. I will write a proper letter soon. Give my love to all, and know how I miss Josh and Juny, and the both of you.

Love, Elizabeth.

THIRTY-TWO

The construction of the *'SCHOOLBOAT'*, as it came to be called, went on to be completed as scheduled. All of a month passed while outfitting, and by the time Dorrie, I, and a couple hundred supporters gathered in good cheer to celebrate its christening, the season was all but finished with September.

It was the middle of October when at last our stove arrived, and we battened down the hatches to cast off from the boatyard. During our stay in Albany, Dorrie and I had made many new friends and acquaintances, the majority of which gathered atop their boats or came to the canal to see us on off. Word of mouth, also known as the *'towpath news'* had brought people from miles around.

"Full freightings, friend! Full freightings, captain!" hollered the other boaters.

"Full freightings!" Dorrie and Carter would reply.

Amid a chorus of cheers, kisses and prayers, the SCHOOLBOAT began its slow and leisurely journey westward 'locks up'. The Schuellers and Gunninks were waving from their coach as they paced us. They too were now heading for Buffalo.

I watched as the warmth of the crowd's affection receded into the background beneath an autumn sky. The days were growing shorter. The clouds looked badly bruised, being pushed about by an arrogant cold-hearted northern wind that predicted winter's coming. It opened and closed its gusty grip, scooping and dropping rushes of multicolored leaves into the water around us.

Overhead, Canadian geese took up their ages-old formation and pointed south for calmer climates. Day skies alternated between chilly ice-blues and thick drab grays. The valley abandoned its luxuriant green mantle in favor of vibrant maple yellows and colorful crimsons blended with the multihued reds and browns of beech and hemlock.

High in the nearly naked branches overhead, departing leaves opened views to balled up nests of bickering squirrels, round and fat from summer feeding. Some sprawled out lazily upon the branches, flattening themselves to absorb the waning summer heat, while others dashed down exposed tree trunks to dart noisily across the crispy ground cover with purpose, burying acorns, and giving yet another tell tale sign of a hard season approaching.

355

Whether my chill was from the wind or my heart, I wasn't sure, but I went below to fetch a wrap.

Impossible as it seemed after all that happened in Albany, we were underway at last and leaving the city and its vibrancy behind. Everyone was in a good mood, laughing and high-spirited. We had gotten off without a hitch and although the boat moved along smoothly, for me the glee was short lived. I had taken my place up by the bow for a better view, and had a good fifteen or twenty minutes of canal life firmly under my belt when I was startled by a boater's yell.

"Low bridge, heads down!"

The warning echoed across the water from a boat that was approaching from the other direction. We were about to pass one another beneath a bridge that appeared wholly incapable of spanning one boat let alone two. I looked at the bridge and new instinctively that we were in for big trouble. My first impulse was to jump ship, but I had to warn the others, so I turned toward Dorrie and Carter at the stern and started running in their direction.

The drawback of the SCHOOLBOAT was in it not having a hold chocked full of goods and so it traveled light, meaning it rode high in the water. So high in fact that from the bow I could see we were about to scrape the bottom of the bridge. It was far too low for our boat to pass beneath, and I was not about to see all our work destroyed in one unlucky moment.

"Hold on! Hold on! We're about to strike the bridge! Dorrie! Dorrie, look out!" I hollered as I descended the steps at the stern. I thought of Buzzy, our new driver walking the towpath and driving the team. I spun around to look ahead in his direction. I raised my hands to my mouth and yelled out his name. He had precious little time to stop the mules.

"Buzzy! Buz—."

Dorrie was walking quickly back from the bows, silently communicating with Carter, the steersman at the tiller. She was

Heads Down

clearly focused on me, and reaching up, she placed one hand on my mouth, while turning me around and pushing my head down with the other. She completely undid my move to warn Buzzy of the imminent danger. lunged for me, grabbed me from behind by the back of my dress and pulled me off balance thereby interrupting my warning to Buzzy. I was too surprised by her actions to be annoyed.

"Good lord, Elizabeth, hush! It's all right. We aren't about to hit anything." She could barely get the words out. It was obvious she didn't believe me for she was laughing hysterically. Carter was laughing as well. "Trust me, I have traveled this canal a thousand times. The boats are built with the bridges in mind. Listen to me, the boat will never hit the bridge no matter what it looks like from a distance, but I can absolutely guarantee that you will get clobbered good should you forget about your head. Watch out for your head, and nothing more. Do you hear me? Do you here me, Elizabeth? *Low bridge, heads down.* Worry about your head."

Dorrie's words made perfect sense. I felt like a complete fool, but even so I wouldn't take my eyes off the bridge. I wasn't about to say aloud that I didn't believe her, but I didn't. I gauged the distance to shore in my preparation to jump ship.

"Yes, Dorrie. I hear what you say, but are you certain?"

"I am certain. Absolutely certain."

I clenched my jaw and my fists, then crouched lower and lower as the bridge came upon us looming solid and unmoving. I braced myself and then was entirely let down, so to speak, for we came quietly upon the other boat, and the two of us glided beneath the stone structure to exit opposite sides.

Dorrie was right of course. She was right this time and every time thereafter, but by little more than two or three inches. It took a couple of days and a number of bridges before I stopped dreading each passing and gave my trust fully over to those with the experience and promises that we would never collide.

I did learn that when it came to collisions, it would be a common occurrence between passing boats and not bridges. As often as not whenever two boats approached to pass from opposite directions they swiped each other. Eastbound boats had right of way, but it didn't matter, we always got the worst of it.

"I guess it's my turn," said Dorrie.

"What do you mean?" I asked as I regained my footing following a solid swipe.

"The lighter boat takes the brunt of the collision. Something has to give way. I'm not used to getting kicked about because after having spent so many years hauling stone, I forgot what it means to take the worst of it."

We learned fast about giving way while on the first leg of our journey, which took us from Albany to Schenectady. This was one of the busiest stretches of the canal. There were some-where near three thousand boats plying their trade on the Erie.

We refused to get caught up in the mad rushes, instead choosing to abide by the law of four miles an hour. We took our time and allowed ourselves to be overtaken if need be. This trip was intended to be pleasurable, a chance to wind down, and an opportunity for me to learn first hand something of life upon the canal, which I noted religiously in my diary.

We spent a lot of our time talking, so much in fact that Buzzy and Carter spent most of their nights sleeping on board instead of bedding down at the taverns as was the norm. Most canalers were hard drinkers and there stood a tavern spewing grog at every lock with a good many in-between. A pint of whiskey cost six cents. A 'foamer', which was a tankard of ale, cost a fip, also six cents. Applejack ran twenty cents a gallon up and down the locks. In spite of the fact that for three cents Buzzy and Carter could get a mug of grog and a night's boarding, they were more inclined to stay with us. They remained respectful of our feelings and understood that impressions would be an

360

important aspect of the SCHOOLBOAT. They stayed sober and dignified.

I aimed to use the journey for spreading word of our intent and showing off the much-expected SCHOOLBOAT. From the get go, we found ourselves well received at every stop with folks lining up at the banks to talk and take view of our vessel. This was in no small part due to the Schuellers and Gunninks who were up ahead spreading word of our approach.

We had no plans to employ teachers until the following spring, and so, Dorrie, her boys, Carter, and I accounted for all souls on board. Buzzy was usually on the towpath with his team of *'long-eared robins'* as drivers often called their mules. Without exception, everyone expressed interest, often asking about attendance for their children. They offered a chorus of encouragement, and more often than not a contribution to help us press forward with our endeavor and their requests for more SCHOOLBOATS.

During those times in which I was not promoting our cause, I was steeped in learning all aspects of keeping the boat shipshape. That included caulking the cabin roof and scrubbing the decks. It meant working in the bowstable, feeding the team their hay and oats or sometimes corn for a treat, as well as shoveling up the soiled bedding and tossing it overboard. It meant helping Dorrie feed Buzzy, Carter, and the boys. I learned how to properly harness the mules and fit their collars and whiffletrees. I mastered sending them on their way down the plank.

On occasion, when we found ourselves traveling after dark, I would follow the mules ashore and walk alongside Buzzy on the towpath. He claimed I was the prettiest *hogee* he had ever seen making *walking passage along the ditch*, which was a canalers term for a driver and his work on the canal. He was especially appreciative after dark when passing cemeteries. He called that the graveyard shift and claimed no driver alive liked walking it alone so far ahead of the boat. I understood why; it spooked the living daylights out of me.

I learned a lot listening to Buzzy while we walked. Boaters who traveled the entire length of the canal during a season were called *'single trippers'*. Those boaters who owned packets and traveled back and forth called their trips *'tricks'*. Packet owners slept on board their boats in cuddy quarters unless they chose to stop the boat at night and go to the tavern for grog.

I learned that the first boats along the canal each spring were part of the clean up group called the *'fog gang'*. As soon as the ice gave way, it was their job to remove all the debris either afloat or submerged before the traffic started for the season.

The towpath upon which we walked was of clay with a surface of gravel packed hard by the thousands of horses and mules that trod upon it. At least once every half an hour throughout the day and night, another boat, either a packet or a freighter and its team would pass us by.

Buzzy would generally drive the mules for about eight hours locks up, putting an average of fifteen miles behind us each day. The distance depended on what happened at the locks. Between Dorrie and Carter, I leaned a great deal about life in the Mohawk valley both on the boat and off, both present and past.

I learned that our journey through the valley would take us three hundred and eighty four miles; that we would pass through eighty-three locks and raise our boat five hundred and sixty five feet from the waters of the upper Hudson to the level of Lake Erie. Dorrie viewed the trip as being made up of four parts. The first, being from Albany to Schenectady.

Buzzy explained that if we were in the business of hauling cargo, a three-mule team could easily tow a boat, which when loaded could haul up to seventy tons of freight. There was talk of canal boats currently being built that would soon haul upwards of one hundred and fifty tons. Our team would only have to haul the weight of the boat itself for the most part, and this would enable us to make good time or great time,depending on whether we went locks up against the wind and current or down.

We expected to arrive at Tonawanda, our final destination near the shore of Lake Erie around the second week of November. The trip would take three or four weeks depending on the wind for we were traveling light. By the time we reached Lake Erie, the season would be at its end and the canal would be drained. The SCHOOLBOAT would either be moved to the middle of the canal and left to wait out winter resting on the bottom until re-floated or else be hauled for the winter lay up.

We headed up the canal to Cohoes and rose almost one hundred and seventy feet going through a number of locks in the space of about three and a half miles. We were moving along the south side of the Mohawk River and passed the town of Crescent, named because of the shape of the river at this location. It was here that we crossed over the river to the north side by means of a sensational aqueduct. It was the longest one built along the canal and measured just over eleven hundred feet.

We followed the river along its north bank for about twelve miles to the Rexford flats, and then crossed the river again this time to the south shore on another aqueduct that measured about six hundred feet. This brought us to the sizable city of Schenectady, or 'Old Dorp' as they called it, the end of the first leg.

Dorrie and Buzzy pointed out a number of interesting things including a very old fort built by the Dutch in the year sixteen ninety-five. This was an area of old battlefields and historic villages. They repeated Silly Billy's claims that in the days before the canal, it was virtually impossible to navigate this stretch of river between Albany and Schenectady because it was so treacherous.

We continued our journey westward past many small villages, some appearing almost overnight along the banks to partake in the growth of business. On the north shore we came to a very famous place in these parts called Guy Park Mansion. It had been built by Sir William Johnson in seventeen sixty-six. A few miles following, we came upon Fort Hunter and Queen's Anne

363

Church, which was built for the Indians and recently torn down to make way for the canal.

Fultonville now appeared, and this place had been well settled even before the canal passed through. There was a blacksmith, a mill, stores, an ashery and sawmill and plenty of other small business, all very active.

"Ya see there 'cross the canal?" asked Carter as he pointed to a small village.

"Yes," I answered.

"That'd be Fonda. When the season's done in, the drivers takes their wages an' drinks 'em up till they're clean broke. This goes on all up an' down the whole canal 'til they's spent out, tired an' hungry. At that point they all comes t' Fonda an' gets themselves thrown in jail. You see, after that they can then spend the rest of winter in a warm place eatin' good an' sleepin' dry till spring. Then they gets turned out walkin' away with full bellies and big smiles. Bunches of 'em do it; it's a fact, you can ask Buzzy if'n ya think I'm stretchin' the blanket."

"I believe you, Carter, I believe you."

"The shenanigans and tomfoolery about the canal is reaching a frightful state with the drinking and all," said Dorrie. "The Puritans and Baptists are all in a fit over the sinful state of affairs, and they aren't alone. There's an attempt underway to stop all activity along the canal on the Sabbath just to keep the day holy."

"Will they succeed?"

"Not a chance, but it's a raging battle to be sure. The amount of trade and travel is so enormous that nothing can stop it. Every couple of days a new town sprouts and all these places use the canal to move about. I can't imagine anybody closing it, not even to keep the Sabbath holy."

Indeed the people of this area were colorful. I grew up learning much about how the English settled the eastern shores of America, but never heard much about the many early French,

364

German and Dutch pioneers in these western areas. It convinced me all the more that this was certain to be a wonderful learning experience for any student that would have the privilege of boarding this floating school.

We passed through the Appalachian Mountain chain and came to the Village of Sprakers. We crossed over the river again at Bauman's Creek near the village of Canajoharie. The Mohawk Indians named this village for a large hole in the riverbed that formed a cistern about twenty feet in diameter. The name meant 'the pot that washes itself out'.

Right across the river was a place called Palatine Bridge that was settled in seventeen twenty-three by early German settlers who came here to escape religious persecution in Europe. I tried to imagine what it must have been like trying to survive here a hundred years ago, fighting the river, the forest and the Indians.

Shortly thereafter, we passed another old fort, this one built in seventeen thirty-eight, and which saw much of that Palatine Bridge hardship and the blood spilled in the French, British and Indian wars.

I watched many old and historic monuments move slowly past on our way to Fort Dayton and the early settlement of German Flats. We passed by Ilion, where the thriving Remington facilities were located. It employed many in the manufacture of firearms and farming equipment. There was industry, employment, and a sense of vigor to be seen everywhere in this area of the valley.

We continued on through Frankfurt, another industrial village settled in the early seventeen twenties. Then came the well-known city of Utica, which marked the end of our second leg. About nine miles west of Utica was the Oriskany Battlefield where General Herkimer was ambushed in August of seventeen seventy-seven. He and his story were one and the same with this place and it appeared as though everything was named after him.

"This is Rome, Elizabeth." Dorrie spoke to me as I observed the town approaching. "This place is significant because it marks the beginning of the old Erie Canal. You see the first part of the canal, when it was constructed, only went from here to Onieda and then directly to Syracuse, which was famous as the 'salt city'. I think we will snub here for the night. The day is unusually warm, the place is friendly, and the kids have a good field in which to frolic."

The fine weather provided Dorrie an opportunity to clean house or should I say boat, without the nuisance of her energetic boys being underfoot. When they didn't stretch their legs and work out their get-up-and-go, they soon became unbearable in the close confines of the cabin, especially after having to watch the passing of such a wonderfully sunny day this late in the year. Jack and Kenneth weren't brats, in fact they were quite obedient and well mannered, but boys were still boys.

Dorrie was not alone in her decision, for other keelboats were snubbed to the bank and engaged in similar activities. A good number of children were to be seen running about, playing games in the sun and raising the dickens. The activity attracted vendors and sightseers, and there was a growing gathering of sorts made up of friends and strangers, and those curious about the SCHOOLBOAT.

I generally tagged behind Dorrie, assisting her in whatever way I might, following her instructions, and happy just to be of help. Once the boat was secured, we released the boys and watched them bound off like a couple of scared rabbits. At the same time, Buzzy and Carter took the mules out to forage in a nearby field.

Only Dorrie and I remained behind. We spent our time chatting away while lazily hauling blankets, towels, clothing, and what-not off the boat to spread about the bank under the warm afternoon sun. The sunlight removed the damp, while a gentle breeze removed the odor of mildew and freshened the fabrics.

As the afternoon wore on, the crowd grew and many more people besides the canaler children were moving about the banks and walking up and down the towpath. New faces appeared among the regular crowd of canalers. They came from town and were anxious to make extra money by selling fruits, vegetables, clothing, baskets, ropes and various other boater's needs. These people moved freely up and down, in and out, and I paid them no mind. Not so with Dorrie.

"Elizabeth." She called to me under her breath, while we stood together with our backs toward the bank. She didn't turn her head in my direction and instead appeared to be occupied in retrieving the push poles.

"Yes?" I sensed something mysterious in her voice.

"Have you noticed the man walking back and forth along the bank, the one that has been watching us?"

I started to turn toward the bank.

"No! Don't turn about," she whispered. "He's heading back this way and watching us as we speak. He's up to no good. I know the kind; I have seen it many times. He is a thief. He's making sure our men aren't about. He'll soon know Buzzy and Carter are gone with the team, and it's just you and me, so you do just as I say. Do you understand?"

"Yes." I was instantly nervous and put all my faith in Dorrie.

"I want you to take the other stub, pretend we are occupied with some chore, but stay close behind me and pay attention. I'll likely be wanting that pole in a hurry."

Dorrie grabbed a 'stub', that is to say a push pole that had been snapped in half at some time in the past and was now shorter, only about eight or nine feet long, hence the term 'stub'. It was useful in tight quarters to push off banks or other boats that came too close in order to avoid a collision, and there were always a few lying about ready for the taking on short notice.

367

Dorrie released the stub from its resting place on the deckhouse roof, raised it over our heads, then turned about and descended the horse plank. She looked down at the ground as though distracted by some object. I reached for the other stub, and as I turned to follow Dorrie down the plank, I glanced quickly along the bank to my right and glimpsed this approaching man of whom Dorrie spoke.

He was a brutish looking fellow of medium build. His eyes were darting in every direction making certain no one was close. In the last second, I saw him focus his attention on our brass galley lantern and simultaneously break into a run. Indeed, just as Dorrie has assumed, he looked to be a thief, and one who had sensed his best opportunity to steal was at hand, for Dorrie was still on the horse plank and I on the boat. I was helpless to do anything, but watch him steal the piece.

His arm shot out, and quick as a fox, he snatched up the lantern and ran past Dorrie just beyond her reach. It was almost a taunt, he being aware of her inability to stop him and even her fear to make such a foolish attempt against the brawn of a grown man.

"Stop! Thief! Thief!" She cried out. Then to my amazement, Dorrie raised the stub over her shoulder and threw it directly as a spear. It sped through the air like a bolt of lightning quickly overtaking the culprit until the blunt end of the pole caught him square in the back between his shoulder blades with a tremendous force and a resounding thud. The blow must have been incredibly painful, for the thief was driven forward from the impact and nearly fell flat on his face. The lantern went flying free of his grip and bounced along the ground, rolling away from his reach.

The brute staggered, momentarily paralyzed, but soon regained his balance. Instead of running off, he was overcome by blind anger and embarrassment and so turned about to confront us. His face was fully contorted with rage, a face smeared with an expression of murder in the making and one that easily convinced me I should run for my life.

He next reached down for the fallen pole and after grabbing it, to my horror; he let out a horrible scream and raced straight for Dorrie. He clasped the pole by its end, raised it overhead, and then swung it down toward her like a giant axe. I feared she was doomed for no person's head or shoulder could survive such a crushing blow.

Her scream "thief" raised attention at once among the boaters, but not soon enough for anyone to come to her aid. They had only just begun to look our way. I was petrified, frozen in place and as worthless as teats on a boar. Dorrie, on the other hand was suddenly facing me, her back toward her attacker. She had spun around and grabbed the opposite end of the pole I instinctively held out toward her. She swung the stub in a large overhead arc, bringing it upward to meet the man's axe-like assault, then deflected his pole and forced his strike straight into the ground. I was utterly astonished. I stood there wide-eyed and slack-jawed. What luck!

I snapped out of my surprise just in time as the pole came swishing past me in a giant sideways arc, causing me to throw up my arms and leap backward out of harm's way. The end of the stub sailed past me and stopped dead at the back of the stranger's knees, laying him out flat on his back and knocking the wind out of him for a second time. Suddenly her move didn't appear to be a matter of luck at all.

Even before the brute had time enough to be surprised, the pole returned to the sky and sliced down through the air in that earlier axe-like fashion to deliver a blow of full force across his exposed ribs. I heard them crack from where I stood a good twenty feet away. He was stunned and unmoving, and so was I. My eyes were big as saucers. I didn't know whether to laugh or

369

cry, to clap or run for cover. I had never seen anything of that sort in my life.

A number of people were now approaching on the run, hollering and carrying on at seeing such a show. They pounded their chests and laughed uproariously, standing directly over the fool and mocking him for messing with a 'canal gal' carrying a 'stub'.

Dorrie didn't retrieve her lantern. She didn't bask in the rounds of applause and tribute. Instead, she turned to walk past me, her eyes flooded with tears.

"If my Robert were here that never would have happened."

My surprise and intended cheers were instantly subdued as Dorrie disappeared into the cabin. I was unsure as to whether it was the rush of adrenaline or emotion that brought the tears, but her comment did bring home the fact that as women we were vulnerable—and also the fact that I really wanted to know how she did those things with that pole!

I left Dorrie to herself, feeling it best to leave her below to regain her composure, and it was a good thing she did because news of her action spread like wildfire up and down the bank and even into Rome itself.

The next thing I knew, the constable, the mayor, the town elders and business leaders were all coming by to offer a contribution to the SCHOOLBOAT along with their apologies to Dorrie for the blemish cast upon their good persons by this scoundrel. Everyone had been waiting for the SCHOOLBOAT, and the elders would have wished for a more dignified reception. As if their wish were coming true, food and tables began to appear, and because people attract people, in short time a large gathering of nearly two hundred people formed to have an unplanned picnic.

As we sat and ate, I listened and learned how Dorrie had come to acquire her skills with the 'stub' or 'staff' as she sometimes called it. Robert apparently taught her the art to perfection through games during their years spent together, and although this was a matter of surprise to the town's folk, it wasn't such a strange notion among the boaters. I recalled on tall ships how the men resorted to clubbing each other with belaying pins.

I made Dorrie promise to teach me the art. She agreed, and I got my first lesson that afternoon at the picnic. She had been asked to demonstrate her abilities and she gave me a pole to hold over my head. She told me to keep my hands far apart when I gripped the shaft and she proceeded to bring her pole down forcefully across mine. She scared the wits right out me with her first blow, and I practically collapsed to the ground after dropping the stub and running off.

"Come back here you scaredy-cat," Dorrie hollered before a crowd that was splitting apart with laughter. "Don't forget your opponent's first objective is to crush your fingers."

"I think she crushed my spirit." I complained to the onlookers.

"Come back here, you fraidy-cat unless you're not woman enough."

The crowd roared. I returned, picked up the stub, and didn't forget. And as the days went by, I strove to learn the use of the 'staff' with eagerness. I loved the wonderful feeling of power and security I received from something as benign in appearance as a stick. The feeling was intoxicating.

The merriment ended in the wee hours of the following morning when the last of the respectable folk left the heat of the fire. Only the young men and drifters remained, many of them falling asleep where they lie. I helped Dorrie shuffle Jack and Kenneth back on board and into their bunks. They were past tired and almost welcomed the order to bed. This last nightly ritual brought finality to the day, which had been a long one and left me all but done in. We retired.

THIRTY-THREE

A late start was the best way to describe the next morning. Buzzy managed to get the team out onto the towpath and start us moving toward the Seneca River. This was a region of marshy lowlands that held great promise for New York because of its thick rich soil. The area boasted some of the most productive fields in the state.

The drawback with so much moisture was mosquitoes. They were absolutely unbearable. They were the most bloodthirsty and persistent pests I had ever encountered. For the sake of my sanity, after being driven below deck by another suffocating swarm, I climbed into my bunk and threw a blanket over my body. I remained hidden there for a couple of hours struggling to ignore the rash of itchy lumps that covered my body.

Dorrie chided me by asking *"what mosquitoes"*? She claimed I was being a baby, for it was late in the year and the mosquito season was long since past.

I gave up my sanctuary only after giving in to Dorrie's repeated pleas to come out and help her catch fresh vegetables from the farms we were passing. She claimed a breeze had come up to hold the pests at bay. I doubted her every word, but out of sheer curiosity, I risked further misery and went topside.

The fall harvest of squashes and pumpkins, apples and corn were plentiful and could be seen stacked everywhere along the banks awaiting transport to Albany and New York. Dorrie was actively dickering over prices with one farmer in particular out of a group that were walking along the embankment. Behind them were rows of grain laid down neatly with cradles and scythes. There were others who were working together fanning and flailing husks or driving horses in a sweep about the pole to power the newer mechanical threshing machines.

"Eight cents voor a pumpkin." He sounded firm.

"Five cents, I can't catch the big ones, and I'll give you three cents each for ten squash."

The man rolled his eyes with disillusionment. "Hard bargain. T'row me jouw money."

"Absolutely not! Throw me your vegetables first."

"What! Furst jou talk me down to nodding, en nowu? How do I know jou'll pay? Maybe jou're dishonest. I don't want no red dogs or bank notes. Women are deceivers," he taunted.

"How do I know you'll throw the vegetables? Fact is, you have a lot more vegetables than I have cash, so you should take the risk."

"A shrewd mind. I pity jouw husbands."

"Husbands! We aren't married. What husband would get potatoes two for a penny? We need husbands about as much as you need bugs."

"Really?"

"Really, and we aren't interested in anything but what you grow."

"I may haaf someding speciaal growing right nowu."

"Oh! You are indeed shameful, sir. Where is your wife?"

"I keep asking myself dat same question."

Dorrie laughed; his companions howled. I was hoping to move quickly through the issue of husbands.

"He's niet married! Jou better watch dat one," they warned.

"Do you wish to sell your produce or not? I'll be buying from the next farm by the time you decide."

"Of course I wish to sell, but if jou drop anyding on deck or in de canal, jou still pay, yah."

"Agreed!"

With the help of his friends, the farmer collected some vegetables, reached for a squash and tossed it our way. Dorrie fumbled for it and handed it to me. The men laughed at her girlishness, but Dorrie left strict orders for Carter to stay at the tiller and leave the two of us to our own device.

The farmers thought the sight of Dorrie and I trying to catch pumpkins and squashes was just plain hilarious. I wasn't about to catch a pumpkin thrown from shore, so when one came my way, I turned about and let it smash against the side of the boat. The men howled with hilarity.

"You best not break my windows!" Dorrie scolded the men.

I wasn't sure whether I was humored or annoyed when Dorrie whispered to continue acting clumsy and keep the farmers laughing. I had no problem in doing that, for I wasn't about to get myself bowled over by a pumpkin. In the end, to satisfy their desire to play with the ladies, we ended up with four times the amount of vegetables we had asked for and this made for a very good purchase. I began to see the wit in Dorrie's madness.

"How about some corn. Twenty ears, I'll buy!"

"Goed deal!"

The farmer tossed another and another, first this way and then that. He kept Dorrie running every which way. The last few he tossed so quickly that she was unable to keep up and they fell to the deck.

"Remember, jou pay voor what jou drop!"

"In no part thanks to you," she hollered. "And don't forget the potatoes, ten for twenty, you agreed!"

"How could I forget!"

The farmer began tossing the potatoes and again for fun tossed a good many extra just to see Dorrie and I scamper about. The potatoes were rolling all about the deck. There were plenty of misses, and between the smashed pumpkins and squash, trod upon potatoes and corn; there were plenty of messes as well.

"I'm not paying for your amusement," Dorrie warned. "If you choose to throw vegetables at us to be mean-spirited then you'll have to swim over if you want them back. I'm only paying for what I asked."

"Don't say het, or I wil bring jou back too!"

"In your dreams!"

"Keep dem! Het was wort' de laughs, but nowu jou owe me en jou haaf fared well voor de price of my amusement!"

"So I have." Dorrie agreed.

Dorrie searched through the potatoes and picked up a perfectly round large one in which she held up so the farmer might see her drive the coins into its meat.

"There you go sir, no red dogs. Have a good day!" She tossed the potato purposely short forcing the farmer to leap frantically forward. His fingers brushed the vegetable but he failed to grasp it. Instead, it fell to the ground where he clipped it with his foot sending it rolling toward the canal like a ball. The men plowed into one another in their attempts to stop it, but this last laugh was to be to ours. It was comical indeed to see *them* stumble about before the potato plunged at last over the edge of the bank and disappeared into the water.

"You need some women to teach you how to catch," hollered Dorrie.

"I know if jou were t'rowing a rolling pin, het would haaf made het te de next county."

"A shrewd mind!" she retorted. "A shrewd mind, indeed, sir!"

We wasted no breath in chiding them all for being a clumsy lot, fully incapable of catching a small potato. And they being of good nature laughed along, none considering the money worth the discomfort of wading into the cold water. They left it to a youngster wishing to earn himself a penny. Even Buzzy was walking backwards along the towpath and taking in the fun.

"Come back te see me!. I want to sell jou someding speciaal!" The farmer yelled as he faded into the distance.

"I will if ever I'm starving!"

In the distance, the farmer cupped his hands about his mouth.

"Promise!"

"I promise!" Dorrie looked at me and laughed.

* * *

We decided to take supper in a basin at Weedsport. The basin was built by two wealthy sons of a successful Albany merchantman at a place where boats could turn about and load or discharge cargo without interfering with the canal traffic. According to Dorrie, it had been the brothers, who began the adjoining settlement of Weedsport. This area of the canal had been finished about eighteen nineteen or twenty. In those days the boats were only running between Syracuse and Montezuma.

Dorrie and I were practicing with the stubs on the bank while the Jack and Kenneth romped through the fields.

"Do you want to hear a really terrible story?" She asked me.

"How terrible?"

"Gruesome."

"How gruesome?"

"Very gruesome, bloody, gory and most indelicate for a lady's ears. Do you want to hear it or not?"

"Spill the nosebag!" I exclaimed. Buzzy was always saying this when he wanted to hear gossip.

"In August of eighteen twenty-five, when they officially opened the canal as completed the whole of it's length and the dignitaries floated through in celebration, locks up and down, the canal was one big party. Everybody was dancing and drinking and carrying on. There had been a lot of preparation beforehand for the event and everyone was looking forward to a good time. One of the events planned was the firing off of a celebrated cannon to mark the occasion. It was a twenty-four pounder and that is one big cannon. Have you ever seen a cannon fire? Have you ever heard one, or felt it?"

"Mm-hmm. Matter of fact, I have." I remembered it well in spite of all the years passed. I was on the deck of the REBECCA as a child, and it wasn't the firing of a cannon, but rather the blizzard of a broadside. It had knocked some of us off of our feet and was an experience one could never forget. It was impossible, and even now I could smell black powder in my mind. Dorrie continued.

"Well, something went terribly wrong and the cannon misfired while there were men standing in front of it. It blew one David Remmington into oblivion, nothing much of him was left found to be buried. And another, one Henry Whitman died a few hours later. Of course, as always, the ones left to suffer are the women and children. There were two young wives with their children, who witnessed it all and were left in a state of horror and despair, not to mention being left from that moment on to fend for themselves. Needless to say, it cast a terrible shadow on the event for all of those who were still sober enough to realize what happened."

Although, I grit my teeth as my imagination played upon her words, I was already grinding my teeth through rock hard bread and an appetite that seemed to have no end.

We practiced another hour or two with our staffs and decided to stay over the night in Weedsport. We continued on the following morning, where a short distance farther we came by a place called Port Byron.

According to Dorrie it used to be called Bucksville after two brothers who settled it in the late seventeen nineties. The name was changed to Port Byron a couple of years back to capitalize on the canal business. Name changing was something that occurred quite often as the canal was changing the nature of life in the region and bringing prosperity to folks doing business with settlers moving past their fields.

As we glided past the village we listened from behind a crowd of curious onlookers surrounding a man who called himself Henry Wells. He was standing atop a stagecoach and trying to drum up investors in an express coach service to the western reaches.

We then arrived at Montezuma where the first boat was built for the canal back in eighteen twenty. It was named after the town itself and carried passengers to Syracuse on its maiden voyage. Just west of here was the village of Clyde and it was named after the river that was the main means of travel before the construction of the canal.

I looked out over a wonderful city called Palmyra. It had been purchased by John Swift and Col. John Jenkins in the seventeen nineties. They had it surveyed into farm lots, and it was well developed and settled long before the canal made its way to their doorstep.

Town after town, so many with historic stories to tell, communities of such interest and so willing to reveal their colorful pasts for the students we hoped to bring to their reach on the SCHOOLBOAT. The journey was full of interest and diversity and I could understand the attraction to labor its waters. We were faced with few incidents or inconveniences, but when they occurred they were usually notable.

One such incident had to do with the aqueduct in the Rochester and Genesse area. It was a very narrow structure and required taking turns between eastbound and westbound boats. Occasionally, someone would err or grow impatient and intentionally take their turn out of sequence. More often than not, like now, as we waited in line, an all fired fist fight would erupt.

378

Between drivers, steersmen and crews, two commercial boats easily carried ten men, and it was nothing to assemble the necessary numbers to form a full-scale riot. We were witness to just such an event, and I swore at times, men caved each other's heads in just to break the monotony of their dull witted minds. It was a scene wholly out of place within the tranquil surroundings of the canal.

"There's no shortage of brawling," confessed Dorrie. "Most of the time its between the boaters, but lots of times its between the boaters and the lockkeepers or landsmen. Lockkeepers can make your life miserable if they don't like you. They can make you wait for cribs of timber to be floated through and you might spend two days stuck at the locks until they let you pass. Then once you are in, they can empty the lock so fast that you fly out on a waterfall of current and go spinning and crashing into the boats down below. I've seen it all."

Another incident I found astonishing left me laughing in disbelief. We were making our way peacefully along just west of the riots in Rochester when we began to ground. I felt the thudding of our hull on the bottom of the canal, and Carter, our steersman, moved us out into the deeper water at the center of the canal as did many of the other boats. I could see Dorrie and Carter, as well as Buzzy, looking about and signaling to each other. They quickly snubbed the boat.

I went to Dorrie who was speaking with an informed intuition. She said the water level was dropping and that meant the canal bank had been breached. As often said, not everyone was thrilled with the new canal. Near this area of Rochester, the teamsters who represented the wagons that hauled freight across land would occasionally sabotage the canal to disrupt the flow of freight handled by the boaters in order to drum up some extra business on land. I saw the bank watchmen and repair crews moving frantically along the towpath. Even so, we sat grounded for two days, much to my amazement.

Without question, the most heartrending part of our trip came as we approached the sandstone quarries. We had reached the Hulberton area. It was an area of new development, all within the last couple of years, and there was a well-outfitted store to service the canal traffic. It catered to the quarry traffic, and it was shortly thereafter that we came to Medina.

There was much boat traffic here servicing the new Ryan Quarry where Dorrie's husband Robert had been working. She broke down almost at once and we saw little of her for the remainder of the day. Although I was very concerned for her, I stayed above deck with Carter and cared for the boys, leaving Dorrie to sort out her grief in as much privacy as I could afford her. When she returned to join us, she did so after dark had settled in so that we might not see the rawness of her eyes. She came on deck with a spread of food.

"Hi."

"Dorrie! How are you feeling? We've been worried."

"I'm fine. I'm sorry I didn't make supper—."

"Don't even say it."

"You should have at least come down and grabbed the bread and cheese. Here, I've heated up the chicken"

"We didn't want to bother you."

"Ohhhh." Dorrie let out a long breath. "I think I have cried out every ounce of my strength. Seeing the quarry was hard."

"How do you feel now?" I asked.

"Oh, I feel better, I guess—tired."

"Come, sit down. Next to me, come on."

"Let's call it a night, Carter," said Dorrie. "We should have done so hours ago. Buzzy must be dead tired. Buzzy! Buzzy! Bring the team in! Let's eat and call it a night!"

Carter and Buzzy were more than happy to oblige. They secured the boat, bedded down the mules and returned. At first we all sat together on deck with the boys and began to eat, but the night air had grown too chilly. We then went inside and sat at the table where we realized just how hungry we really were once the food touched our lips. We ate until we couldn't breathe, moving one final time only to find our bunks.

* * *

The closing of our journey along the Erie Canal commenced with a pass through the Rock Cut, which was a particularly dangerous place along the canal for man and beast alike. The vertical granite walls rose high over the canal having been carved into the cliffs. The drag of the boat, rope, wind, current, or just a misplaced step could spell severe injury or death from a fall off the narrow towpath. I was very nervous for Buzzy and thanked the Almighty when he passed through safely.

It was soon after, that we entered the crooked flow of Tonawanda Creek and tied up in a town of the same name. Tonawanda was bursting at the seams with growth. It was more like I might imagine a frontier town to be. It was thriving and yet everything seemed only half-finished. There seemed to be too little time to attend to details.

Lumber mills and wood working businesses were gaining a firm foothold in this area because lumber was being funneled through Tonawanda from the Great Lakes regions, upper New York, and Canada. All variety of establishments were opening their doors to turn raw lumber into finished furniture. There was much work in progress to meet demand and the call for workers attracted immigrants of every nationality.

Tonawanda was a good prelude to Buffalo, where we arrived after a short jaunt the following morning. We had reached the end of our journey, and were met with great fanfare by the

Schuellers, Gunninks, and a sizable crowd of supporters and curiosity seekers.

Between Dorrie, Buzzy, and Carter, I was introduced to the Erie canal and upper New York in such an intimate fashion that I found it every bit as interesting and spellbinding as my travels past the Adirondacks and the majestic mansions of the Hudson.

The slower pace of the canal offered me ample time to appreciate all I was shown. It gave me time to stuff memories into my diary pages, to convey accounts of the wonderful sights to Mary and Allen in my letters, and also to search for Christopher. I did in fact find signs of him as of late along the way. He had been especially active in this area about Tonawanda and Buffalo, leaving in his wake a lumber mill, a store, a furniture manufacturing facility, and a boatyard.

Back in Boston, I hadn't dreamed of the attraction that the canal would have presented to Christopher. He had passed through my life on his way out west long before the waterway was built, but it was obvious he had returned to investigate the potential for profits in this region. I found no one who could claim to have seen Christopher in the last couple of years, but I was growing more confident than ever that I would eventually find him.

I had now traveled as far into the interior as had any of my close friends or family. Only those orphans I knew through my letters lived in these borderlands and beyond. I made every effort to locate Jennifer Laketon who wished very much to see me, and at last correspondence was living in the Buffalo area.

My inquiries proved disappointing. Jennifer and her husband were presently trapping in Canada according to what I had been told by those who knew the couple. I have no doubt she expected me and was heartbroken at my failure to arrive when planned, which should have been months earlier if I made it as far as Buffalo. Who could have foreseen the events in Albany that would change everything?

"*Everything* has changed."

I said the words aloud as I stood upon the shore of Lake Erie and saw nothing before me but an endless sea of water. I stared at the distant horizon, beyond which lurked stories of mountain men, trappers and Indians, riches and dangers unknown. I felt no trepidation, only the curiosity and wonderment of my youthful years, for that flat featureless body of water served to forewarn me of how vast was this country.

Somewhere out there was Christopher. For all the space that might exist between the two of us, I felt closer to him now than at any time in the many years past. My ages old devotion to this man had been fully rekindled and the anticipation of seeing him again brought me only happiness and peace of mind. I had made him my heart's destination, and I could feel myself being drawn to him. It was though I were fulfilling some unknown but necessary need deep within my being.

THIRTY-FOUR

Sunday the seventh of November was an exceptionally nice day and belied the typically chilly, grayish gloom that was normal for this rainy season. All up and down the bank, children of the canalers were squeezing out the last of a lost summer's day.

Dorrie and I practiced with the stubs for a while, but then took a break to catch our breath and make the best of an unexpected opportunity to escape her maternal obligations and leave the boys on their own for a spell. So rarely did we find time to ourselves that nary a second was wasted in efforts to get away from the boat. Once assured that Jack and Kenneth were playing safely with friends under the watchful eyes of trusted parents, we disappeared.

Over the last two months, my friendship with Dorrie had fully blossomed, becoming both close and personal. I missed Mary dearly, and I suppose it was only natural that beneath the surface of my business façade, I should invite the nearness of another. I was feeling sisterly and the two of us were bubbling with laughter and babbling away in conversation, making the best of our time beneath the warm and sunny sky as we trekked into town.

It was a Sunday and everything was closed as expected, but we were content to stroll the main street bidding a good day to passersby until reaching the north end of Buffalo. There, to my delectation, I spotted another of Christopher's concerns. A marquee affixed to the building above two large barn-like doors advertised Claussen Supply.

I didn't hide my joy at this happenstance; for whenever I saw the Claussen name, I took it very personal. I felt duly attached to the signature, believing it was a part of me and that I belonged to it. In my mind, I held certain rights, certain claims. Inwardly, I was sinfully proud of being associated with the Claussen name, its reputation, and all the weight and good that went with it.

My face must have clearly reflected this delight because at that moment, for the first time ever, Dorrie questioned me pointedly about Christopher. To my surprise, she was deeply curious about my relationship with him, and although she was delicate in her probing, she freely admitted to finding it most mysterious and hoped this once for some answers.

"What I am trying to say, Elizabeth, is this; I have listened to you speak of Christopher as though he is a person very close to you, very close to your heart, like a stepfather or maybe a dear uncle. Yet, when you find something of him, such as this marquee, you act as though you haven't seen hide nor hair of him in *years*."

I listened with amusement. I couldn't help but to smile and encouraged Dorrie to continue. "Go on. What do you mean? Tell me why do you think that?"

"Well—it's like when you offered to pay for the repair of my boat. You spoke of Mr. Claussen as though he were merely a town or two away and that his funds were readily available for your use, but that you still needed his approval, or at least you were very concerned about having it. It was as though he were watching your every move.

"I always assumed he was just out of sight, across the street or down the hall. I mean, why would I think different? Then something is said and this impression falls apart leaving me with a feeling that he's a million miles away, someplace far beyond your reach. I mean, to be frank, we have spent all this money and I have yet to see a glimpse of the man. I find it all puzzling and mysterious, and have paid closer attention. Often I wonder if you are searching for something hopelessly lost, which makes no sense to me because I can't imagine you to be a dreamer or one to run about on a wild goose chase.

"I can't imagine it, because you are too sensible. You are so polished, Elizabeth, so upper class. You know, educated and confident. All those things, that is why until today I have never asked anything personal. Even now, just asking about this is difficult for me. I know at times I can be short on manner, and the fact adds to my fear that you might think me rude and nosey or even worse. I know, I am a commoner—."

"Oh, Dorrie. I could never think that. I admire you. I have from the first day we met. I know I must come across haughty, but I don't mean to. Honestly. It's just that my younger years were spent in training to be a perfect maiden in service. The things one learns at such an early age stay for life. Nowadays, if I don't carry myself just so, or do everything just so, I feel—I don't know—like a bad little girl."

"Oh, please, Elizabeth! I have never thought of you as being haughty. You are anything but. Perfect? Yes. Perfect in every way, I swear… but haughty, *never*. Your life is not my business, and mostly I want you know how grateful I am for all that you and Mr. Claussen have done for me during these past months.

They certainly would have been the worst weeks of my life, and I can't imagine how I would have managed without the two of you. I have no wish to meddle in your affairs, but so much of the time I feel uncomfortable, even cheated I would say."

"Cheated?"

"Yes, in a way. You see; I accept you, Elizabeth, perfect as you are. Your help, your advice, I love you for all that you have done in my behalf, for all that you have done for Jack and Kenneth. I have taken you into my heart. But it is unsettling that you should know the most personal things about me and my boys, not to mention those intimate things I've told you about Robert, yet I hardly know anything of you. Do you understand what I am saying? The arrangement isn't fair.

"I mean, I answer most every question you ask of me. You know me inside and out, and yet, when it comes to my knowing you, even after two month's time in each other's company, I am only slightly less confused today about who you are than I was the day we first met. I never feel comfortable asking anything of you. I'm always going about talking to myself or asking questions to my broom or a teacup."

Dorrie spoke her piece. She had let loose her feelings with hope that I would be kind. I felt very good about Dorrie, and I turned toward her with warmth and understanding. I took her arm, pulled her tight to my side and laughed. I thought it very funny what she said.

"Oh, Dorrie! I promise I'm not trying to hide anything, but I swear I am probably only slightly less confused than you. I gave up trying to figure out my life, let alone my relationship with Christopher, years ago. And no, I don't think you are being nosey or rude. I never realized you desired to know something more about me. I have only paid mind to helping you overcome this ordeal, and I never gave thought to the idea you would wish to be bothered with my concerns. How inconsiderate would it be for me to carry on about my goals or my frivolous disappointments when your entire world collapsed? I haven't lost a husband, Dorrie. I haven't lost a son. My issues can't compare."

"Oh, but I do desire to know, Elizabeth. I've always wanted to know more about you. You seem so universal to me, so wealthy and yet so mysterious. Often I think of you as being supremely kind and yet sad, like a lost angel that has fallen from the sky. I see it in your eyes when you look at Jack and Kenneth.

"Now, if we had been sisters, I would have sat you right down and said, 'Hey! Who are you exactly? And why are you sad, and what is going on here between you and this Mr. Claussen, and what is he to you anyway? How come you're not married—or are you married, and what about kids. Where are your kids? Where you ever in love? Did you ever sleep with anyone? Was your heart broken by the only man who mattered? No secrets between sisters, Elizabeth. I would want to know everything down to the smallest detail!'"

I took no offense to Dorrie's directness. To be truthful, it felt wonderful to have someone who might ask such personal questions, someone who was sincerely interested in my life now that Mary was no longer at my side. I liked to talk about Christopher, but why would anyone want to listen. Why would they care whether or not he played a major role in my life? It was unusual to find someone genuinely interested, and I was more than happy to explain something of my past.

"You would want to know everything, but there just isn't that much to tell when seen from a distance. I'm sure I've told you most everything. My life is routine, simple, full of accomplishments and material wealth and empty of heart. Honestly, there just isn't that much to tell.

"Now as for Christopher, that's a different story. What can't I say about Christopher, but that he has cared for me in every possible way since I was about nine or ten years of age, since first I first came into his employ. At that time we lived in Sweden. My mother had been sick for a long time and my father knowing he could no longer keep the family together, sent me off to the Claussen estate, telling me I was to go on a short holiday. My mother died soon after my departure."

"I'm sorry to hear that."

"It was a long time ago. Actually it was Christopher's wife, Lady Rebecca, who took me in and cared for me. She was English, as was my mother. Somehow they had met, maybe at the market, I don't know, but they had become friendly toward each other. Lady Rebecca was a most remarkable woman who was orphaned at birth. Like Christopher, she also was generous, and she was devoted to me. I loved her dearly.

"When it came to Christopher, in the beginning I was scared to death of him. After awhile, I accepted him as something of a father figure, but I always thought of him as more of a god. He was like a great king to me at that age. I believed with all my heart that he could do anything, catch stars, calm the seas, feed the multitudes; it made no difference. I was utterly convinced he had magical powers, and I lived in awe of him from the very first day I stood at his table to serve.

"I remained at the estate in Sweden for only a short time, after which he brought me to America to attend to Lady Rebecca, and although I was only a maiden servant, he raised me as his own. He was a wonderful master, stern, yet forgiving, dead serious, but funny, a generous man in every way. He was especially fond of children. During my growing years he lavished me with gifts, but most important, he and Lady Rebecca showered me with love and gave me a home in light of my mother's passing.

"I was very close to Lady Rebecca and seldom left her side in my younger years, but I was inexplicably attracted to Mr. Claussen. He was a giant of a man, and I would sneak around to spy on him. I watched his every move with mixed feelings of fear and excitement.

"Then, as fate would have it, Lady Rebecca fell to an untimely death, which turned my whole world upside down and left both Mr. Claussen and I devastated. He arranged for me to be cared for by his first maiden servant, Mary, who raised me and is to this day my best friend ever. As we speak, she is most distressed I have not returned home.

"Anyway, it wasn't long after Lady Rebecca's passing that Christopher left to sail the seas. He was gone for years, and I used to write him letters that were pages long, me whining about my trials and tribulations or bragging up my accomplishments. He never forgot me, never let me down, and always responded with advice and encouragement, no matter what corner of the earth kept him away.

"Over time, growing older, and seeing things differently, my perception of him changed as one might expect. He was no longer that king, nor even a father so much as a best friend or something of the sort. Maybe soul mate would best describe him. I could talk to him about anything, no matter how personal, and that's what we did for years by letter.

"Christopher drove me to better myself. He magnified my every triumph, regardless of however trivial. The fact that I was a woman never altered his ambitions for me. He had me convinced that I was capable of anything. He encouraged me to chase my dreams. He gave me my dreams."

As I spoke, I was unexpectedly caught up in a wave of emotion that both surprised and embarrassed me. I had to catch my breath, and turned away in a failed attempt to keep Dorrie unaware. I faked a cough to clear my throat.

"Forgive me if I have pried too deeply...."

"Oh, no—something in my throat." I patted my chest. "I was only going to add that it is hard to find a man like that anywhere. Believe me, I have looked. You seem to have been luckier."

"Nobody gets that lucky. Does he have any unmarried friends?"

We both laughed. To hear Dorrie joke about an issue regarding men so soon after Robert's death caught me off guard, and I realized that she was trying to accept her loss in stride, trying to put the tragedy behind her. I could only imagine how difficult was the task. I thought her a brave one as I dried my eyes.

"Actually, it's funny you should say that. I have often wondered if Christopher had any friends at all. I have only known him to be a loner. His wealth has been his burden. He told me that many times. He knows a multitude of people, everybody who is anybody, but stays to himself. We were close when I was young, or so I thought, but I have come to question that more and more as time goes on. Maybe I just thought we were close. I don't know, I may be wrong. Somehow, we lost touch and at least for me, I can say that my life has been the worse for it."

"Maybe, I should envy you. The relationship sounds heavenly. A confidant, a mentor, a little distance to keep the heart longing; if Mr. Claussen were a husband, he would have taken you for granted ages ago, believe me. I mean, I loved Robert with all my heart, but men are men and they are mighty annoying most of the time."

"So I have been told. I suppose my view of Christopher is distorted because so much of it was seen through the eyes of a child. I don't know. I just remember him directing my affairs, giving guidance and all. After Lady Rebecca died and he sailed off, I only wanted to die.

"I remember that most of all. It was rough at first, very rough, but I was young and the young survive. Fortunately, I had Mary and Allen to support me. They were wonderful. They made my life rich and happy. There was no lack of love and affection or caring from either of them. Even so, there was always this little pain of sorts, it would come and go. From those days on, I have always been a little bit lonely. I go on with my life as must we all, but I never forget. I wonder endlessly about him. I miss him."

"I can't believe you never married, Elizabeth. You are so beautiful."

"Married! Oh, Lord have mercy. The great state of matrimony! The great failing of my life, indeed." I rolled my eyes. "No ma'am, never was, never will be. That's a story of delusion. I was told I had brains, I was told I had beauty, I was told I would fall in love and be swept off my feet. Someday my life would be filled to the brim with bliss and I would live happily ever after with my one true love. Wrong! Never even came close."

"I'm sorry, I didn't mean— ."

"No, no, it's nothing for you to fret about. I am a spinster, Dorrie, and I have gotten used to it, learned to accept it as my lot in life a long time ago. And besides, it has certain benefits. I am free to do things like travel the frontiers and meet the likes of Dorrie Anne Whipsman. Couldn't do these things if I were married."

"That is true, but I would still rather be married. I don't like sleeping alone at night. I tend to worry about every little noise. I get lonely."

"Loneliness is just another form of pain, Dorrie. You look for things to distract you from thinking about it. If I pinch this hand, the other one doesn't hurt."

"Why is it *that* important you find Christopher now? I mean, after all these years."

I took a deep breath and thought about the question.

"Honestly, I don't know. The easy answer is that I was bored with my life and it always seemed to me that things happened around Christopher. I thought searching for him would bring me back some of my youth and the excitement that was so much a part of it. So far, I can't complain.

"The 'not so easy' answer isn't as clear. Something pushes me his way. I can't explain it. I just feel it. I am drawn to him. I get almost desperate to see him on some days. He keeps me restless much of the time. Now he even has me wandering the earth." I laughed.

391

"So you have no idea where he is?"

"None, whatsoever."

"And you are off on your own to seek him out? Are you not even a little bit afraid for yourself? I mean after all you are a woman and traveling alone. I would think that very dangerous. I don't believe I could do such a thing. I would be too frightened."

"Really? It surprises me to hear you say that. I find you so capable. I mean you travel all the time, and god help a man should you have a stub in your hand."

"I travel, Elizabeth, but I know every inch of this canal from one end to the other, and I know the boats and families. I know the towns. I know what to expect and who to meet, and who not to meet. It's no more than a big back yard to me. There is nothing here to fear. I don't see it that way for you. I would be scared to death to do what you are doing."

"I am not sure what to say." I shrugged. "I hear the same concerns from others as well, but so far it's not been bad. The people I meet are always friendly and helpful. I jot down their names and addresses in my journal and I feel I can count on them should I run afoul. I have made a trail of friends and acquaintances. And then, each time I stumble upon another of Christopher's concerns, I feel I'm in his backyard. Actually, in an odd sort of way, the farther into the frontier I travel, the closer I feel to him and the less worried I become."

We stopped before Christopher's building and I fell silent, enjoying that sensation of closeness that I had described to Dorrie. The place was closed for the Sabbath and stood in a row with many other establishments to soak up the deep pumpkin colored rays of a late autumn sun. The day was truly a 'left over' from October's Indian summer and utterly void of the depressing nature of November.

I felt good, and wishing to absorb more of Christopher, I decided to look about the lot.

"I'm going over to that window to see what's inside. Do you want to come with me?" I pointed to the side of the building.

"Sure."

We left the street and walked alongside the building to its small windowpane, so I could have a look and see.

"What's in there?" Dorrie asked.

"It's so dark in there I can hardly tell, and this glass is awful, too wavy. Everything is so distorted I can hardly make sense of anything I see. Here, you look." I backed away so Dorrie could take a look.

"I can see a stack of logging hardware—a lot of crates—chains." She rubbed the glass clean and looked again. "There must be another window at the back because there is light coming in over there."

"Is that so? I'll go around back and have a look. You wait here."

This I did, and as Dorrie assumed, another window came into view. Unfortunately, about seventy or eighty newly made wooden barrels that were standing on end about waist high were between the window and me. I would have to traverse the lot in order to make my way to the pane for a look inside.

At first I wasn't sure it was worth the effort, but I looked about and saw no one who might think me up to mischief, or who might observe me performing an unladylike act. And so, I turned my back to one of the barrels and pushed myself upward in order to sit upon it. I rose to my feet and stood atop the first row of barrels. Stepping carefully from barrel to barrel, I made my way toward the rear window.

The barrels were large, empty, and unstable. They wobbled beneath my every step forcing me to keep my eyes upon my feet in order to avoid a fall. And so it was, out of the corner of my eye I sensed something amiss only after it was nearly underfoot. It was a space between the barrels that lay a short distance ahead.

The space made me suddenly wary. Had something moved? Had I heard something? Was it just my imagination that spooked me? I was troubled enough to stop and study the shadows that filled its area.

I was aware that Dorrie could not see me, and if there should be any foul play, I would be the worse for it. So working up my courage, I stepped cautiously over to the next barrel and only then slowly on to another. My eyes remained fixed upon the crevice between the barrels.

A bolt of fear sliced through me. Something moved! This time I was positive, and although it was slight, it stopped me dead in my tracks. I stood motionless and stared. I wasn't up to calling out for Dorrie lest I discover an old alley cat or sleeping dog bound to make me the fool. But what if it was a mean dog?

I glanced quickly behind and prepared myself to turn and run at the drop of a hat. With a foot ready to move either way, I chanced another step, another barrel. I leaned forward and studied the shadow, my eyes fixed upon the darkest region. There was definitely something there. The devil being my curiosity, I was driven one step closer to make better sense of what I was seeing. Slowly, the form became recognizable.

Lo and behold! My realization came as no small surprise. Before me was a black woman huddled upon the ground in that crevice-like space between the barrels. I watched her for a moment and wondered if she was sleeping or worse. I called out to her, but she did not respond. I stepped across the last remaining barrels and looked directly down upon her. I called again, but the young woman was either sound asleep or unconscious.

She lay there curled up within the folds of a large tattered shawl. She was dressed in rags, the remains of formerly fine clothes representative of a servant in good standing. She seemed unaware of my presence, so I dropped to my knees and studied her. Upon closer observation, I saw she was mumbling incoherently. Then she lifted her head and looked at me, but I wasn't sure she realized I was standing over her. By action and appearance, it was apparent she was in a bad way. Her sunken features led me to believe she was very sick, dehydrated, clearly half starved, and one could only guess what else. Judging by all that I saw, I suspected her to be a runaway slave.

I rose to my feet and casting caution to the wind; I ran across the wobbling barrel tops to their edge and dropped to the ground. I raced around the building toward Dorrie, who was now leaning up against the window with her back toward me, and looking out across the street while awaiting my return.

"Dorrie, quick, quick, come quick. I need your help!"

"What's the matter?" She turned to face me.

"There is a woman back there who is in a bad way. I need your help." I reached for her arm.

"What woman?" She asked nervously.

"I don't know—a Negro woman, a servant or a run-away, I think. I'm worried she might be dying. If she isn't, she must be frightfully sick. Come on, hurry up." I pulled on Dorrie's arm as I headed back toward the rear of the building. Dorrie pulled back at once.

"A Negro woman?" She hesitated and even then would only be dragged along with a good measure of restraint.

"Yes, she needs our help, come quickly now."

Dorrie followed me to the back of the building, but made no attempt to hurry. I scaled the first barrel and prodded her to do likewise. I brought her back to the small space where the woman had crouched in hiding or so it appeared. We stood there looking down at her, unsure of what to do next.

"She looks terrible," said Dorrie.

"Doesn't she though. We have to lift her out and get her back to the boat. She needs attending."

"Why don't we just fetch help and let a doctor 'tend to her?" Dorrie was visibly nervous. Her reaction to the urgency of this situation had been standoffish from the start and seemed contrary to the character of the woman I had come to know.

"Dorrie, your hesitation surprises me. This seems so unlike you. Do you dislike Negroes, or is there something here I don't understand? Are you afraid to assist this woman?" I asked these questions in all sincerity. I never thought of Dorrie as dim-witted, and I could only assume she had good reason to behave in such a manner.

"She's probably a runaway slave, Elizabeth. You must be careful—so very careful," said Dorrie with concern most visible upon her face.

"Well, the thought had crossed my mind, but that doesn't change the fact she needs help."

Dorrie seemed to reinforce her warning by looking around fearfully. "We'd be in a whoop o' trouble, to say the least, if it was said we were found to be helpin' her get away. It's a sensitive issue in these parts. She is not the first I have seen by any means. A lot of runaways come north through Pennsylvania. They're all around here workin' their way along the canal, headin' to Canada or Indian lands, or the free states of Ohio and Illinois."

Dorrie studied my face as I listened to all she was saying. No doubt, she expected a reprimand from me, but I understood her concerns, yet, that is not to say I wasn't a little taken aback by her reservation in helping this person who was so obviously in need. I goaded her a little.

"Is this not the *free* state of New York? I thought it was here that passions ran strong to abolish slavery. Is it so dangerous to help a sick woman?"

"Passions are strong here, but that doesn't mean everybody embraces abolition. And even if everybody did, the law states clearly that a runaway is to be returned to its rightful owner and anyone found assisting in the escape of a slave would face the penalty of law, free state notwithstanding. And, the law is strict about it. It makes no difference what I think, she is still property to someone and it's our necks that are in the noose."

"Well, I hear what you say, Dorrie, and you may very well be right. However, as arrogant as this might sound, I must tell you that Mr. Claussen will never allow harm to come my way so long as I am employed in the work of helping others. He has the finances and resources to save me from whatever misfortune this encounter or any of my actions might bring about. It has always been that way, I have no doubt it still is, and it probably always will be. So, I will not be deterred. Now, help me lift her out of here." I took the upper ground, and reached down for one of her arms.

Dorrie shrugged, and with a head full of apprehension, she reached down for the other arm.

"I hope you're right, Elizabeth. I have never run afoul of the law and this scares me."

"Me too. And, I hope whatever it is she's got, it isn't contagious."

"Oh!" Dorrie dropped the woman's arm at once.

"Dorrie?"

"Please, I beg! Scare me half to death! You have nerve, Elizabeth. You have some nerve, indeed!" Dorrie was hardly amused as she reached down burdened further with additional thoughts.

The woman was very frail. There was no weight left to her frame, and she lifted as easy as a child. The only difficulty was in walking her across the barrel tops without us stumbling over each other and falling in-between, for the woman was unable to stand on her own.

It took some effort to get her down off the barrels, but once on ground, our task became manageable. Pulling her arms up over our shoulders, I looked her way and she reminded me of Christ as her head hung lifeless between outstretched arms. I thought her very attractive for a Negro woman. She was fair skinned, possessing doll like features, dainty and becoming. We started back down the street toward the canal dragging the woman's feet as we went.

As Dorrie feared, it was only moments before we drew the attention of others, and only by Dorrie's quick wit did we avert a potentially unpleasant situation. It began with the approach of a large man driving a wagon our way.

"Ladies." He tipped his hat. We nodded.

"See yer in need o' some help. Gotch yourself a runaway, eh?" He shook his head in disgust. "Them slaves all figured they had it bad 'til they were set free to strike it out on their own. They just don' understand it takes a heap of brains and common sense to make good of it. Ya jus don' walk off with a hand full a papers and begin a new life." He shook his head again and snickered.

"I can't say I know she's a—." Dorrie jumped in and cut me short.

"Yes, sir! She's done it before, gets a fever and tends to wander off. Not a runaway though, never been a problem, or one to give us a fit o' concern. We just light out and fetch her back. Couple days of nursing and she'll come around good as ever. She's been worth every dollar paid, but I wouldn't want to be getting' too close to her if I were you. No point in getting yourself sick." Dorrie gave me a stern look, which demanded in no uncertain terms that I keep my mouth shut.

"How far ya gotta bring her?" he asked.

"Just a short ways. We're moored down at the canal. If your of a mind sir, to be aiding us, we would be most appreciative of your wagon," Dorrie whimpered.

"I wouldn't consider anything less. Randall is the name." His voice was deep and fitting for his size. He tipped his hat again then stepped down from his seat unconcerned about sickness and took the woman from us. He lifted her effortlessly from our grasp and placed her gently into the wagon upon some straw.

"Ain't much to her. I guess she don't eat ya outta home and hearth."

"No sir, she's a good one," said Dorrie.

He signaled us to climb into the wagon as he climbed back up onto the bench. We situated ourselves for the ride back, and Dorrie placed the Negro woman's head upon her lap. With little else being said, Randall snapped the reins and we began the short trip back to the SCHOOLBOAT.

Once arrived, Randall removed the woman from the wagon, carried her across the plank, and brought her down into the cabin. He laid her on the bunk with care. I was struck by the thought that maybe his words belied his heart. Maybe he too was an abolitionist, for he showed no reservation about handling this woman we claimed had the fever. We thanked him profusely for his assistance and then turned our attention to the stranger lying delirious within our midst. Dorrie turned to me and whispered.

"I apologize for interrupting you on the street." She was concerned.

"My word, Dorrie. That's all right, don't you fret. You seemed to know best what to do," I replied.

"I was just nervous. It seemed if we went along with his thinking, he would feel confident in his own figuring of the situation and that'd be that." Dorrie looked away.

"Dorrie." I placed my hand on her shoulder. "I agree entirely. You've done what's best. You can't go on being so worried about my feelings. We are friends and it's good you took charge. It all worked out exactly as you expected and we are now returned to the boat, safe, and none the worse for wear. Now, worry less about me and more about how we best attend to this poor soul."

The stranger was clearly ill. She suffered from fever heat and chills. It may have been due to the ague or lack of sustenance and exposure. We began by removing the woman's clothes and effects in order to bathe her. Her ribs were clearly visible making it obvious she was half-starved. She remained delirious all the while we washed her. We toweled her dry, dressed her in nightclothes, and then settled her back into the bunk. We covered her warmly with blankets and saw to everything that might bring her immediate comfort. She seemed to fall into a deeper sleep.

The last thing I did after tucking the woman into bed was to replace a medallion I had earlier removed from her neck in order to wash her hair. After refastening it about her neck, I rolled it about in my fingers. It was not an inexpensive piece.

I was suddenly struck by the fact that her medallion was similar to the one I had seen about the Indian's neck in Albany. The coincidence was cause enough to astonish me and I had a closer look. It seemed the same design fashioned of gold and silver. I turned it over and read the inscription 'CALEB' engraved across the back. Unlike the Indian medallion this one was on an attractive gold chain instead of a leather lace. I laid the piece back upon the stanger's breast and shook my head in wonder. I was amused, for it was a supremely odd coincidence.

THIRTY-FIVE

"Hwere am I?"

A weak raspy voice broke the stillness of the cabin. I turned to see our unknown guest trying to focus upon me. My eyes darted at once toward the hatch where Dorrie had just stepped

400

outside. I looked back at the stranger. The woman had regained consciousness, but was clearly confused. Watchfully, I went to her side and seated myself in a chair that had been placed next to the bunk. I was unsure of her condition, but thought it best to console her by answering the question.

"Everything is fine. You have nothing to worry about. You are on a canal boat in Buffalo and safely out of harm's way. You have nothing to fear. Do you understand?" I looked into the blank stare of the woman's eyes and questioned her lucidity. "Do you understand what I am saying?" The woman failed to reply but I continued. "You have been deathly ill, and I must say, I am very pleased to hear your voice. It means your health is returning. Do you understand me? How do you feel?" Still, there was no response, her eyes yet unfocused. "Are you well enough to eat? Would you care for something to drink?"

The stranger was not up to answering, but I could see how she was struggling to make sense of me. Her eyes were coming to life, drifting around the cabin and then returning again and again to center on my voice until she finally met my eyes. She was becoming coherent. I tried to read her expressions as she studied my face, and was caught quite off guard when she returned to reality with a sudden look of dismay and a question full of tortured disbelief.

"I'm still alive?"

The disparaging whisper of words came thick and dry. She rolled her head weakly in a show of painful disappointment. "I'm still alive," she repeated to herself. "Even the Lord rebukes me." A disheartened sigh crossed her lips, afterwhich she closed her eyes and appeared to drift away.

Clearly, I was taken aback by her words, as would be anyone that heard such pronounced disillusionment. Her disposition quieted me at once and being somewhat unsure of what next to do for our guest, I arose from the chair, feeling it best to summon Dorrie. I could now hear her walking about on the deck, and so stuck my head outside the hatch.

"Dorrie!"

She looked my way. "What?"

"Our patient has awakened." Then under my breath, "For whatever reason, she is deeply troubled. It seems she had hoped to die."

Dorrie winced. I stepped back down as Dorrie leaned in and looked toward the black woman still lying prone atop the bunk. Dorrie then descended the steps to stand alongside me, and together in brief silence we considered the woman before walking over to her side.

It was now Dorrie who settled into the chair. I noticed how there was no longer any sign of the apprehension she had displayed days earlier about harboring Negroes. After a passing thought, she drew herself up close to the bunk and addressed the stranger.

"Is your name Caleb?" Dorrie asked softly. The woman appeared to have been jolted by the question.

"Hwo?" She opened her eyes again.

"Caleb. Who is Caleb? It's the name on your medallion."

The stranger raised her right hand, placing it upon her chest as though to reaffirm the presence of the piece. She stared at Dorrie.

"No."

The woman said nothing more and turned her head away from us. Dorrie lingered, still leaning across the bed. Then wishing not to irritate the stranger, she sat back straight. I too dismissed questions about the medallion for the sake of curiosity, thinking it more prudent to wait. Dorrie started to rise from her chair, but the woman's hand fell away from the medallion and landed upon her arm as if to stop her. The woman cleared her throat.

"Thank you for hwat you done."

402

Dorrie accepted her words with a smile. "You'll be fine, I promise." She clasped the woman's hand firmly and turned to me with an expression both hopeful and perplexed. She said nothing, but we were most certainly thinking the same thought. The stranger spoke in an unusual tongue of southern black graced with a notable English accent. My mind considered the possibility that our patient was a learned person, for this was clearly not the language of a Negro, let alone a slave. Maybe she was a freed person or a foreigner. Maybe she came from Canada, where there was a strong British presence, I thought to myself.

"Would you care for a drink?" I asked.

"Yes, thank-you. That would be nice, yes" she whispered.

I signaled Dorrie to stay put while I scooped out a cup of water.

"Hwere you takin' me now?" the stranger asked in a stronger voice.

"Taking you?" Dorrie repeated. "We are winter bound. We go nowhere."

The woman said nothing, but looked around the cabin as before, only this time with suspicion until bringing her gaze back to Dorrie.

"Hwy would you be helpin' a Negro woman?"

"You must ask Elizabeth. It was she who found you and not I. When she's of a mind to help, there's no other way. Believe me, ...I know." Dorrie's voice broke quite unexpectedly. Curiously, the stranger sensed this.

"You burdened yourself, ma'am?" She asked.

Dorrie nodded her head, quickly regaining her composure. "It's nothing time won't heal, but like you, I also have much for to thank Elizabeth. In the meantime, you must call me Dorrie."

"Thank-you, Miss Dorrie."

"You're welcome."

"Here, drink this slowly." I handed over the cup of water.

"I haven't means to repay your kindness."

"Shush, don't you be thinking any such thing," said I.

"Are kinsmen about?" the stranger asked.

"No," said Dorrie. "Just Elizabeth, myself, and the boys—young-uns."

It was apparent how this news relieved the woman. She was now fully awake and appeared to be quickly regaining her clarity of mind. She was feeling more at ease, and after taking a drink, she began to speak; slowly, softly, but her first words drew our immediate and undivided attention.

"I wanted t' die in worst a ways, Miss Dorrie," she whispered. "I got nothin' left to live for. Nothin'. I thought I woke up in Heaven 'til I saw both o' you an' noticed you were hwite folk. Then I thought, change o' chains, change o' chains. I awoke in Hell an' ain' that a day's way. It was punishment certain for a wantin' to end my hard times.

"Please don' take offense t'hwat I say, I just assumed Heaven would be my own kind—that is, if I have a *'kind'*. I understand now you bin' most merciful, yes, an' that the Lord has decided it is not my time. Hwy, I can' imagine. My life is of so little worth." She drifted off into her private thoughts for a moment then questioned Dorrie anew.

"Hwat is it that weighs so heavy on your heart, Miss Dorrie? It would do good you tell me. Sharing one's sufferings soothes the soul, yes."

I was astonished to witness such a sickly person open her heart for the purpose of consoling another. Dorrie was suddenly the patient and visibly uncomfortable. She withdrew as she contemplated discussing her own loss openly for the first time with a stranger. I felt the issue to be most sensitive and elected to step back from the conversation out of respect. I wished to offer the two of them something of privacy.

"Excuse me a moment, I am going to put on some tea."

I turned my back to both as I went to the stove. There was a brief pause, an awkward silence that pressed Dorrie into motion. She stood up from the chair and worked to assist the black woman into a sitting position so she might drink her water with greater ease. She averted giving a direct answer to the woman's question by asking a question of her own as she brought over extra pillows.

"May I know your name?" Dorrie positioned the pillows

"Oh, yes, yes, yes. Forgive me. Neither mind nor manners are with me. I go by Rachel, Rachel Cook."

"It's a pleasure to meet you, Rachel. I am Dorrie Anne Whipsman, and this is Miss Elizabeth Claussen." Dorrie motioned in my direction. "What I said was true. It was Elizabeth who rescued you and brought you back here to the boat. I was too scared to get involved. I am so sorry. I thought you might be a runaway, and that frightened me. I wish I could say different. But, Elizabeth, she pays no mind to that kind of thing. She scooped you up like a baby, in the blink of an eye, and never gave a second thought. It's just not in me to be that brave. I pray you'll forgive me."

The woman turned to study me. "*Elizabeth.* Always been one of my favorite names, yes. Hwen talked about havin' names, Miss. Dorothy often said she'd a sister named Elizabeth. She'd said Elizabeth meant 'God's promise'. She'd said Elizabeths were chosen by God for to do his work. She'd say chosen, chosen for an almighty purpose. Then she'd say, '*unfortunately, my sister never entirely perceived the Lord's message*'. She'd said in spite of her sister it was still a good name. I have always felt it sounds very English, yes, a very proper name I think."

"I'm glad you like it." I responded.

"I am grateful, Miss Elizabeth, for bein' blessed with such kind folk. Truly, I am embarrassed to have burdened you—."

"No, no, don't say such a silly thing," Dorrie interrupted. "You mustn't feel that way."

"You're too kind, Miss Dorrie." Rachel looked at Dorrie in earnest. " I must tell you although my mind is clouded with uncertainties, *this* I swear. I am not a runaway slave. Don' be a fearin' such things. I have no papers, yes, but I swear before God Almighty an' all his saints, I am not a runaway—at least not in the way you should think."

"It's of no matter for now, Rachel. Whatever misfortune has befallen you, we will remedy it, I promise. You just rest up." I did my best to reassure her. She returned a desperate smile, one quivering with doubt before turning back to Dorrie.

"And hwat is it that saddens *you*, Miss Dorrie?"

Dorrie swallowed hard, but this time faced the question.

"I lost my husband and a son. It was an explosion …both died. It was my youngest son, Jerry. I have been trying hard to accept God's will, to be strong for my remaining sons, but if it hadn't been for Elizabeth standing by my side…. " Dorrie stopped short, her heart in her throat, and said nothing more.

"Your son *and* your man?" Rachel said as if stunned. She shook her head in disbelief. "An' jus' so recently? Ohhh, ain' it a day's way."

Dorrie looked back to Rachel, while holding on tenaciously to what little emotional control she possessed. She nodded it was so.

"Now, if I may say. For myself that is an amazin' thing to hear, Miss Dorrie. The Lord Almighty is a showin' me the error of my ways, for certain. Yes, he must be. I too have lost a husband and a son. Onliest, I wasn' strong like you. I couldn' see no reason to go on a livin'. I didn' believe it possible to go on without those I love, so I gave up. Yes, I said, no more. No more! I wanted nothin' but t' lie between those staves an' die. I prayed hard to step over, prayed hard, Miss Dorrie. I thought certain I would freeze to death, yes, but instead, I awoke alive an' well in a warm bed to bear witness to your own loss. Change o' chains, change o' chains, Miss Dorrie. It's the Lord's mysterious way o' showin' me the righteous path.

"I believe the Lord has said, 'You ain' alone, Rachel girl, you ain' alone, honey'. Yes, I feel that I am suddenly grown stronger. For hwatever reason, I believe the Lord has brought us together, Miss Dorrie. D'you suppose we're meant to be pillars o' strength for one another to lean upon, even if only for this one moment an' nothin' more?"

The two women looked at each other for the longest time lost in feelings that only they could share. A bittersweet bond was forming between them.

"I am sorry for your loss," said Dorrie with sincerity.

"Yes. And I yours, Miss Dorrie. I understand your pain. I do, I do, Miss Dorrie." Rachel smiled warmly, and I could see the heart of a loving and caring woman behind her eyes.

"Tell me about your medallion. Is it then his name we observed, the name of your man?" asked Dorrie.

Rachel stared as though she were frozen in memory, as though she were falling backward through a thousand scenes from her life, a thousand tragedies. She grabbed a hold of some place in time and then spoke slowly, her words weighted with grief.

"You can' imagine hwat I've been through to keep this. I've had to hide it day after day…in my mouth, in my womb", she whispered. "Yes, Caleb was the name of my man. I pray the Lord watches over his noble soul. He was a fine man, a good father. I worry everso for his well being. Yes, this here medallion was a farewell gift from Miss Dorothy to Caleb an' myself hwen she left for England. I treasure it with my heart. It's the onliest thing left I have of him." She raised the piece to her lips and kissed it.

"Tell me about your husband," said Dorrie being openly curious. Rachel turned to look at her with mild amazement.

"You want t' know about my man?" Rachel asked incredulously.

"Of course. Why not, I'm a woman. Don't we all dream about a good man, a good father? You make that sound so strange." Dorrie was amused and awaited a response from Rachel. Rachel, for all her appearances of frailty within the pillows and blankets that engulfed her slight frame, was plainly studying the caring individual sitting before her. She then answered Dorrie in a measured fashion that seemed too powerful for the woman in our midst.

"Yes, Miss Dorrie. That is strange, strange indeed. Nobody asks a negress 'bout somethin' like that. Black women are mostly slave women, slave women don' get husbands. Slave folk don' marry. You know we can' marry, Miss Dorrie. It's against the law. You know that."

"Well—I guess—I never really—Maybe I forgot—." Dorrie was taken aback, suddenly struggling to find the right words. "I...I...."

"Slave folk can' be goin' round holdin' contracts, Miss Dorrie. Contracts would make us reg'lar folk, an' onliest the likes o' reg'lar folks have rights in courts o' law. An courts o' law are too busy to take on matters that ain' party to reg'lar folk. Yes, that's hwat they say. Animals an' slaves have no rights b'cuz instead o' bein' reg'lar folk, they's property. Marriage is contract, an' 'cause animals an' slaves ain' reg'lar folk, we can' be party to contract, we can' marry. So says the law. Our children, they always be illegitimate. They always be property. We ain' reg'lar folk so we can' own property, so we can' keep our babes, we can' keep them children. That's how the law says it."

The room went silent after the not so sublte point of fact. There was a notable bite to Rachel's words. Dorrie was profoundly embarrassed, and so too was I. She shrugged her shoulders and turned away from Rachel to face me. "I was merely curious about Caleb, that's all," she said apologetically.

I stepped forward to rescue her. "We don't mean to meddle, Rachel. We're opposed to slavery. We simply thought you might like to tell us about your man and nothing more. We're all three women, and we all know about love and hardships." I lied, for I alone knew little of love.

Rachel rubbed her forehead nervously. She closed her eyes. "Yes, yes, yes, I am so sorry. I beg you both forgive me. It's just a day's way. My bitterness runs deep, yes, but my tone was uncalled for. Better I bite my tongue than offend you folk. I meant nothin' by it. I know you be good people, an' I would like, yes, t' tell you 'bout Caleb. I hardly know hwere to begin; yet, I need someone t' know hwat's happened. Someone who might understand. I've hadn' spoke to a soul 'bout these here things ever. I never come t'think anyone would care one way or another. Why pay mind to a slave girl? Yes, it is so much harder hwen everythin' stays bottled up inside, hwen it can' be shared. It hurts."

"Oh, my word, Rachel, please, please, do tell," Dorrie implored. "Tell us. Tell us all you shoulder, should it make you feel better. Tell us everything, I beg you. We have nothing pressing, nothing to do but tea and talk, so tell us all you will, speak your mind at once and free your heart of this pain. You are safe here, I promise, and Elizabeth and I are good listeners to be sure. We are very good listeners."

After stuffing another log into the black stove's belly, I brought over tea, lemon, and a plate of sugared biscuits. Dorrie offered me her chair and went for another. Like the pouring of tea with its aroma, Rachel's words began to flow and fill the cabin with a hypnotic resonance that captured our hearts and souls.

"Promise t' stop me if I should ramble on aimlessly, yes. There is so much t' tell I am unsure hwere t' begin."

"We promise. Be sure to leave nothing unsaid," said Dorrie.

"Here, try and eat a little of this." I handed Rachel a biscuit. It'll help you get your strength back."

"Thank you, Miss Elizabeth." Rachel accepted a cup of warm tea and took a sip. She nibbled at the biscuit. "Oh, yes, this is wonderful."

"Eat what you can. You're all bones." I encouraged her as I sat down in my chair.

"Tell us what's happened to you," said Dorrie. "Where is your man, Caleb, and where is your son? How did you come to be so desperate?"

Rachel took a breath. "Believe me, Miss Dorrie, it don' take much to be desperate hwen you're black folk. You don' have to be a slave to be down n' out. Bein' black is bein' shunned an' freedom may do wonders to fill your soul, but it's mighty poor at fillin' your belly. Bein' free can be hard even for the likes o' me. What I mean to say is, you probably noticed my features, yes, that I look a good deal more hwite than anything. I little doubt but my father was a hwite man. Times told, Miss Dorothy'd said my mama was a fair skinned woman, pretty as could be. Could be my daddy was a plantation owner, or maybe an overseer who had his way with slave girls. You can be certin' there's many about like me. I've seen 'em. I imagine hwen the man figured my mama was with child, he probably hurried her off for sale quick-like so avoidin' rumors n' such. You know, questions 'bout babies that ain' lookin' slave kind. I can' say it for fact, but it happens often, an' a judgin' by the looks o' me, yes, I feel it in my bones. Yes, Miss Dorrie, I feel it close to God's truth."

Dorrie nodded, as if to lend support to Rachel's convictions. She sat staring at her patient, transfixed, eagerly awaiting the next word to come forth. Rachel obliged.

"Well, whatever. Times told, Master William Plackerton an' his woman, Lady Dorothy, we called her Miss Dorothy, purchased my mama who was at that time expectin'. They were

410

two upright people, the Plackertons, fine folk, gentle folk, they were fair, an' commendable, an' I was born an' raised on Plackerton's land. Never laid eyes on anythin' but. Theirs was an upland farm, out a ways from big plantations. It was a small place hwen compared to plantations down country, yes, but it was all of a hundred and sixty acres respectable. Times told, it had been planted tobacco, but cotton proved more profitable an' so Master Plackerton replaced the old crop. Plackertons were from England an', yes, that is hwy I so like the name Elizabeth."

"That explains why you speak the way you do," I commented.

"Yes, we noticed it right away," said Dorrie.

"Yes, that too. I heard it said many a time that I speak entirely wrong for black folk," she laughed. "Of course, it seems to me that all black folk in England would speak in such manner, wouldn' you agree?"

"Seems certain to me," said Dorrie.

"Yes, yes, I would think. Anyhows, Plackertons never were blessed with young-uns. Fate can be terrible cruel an' that is easy enough t' see with folks as kind-hearted as the Plackertons. But for this lack of kin, I 'magine they turned attention to field hands. They purchased mama for a ginnin' cotton, an' fact she was with child was no concern in that chore. Miss Dorothy'd said, *'I like your mother, she is a fine person'* an' yes, she'd said, *'Hwen you were born, I was as excited as the next'*. She held me in her arms even before my mama.

"Anyhows, in a day's way, mama took sick, got the fever an' passed on most unexpectedly hwen I 's goin' on three years in age. Miss Dorothy, good-hearted was she, took me into Master's house an' cared for me as her own. God bless her noble soul. Maybe bein' light in color, as I was, she viewed me differently. To speak truth, as of late, I often wonder if my color was blessin' or curse, yes. Anyhows, I grew up a learnin' well chores of a server an' seamstress, spendin' most of my time inside the big

411

house a learnin' to sew, cook, an' clean. Have you ladies ever been up to a large plantation?"

"No," said Dorrie.

"Not often," said I.

Rachel nodded her head, unsurprised, and continued. "Unless you lay up time on a big place you will never know hwat is slave life. It looks peaceful enough from master's house or road. Oh, yes. On high, life looks good as sun shines down on fields of hwite cotton, rows that stretch far as eye can see. Yes, how sad is truth. Peaceful it rarely is, especially hwen times are bad, an' times are always bad on plantations.

"Lucky me, not to be raised on a plantation, but rather a farm. My life was different. Mine was a smaller world, a world hwere everyone had a name to be known. Nobody knows your name on the big estate, less'n you be in trouble. On plantations, slaves make their own meals. It has to be, but wasn't anythin' like such at Plackerton's. We were only thirteen Negroes on the farm, an' so Miss Dorothy prepared meals for everybody, or better I say she preparation of meals for everybody. She insisted her help an' all hands learn table manners. An' that we did, yes, yes, yes, or we didn' eat at Master's table nohow.

"Miss Dorothy was a woman of determination. Oh, my, yes she was. She had her own way o' doin' things, her own mind to be sure. She'd said England had abolished slavery nearly a hundred years before, an' that France an' Spain agreed to do same. She spoke freely, voicin' her thoughts an' many a grave reservation 'bout ownin' slaves. That is, unless she was in earshot of Master Plackerton. It ain' that he was unkindly. Indeed, he was a considerable man. They just looked out different windows so to speak.

"For example, after a day's work Master Plackerton preferred we'd rest up for the morrow, hwereas Miss Dorothy encouraged us to hire out an' make money for ourselves. Yes, she wanted somethin' better for us. Master Plackerton worried about our health, an' Miss Dorothy worried about our hearts. She came with her English ways an' points o' view to the farm, to the table, an' to the ear of anybody seated to eat. Yes, ma'am, that she did.

"Miss Dorothy always plained that life on a farm was as borin' as scrubbin' baby britches. She rather enjoyed a gatherin' everyone up for a meal in order that we might sit together an' have a laugh. She wasn' a resentful sort, far from it, but she wasn' suited for the slow pace of Virginee. Yes, she tried, but we knew she longed to return to her home in England. Her heart yearned for her family, the bustle of city life, the crowds, an' the attractions. I hardly blamed her, for she would tell stories an' speak of England at the dinner table. We loved to listen, for it seemed a magical place with great buildings, an' courts, an' kings 'n' queens.

"Anyhows, hwen I was about eleven, twelve years of age, Plackertons brought home another family, Cooks, to work fields an' sit to our table. Three in all they were, father, mother, son. Boy's name was Caleb; he's 'bout thirteen at the time. I cottoned to Caleb like bees do blossoms. I mean, I *really* cottoned to that boy. I didn' know nothin' about love ways of course. I was too young, but I was always a lookin' to find him, yes, yes, a followin' him everyhwere up hill an' down dale jus' like a little puppy do."

Rachel stopped talking and looked at us.

"I'm a natterin' like a ninny aren' I."

"No, no, not at all! Go on. Don't stop now." Dorrie came half way out of her chair. "I wish to hear more. Please, do tell", she insisted.

"Please do, Rachel, unless you feel poorly or prefer not. Truthfully, you speak of a world in which we know little more than secrets and hearsay. Like Dorrie, I too am most intrigued by everything you put across."

Through the corner of my eye, I watched Dorrie. I believed she was clinging to the memories of love and romance that she

413

once enjoyed with Robert and therefore cherished such stories of the heart. Rachel kept looking at me as though expecting me to understand these unspoken feelings of lost love in the same way that did Dorrie, but I could only nod my head and pretend.

As always, for me it was different, that kind of love being something to which I could not relate. For me passion proved to be nothing more than an embarrassment. I was far more interested in the unspoken experiences of a Negro or slave. I wanted to know what hardships they endured. I wanted to know if this woman was witness to any of the horrible events often rumored.

Rachel took a drink of her tea and set the cup back down with a weak quivering hand. She took a moment to work up her strength.

"Rachel, are you all right? Do you feel all right? Maybe, it's better you rest. I am most inconsiderate in the way I have begged you to proceed. I don't wish you to overdo," said Dorrie.

"I'm fine, thank-you. Sometimes, one needs to talk more than one needs to eat or sleep. Yes, sometimes, silence is the worst sickness to endure."

"Tis' true, but take care not to unduly fatigue yourself."

"I'm fine."

"Very well," said Dorrie. "In that case, we won' stand for silence here." Everyone laughed and Rachel then continued.

"Yes. Well, I never give it thought at the time, but in later years I supposed Miss Dorothy brought Cooks aroun' jus' so I might have Caleb for a man. There was no other man of suitable age on the farm. Never had been. In particular, I supposed this design due to Cooks also bein' very light skinned, same as me. Caleb an' I could have passed as brother an' sister. One time, I said as much, an' Miss Dorothy just laughed 'bout nonsense I spewed, but she never actually denied it, Miss Dorrie, no she never did.

"Yes, I know in my heart that Miss Dorothy brought Caleb home for me. Plackertons had complete say over who set foot upon the farm, an' everyone that came by for work was carefully considered by Master himself. First day there, it was decided Caleb would be a livin' in the big house an' be taught servitude like myself. It was Miss Dorothy who showed him how to barber.

"He learned about placin' settings, servin' repast, an' layin' out clothes for Master. Over years, we both learned not only table manners an' how to dress up proper, but also how to speak standard English of sorts an' somethin' else—yes, somethin' special. You see, Plackertons taught us both how to—." Rachel halted suddenly, caught in a visible state of indecision. Her eyes darted back and forth between Dorrie and myself before finishing her sentence with much reservation. "—read an' write." Then slowly, "Caleb an' I spoke an oath before Master and Miss Dorothy never to reveal this secret because we were told it would upset others, bein' they weren' learned." Rachel watched for our reaction.

"It's all right Rachel. You have nothing to fear in our company. You know how to read and write. That is wonderful. Maybe you can teach me as well," said Dorrie.

The woman looked at Dorrie as if to gage her sincerity. Her revelation had clearly been a mistake in her mind, and she seemed to be again evaluating us before relaxing enough to enter back into her story.

"Maybe—I will sometime. I think I might not have learned it good enough to do that. Honestly, I'm not very good at it."

"Go on, don't be shy. I am certain you read very well, but right now I just want to know what happened next? And, that's all." Dorrie offered assurance, but there was still hesitation.

"— Yes, well, I must say it isn' that Caleb an' I wanted to read or write or anythin' of the kind. You do understand, we were told what we had to do. And Caleb an' I were asked to read aloud by the Plackertons every candlelight. An' this we did for many a year. I think mostly because we were young an' had the onliest good eyes to see in dim lamplight. We mostly read journals an' news newly arrived from England, hwich both Master an' Miss Dorothy enjoyed before all else. We would read 'bout things that brought back good heartfelt memories an' mentionin's of old friends an' acquaintance. I would read recipes an' social events to Miss Dorothy, hwereas Caleb read news an' finance to Master Plackerton. Yes, I realize Plackertons would have been in frightful trouble had it been found out they taught slaves a readin' an' writin'. Such things was not welcome in those parts then just as now. Ain' nothin' changed.

"Fact of matter is, onliest of late did it occur to me how often Plackertons cut away articles from pages we were to read. For certain, I now can see that there were things about slavery dealin's Plackertons wished kept quiet. I suppose much of it was to keep us unawares, to keep us happy. Hwat we didn' know, couldn' trouble us. Hwenever I asked about cut-outs, Miss Dorothy would sour on the matter insistin' they were unpleasantries. Times told, she'd said, '*these postings served nothing save injury of conscience, suffering of souls, and certain rise to the Lord's indignation. It was so much the better these things be left unread'.*" Rachel held a private momentary thought. "Can you imagine?" She laughed miserably. "I can safely put forward, she was correct in her opinion.

"Let me be clear, Miss Dorrie, I never realized any of this hwen I was young, an' even afterwards when older, I paid but little mind to my bein' a slave., We were set apart from the outside world, secluded, an' so ignorance was bliss indeed. I liked my chores better than that of field hands, I had Caleb, the love of my heart, a room in the big house, an' so for me life was very good. I never knew any other way an' I wanted for nothin'.

"Yes, I can see now, I should have paid mind to clues a comin' from slaves who visited our farm onliest durin' pickin' seasons, ones passin' through. They dared stories on occasion, incredible, horrible stories that seemed far removed from our way of life. Tellin' such tales was greatly frowned upon by

416

Plackertons an' some of the others, an' rightly so. It upset children an' those timid folk. Wouldn' take but a minute an' menfolk would holler, *"shut pan or you'll be seein' a sockdologer certain!"*. No person took kindly to a body stirrin' up fear.

"Let it be said, I rarely heard the word 'slave' around the farm. To me, sayin' I was a slave was like sayin' an In'jun was a red-skin. Yes, sayin' so was true, but such sayin' was particular to hwite folk. If someone said, *'Rachel, so-an'-so don' like slaves'*, I never felt so-an'-so didn' like me. If they said so-an'-so don' like Negroes, well, then I would respond by sayin' I didn' like Irishmen. I took the remark right to heart. I didn' even know hwat was an Irishman, but Plackertons held 'em in low regard an' that was good enough. It must be confest, that I was nothin' more than an innocent child Plackerton's sheltered from life's hard ways.

"Hwen I turned sixteen, I was coupled with Caleb an' we were given a room to ourselves in the House. I was so happy; I loved Caleb crazy-like. It wasn' but a year's time before I gave Caleb a son, Isaac. We three lived together an' shared work day to day without reason for plainin'. The work wasn' so much hard as it was unendin', just like passin' of time. My life was free from worry an' I knew nothin' of fear until that terrible mornin' hwen Master Plackerton dropped stone dead.

"His passin' came without warnin' in a day's way. Yes, I remember how women came runnin' cross lots from the field a screamin' an' cryin' an' as I looked out across rows of cotton, I saw men carryin' Master Plackerton above their shoulders, slowly, solemnly, with respect. Not a soul so much as hwisperin' a word. They returned Master Plackerton's body to the house, hwere they stopped before the great porch an' stood silent, waitin' under a brilliant sun.

"I recall leanin' on that porch railing an' lookin' up from the fields toward the sky. The heavens appeared so blue an' clear; it seemed impossible that death could be stalkin' about on such a magnificent day. It made no sense to me whatsoever, for it was said Master Plackerton's heart just plain quit for no reason. I remember a thinkin', I'd never seen him take ill a day in his life.

"The Master was a good man, a truly good man who was both kind an' fair. Nobody about the farm ever feared Master Plackerton's ways. He allowed menfolk to carry guns because he'd said *'only food fit for eatin' was fresh killed food'*, so menfolk did huntin' an' womenfolk helped Miss Dorothy with fixin's an' doin's.

"Hwenever Master Plackerton bought home a new hand, he would send him out with the rest an' pay him no mind hwatso-ever. He wouldn' be bothered because if the man were a slacker, field hands would row his sorry black butt up Salt River. Master Plackerton was one to work hard, an' so we worked hard, an' we expected those in our company to do same. He was the center of our universe. He did us right an' we did our best in return.

"Yes, it was terrible hard for me to let him go, but to other folk on the farm, his passin' caused more than grief. The effect of his absence was everyhwere. Folks became restless an' moody—nervous. They were fidgety an' short on patience hwenever beyond Miss Dorothy's sight. I never saw such concern about days a comin. Yes, Master Plackerton left us with broken hearts, but he also left us with good land. An' so, I thought it almost comical the way in hwich others went about a frettin'.

"Change o' chains it was. Yes, I was to find out that there wasn' anythin' comical 'bout it at all. I could say soon thereaf-ter my world began to fall apart. It wasn' because of grief. Although, he was like a father to me an' for weeks I wept for him alongside Miss Dorothy. No, it was because of Miss Dorothy's wish to go home.

"Miss Dorothy held her head high, but because everythin' about the place was about Master, she was surrounded by all them memories that held her down. I know, she always possessed a heart that longed for England, an' so it came as no surprise hwen one day she approached Caleb an' I, a confessin' her wish to return to the home of her youth. She was troubled deeply by guilt, a believin' herself to be abandonin' us. Of course, we understood, an' Caleb agreed to look after the estate an' oversee arrangements for sale of the place much to her betterment.

"With Miss Dorothy's permission, an' by her insistence, Caleb saw to it that workers were sold as families an' not split up. She never pressured Caleb into any sale, for profit or otherwise, an' he made sure all field folk went to owners who were known by word of mouth to be kind. They went to small farms, not a one went to an overseer. An' so it went, until just four of us remained.

"The land, hwich had been let out for next season, was finally sold to neighbors who were forthright an' gave a fair an' commendable price. It was agreed that we could stay on as long as need be, but Miss Dorothy had seen to harvestin' fields an' ginnin' crops an' so planned to be out before or soon after next spring plantin'.

"Hwen Miss Dorothy did finally close her accounts an' settle her affairs, she presented Caleb an' I with a generous gift of cash an' a set of papers. Yes, I could read of course, an' understood the papers to mean we were set free by her hand. She'd said we was to be called Mister and Missus Caleb Cook. We were married jus' like regular folk. She had been stern in her warnin' to take proper care of them papers, an' to never reveal their existence unless the devil come a callin'. She encouraged us to leave Virginee an' accompany her north to the free state of New York hwere we could start life anew. She was desperate that we should heed her advice hwich, for her sake, we were most happy to do.

"At the time, freeman's papers were nothin' more than a novelty to me, humorous articles that in my ignorance; I actually laughed about. Caleb, bless his noble soul, didn' share my ignorance. Bein' free meant nothin' to me until much later because I never felt as though I were enslaved. I had always lived a good, happy life filled with friends an' family.

419

"The first indication that things weren' quite as I had figured them, came durin' those days hwen Caleb was sellin' off the others. Yes, I fully understood the meanin' of *'sell'* an' although that word always rang peculiar. I accepted it as just a way of doin' business an' makin' a livin'. I knew field folk as good hard workers and, yes, it seemed only natural to me that they would be worth a considerable sum of money for their knowhow. Fetchin' a good dollar was prideful in a way. If you wanted to have good workers, then you had to pay for 'em fair enough. If a man possessed a trade, his employer often paid an extra amount to own his skill. I had often heard field workers brag about hwat was their worth. Worth was akin to rank or status. It earned one favors.

"Yes, yes, I do say, hwat opened my eyes wide was somethin' more sinister than fear an' nervousness of bein' moved-on that I saw risin' about me in them final days. It was the learnin' that families could be forever split up. At first, I didn' fully grasp how Caleb was tryin' hard to place our friends, they bein' mothers an' fathers an' children, as a family. How else would one do it? I couldn' imagine my goin' anyhwere without Caleb an' Isaac.

"To be sure, I soon understood how this was reason enough for the disappearance of good times an' laughter. Yes, I was understandin' now why names were the same, but faces were changed, tormented, an' dispositions were different now as night an' day. An' yet, still, time n' again, I'd get the sharp end of a tongue for not havin' sense enough t' keep my high spirits to myself.

"I began to learn that changes in those about me came not so much from a mournin' Master Plackerton, but from somethin' much worse. It was fear of the unknown, fear of uncertainty. A fear of questions that had no answers, questions that even I was beginnin' to form. Yes, I was beginning' to wonder ifn' I should be worried after all. An' yet, I refused to face these concerns, but for carin' little to accept *misery* as the new world

420

I was about to enter with Caleb an' Isaac once departed from the farm.

"I'd never asked nor pried into pasts of field folk. I was raised by Miss Dorothy never to be nosy about other people's doin's. There was times at the dinner table I sensed issues of the past unmentioned, memories kept hushed, dark things unforgotten even durin' good years an' light of day.

"I was a thinkin' it had been those dark things unspoken, those memories that I witnessed surface an' unfold into meanness. Yes, I saw tears of joy an' profound gratitude given Caleb for placin' folks on good farms with kind masters an' assurances that families would remain together. This news bein' the only times after Master Plackerton's death that smiles briefly returned. Who would break up a family? Yes, yes, I asked myself so many times. Who could do such a thing?

"Even then, hwen all was said an' done, an' others were happily settled in with their new masters; I felt much of the tears an' talk, much of the cryin' an' hysteria to be mostly for naught. I questioned if it wasn' but simply fear o' change that upset people so.

"As for me, change was anythin' but fearful. An' so havin' wiped away what signs of our lives be left on the farm, I found myself wide-eyed excited for the future as we four strapped our belongings onto a coach an' headed north. In this way, we stayed together as long as possible until Miss Dorothy felt us safe in the free state of New York, an' she able to depart for England with clear conscience. It was then she gave Caleb an' me the split medallion. I cried hard as might a child, for as Master Plackerton had in every way been my father, so too had Miss Dorothy been my mother.

"Yes, it would make sense that I carry Caleb's name on my heart, an' he carry mine, but that wasn' how it was meant to be. No, ma'am. Miss Dorothy had our names inscribed on both halves of two medallions—Rachel twice on one heart, Caleb, twice on the other. She then kept one half of each heart for herself. Our two missin' halves formed a complete heart, hwich she took back to England as a keepsake to remind her of us. It was only after Caleb an' I were abducted, that we exchanged our names between us."

"You were abducted!" Dorrie's eye grew wide.

"Yes. Oh, yes, Miss Dorrie. I was indeed, an' it was a terrible thing, as you shall hear should you wish."

"You were abducted in New York?"

"Yes, ma'am. In the middle of the city, in the middle of the day."

"Let her speak, Dorrie. How will we ever hear it if you don't keep quiet," I spoke out. "Go on Rachel, what happened next pray tell."

"Yes. Well— Caleb an' I sold the coach an' kept proceeds as instructed by Miss Dorothy. It brought into our possession a tidy sum indeed. An' there we were a standin' in the free state of New York, sad, but happy to be startin' a new life, just three of us left to our own device.

"Caleb found work within a day of our arrival doin' construction, hwich was visible everyhwere one turned. New York was boomin', an' most important, slavery was abolished in twenty-seven so it was possible for a black man to earn a livin'. So much help was needed to keep up with growth that wages all over the city proved to be generous no matter hwat one's color.

"I took on work as a house servant. Between my speakin' with an English accent an' bein' knowledgeable in southern manners an' hospitality, I found myself much in demand. I quickly earned top wage almost from the start. In truth, a good deal more than even Caleb might muster. It wasn' long before he too gave up rigors of construction an' began servin' himself. The work was far less dangerous an' earnin's were too good to pass up. It was ironic that we performed exactly the same service we did as slaves. We couldn' deny our trainin' an' advantages it brought.

Caleb an' I finally let a small place in Brooklyn an' enjoyed a simple life raisin' our son Isaac.

"It may be supposed that onliest after I spent time in New York did I truly began to fathom somethin' of the horrors of slavery while the institution remained comfortably distant. Our good fortunes gave me time an' opportunity to read about social issues of race, politics, of slavery, an' the relevant color of my skin, hwich I looked at repeatedly. I looked at Caleb an' I looked at the beautiful shade of Isaac's skin. Why hwite folk thought this darker skin made us unworthy was beyond me. I simply didn' understand. No matter how hard I tried, I could make no sense of it. But there is was bein' argued by the high n' mighty, we was but animals, like dogs an' mules.

"Yes, it was as if I was bein' born a second time. It was as if I were openin' my eyes for a second time. Only, this time I began to see everythin' differently. This time I saw much of the pervasiveness of this sin called slavery. The absurdity of intelligent individuals viewin' Caleb an' I, an' my boy as bein' animals, literally beasts of burden. This time I realized how far across our nation this infection poisoned good people.

"I understood at last how in spite of dark murmurin's an' fearful glances of field workers, Miss Dorothy managed to protect me on one hundred an' sixty secluded acres of peaceful ignorant bliss. I found myself torn between a sense of love an' a sense of betrayal. The more I learned about who an' hwat I was expected to be, the more I was troubled an' fearful. It was as though the brighter my day, the darker my night.

"Yet, in spite of many fearful issues of my new found aware-ness, those next months marked some of the best times of my life. New York was thrillin'. It was impossibly excitin' for someone such as me, who had spent her whole life a livin' the monotony of day-to-day farm life. I knew at once hwy Miss Dorothy longed for England with its kings an' queens, with its castles an' House of Parliament, with its bustlin' shops. Just as I had always imagined England, everythin' here was an attraction to behold.

Everythin' called to me an' yet I didn' have to answer to anythin' or no body. I don' mean just as a slave, I mean even as a daughter.

"You see, Plackertons were very good to us, an' I loved them both dearly. I did think of them as my parents, but even parents had to be reckoned with until now. Now, it was New York, Caleb, Isaac an' me. We were free, wonderfully free, settin' our own course until in a day's way fate finally struck us down."

The pounding feet of Jack and Kenneth were suddenly crossing the plank as they boarded. Rachel was visibly frightened by the sudden noise.

"It's the boys," I said. "Nothing more."

"Jack and Kenneth, they are my sons," said Dorrie.

Rachel heard us, but clearly held her doubts. She strained to raise herself higher onto the pillows as if to prepare herself for the wolves. Dorrie reached out at once to comfort her.

"It's all right, Rachel. It's just my boys. Don't worry." Dorrie stood up and headed for the hatch to meet her sons while I went for the teakettle to warm up our tea. The hatch flew open with an inconsiderate slam, just as Dorrie made the steps.

"No! No! I don't want you boys on the boat right now. Jack, Kenneth; you boys stay out a while longer. It's nice outside. I don't want you in right now."

"Mom!" They began to protest.

"Mom, nothing. Go play for a while. I'll call you when I want you to come in. Now, get!"

"Mom, we're hungry! We want something to eat," said Kenneth.

"Yeah, we're hungry!" said Jack.

"Listen to me! Rachel has just come around, and I don't think she is up to all your noise. You can take the biscuits with

424

you, and don't bother me again until I call, or I'll take a switch to your bottoms for sure. You understand?"

"Yes, ma'am."

"Here, now get!"

Jack and Kenneth's eyes opened wide with delight after being handed an entire bowl of sugared biscuits. They stampeded back across the deck and down the plank howling like banshees. With a sigh of relief, Dorrie closed the hatch to the cabin and sealed out the distractions beyond.

"Boys!" Dorrie exclaimed with a parting breath. She sat back down. "Now, where were we? Did I miss anything?"

"Not a thing," I answered. "Here, I warmed your tea."

"Good! This is a story, indeed! So, you were saying, Rachel, fate struck you down."

"Dorrie!" I exclaimed.

"What?"

"A good story? You almost sound flippant. It bothers me to think of this as a story. It is her life and I fear her accounts will grow all the worse. Story sounds so terribly inconsiderate." I complained. I stared at Dorrie, who turned to look apologetically at Rachel.

"I meant nothing by it, Rachel. God forbid, I don't even want to know what comes next. I'm just going to cry. I know I going to cry, but I can't help myself."

"No harm done, Miss Dorrie. I am touched by Miss Elizabeth's concern. She is a sensitive soul, but my ramblin's would be nothin' more than a story to anyone else, so hwy not you. Don' think twice on it."

"Bless you. So tell me about fate. It was cruel, just like Elizabeth fears. It was, wasn't it? What happened on that day?"

"Yes, yes, it was indeed. It was very cruel. As we say, change of chains, change of chains. One misery to another, bad to bad. It was the day hwen my naive view of life with its bright sunny days, its high hopes an' laughin' children came to a crushin' end. It was a day I was damned to live in fear an' dwell forever in a world of shadow an' suspicion, a world of mistrust hwereby I would always watch over my shoulders. It was a world hwere I no longer had a man or son. A world without the love an' comfort of my family.

"Yes, Miss Dorrie, that day was August eighth. It was the first time in weeks that neither Caleb nor I had to work of a Sunday an' so he decided to take Isaac a fishin' down on the Hudson. I packed a basket full for a picnic lunch an' brought a blanket, hwich we planned to spread out in a nice shady private place so Isaac could frolic without bother.

"I remember a growin' mighty impatient with Caleb because I was tired of carryin' the basket back'n forth across the same stretch o' ground hwile he went on undecided about findin' the perfect place to fish. He knew I was annoyed an' to mollify me he settled down at a place he figured had some possibilities. I remember him goin' on about not makin' any promises an' leavin' me to understand that if Isaac should come up empty handed, it would be entirely my fault.

"Little did I know, Miss Dorrie, we weren' the only ones fishin' an' hopin' not to come up empty-handed. We never gave thought to the fact that other Negroes lookin' for the same kind of secluded spot frequented this place many times in the past. I suspect the place attracted black fishermen like worms attract fish because it sure attracted slavers.

"Who could o' imagined that in New York just such people would be hidin' in woods waitin' for the likes of us, but there they were. An' hwen best to their advantage, they jumped out of the trees an' grabbed my boy Isaac. Yes, I was absolutely dumbstruck. Terrified. Neither Caleb nor I had any idea hwat was happenin'. Hwy would we think to worry about slavers in the free state of New York—in the city—in the middle of the day? We was just fishin'.

"At first I thought they were robbers, an' then I thought *kidnappers* meanin' to steal Isaac away, an' I began screamin' for all I was worth. Caleb started for the man holdin' Isaac, but the man pulled a knife, hwich he placed at Isaac's throat, an' Caleb stopped at once. He dared not move, but the sight of the knife made me hysterical. I went out of my mind screamin' for help 'til one of 'em hit me backside the head so hard, I hit the ground insensible, wits knocked right out of me.

"There was four hwite men all told, an' as I lay on the ground gropin' for my brains, I overheard 'em talkin' between themselves. I come to realize they thought we was runaway slaves. Yes, I can' tell you the relief I felt once I understood it had all been a terrible mistake. I attempted to rise to my feet an' approach one of the men to point out the misunderstandin'.

"Caleb stepped forward to shush me, but he was restrained, an' for the sake of Isaac, I wouldn' be quieted. I put forth that we were freed slaves an' I produced my freedman papers. I had our licenses an' receipts in good order to prove all that I said was true. In my nervousness, I read the dates an' some of hwat I handed the men. There could be no question to hwat I said for it was printed out plain as day. I'll never forget the way Caleb dropped his head with resignation.

"The men grew silent. They gathered around to look over the documents. The man holdin' our papers called out to the others an' asked if anyone could read. They all laughed and began cursin'. He looked back at me with eyes burnin' in anger. His teeth were clenched right tight when he next spoke.

'It's a bloody sad day when an uppity nigger can read an' write. Now let's jus' see what good that does ya.'

"Lookin' straight into my eyes, he then slowly ripped the papers into long strips an' let them float away in the breeze. It was their word against ours an' that was the end of it. Caleb had

427

foreseen this. He knew from the start hwat in my state of fear, I had failed to consider.

"From then on, we did only hwat we were told, for we were sick with worry over Isaac. Caleb told me they was slavers, an' for Isaac's sake, not to make 'em angry. They kept our boy out o' reach, makin' sure we didn' fuss 'bout bein' bound an' gagged. After that, we were led through woods an' along a path that come up to a wagon. We were ordered to lie down on our backs, so our wrists an' ankles might be chained to the bed. I never opened my mouth again. Caleb an' I only listened to hwat was bein' said.

'Maybe we ought sell her here in the city. She don't look too bad. She's fair skinned for a nigger. I'll bet she'd turn a profit in no time.'

'Are you kiddin'? What are you thinkin'? Are ya corned or somethin'? For one thing, she knows the city too well. For another, she's not a virgin. They only want virgins, ya coot.'

'I never could figure that out, why virgins when—.'

'Good night, Ben! They don't gotta be virgins, but they can't have given birth, get it? They're too stretched out ya daft shuck. It ain't worth takin' the chance. Besides, how long ya think we're gonna keep that nigger kid quiet without his mother bein' round.'

'Yeah, you're right about that. You guys'll go nuts listenin' to that brat screamin' for the next five hundred miles. Ain't worth it, Ben.'

'Yeah, I guess.'

'C'mon, Ben, get in the wagon 'fore ya get my ass in a pucker an I end up knockin' ya into a cocked hat. Let's get outta here now, full chisel, ya hear me, full chisel.'

"Yes, I was numb, Miss Dorrie. Scared to death. Every tale, every fear, every rumor ever hwispered in fields at Plackerton's an' dismissed by me as much to-do 'bout nothin' was right now fact. Every article ever read in the paper that seemed crazy an' unthinkable was suddenly true. I was about to begin livin' the

428

life that was supposed to be mine. I was a Negro an' therefore I was a slave.

"We started our journey out of New York on our backs sweatin' in the heat of day hwile hidden under a pile of mats an' baskets. Two of the men were heard to leave, an' two, this Ben an' a man named Warren, remained to head up the wagon.

"My eyes were swollen in no time, irritated by sweat an' dust until I could no longer open them to see. The back of my skull was soon rubbed raw from slidin' an' slammin' upon the bed of the wagon as it jounced about crisscrossin' ruts an' rocks. My hair was caked in blood an' my head split with pain from the jostling.

"Yes, but that was only physical pain. Change o' chains. There was much worse pain to be had. Once we left the city, drivers had their way with me. It seemed they were impatient to get on with it. They were as pleased with rapin' me as kids enjoyin' iced cream on a hot summer day. I was raped many times durin' the first two weeks on the road. It was made clear that I would comply with hwatever demand, hwatever their pleasure or Isaac would be sold at once to the first bidder we come upon. The fact that Caleb an' Isaac were watchin' meant absolutely nothin'. I could do nothin' but cry, an' I tried by best not to. I wanted to be strong for Caleb's sake. The poor man was beside himself with worry for me, but shackles kept him from doin' anythin' more than touchin' my fingers with his.

"Twice a day our wrists were unshackled, but not together. If one should choose to run, the other would be held to pay. We were given a drink of water with a piece of bread, once early in the mornin' an' once again after dark. We weren' allowed nohow to relieve ourselves or do anythin' that might draw attention. The slavers feared most we might be seen by abolitionists an' so kept us shackled for hours in our own filth, hwich caused our skin, rubbed raw from the bed of the wagon, to become covered with rash an' infected. Onliest if we came upon runnin' water did the men take buckets for to flood the bed an' clean it out.

"Yes, we suffered until we were well away from New York State an' well into Marylan' at hwich point we were uncovered an' fastened to a chain that trailed the back of the wagon. We now were forced to walk. Hundreds of miles seemed to pass us by, wearin' our shoes down into little more than sole-less scraps of leather, an' our softened feet into bloody sores. Still it was better than bein' shackled on our backs. We picked up more slaves as we went until there were eight in total.

"Time an' time again I thought as I spied the country about me, how ironic it was that the south should have always been a place of wonderful memories for me. Virginee was the place Caleb an' I were coupled. It was the birthplace of Isaac. It was the place of my youth—*a place of ignorant bliss.* May I have another biscuit?"

"What?"

"May I have another biscuit?"

"Oh! Of course!" Dorrie snapped out of her trance and quickly passed the plate to Rachel.

"These are delightful. Did you bake them?"

"Actually, Elizabeth did this batch. She can hold her own at a stove."

"Yes, she can. They have my mouth just a-waterin'. I am startin' to realize how hungry I really am. Honestly, I forgot the last time I ate."

"I'll fix you a right proper dinner tonight if you're up to it," said Dorrie.

"Oh, imagine havin' food on a table instead of a branch! I don' think I can imagine." Rachel bit off a piece of the biscuit. "Mmmmmm". She savored the morsel, lightly licking her lips. "I am of a mind to say, I'll be soon on my feet, an' so long as I shelter under your roof, I will fix you the finest fare in these parts. Yes, I love to cook an' if you will excuse my boastful pride, I take second seat to no one at a stove, an' I might add that is one

430

fine lookin' stove you have there. Of course, that is onliest if you allow it."

"Allow it! You must be kidding. I would gladly let you and Elizabeth share the cooking. Fine with me."

"Ahh! What do you mean *'you and Elizabeth', "* I protested. "I didn't volunteer to cook anything."

"Fine, it's settled then. You shall eat like queens, it's the very least I might do to show my appreciation for your takin' me in." Rachel glowed.

"All right, all right, now that that's settled, *puh-leeeze*, what happened next after you arrived down south? Am I the only one dying to know?" I looked directly at Dorrie.

"Don't look at me," said Dorrie. "No more biscuits, Rachel."

Rachel laughed as she swallowed her last mouthful. She took a drink and let out a breath. "Yes. Well, from hwat I had gathered, our destination turned out to be a large auction house located somehwat west of Richmond. There were three buildings in particular. Three pens, slave pens, or of'entimes in the south they are called dens. One for men, one for children, an' one for women an' mothers with nursin' babes. Caleb was unhooked from the coffle an' taken away. I never saw what become of Isaac.

"I was taken to join others standin' before a low built hovel of sorts. Hwen I entered the den, I passed through a door at the left corner of the buildin'. It was a low squarish shack with barred windows spaced high across the wall. The door opened into one end of a corridor situated along the same outside wall with barred windows up high. This wall was now to my left as I walked. To my right was a cage of black iron bars supportin' a gate-like door, much as one might see in a jail. Yes, these were small buildings with ceilings so low in places we had to stoop. There was only one other openin' to the barred room in hwich we were locked. It was low to the ground an' meant for flushin' out filth that collected on the floor.

"I shared this pen with about sixty other women an' children, an' a god-awful swarm of flies an' mosquitoes, for there were no chamber pots let alone privacy. Each mornin' we were made to scrub the floor clean of filth, sweepin' it out through the small opening, but by day's end the effort seemed pointless for the stench was utterly overwhelmin'.

"We were to remain locked up for a few days in order to recuperate from hardships of travel. The slavers wanted our wounds to heal an' for all o' us to be fattened up best we could. We were fed as much as we could eat in order to improve our appearance. *'A pittance in food, a pound in flesh'*. In other words, a healthy lookin' slave would fetch a good deal more come auction.

"The womenfolk eased my worries by assurin' me that Caleb an' Isaac were most likely still in pens for men an' children. Yes, but I was sternly warned to summon all my strength because it was here that families were pulled apart. All about this area, tobacco plantations were failin' an' slaves were bein' sold to cotton plantations in the west. Every year hundreds of children were taken never an' never seen again. To hear of it stiffened me with dread.

"Durin' afternoons, the den was unbearably hot. Bein' cramped so tightly did nothin' to ease the stiflin' humidity. There was no means for movement of air. We remained locked up in this dreadful state until the followin' Saturday afternoon, hwich was five days later. Yes, I swear before God an' all saints in heaven, I learned more in those five days about slavery than in all my twenty years prior. Yes, I learned more than I ever wished to know.

"My lessons began soon as I entered the den an' found myself starin' at this woman standin' beside me. She was tall an' attractive except for a terrible scar centered upon her cheek. It was a large letter 'R'. The woman took note of my fixation an' told me she had been branded 'cause she wouldn' be broke. Times told, master said stay put, but she was always runnin' away.

One day he held her down and branded her face so all would know was an untrainable runaway. It was mostly done as a lesson to others on his plantation.

"The idea of such barbarity was simply beyond my ability to believe. The thought of such searin' pain upon one's cheek. As I stood there starin' at her, an older woman turned to me an' lifted her shift, revealin' her nakedness. She lifted one of her large breasts upward an' showed me hwere she too had been scarred by branding. She wasn' alone. She was a part of a larger group of older women who all had brand marks burned into the bottom of their breasts. Yes, I began to tremble. Yes, I was terrified, indeed.

"This older woman went by the name Jersey. She took kindly to me an' tried to ease my anxieties. She was quick to see not only my fear, but how I spoke an' acted different than the rest. She told me not to worry so because although it was harsh, it was easy compared to many other things I might have faced.

"Then she began to give account of her trip to Carolinas from Africa as a young girl. She told me how slave traders had built this fancy new ship for transportin' slaves an' how the company was thrilled about the number of slaves it could carry, an' about how profitable a ship it would prove to be. She had been happy to hear it was a new ship an' wouldn' sink, for she was deathly afraid of water an' monsters that lurked beneath.

"Hwen her people went aboard, they were stripped of their clothin' then branded with a hot iron on their stomachs. This was so the wound wouldn' become irritated hwile lyin' on their backs. They were forced to lie down tightly against one another, shoulder to shoulder, one person's head between the ankles of another. Folks were then shackled to wooden decks by the neck or ankles, or both.

"Yes, if a woman was particularly attractive, they said she was branded on the bottom of a foot an' left unshackled so as not to diminish her beauty. These women were sold for high sums to masters who owned sex houses in the north, places like New York an' Boston.

"Jersey told me that unlike older ships, this new ship had been made with many decks, each only four or five hands high. Hwat builders of the ship never thought was how at very least, people needed fresh air an' in such small spaces it was impossible to breathe. An' so it was, she said, that a tremendous din arose within the hull an' the owners were obliged to bring folk up from below in order to put a stop to it.

"Jersey spoke on how them souls appeared hwen they reached the upper deck. *'They were foamin' at the mouth an' filled with madness from near suffocatin'.* She'd said people were killin' those lyin' next to 'em in order to get more air, an' some of the stronger came above draggin' one or two dead bodies behind 'em. Others came up in groups havin' completely lost their minds. She'd said how women came up bloodied, stabbed or shredded by nails that had been pulled up from wooden decks but for them tryin' to kill each other in order to get air. She'd said out of five, six hundred people that were squeezed into the ship, fifty had died outright before even raisin' anchor.

"Jersey said to me, *'Rachel, first I feel lucky fo' havin' been chackled onna upper deck an' all, near an open hatch tha' letst in air.'* Then she said, *'Child, it was nothin' but a change o' chains. Nothin' more than a change o' chains.'* She lived through the first day, but only to suffer the voyage. The ship pitched back an' forth, Miss Dorrie, endlessly, like this, makin' sick all in the holds." Rachel raised her hands then rocked them back and forth to show the motion of the sea.

"The wretched folk were unable to move or even sit up in the low space that kept them. Yes, she told me everything. She told me how they had to lay in their own vomit an' filth, an' how they had been given no food to speak of an' only enough water to keep them barely 'live. Jersey spoke how those poor souls were so stiff from days spent on their backs, an' racked with such pain, that few could manage walkin' hwen brought up on deck. They had to be carried up if they's to see sunlight.

"There was no sun shinin' down in the holds, but it beat down upon upper decks an' drove heat below until the ship's innards were like the inside of an oven. The lack of sufficient water only served to bring more death with each passin' day. So many died, their bodies were left shackled hwere they lay because the masters couldn' stand the stench in the holds. It was too much work to remove bodies, but for the shacklin' an' unshacklin' an' stirrin' folks up every couple of hours, so, dead folks were left to rot next to livin' until there was little choice but to haul 'em out an' throw 'em overboard. This chore was left to slaves of course, a man throwin' his woman to sharks, a mother her children.

"Yes, Miss Dorrie, I heard it all. This one particular women stepped toward me so she might tell me what she saw shortly after traffickin' of slaves was made illegal. By her own words, this old woman said a ship's master who had been found out an' was now bein' chased down by the law, shackled all his slaves to the ship's anchor an' threw it overboard. In less than a moment, he cleared his decks of any sign of slaves or wrong doin'. Them folks were dragged fiercely off decks an' down into the black depths to suffer their horrible deaths. *'Can you imagine such a thing?'* This the old woman asked me. How could I possibly imagine such a thing?

"Jersey looked me square in the face an' said *'It was but for all the death an' dreadfulness of my journey that I thanked the Lord for havin' arrived in America in chains'*. Yes, in those few days, I heard tell things I feared to consider, things I could never have imagined true, all manner of torture an' horror. There was no fat'nin' me up, Miss Dorrie. I couldn' eat for days."

Dorrie and I sat silent. I was nearly sick to my stomach as I imagined suffering such miserable fates. I found myself holding my breath without being aware. I shuddered at the thought of plunging into the depths of a watery grave. I remembered my first walk across a boarding plank and how I stared fearfully into the murky depths beneath me. I tried not to think of their terror.

Rachel sipped her tea. She studied us a moment, maybe wondering if we could ever truly understand.

"You know how you hwite folk say the cotton gin has changed everythin' in this country for better. Well, let me tell you how for some folks, it made things worse. Many of the women I stayed with told me they were bein' sold because they were too old to breed. They had been bred over an' over soon as they commenced to bleedin'. Some of 'em had give birth to many as eighteen children, all taken an' sold. Yes, I learned that breedin' black folk is big business.

"You see that cotton gin set the south an' west on fire. It cleaned cotton faster 'an ever, faster'n it could be picked, an' that meant onliest one thing, more hands needed for pickin'. Problem was, transportin' slaves across the ocean had come to be against the what the law says. It was made illegal, hwich left but one concern—*breeding*.

"Jersey'd said that breeders handpicked their slaves for size an' strength an' then mated them for young-uns to sell. She said masters who had been raisin' tobacco, an' were now losin' out to cotton farmers, made more money from breedin' strong healthy slaves an' sellin' them to cotton plantations than they did by harvestin' tobacco. She'd said they liked the business because the masters only needed a few good strong bucks an' the rest were women who weren' as apt to give trouble. If a woman died givin' birth it seemed more an act of God than did death from overwork an' hardships in the field.

"In a day's way, I learned it all. Yes, I learned more than I care to say. I saw more than I dare to speak. For certain, it wasn' always bad for all, but it had been plenty bad enough for many of 'em waitin' in that pen. Even knowin' how my life had been easy an' sheltered, them women what been through the worst of times were the ones that comforted me most. I guess they were strongest. I guess they had long since learned how to forget feelin's for their young-uns, an' for love, an' for hope so to survive.

"That was somethin' I had yet to be taught. I cried every day for Isaac. I cried for Caleb, who I hadn' seen since our arrival, but I knew he was nearby an' that made it all the worse. I might have entered the pen terrified, but after a week I too began to feel less. I began to grow numb to it all.

"On Saturday mornin' we were led to a barn an' ordered to strip off our shifts an' file into a straight line, one behind the other. We were ordered to climb into a tub of ice-cold well water an' to scrub down, afterhwich we were ordered to stand in a second line accordin' to height. I was heard men an' children were also bein' told to bathe as well. We were given no towels to dry ourselves, an' forced to stand in chilly mornin' air without benefit of sun as buyers in fine dress an' overseers from neighborin' plantations strolled patiently about to inspect us.

"As I stood there shiverin' an' witness to all takin' place, I once thought about how I had read arguments of abolitionists durin' my time of freedom in New York, an' how those issues had seemed so distant. I suppose knowin' that New York was a free state, made me feel too far removed to be bothered. I thought about growin' up in Virginee, hwere I had only known kindness on the Plackerton farm, a place from hwich I had never strayed the whole of my life.

"Now, it seemed thinkin' was dangerous. To think was to hope. This was not a place to hope. Here one was clobbered by reality, horror-struck an' humiliated beyond all measure. Now, I stood barefoot on the cold stone floor an' shakin' in drafts of a mornin' breeze. My flesh was tight with goose bumps an' my nipples were hard. I suspect because I was younger than Jersey an' the rest, overseers were drawn to me from the start, an' they delighted in rubbin' my breasts an' squeezin' my nipples painfully as if I were a prize milker. They rubbed their hands over my back an' buttocks an' checked my teeth. This done for the sake of inspection, so they said, as if one could believe dealers hwo

437

eagerly pointed out my youth an' firmness—inspection, yes indeed, a close inspection at that. A woman knows well the look in a man's eye an' thoughts that possess him, an' I was no exception.

"I will tell you both, my lesson was late in coming. An' it was a most brutal lesson that I learned fast an' first hand. Bein' a slave was all about fear. It was all about livin' in fear. It was all about not existing, about bein' nothing. I wasn' supposed to feel pain of lash, or loss of a child, or grief of death, or embarrassment of a gropin' hand. Men would rub my belly an' buttocks as one would rub flanks of a horse.

"My tears were only a curiosity that raised eyebrows an' remarks, a sign that I was more pure of spirit an' less ravaged, that I was fresh an' easily trainable. It had nothin' to do with worry for my son who was merely a small version of a larger animal in their eyes. My tears couldn' reflect feelin's of a mother that were considered to be no deeper than that of a cow for its calf. Mooooooo!

"Hwat matter did it make, is was nothin' but a change o' chains. That afternoon put an end to it all. After bein' inspected an' all, we were bound an' led into a courtyard in three lines. One line was for males, one for females, an' one for children. This was the first time I had seen Caleb or Isaac, an' first sign of separation told to me by Jersey. I could read desperation upon Caleb's face. I knew how he had worried himself sick over our well-bein'.

"Then I observed as one by one men were unhitched from the coffle an' led to the raised platform. The auction began, an' I stood chained an' mute. Through my tears, I watched as my man was auctioned off for three hundred dollars, a poor price. He had never been a field hand an' wasn' as massive as some of the others. Maybe I should have been shamed for he was worth so much more to me. He never saw the look on my face, an' I never saw him again after he was taken away.

438

"As difficult as I thought it was, an' as much as I loved Caleb, it was nothin' compared to the pain of seein' my son sold on the block an' led away. All that I lived for could be found within the eyes of my boy. Hwen they led him to the block I would not be silenced, an' this time I screamed an' I pleaded, I beseeched them with all conviction of my heart not to separate us, but it was to no avail. I was only one voice of despair among many. My boy was lookin' at me an' smilin' all the hwile.

"At the same time Isaac was led away, a couple of auctioneers approached me an' began askin' me questions about my past. I paid them scant mind, but for my misery an' sobbin'. Just as did the both of you, they took quick notice of my English accent an' the manner of my speech, an' I was immediately removed from the line.

"I thought that maybe here was a chance to explain the tragedy of hwat had taken place. I told them I was not a slave but a freed person. I explained how we were kidnapped from the river in New York an' how my license an' receipts had been ripped up, an' how I had been brought to Virginee against my will. I pleaded with them to believe me an' allow me to contact my employer for his testimony. I pleaded with them to reunite my family, but they were utterly deaf to my beggin'. There was no hope. I fell silent an' the men simply informed me that a Negro without papers in Virginee was a slave no different than anyhwere else.

"Due to my articulation an' manner, I alone was dressed proper in maiden's attire an' saved for a special auction given to preferred customers. Two days later I was sold privately to a Mr. Henry Jacobson for eight hundred dollars. Half again more than any of the field hands auctioned on the block an' three times the price fetched for the women. Miss Dorothy had taught me well. There was now bitter irony in my recollection of havin' believed that if one wanted a slave who knew her business well, then one would have to pay fair enough."

Rachel took her tea slowly. Dorrie and I sat stock still, both of us appalled and mesmerized until I was blessed with enough sense to warm Rachel's tea. Neither Dorrie nor I uttered a word. There was a filth, a shame that choked out the light of day, the light of hope. I felt myself trapped in a place between crying and vomiting. We just stared at this stranger before us and waited for whatever next she might say.

"I don' think it's possible for me to describe in words hwat misery beset me. Never in my life had I been scared as I was durin' the abduction an' hwile waitin' in the slave den. Never in my life had I experienced anythin' like the pain of havin' my loved ones taken away.

"My world was nothin' if not a cloud of confusion an' uncertainty, but I believe the worst shock of all was wakin' to the reality how worthless I was as a human. I read many things in papers of New York. I knew of injustices presented to slaves, but like a fool, I never thought myself to be anythin' of the sort 'til I realized the way hwite folk looked at me. I don' believe I ever saw hwite men look at a pig with as much disregard, as how they looked at those folk around me.

"Worse yet, I fit nohwere. I was a half-breed, half caste, mulatto, half hwite an' half black. Some black women scorned me as much for bein' fair skinned as for my trainin'. I was of'en given preference by hwites an' there were black folk hwo resented it bitterly. They knew nothin' about me an' yet I was despised because light skins worked in the big house, hwile dark skins worked the fields.

"Times told, I heard Master Jacobson was as cruel as they came, an' his wife, Mrs. Jacobson was every bit as mean. A truly fine pair they made. They dressed fancy an' proclaimed to be people of God, yet first thing a slave was told upon arrivin' at the plantation was four slaves had been killed for crossin' the master—two after a hwipping, one from a press, an' one by the dogs. Punishments were made clear upon arrival."

"I know I will regret asking, but what's a press?" asked Dorrie.

"A press? Well—it's like a large table with a platen, it bein' of same size, hwat hangs overhead, atop the table. The platen is lowered onto the table by turnin' a large handhweel. The press is used to squeeze cotton down from fluff to hard packed bales for loadin' on wagons an' boats an' such.

"I never saw a man get the press, but I heard they never used it to kill a man. Instead, they would squeeze 'm with the platen until he was unable to move then they would walk away leavin' him there in crushin' misery. I hear after about fifteen or twenty minutes the pain is unbearable, an' the poor souls are left to suffer for hours. The worst pain comes hwen the platen is raised back up. If a man lives, he lives, if he dies, he dies."

"I think I'm sick." Dorrie grit her teeth and looked squeamish.

"That would be plantation life. I was told first day penalty for visitin' another plantation was ten lashin's. Bein' caught on horseback, would get me twenty-five. Bein' caught keepin' a club, or carryin' one, or out after dark without a pass, I would get forty lashin's. If I persisted in my ways, I would get the brandin' iron. If I should choose to run, they would let loose the dogs.

"The Jacobson plantation was everything opposite the Plackerton farm. It was enormous, some eight hundred acres, a mix of tobacco an' cotton. I never knew exactly how many slaves worked fields but there were eight includin' myself that were assigned to Mrs. Jacobson alone. We stayed at the house. I guess upward of seventy or eighty slaves stood under the hwip of the overseer, not countin' those hwo came an' went accordin' to season. There was no such thing as friendship or eatin' together, or table manners to be learned at this place. There was only pain an' fear. For field hands, mornings an' evenings started an' ended with lashin's.

"My fear was not to be one of lashin', but rather the attentions of Mr. Jacobson, hwich began immediately with his inspection of me in the auction house. He liked to have his way with the help. Mrs. Jacobson keenly aware of my light skint. She insisted I be her personal maid so she might keep me close by an' watch my doin's.

"Realizin' how perilous was my situation; I made every effort to be invisible before Mr. Jacobson, an' stay under Mrs. Jacobson's nose as much as possible. Although, I worked my fingers to the bone so as not to raise complaint or attention, Mrs. Jacobson had no likin' for me hwatsoever. The more her husband came sniffin' around, the more she stood about starin' at me.

"There was no time to grieve for Caleb an' Isaac. As soon as I arrived, I was ordered to bed an' put out to work before sun-up followin' mornin', hwich happened to be a Sunday. The fact did not escape me. I kept remindin' myself that it was the Lord's Day, a day I had always kept sacred. I wondered many times over hwether the Lord thought my praise to be human or animal.

"I never knew the answer. All I could do was wait an' wonder. Time moves slow as snails hwen life no longer seems worth living, but even for my broken spirit a year came an' went. I could never escape my mulatto features, an' all the hard work in the world failed to hide me from Jacobsons or anyone else.

"I always been a curiosity to hwite an' black alike. I like to think it was my hard work playin' a role in earnin' me a measure of respect on the day a servant who went by 'Licky', an' I were summoned to Mrs. Jacobson's sittin' room. It was there that she informed us we would be accompanyin' her on a trip to New York for purpose of business.

"Neither Licky nor I gave any sign of feelings hwatsoever. I knew for a fact that Licky dreaded the idea of bein' confined in a coach alongside Mrs. Jacobson for such a long trip. She would be a nervous wreck. I, on the other hand, heard little else of hwat Mrs. Jacobson had to say because I was deep in prayer, thankin' the Lord for helpin' me to keep my mouth shut, an' for my never havin' mentioned to anyone that I once let a place in that city.

"If anyone had known beforehand that I had lived in the free state of New York, I would have never been considered for this trip. The Jacobson's had paid way too much money for me to chance my runnin' away. It was purely fear that had kept me from revealin' anything of my past in this place, for I learned early on that secrecy made no friends, but a loose tongue could be one's worst enemy.

"From first hearin' of the planned trip, no other thought was allowed to enter my mind. New York was my obsession day an' night an' I would not be distracted. I had pleaded with the Lord every night hwilst layin' in bed that Caleb an' Isaac would someday escape an' find their way back to me, an' I knew that meetin' could only happen in New York, the place all three of us knew as home. I swore an oath to God that if ever I should reach New York again I would become a runaway slave for real.

"My greatest strength lie in my ability to read, a fact that remained unknown to all, an' a fact that always served well to build my confidence. Miss Dorothy's stern warnin' about my education rang forever in my ear, an' I kept my secret close to heart behind sealed lips. Mrs. Jacobson was most suspicious an' mistrustin' of her servants, as was Master Jacobson of his slaves, an' I learned from papers lyin' about that an educated slave could not only cause embarrassment, but also put the fear of death into an owner.

"I soon realized that I was not accompan'nin' Mrs. Jacobson to New York because of any reward for my performance as a servant, but for other reasons. In public, she would say I was goin' because she believed I could hold up to the added burdens we would face hwile travelin' an' because my manner would lessen her chances of embarrassment by an ignorant slave. Mrs. Jacobson liked the idea that I could speak in a more refined manner. It was a novelty like no other.

"Hwat she didn' say in public was that to leave me alone with Mr. Jacobson would have surely brought forth an unexplained pregnancy into her home. The thought of it rankled her to the

443

core an' I believed she delighted in stealin' me away from his reach. She held no reservation about tellin' me to my face that I was a black hwore no different than any other, an' would spread my legs without shame for nothin' more than a day off. She would rant about how me an' my kind ruined the morality of half the south's most respected men.

"I was no whore, but I certainly agreed about the pregnancy. An' so I willingly sat beside her hwile watchin' the many miles of rural Virginee, Marylan', an' Pennsylvania pass by me for a third time in as many years. I felt for Licky. We were utterly trapped with Mrs. Jacobson in the boundaries of her coach, an' she seldom spoke a word unless to reprimand. It was Licky's worse nightmare come true.

"Licky did manage to endure the weeks of anxiety before New York City raised its mighty head. Her face showed all the emotion of seein' the city for the first time, hwereas my face remained unmoved in order to hide a heart racin' to again see the place I called home. No matter how unpleasant Mrs. Jacobson, I could enjoy knowin' I'd not returned to New York shackled to the bed of a wagon.

"Mrs. Jacobson's vacation was termed business, but nothin' could been farther from truth. By her conversations, it was clear that she was here to visit friends livin' on the Hudson River an' shop the city for the latest in dress. We wasted no time gettin' down to the chore of shoppin'.

"At first, both Licky an' I were ordered to accompany her, but as the coach began to fill with items purchased, Mrs. Jacobson became more inclined to keep an additional guard posted at the coach to watch over her belongings. She trusted her drivers even less than her house servants.

"Neither Licky nor I cherished the idea of bein' left behind to wait in the coach, much preferrin' to go into the stores, so it was a matter of turns to be taken. Bein' that I accompanied

Mrs. Jacobson to the first few stores, it was now my turn to wait, an' with nothin' to do but stay put; I found myself sneakin' peaks through one of the daily journals layin' next to me upon the seat.

"I kept open a wary eye for folks nearin' the coach whilst I slipped through pages scannin' articles an' findin' interest in anythin' written about New York or news in general. But I was now especially sensitive to articles about slavery an' abolition, an' especially on slave riots, an issue that drove fear of death into virtually all hwites because they were badly outnumbered in the south.

"In meantime, hwile I was occupied within pages of print, Mrs. Jacobson had finished her business an' approached the coach. Hwen I looked up, I realized she had already observed me readin' paper an' was clearly enraged. The minute I saw her face, I put the paper down, but the glare of her eyes predicted hwat was about to come. She was furious. She was beyond furious. She was all-fired burned.

'Get in Licky!'

'Yes, ma'am.'

"Our driver closed the door an' at once Mrs. Jacobson bore down on me without mercy. She struck the back of my head with her hand.

'What are you doing! What are you doing!' She forced the words through her clenched teeth. 'You are a learned slave aren't you? I knew it! I knew it all along!'

'No, ma'am. I'm not. I swear. I was just lookin' at the pictures. I swear. Just the pictures.'

'Don't you lie! Don't you lie to me, or I will have you whipped bloodless. Now, tell me! I insist you tell me this very second. I knew from the start that you were one to be watched. You can read, can't you?' she railed.

'No ma'am. I can't, I swear. I was only lookin' at the engravin's. I was bored an' fidgety an' I picked up the paper to see the engravin's. I meant no harm ma'am, I swear.' My tears fell an' I blubbered out my lies through convincin' sobs, for I was in fact truly scared half to death.

'So help me, if I ever see you so much as look at a paper....'

'Yes, ma'am. I deserve to be hwipped. I understand. I was wrong. I am sorry, ma'am. I am very sorry. I will never look at engravin's again. I promise, I promise I never will, no, ma'am. I promise.'

'Humph!' Mrs. Jacobson settled down some. 'How do you think it looks to these people in the street when you sit in my coach and appear all uppity reading a paper without the slightest bit of concern? Have you no sense? Did it never occur to you the trouble such foolishness might bring me, let alone the embarrassment? Of course not! You haven't the brains to consider such a thing! God help me, why must I even ask? One needs the patience of a saint nowadays.'

'Yes, ma'am.'

"She sat there starin' at me, filled with suspicion, indecision an' frustration that she couldn' sufficiently vent. She most certainly was mullin' over the seriousness of my actions, but in the end decided to forego the exasperation an' let it go after one more hellish warnin'.

'Don't you think for a minute that you will pull a fast one by me, Rachel. I don't trust you for a second. Your manner, your speech—there's a good deal more to it than meets the eye. I find you much too refined for your own good, and I will be watching. I will be watching your every move, Rachel. Do you understand me?'

'Yes, ma'am, I understand. I understand perfectly.'

'Good!' She leaned back upon the seat, let out a breath of frustration, an' then turned to look at Licky. Licky came as close

446

to bein' invisible as I ever saw. Mrs. Jacobson raised her fist and as Licky raised her arms in defense, she rapped on the cabin side.

'Let's go Zachary! I have wasted too much time as it is.'

"The coach moved forward.

"If I had been back on the plantation, I surely would have been hwipped for even lookin' at a daily journal. Hwether I was right or wrong, the act was strictly forbidden an' a hwippin' would have served as a lesson to others either way. But we were travelin' an' hwippin' a slave in the middle of the city would have been distasteful enough, without it bein' the free state of New York. The incident put Mrs. Jacobson into a foul state of mind, an' I remained the source of her irritation for some time before she became fully distracted by the sight of a newly opened store.

"It must be confest, although scoldin' had badly frightened me, so too, had it emboldened me. Through my show of tears an' sobs, I had feigned a good deal of my fear an' remorse, for I wished no unnecessary trouble from Mrs. Jacobson. I needed to put an end to the episode as soon as possible because above all else; I did not wish her attention. I knew we were about to leave the city an' begin headin' north upriver along the Hudson, an' I had worry enough without addin' Mrs. Jacobson to my concerns.

"I was becomin' frantic knowin' that time was a runnin' short an' if I had any notion hwatsoever of makin' my escape it would have to be in very short order. I was so racked with anxiety that I was positive Mrs. Jacobson could see right through me, straight into my plottin' soul with her suspicious eyes. I prayed she would think my nervousness due only to the issue with the paper.

"My confidence soon swelled as I recognized streets that I had walked many times with Caleb an' Isaac. We were now close to neighborhoods I knew. I felt as though things were turnin' in my favor an' I would be able to hide an' find my way about. I knew this city. I could feel it pullin' at me. It was only a matter of courage, but hwen it came right down to it, in spite of my oath, I was terrified. I was thinkin' like a slave.

447

'Are you ill, Rachel?'

'Hwat?' The question caught me off guard an' frightened me. Mrs. Jacobson was starin' at me.

'I asked if you were feeling ill. I see you are trembling, are you ill? It's a simple enough question.'

"I knew her concern was not for my health, but for fear the trip might be burdened or worse, be delayed by a sick servant. I tried to appear glum an' reply in a troddened spirit that belied my fear an' anxiety. Inwardly, I was barely able to answer her, but for a racin' heart an' nervous breath. I felt certain she was readin' my thoughts.

'I am only nervous ma'am. I am upset that I caused you so much trouble over the journal. I didn' mean to do so.'

'Yes, well, see to it that it doesn't happen again.'

'Yes, ma'am.'

"Havin' lied an' bein' unable to meet her eyes, for fear of bein' found out, I quickly turned away to look again out the window of the coach. It was just then there came into view the very last thing in the world that ever would I have imagined. A miracle would have made less of an impression, for across the street, painted on the wall was a large half heart containin' the words:

RACHEL

GO

TO

ALBANY

$350.00 REWARD

Immediate payment for return of my negro maiden servant slave!

Rachel Cook

Ranaway from subscriber Sept. 27 last.

Handsome mulatto woman aged about 25 in years. Fine featured, light eyes & skin. Active by nature, genteel in manner. Well trained and articulate. Will likely claim to be a freed person. Leapt from my coach on Jesey St. between Astor's Hotel and Washington's Market. Last wearing long sleeved black dress with white collar and ruffles. Leave word at front desk of Astor's Hotel until 15 Oct. Mrs. Henry Jacobson

"I went numb to the point I thought I would faint. My eyes flooded with tears at realization Caleb had somehow managed to get free an' was here waitin' for me. Before I even knew hwat I was doin', I threw open the coach door bolt an' leapt to the street. I fell flat on my face an' rolled along the pavement. I would most certainly be bruised, but blessed me; nothin' broke.

"I suspect Mrs. Jacobson must have thought I fell out an unlatched door as she stuck her head out the open door with a look of utter astonishment. However, once I got to my feet an' lit out, her naturally suspicious mind knew precisely what was happenin' an' she began to scream.

'Slave! Runaway slave! Runaway! Runaway slave!'

"As her voice echoed in the street behind me, I could see a number of hwite men movin' quickly in my direction, an' I knew although slavery was abolished in New York, runaways were not tolerated. New Yorkers weren' warm to the idea of an influx of Negroes in their city.

"Much of the north, especially along the east coast, renounced slavery an' voiced their outcries publicly, but privately they often supported the south an' offered scant condemnation for its practice of slavery because the plantations provided enormous amounts of cotton for northern mills. Slave labor in the south transformed itself into well payin' jobs in the free states of the north. I knew this because I had read all about it.

"I was light an' quick an' by dartin' this way an' that, I eluded the reachin' arms. I needed to get off the street an' so I sped down an alley, lookin' back only briefly to see who was in pursuit hwen I slammed into the likes of a wall. The air gushed from my breast after plowin' into the broad chest of a very large hwite man.

'Whoa, girl.'

"He had stepped out of nohwere an' lifted me clean off my feet payin' no mind as I struggled with every ounce of my strength.

'No! No! No! Let me go! Let me go! I'm not a slave! I'm not a slave!'

"I pounded him with my fists like a mad woman. I sank my teeth into his arm, but he grabbed my throat an' choked me into submission at once. He held me firm. The sky swirled about me an' the buildings swept around me like horses on a merry go round. He was runnin' an' he threw me forcefully through a doorway, hwich he slammed shut an' locked.

"He spoke to me in a restrained voice, *'Shut-up! Or they will surely find you. Follow me, quickly! We have no time to waste.'*

"I was so scared an' confused; I did exactly hwat he said without question because I knew hwat was in store for me should Mrs. Jacobson get hold of me once again. I wiped away tears of panic so I might better see. He led me through a maze of rats an' dimly lit tunnels, windin' their way through a myriad of foundations that supported freshly bricked walls of New York. Eventually we came to another door that opened to the outside, but a good distance away from hwere Mrs. Jacobson had been screaming.

'Who are you?' I asked this man.

'It doesn't matter.' He said to me. *'I'm an abolitionist and just doing my part.'* I noticed blood runnin' down his arm from the wound of my bite an' I felt terrible.

'Look at your arm. I have made a mess of it. I feel terrible, but you scared me to death. I thought you were—.'

'It'll heal, now come along.' He cut me short.

"We stepped into the light an' walked through a labyrinth of back alleys until we arrived at a secluded courtyard.

'You will have to ask yourself if you believe you can trust me. The open road is right there through the gate as you can see. You are free to go, but if you stay for a while, I will return, and I will bring you some money and food—and possibly help you get to a safer place. Trust your instincts.'

"Then he left me sittin' there all alone fightin' an unbearable urge to run an' hide. But havin' not a penny to my name an' without food or clothes, the impulse was foolish, if not dangerous, an' so I waited an' prayed to God for guidance.

"After about twenty minutes, he returned with three Negroes, a man an' two women. They had packed a carpetbag with food, clothes an' money an' they came with a smile. One of the women spoke to me.

'Hello chile. How you feelin'?'

'I'm fine thank-you. Scared. I'm mostly scared I guess.'

'I don' doubt. We don' tell no names, honey, buh we's here t' help. Where you from, talkin' like that?'

'Virginee.'

'Virginy! I don' never heard a soul talk like so in Virginy, no ma'am. You soun' like white folk. You live in da big house or you gots some white in ya, chile? You looks like a massa's chile, you do, yes'm. You's light.'

'My father.'

'A white daddy, yes'm I though' so. You look it. So, tell us where you be headed, hon, Pennsivania?'

'Albany.'

'Albany. Oh! Thas good, hon, buh choo gots t' be careful. I say, has you got famly or fren's waitin' on ya up that a way?'

'My husband.'

'Oh! Thas good. Ver'well, you jus' eat an' rest for now. You jus' calm yo'self, an' we'll come fer ya at candlelight t' fetch ya along.'

"And so they did under cover of dark. The trip by wagon was difficult, but much safer than by river, hwich was the customary means of travel to Albany. I traveled with a hwite man who used the name Sliver. He too was an abolitionist an' very sympathetic

453

toward the black man's cause. He was one of many who helped transport runaways from the South to freedom in Canada.

"We'd had plenty of time to get to know one another an' I liked the man enormously. He was smart an' funny. He kept me laughin' an' raised my spirits a good deal. We conversed at length, but he only gave me glimpses about his personal life, this for the safety of his family. He told me he had made this trip six times before. He said I was lucky because he would be takin' me as far as Kingston hwere we planned to meet another man who would take me the rest of the way to Albany.

"These plans were never certain an' I had been told onliest the possibility existed. We waited the day an' no one showed. Sliver asked me to understand the dangers involved an' to understand there were many reasons hwy the other man might not have been able to meet us. He himself was unable to stay any longer an' needed to return to his job in New York.

"I thanked him from my heart for all his help an' pleasant conversation. He had treated me as a person at a time hwen I needed the recognition as much as food an' water. We parted company an' that marked the last bearable day of my journey north.

"From there, I was on my own. I said a prayer an' started walkin' toward Albany. Mile after mile after wilderness mile, I walked in fear of animals, of hwites, an' my own imaginin's. My legs were scratched an' bleedin' from my ankles to my knees but for the amount of time I spent walkin' to the side of the road. I waded through brush, briar, an' thistle, for fear of bein' seen.

"I ran out of food long before I ever reached Albany, an' was left foragin' for roots an' berries best I could, but found very little, it bein' late in season. I spent the last of my money on bread. I traded my carpetbag for food at a backwoods farm. The worst part of all was the cold night rain. I couldn' keep dry an' I couldn' dry out. I caught a death of a chill an' was sick from then on.

"By the time I finally reached Albany, I was in a frightful state. I was tired, hungry, cold, plum wore out, sicker than a colicky horse. I was scared to death I might be seen in the city without a master or overseer. An' to make matters worse, I realized there is a real drawback to bein' black an' knowin' how to read.

"So many slaves are headin' either north to Canada or westward to the frontier that this place is literally papered with placards. I could read every poster announcin' runaway slaves, an' rewards, an' bounties, an' slave hunter services beyond count. They did little for my spirit. I hadn' eaten a thing in days, but I figured Albany was just crawlin' with slave catchers, an' I was too scared to ask anybody for anythin', so I jus' went without.

"Caleb left his half heart messages in many places, not only around our apartment in New York, but also in Albany. The half hearts in Albany never said hwere to go, an' for that reason alone I was never able to find him. At first I thought him stupid, wonderin' hwat he expected me to do, but after seein' all the placards posted about the city, I understood no slave in his right mind would say hwere he was hidin'. I could only wait nearby his signs an' in hopes he might appear.

"Days went past hwile I waited. I had managed to corner a few freed slaves hwo took great risk in talkin' to me. They believed I was a free person because of my speech, but I had no papers to prove it an' that made it against the law for them to speak with me. They did tell me it was said that a good many slaves were gainin' shelter by workin' in loggin' camps at the west end of the canal, in forests north of Buffalo an' Tonawanda.

"I have no idea how I made it from Albany to Tonawanda, but by the time I arrived, I was so run down an' nights were so bitterly cold, I accepted the fact that I could go no farther. As a rule, I slept in the warmth of the daytime sun an' kept movin' at night to ward off the chill, until it became useless. I had a choice of turnin' myself in, or freezin' to death.

"Fearin' the slave catchers an' the fact I would never see Caleb or Isaac again, I worked my way amongst the barrels for the last time. The sun was so warm that day it was just like summer, an' the wind couldn' reach me. I wrapped myself in my shawl an' prayed the Lord might take me to heaven before came the cold of night. I was so tired of living. Lord, but I was tired an' was soon fast asleep—peaceful sleep in the warmth of the sun. An' then I woke up in this bed." Rachel looked at us with resignation.

* * *

So engrossed was I in her story that my cup was still full of tea—*cold tea*. I don't think anybody alive would have known what to say at that moment. Dorrie and I could do nothing but sit there in a stupor trying to imagine how anyone could stand up to such a godforsaken fate.

I had seen slaves, had read and supported their cause, had fed and clothed them in shelters, but had never really interacted with them on a personal basis. Slavery had been outlawed in New York for some time and was never allowed to take a firm root in other parts of the north. Years back when I was active on the street, I had on occasion visited orphanages for black children, these institutions were more noticeable the farther south along the coast one traveled and I never traveled much below New York State.

I had read many articles by the abolitionists who exposed terrible atrocities and injustices, but I had never been so close as to sense first hand the sickness of it, never so close as to take it personal, so close as to feel the emotion and shame of having done nothing more to help these people. This was a sobering experience and I found myself both guilt ridden and bleeding for this woman.

* * *

The days moved forward quietly and their peaceful nature along with plenty of good food quickly brought strength back to Rachel. She regained her weight and was soon up and moving about as though she had never been down. I found Rachel to be well read and a woman of great insight. Dorrie and I enjoyed her company immensely, for she added a whole new dimension to our tiny space inside the SCHOOLBOAT.

However, as always, there were those areas where I was incapable of conversing with conviction, specifically the realms of men and babies. It was in these areas that Dorrie and Rachel shared common ground and a similar fate. And so they spent a good deal of their time working together doing chores, sharing stories about their children and finding a way to accept their losses. Dorrie and I grew apart but I understood.

THIRTY-SIX

The waters of the Erie Canal were cold in these shortened days of late autumn. During the warm summer months our habit was to jump in the canal, wash, and call it good. Now however, washing was a ritual we shared every Saturday evening, at which time we dragged out the tub and heated water on the stove. The three of us rotated turns, allowing ourselves a half an hour each to soak in blissful comfort, while served a cup of hot tea before retiring to bed.

This particular night I was first to bathe and after a heavenly soak and relaxing cup of tea, I arose, clean and refreshed, leaving the tub skimmed and reheated for Dorrie, who was next. I refilled the pots to boil for Rachel's bath and saw to the boys, tucking them into bed. After a short chat with Dorrie and Rachel, I decided to leave the two to their baths and take a short stroll along the towpath for some fresh air.

There was a buffeting breeze that foretold of an approaching storm. This always excited me and I was easily drawn out of doors to enjoy the wind upon my face. Summer was long since past, having fought its battle and lost, but in its death throes, it wheezed and coughed and gasped a warm dying breath from some distant southern place. It filled me with sadness and comfort at the same time.

I threw my head back and listened to the wind blow through the leafless branches. I felt it kick up the fallen leaves and roll them out of the shadows to cartwheel across my feet. The countryside went from blue to black and back again as the moon dodged and sidestepped a herd of stampeding clouds. It was an impossibly warm evening, a surprise—a gift best not taken for granted. After all, this was November and one should not be fooled by a warm windy lullaby.

I began to walk eastward along the southside towpath, and with every step I moved farther away from the boat and closer to the impending storm. The wind took on a life of its own, talking in low tones, whistling and howling in the darkness. It spoke from the surrounding woods and the farther from the boat I ventured, the spookier it became. I was covered with goose bumps, but I loved the daring sensation. I bundled up tight in my shawl and shivered.

The wind cuffed my ears and whipped my drying hair about my face. I stood at the bank and looked back along the canal toward our boat lanterns flickering off in the distance. The moon forced its light down through a sieve of ominous clouds, and its beams cracked like ice across the ripples of agitated water. I closed my eyes and leaned back against the push of its unseen current. It smelled of rainwater, and I let myself be rocked by its rush to pass me by.

The wind in my ears veiled any sound that might have fore-warned me of the massive hand that reached out to completely cover my face. I was lost in its size and not only was I unable to scream; I was unable to breathe. Frantic, I attempted to pry away the fingers with my own, which were twig-like in comparison and no match for the man's strength. I dug hard into him with my nails and attempted to bite his flesh, but he lifted me off my feet and carried me backwards away from the towpath and into the darkness of the woods.

My struggle now was only to breathe. I was numb with fear knowing Dorrie and Rachel were soaking in a hot tub out of earshot and oblivious to my being swept away. I was powerless against the strength of my abductor and convinced I was about to die or worse, be hauled away in chains like Rachel. I looked up to heaven uttering my first words for mercy and forgiveness when the man spoke.

"Shhh. I not hurt you. I friend. We meet in Albany. You bring gift to Indian girl. I bring gift for you. No scream. I not hurt you." Slowly he let loose his grip. I was shaking so bad I had to hold on to him to keep from collapsing. I turned to the stranger in the darkness, but was so badly frightened I didn't realize at first who he was. The moon flickered once again and its light bounced off the half heart medallion upon his chest and instantly I knew.

As was often my nature in abnormal situations, I filled with rage and lashed out, striking the man in his ribs with my clenched fist and all the might I could muster. He moaned from the blow.

"Don't you ever, ever, ever scare me like that again! Never! Do you understand me? Never!" I screamed as I delivered a second forceful blow.

"Yah." He took my rage without complaint.

"My god! I thought I was about to die. You should be shot!" I stepped back away from him in order to regain my wits.

"Yah. Sorry." His voice filled the shadows.

He was almost invisible in the darkness of the woods. I tried to make out his face, but it was pointless. I settled down out of necessity; I needed to get my breath back.

"What are you doing here?" I finally asked him.

"I look for you. I bring gift."

"Gift! My god! It better be a good one." I tried to stop my shaking. "What gift? Why are you bringing me a gift?"

"Spirit gift."

"Why Spirit gift?"

"Brush. Good medicine."

"Brush?" I frowned and then it came to me. "The girl is well, yes?"

"Girl is well, yes."

After so much worry on my part, I was genuinely pleased by the news.

"That is wonderful. She is strong, yes?"

"Strong, yes"

"Lord! You scared the devil right out of me. Is she with you?"

"No."

"Are you alone?"

"Yes."

"Come with me to the boat and rest."

"No."

"Yes, I insist. You must come back to the boat and stay. You can eat and rest."

"No."

"Why no?"

"I go now, back to Albany. This for you, gift from mother."

He produced an amulet, which he handled with respect and pointed out two locks of hair in particular among an assortment of oddities.

"Hair of mother and daughter, Snow on Ground and Little Deer. They go with you, many prayers, much love, strong medicine, good medicine. Coyote hair bring courage, bravery, and smart. Dove feather bring love, peace. Redbird feather mean blood, life, heart. You wear. It is good. Great Spirit go with you, Snow on Ground, Little Deer go with you."

In the darkness of night, the amulet was difficult to see, but it appeared as though the small bundle was tied with a fine piece of sinew strung through small decorative beads or seeds. He placed the amulet about my neck and tied it. I looked up onto his face and could see that he was very pleased to have presented me with the gift.

"Thank-you. Thank Snow on Ground and Little Deer. Now, you come to boat. Rest. Eat. Come with me."

"No. I go back."

"Why not come to boat?" I asked.

"Many white men. Not good. I go now."

"Wait. I will bring you fresh food and drink. Food, do you understand?

I will bring you food. Stay! Will you stay?" He looked at me and glanced around.

"I stay."

"Don't move! I will be right back. You stay."

I ran back to the boat and stormed down the steps startling both Dorrie and Rachel.

"Good Lord, Elizabeth! You scared the wits right out of us," said Dorrie.

461

"I need food. I need food. What do we have to eat? I need it quick!" I ransacked the cupboards much to their concern. I reached for a bowl of muffins. Dorrie turned about in the tub to better see me.

"Elizabeth, what on earth are you up to? Is everything all right?"

"I'll be right back. I'll tell you about it in a minute!"

The two of them looked at each other in surprise, and then back at me as I threw the last of whatever I could find into a sack and stepped back into the darkness.

The Indian had waited as I asked, but he wouldn't eat in front of me.

"Little Deer is fine. I am very happy to hear this. I prayed for her."

"Yes, Little Deer strong. She laugh now. Snow on Ground very happy yes."

I could see that the Indian was edgy and impatient to vanish back into the darkness. I decided to let him go. But first—.

"What is your name?"

"Taa'sooma'hane"

"Taa—Taa—."

"Taa'sooma'hane", he repeated.

"Taa'-soo-ma'-han-e. What does the name mean?"

"Night-shadow-killer-hunter."

"Night killer? Oh, terrific. That's just what I would expect an Indian to be called. No thank-you. I'll go with Shadow Hunter, a fitting name that you have certainly done justice." He looked at me without understanding what I meant.

"Never mind. Tell me, Shadow Hunter, where did you get this medallion." The Indian stood momentarily mute, as if he didn't understand my question.

"Found it." He replied after some hesitation. I reached for it and turned it over. I could feel the engraving upon the backside. I scratched it with my nail, but I had to wait for the flickering moon to cast its light upon the medallion. When it did, there before my eyes was what might well have been the name Rachel, or just wishful thinking, for it was hard to make out anything in the intermittent moonlight.

"Shadow Hunter, I remember this medallion. You were wearing it when I went to your camp. Where did you get it? I must know."

I grasped it firm in my hand, and because of my nearness to the man I was able to sense his unease about my question. I understood that he would only lie to protect himself so I explained further.

"Shadow Hunter. Listen to me. I know Caleb. He has squaw. He has wife. She is Rachel. Rachel hurt like small girl. Rachel needs Caleb. You bring Caleb here. You bring Caleb to me. This is good. This make Great Spirit happy. This make me happy. I pay you much. I make you happy. Yes?" Shadow Hunter only looked at me.

"I go now."

"Yes. I pray for Indian girl and for Caleb. Tell Caleb Rachel here. You bring Caleb to me. Yes?"

"I go now."

With no positive assurance that he might do my bidding, Shadow Hunter disappeared into the nighttime forest. He was as silent as his name implied. I remained still, standing a short spell upon the towpath in order to think over all that had just taken place.

The medallion seemed an incredible coincidence, but certainly explainable, and I would not have been the least bit surprised to know that Caleb was with the Indians. Not that Shadow Hunter would ever say so, but I recalled seeing Negroes run into the thicket when I first entered the camp. There were Negroes living among the Indians.

I recalled how Rachel had said she made her break as soon as she arrived in New York—how she knew Caleb had done the same and left messages in the streets around their boardinghouse instructing Rachel to look for him in Albany. Why Albany? Maybe he couldn't stay in New York any longer. Maybe the slave catchers were on to him. Without documents, he would have been in constant fear. He must have been heading for Canada. That made rightly good sense.

I wondered how long he waited in New York in hopes of seeing her. It must have been difficult knowing the chances of her escaping and returning to their home were next to none. He probably didn't wait at all. It would have been pointless. It would have made more sense to find a place of shelter and leave signs for Rachel to follow. Rachel did exactly that and went to Albany.

Meanwhile, he found temporary shelter in the one place he might be welcome—an Indian camp. They were known to be sympathetic toward slaves and free blacks. Even in Albany, Caleb wouldn't be able to travel openly and make himself visible for Rachel without documents. The Indian camp would be an attractive place to hide out and keep up on news of who else was on the run. The camp would be the perfect place to wait before crossing the border. I had overheard at Van Meriden's, Indians made good money by guiding slaves through the back-country en route to Canada or the frontier.

Rachel on the other hand had left Albany for Tonawanda because the free blacks had told her of the logging work in this area. Something told me that Caleb was still waiting for her in Albany. Of this, I was absolutely certain although at first I couldn't say why. It must have had to do with Shadow Hunter. It was something about him that told me Caleb was in the camp.

I could feel it inside. I could feel it in my heart, and I knew Rachel's spirits would be resurrected with a little help from the Good Lord. Smiling to myself in the dark of night, I started back for the boat.

Both Dorrie and Rachel were awaiting my return. They had cut short their baths and ventured outside. They were walking cautiously along the towpath searching for a sign of me. I stepped out from the woods into plain sight and headed in their direction.

"My gosh, Elizabeth! Where have you been? We were really beginning to worry," exclaimed Dorrie.

"In the wood talking to an old friend."

"In the woods?" Dorrie repeated with a questioning tone, finding that a bit odd.

"Yes, yes, in the wood. Go on inside and I'll tell you all about it."

They were both anxious to know what had happened and quickly went below. I followed them back inside and after preparing a fresh brew of tea, gave a less than full account of what had taken place. I simply told them how excited I was to see my old Indian friend and receive news of Little Deer's progress. I told them how I wished to help him on his way. They were fixed upon my story nonetheless, for any association with Indians was a matter of interest.

"I couldn't imagine what you wanted with all that food," said Dorrie.

"It was the least I could do. He traveled all the way from Albany to give me this spiritual amulet. It was their way of saying thanks."

I opened up my shawl and revealed the amulet. Dorrie and Rachel leaned forward across the table and were at once fascinated by the odd bundle of hair and feathers. Dorrie was very familiar with the details of the accident, as it was connected with the explosion. I had mentioned many times the burden brought

465

to my heart by the little girl's injury, and how I had gone to great lengths to find her. I answered all their questions the best I was able, but contrary to what is said about a woman's ability to keep a secret, I made no mention whatsoever about my discussion with Shadow Hunter regarding Caleb.

After tea and talk, it was late and we retired for the night. I removed the amulet from around my neck and studied the curious object. I was amused by how readily I accepted the notion that it held great protective powers. I supposed I cherished the thought of someone or something to watch over me. It gave me a sense of security and peace of mind. I felt compelled to keep it near. The absurdity of such notions made me feel foolish, and I laughed at myself, yet I willingly placed it under my pillow for no sound reason.

As I proceeded to climb into bed for the night, the meeting with Shadow Hunter and our conversation about Caleb played over and over in my head. I said nothing about Caleb to Rachel or Dorrie for fear of building up hope that would sink Rachel beyond reach if something went afoul. I felt good about both keeping the secret and proving to myself that I had the backbone to bite my tongue in spite of possessing such wonderful hopes. I repeated my vow to keep quiet as I drifted off to sleep.

It may or may not have been because of the way Shadow Hunter locked his strong arms around me, but I dreamed of Christopher and found myself blissfully within his embrace. It was an embarrassingly sexual dream, maybe even sinful. It was as real as life itself, and I reveled in the rapture of his attentions. I was utterly devoid of any will to resist his advances, utterly helpless against his power to sway my heart. He fulfilled my nocturnal desires. He brought me a sense of security and peace. He made me feel whole.

I awoke the following morning with a heart full of bitter sweetness. I had been on such a wonderful journey, having felt all the emotions of love that I craved in my real world. I lay in bed not wishing to move, only relishing the last vestiges of passion with a joyful smile long before I opened my eyes. I was in the best of moods. I couldn't imagine why I had been blessed with such a dream, but determined it must have been due to discussions the night before about the amulet and the powers of protection and love it was supposed to possess.

The days passed and we were all blessed with improving health and spirit. While Dorrie and Rachel spent their time knitting winter mittens and socks for the boys, I spent mine writing Mary and Allen, writing in my journal, or seeking out information regarding Christopher. My best lead came from a man named Randolph, the administrator of a lumber mill at the west end of Buffalo. I had been directed to see him by the manager of the supply house where Dorrie and I had found Rachel.

* * *

"Yes, ma'am. I've met the man. But it's been a good many years I seen 'im last. He was attendin' to business here in Buffalo includin' lookin' over this mill t' see how many board feet we could work. He was stoppin' here b'fore headin' into Michigan Territory to survey. Said he was a plannin' t' search for waterways an' timberland t' be milled at a later date. I 'member folks was laughing heartily around here they wuz thinkin' him rather peculiar t' be so interested in Michigan timber, they sayin' it was worthless. Ya can't give them trees away.

"I figure it'll be centuries 'fore anyone'll look to Michigan for timber. Too much wood available here in New York, an' back east, comin' from Maine, an' Pennsylvania t' make the Michigan stands worth the effort. Even with the canal, gettin' them trees back east jus' would never be proft'ble."

Randolph cocked his head to one side and looked up at me with a devilish grin. "I ain't sayin' the man is an idiot, mind ya. For sure he's done well for his self. Ya can tell that jus' by the way he talks, ya know what I mean? I reckon he's got somethin'

467

up his sleeve cuz a what he said when I was laughing 'bout him buyin' trees in Michigan. He looked me straight in the face and said, *'Ever hear of a place called Chicago?'*

'Most certain,' says, I. *'Fort Dearborn, the Chicago Massacre, heard plenty. Never been there myself, don't care t'go, too many Indian troubles, but Buffalo ships off and on to Chicago.'*

"He says, t'me. *'Chicago will be one the great ports of the world. It's just waiting for someone to build it and where do you suppose is the closest place in the country to supply the lumber?'*

'Michigan?' says I.

'Michigan,' says he.

"Would you know where in Michigan he might have surveyed?"

"No, can't say I do. Ya see, he was also partic'lerly interested in rumors 'bout large nuggets o' copper, said to be a ton apiece lyin' about the south shore of Superior. That's way up north in Siberia. He was askin' a lotta questions 'bout those nuggets. He was talkin' some about smelting an' formin' copper nails for the furn'ture industry, and cladding for ship hulls, which he could both use for his fleet an' sell for a handsome profit as he put it. I 'member he did assemble a team here in Buffalo to head up Michigan way, but that's about all I can tell ya. I only remember all this cuz he wasn't the kind o' man one soon forgets. He seemed t' be interested in everything."

Randolph went on to mention Christopher's intention to go to St. Louis in search of a route through the Stony Mountains. His comments brought back memories of Christopher's excitement when he conveyed those ambitions to me in Boston years ago.

Randolph proudly produced a crudely embellished map of his own making that he kept readily available for conversations the likes of ours. He was clearly thrilled to discuss the mysteries of the western frontiers with anyone interested, and from his conversations with travelers along the canal, he had drafted his own version of what he believed the western unknowns looked to be.

"Here. Look at this." He cleared the countertop, unfolded the sheet and carefully laid out his map before me. "Them territories out west are uncharted. I gotta good idea 'bout how things look, cuz I've spent so much time talkin' to Indians 'n traders goin' back an' forth."

He drove his digit down atop the name Buffalo and from there began sliding his forefinger back and forth across the sheet showing me visually to the best of his knowledge how Christopher planned to head into the Northwest by way of the Missouri River.

"Now, I know for fact he was plannin' to head into them territories. That I know for fact cuz I remember thinkin' *what a dreamer*. Thing is, I don't know for fact he was headin' straight west 'long the Illinois River t' get there. Seems he had business on the Ohio. He was goin' on 'bout boats and such. He might o' gone down here like this."

Randolph dragged his finger from the south of Michigan down along the Wabash River on the western edge of Indiana. He then jogged hard to the right guided by a squiggly line that represented the mighty Ohio River.

"Otherwise, it wou'da been shorter t' go by way 'o the Illinois River, like this here, 'specially if you happened to be in Chicago." The man raised his finger to a more northern position upon the map. "Ya see what I'm sayin'?. It's a more west'ly direction that goes dreckly t' the Mis'sippi an' darn near straight 'cross t' the Missouri an' St. Louis. Mr. Claussen made no mention o' goin' either way. but I'm here t' tell ya, it's cert'in he planned to end up in St. Louis. If ya don't fine 'im there, ya can darn well bet yer hot on his heels. He'll be close by."

"Lord!" I let out a deep breath. "It's certain you have talked with Christopher, I can see that. But in all honesty, I am not sure what I should do next."

469

"Ya mean where to go?"

"Yes. I mean exactly where to go. You have him all over the map. I had thought maybe Cinncinati, maybe toward the Ohio River."

"Wouj ya like to know what I'd do?"

"More than you can know."

"He talked, trees, copper, mills, Chicago, boats, but he was clear on St. Louis an' the Stony Mountains. Everythin' else was kinda in the air. If I was you, I'd take a steamer t' Michigan for sure. They're opening land offices all over. There's one in Monroe, Detroit, there's one in a place called Kalamazoo. I'd go to Detroit. If he ever bought up any land it'll be in the records at the land office. An' if he didn't, ya can travel the old Sauk Indian Trail from Detroit t' over Chicago way, they call it the Chicago road. If ya wait til winter sets in, it shouldn't be too bad. Get outta Buffalo an' across the lake soon as ya can, for the season ends, but wait in Detroit until the hard freeze, then go for Chicago. For one thing the In'juns should be farther south by that time an' not so apt to give ya trouble. I figure no matter where he's been, Chicago will give you plenty o' choices on what t' do next."

* * *

I listened to all Randolph had to say and left in something of a depressed state of mind. Maybe Christopher would be impossible to find. I could barely fathom any prospect of traveling to the upper regions of Michigan even if it meant additional clues to his whereabouts. That was horrifically difficult country. Aside from Detroit and a few French, there were no whites living in the territory anywhere to speak of— *only Indians.* I was relieved to think it had been years since he

470

was in that area. I much preferred to think about going straight to St. Louis.

It was with heavy heart and contemplation that I left the lumber mill to head back to the SCHOOLBOAT. While en route, I was forced from my thoughts by a gang of children who had stopped their activity to study me. They stood staring as if to know me, and it gave me a most peculiar sensation. It made me very self-conscious for I knew of no reason I should be the object of their attention. Then, as quickly as they stopped their business, they carried on with it, and paid me no further mind. I looked over my shoulder in their direction a time or two.

Whether the children thought they knew me or were of a mind to beg for a handout, I couldn't say, but in my morose frame of mind the kids caused me to consider how pointless seemed these efforts of Christopher to go laboring through life amassing ever-increasing fortunes when he had no heirs. No sooner thought, however, than a second woefully dismal consideration came to mind. I reminded myself that I really had no idea what Christopher had in the way of heirs considering his travels all over the globe.

Not only did this thought not sit well with me, but also much to my surprise, it made me feel jealous of all things. Jealous, pure and simple, and it left me with a sudden sensation of having been left out in the cold. I was so wrapped up in my relationship with Christopher, so selfish and short-sighted that I never gave the least consideration to the possibility I might not be the only purpose of his affection, for it had always been Christopher, Lady Rebecca, Mary and I. Furthermore, I had to ask myself how much affection could the man have for me if he let me slip from his world. I felt my spirits sink to rock bottom, yet they didn't diminish the overwhelming urgency to find him and re-secure my place in his life, the sooner the better.

471

THIRTY-SEVEN

Taa'sooma'hane dropped back into the dark of the woods and stood stock still, as if one with the tree trunks about him. He was in plain sight of the white woman, but he knew she would never see him. He watched her pause now and then, peering into the underbrush, straining to see through the shadows for a sign of his presence.

He observed her moonlight mottled face as she stared directly at him. He smiled. She had great powers and he knew she sensed his being there, but he was invisible to her. He watched her walk back and forth along the bank of the canal. He understood by her side-glances that she was growing wary of the night and things unseen, and as he expected, she soon went back to the security of her boat.

He rubbed his ribs. She had delivered a respectable blow to his chest, but he only admired her all the more for her action. She was spirited, and he liked that in a woman. She was brave. He recalled how she dared to enter his camp alone, how she handled the stolen brush, and the way in which she refused to hand him the gold coins, instead demanding to give them to the chief herself.

The last thought made him chuckle out loud. There was no chief in the motley collection of left-behinds that dwelled within the clearing that was his home. They were all lost souls once looking for shelter and now clinging together in order to survive. But the old man played the part well.

It was understandable to him that the Great Spirit guarded 'Ezlbeth' and this was reflected in her character. She was of strong medicine and he was careful to respect her from the very start. Yet he liked the feel of her, the smell of her. She had just bathed. Her hair had been damp and her warmth and cleanliness were appealing. He looked down at the sack of food. Not only was the woman strong and favored by the spirits, but also she was generous and of good heart.

472

Taa'sooma'hane sat down within the security of darkness and opened the bag. The aroma of bread and chicken drove a sigh of pleasure across his lips. He brought the food to his nose and his saliva flowed heavy. He had eaten only jerky and pemmican for the past week since leaving Albany. Time had not been on his side and this prevented him from hunting for fresh food. His only option for variety was to steal fruit and vegetables or dig for roots. He placed his nose over the bag and inhaled. Nothing eased hunger like good bread.

He knew from years of living and working about the canal that the boat would soon be hauled ashore for the winter season and the white woman would most likely shelter elsewhere. He had been under pressure to find her before she left the canal, and so he spent his nights riding and his days hiding and sleeping. It had been much to his advantage that the days had grown shorter and the nights long, for he had been bound by his word to find this woman.

Taa'sooma'hane broke off a small piece of chicken and raised it to the sky. He lowered it to the earth. He held it up to the four directions and then set it upon the ground, leaving it untouched as an offering to the Great Spirit. He then stuffed his mouth with the fowl. He repeated the ritual for every offering, muffins, preserves, fruit, and cake.

He could easily have eaten his way through the entire contents of the sack, but he knew over the course of his return trip, he would regret his greed. Instead, he finished off the chicken so it wouldn't spoil and slipped the remainder of the foods into his parfleche. It was always best to stay a little hungry and sharp.

Taa'sooma'hane now felt invigorated, revived both physically and mentally. He lit his pipe and thanked the many gods that watched over him. He acknowledged the spirits of the wood, the sky, storms, and earth for helping him achieve his goals. It was a good night. He had filled his stomach and met his obligation of oath.

473

He leaned back against a tree and relaxed. He noticed that the moon was flickering less and shining more. The clouds were thinning. Maybe it wouldn't rain after all. He looked along the canal to his left, toward the boat that belonged to Ezlbeth. He stared at the twinkling lantern and he wondered about the white woman.

She asked him to bring to her the black man, Caleb. Was he her slave? Had she originally come to his camp to find Caleb or to help Little Deer? Taa'sooma'hane still believed it was for the benefit of the little girl, but the white woman knew of the medallion. It meant something to her. It was true she didn't try to take it from him, but still, it meant something to her.

He thought about how she spoke of *'wife Rachel'*. These words were also true. Caleb always spoke of finding his wife, Rachel. Caleb had said that a woman owned him and his wife. Could this be the woman? Of course not, Caleb would have known her when she entered the camp. He tried to make sense of it, but it was too confusing. It may have been the work of spirits. He decided he would tell Caleb about these things, and let the black man make his own decision. He would be happy to bring Caleb to Ezlbeth and collect the reward should they go to Buffalo. That would only be a fair trade if it were he who brought good medicine to Caleb.

The journey back to Albany was more agreeable. He was no longer bound by his commitment to Little Deer's mother. He also now traveled with the wind at his back. He traveled at a more leisurely pace, taking what time he needed to hunt for food, to rest, and to gain back his energy and stamina. He had reached Buffalo from Albany after more than a week of hard riding, but was taking twice that time to return, dragging with him the winter season close behind.

Taa'sooma'hane always preferred to ride under cover of night whenever traveling. He believed given half a chance, the whites would go out of their way to make his life miserable. He viewed white men as an arrogant breed that possessed little if any compassion for anything but greed. They took everything that belonged to his people, stripped them bare of a livelihood then insisted that they "dress proper", go to church, and live like the whites. For those who failed to conform, it meant banishment, sometimes the slave block, or more often than not, a suspicious death.

He understood that since the arrival of the white man, his people had been uprooted and were in constant battles with the English, the French, the settlers and each other as they fought to find or protect land on which to survive. The strength and numbers of the white man continued to grow while his people dwindled away from disease, drunkenness and depression.

Even when his people tried to adopt the white man's ways, they were harassed and shunned. They were forced into pockets of wilderness that were out of the way and out of mind for ever shorter periods of time. His ancestors had fought the settlers hard. They had been brave and willingly gave up their lives to save the land and their people.

Unlike Indians, who respected their opponents' bravery, the white man despised the Indians, their ancestors, and their children. The white man's government had offered money for Indian scalps. It was barbaric, but not surprising. As far as he was concerned, white men hated Indians, always had and always would. That was the long and short of it.

The days of tribal distinction were disappearing in this part of the country. He and his kind were often being forced at gunpoint to move westward into less desirable lands that were as of yet unwanted by the whites. Those that remained behind were corralled into small reservations, or sought refuge in camps much like his.

The camps were comprised of many different tribal bloods that now intermarried and further blended the distinctions. His people no longer knew themselves. The old ways were disappearing. Their culture was crumbling. They were leaving the earth, becoming one with the wind to blow around invisible.

These troubling thoughts played heavy on his mind as he passed the many new towns sprouting up along the canal on his way back to camp. As he turned away from the canal and the white man, he worried about the future of his family. As he entered the woods of his lodge, he worried about his children and asked the Great Spirit would he live to hear their laughter or their cries.

He was deep in contemplation, unaware of his surroundings until overcome by a sudden sense of disorientation. He looked about. Had he somehow lost his bearings? His mind had been wandering far away with worry, but not fear, for his horse knew its way home. Mentally, he backtracked along his course of travel to reassure himself his horse hadn't been daydreaming as well and taken a wrong turn, impossible as that may have seemed.

His thoughts became lucid, snapping back from his mental meanderings, he looked about to confirm his bearings. There was no doubt; he was where he should be. He was supposed to be home, but something was amiss. Had he eaten some bad food or was a forest spirit playing a prank? A feeling of concern coursed through him. He stopped his horse and looked ahead.

"Héehe'e." (yes) He spoke aloud.

He was where he should be, but where was the camp? The trees were bare, and instinctively, he knew there should have been a fire in the distance, or smoke snagged in the branches as it hung low in the cool night air. He listened. Nighttime was the Indian time for eating and merriment, but there were no sounds of laughter, no sounds of children playing or dogs barking. His confusion was quickly replaced by a disturbing premonition— *the whites.*

He rode a ways farther along the trail until he reached the creek that snaked along the perimeter of the camp. He stopped and looked across to the clearing in astonishment, for the camp no longer was. Everything was gone, lodges and all! The smell of old firewood and wet ash permeated the air.

He dismounted his horse and walked over to where the great fire had always burned. He stooped down and sifted the dark dust with his fingers. It was cold. The earth below the ash was cold. It had been out for many days. It was too dark to scout the ground, but he knew the heel marks of the white man's boot would be found in great number.

Taa'sooma'hane rose to his feet and looked around. He was alone. He thought of Little Deer, and Snow on Ground. He thought of Hard Foot and Jimmy Black Crow, the old man and all his many friends. He was saddened and distressed. He walked across the barren ground through a world now invisible and silent. He moved to the place where his lodge had stood and saw the faces of his people moving about him like ghosts in the night. In the dim light of the moon, he was able to make out the blackened image of scorched earth and the stumps of burned poles that once formed the walls of his home. His lodge along with all the others had been torched and only these charred posts remained.

It was a disheartening event that had taken place during his absence. It was more than just lodges destroyed by a fire. It was years of memories in this place he called home. Many of them good like the birth of Little Deer, many of them troublesome and serving to bring strangers closer together. His people had been living under the threat of eviction for as far back as he could remember. It appeared as though the whites had accomplished their goal at last. His people had been run off the last camp.

Like all people who lived in the lodges, Taa'sooma'hane knew that the area about Albany had become well settled, and it was only a matter of time before something like this would happen. Every day more whites crowded in and spread out along the canal in search for opportunities as business expanded, buildings multiplied, and open land disappeared.

The Indian community irritated the whites. They believed his people to be an affliction and an obstacle to the development of the land. The white man's Congress had passed the Indian

477

Removal Bill and all eastern tribes could now be legally forced off their land and driven west of the Mississippi.

One lodge after another was burnt down, and its occupants evicted for not having title to property, which they inherited from their fathers and their fathers before them. Time had come, and now it had happened to him. He needn't be told anything further. His people were growing distant, and now he only worried for their well-being. He would have to find the women and children and give hand with the other men to ease their suffering.

Taa'sooma'hane suddenly raised his head to the wind. He had picked up the scent of a fresh fire. Smoke wafted through the woods mingled with the unmistakable aroma of roasting meat. He stood one with the stillness of the night and listened for the sounds of man. There was nothing to be heard nor seen. He looked for the glow of firelight in the trees, but saw nothing.

Yet, someone was nearby. He felt certain it wasn't white men, for they had no reason to be quiet or hide. White men would have had a roaring blaze, and a lot of commotion would be heard echoing through the trees. This was different. This was hiding out, probably someone left behind, someone not in camp when it was burned down. Someone, who might have run to hide, and could now tell him what had taken place. He slipped into the underbrush.

Taa'sooma'hane earned his name at an early age after displaying a notable shrewdness when moving about after dark in an unfriendly white man's land. It was the best time to scavenge. As an Indian, he was seldom offered work, but still he contributed much to the welfare of the lodge. He was a silent and cunning thief, who made his ancestors proud. Those skills came to him naturally and now without thought, he became one with the night that surrounded him. He moved quietly through the trees and headed forward with his nose to the wind.

The glow of a campfire quivered among the upper branches of a tall stand of oak, and after cresting a rise, he looked down into a creek bottom not more than an arrow's flight away.

Slowly, he worked his way down the slope, moving in the direction of the fire. Careful not to snap twigs or rustle the dried leaves, he picked his way down to the creek and toward the light.

When he was close enough to hear voices, he dropped onto all four and laid low. He listened and the sound of the voices brought a smile, he recognized the three black men as friends. Although his heart weighed heavy, his questions were many and his mission serious; he was unable to resist the sport of the moment.

Slowly, Taa'sooma'hane inched his way forward. Testing his ability to be silent, he advanced only when the wind moaned and the branches rubbed in complaint. He laid his belly on the ground and filled his lungs with the scent of soil. He imagined himself to be the leaves, the roots—the dirt.

He called upon the lizard spirit for stealth. One arm up, then down. One leg up, then down. He called upon the spirit of the earth to lie quietly as he passed over its leaf-covered face. He called upon the spirit of the forest to make him in invisible behind the branch of leaves now clenched in his teeth. He calculated each measure of ground, each move to be made. He sensed each muscle in his body. He called on them one by one, directing his body to the next position, steadily and imperceptibly closer to the three men.

Caleb, Johnny, and Birdie were settled around the fire talking in quiet voices, sometimes complaining, sometimes joking, which brought forth an occasional laugh. When Taa'sooma'hane was little more than a tall man's stride away from the three men, he arose from the leaves to stand tall before them, glowing in the light of the fire as the oak leaf branches dropped away to expose his massive frame.

"Ah Ho!" He greeted them with his booming voice.

Caleb and Johnny both fell backwards and away. Nearly paralyzed with fright, their eyes opened wide like bright white buttons. Birdie had the misfortune of sitting with his back toward Taa'sooma'hane, who intentionally brushed the back of his head with the leafy branch. He never turned around, but launched himself across the hot coals in a desperate 'do or die' scramble for his life.

Taa'sooma'hane looked down at the three of them sprawled in fear upon the ground, and broke into face-splitting grin. The three men, on the other hand, were thoroughly disgusted with him to the point of anger.

"Damn you Taa! Hwat in god's name is the matter with your head! Ya scared me half to death." Caleb shouted, still badly shaken.

"Taa'sooma'hane, ah gotta mine t' club ya wit dis here stick for bein' so mean. I done burn mah hands an' all. Ah swea' I gotta a mine to scalp yo hea' mahself." Birdie was now on his feet with a chunk of firewood gripped firmly in his hand and fuming.

"Lucky, I no slave catcher. Yah? Ha-ha!" Taa'sooma'hane laughed good and loud, pleased by his acumen.

"Lucky fo you, ya re'skin devil. I 'bout ready t' club yo hea' flat an' put ya in da groun'. I come dis close t' poundin' yo ass right down inta da grave fool, yassah! I come bu' dis close." Birdie held his fingers close together on one hand, while swinging the club in a threatening gesture with his other. He clenched his jaw and snapped his head with short jerks, as he spoke. He was as red faced and fired up as a black man could get, and hotter than the coals he had just passed through.

"You fight better you hear, I hope, yah?" Taa'sooma'hane teased him then sat down before the fire, oblivious to Birdie, his club, and any sense of fear. The three eventually sat down as well, and within a moment's time they all began to laugh uproariously recounting Birdie's flight across the fire pit. He was still rubbing his burned hands. It was their last good laugh for Taa'sooma'hane wasted no time in asking about the camp. Caleb spoke for the three.

"Times told, it happened jus' like you always said it would, Taa. They come ridin' in early, before sunup, an' surrounded the camp. At first break of light they charged in an' rounded up everybody. We were all sleepin' sound and most everyone had to get dressed.

"Johnny, Birdie an' I havin' no family just hightailed it into the woods. Everythin' was turned upside down an' in a state of confusion, an' it was still dark enough for us to slip into the underbrush unnoticed. I always worry about them damned slave catchers so I sleep with onliest one eye closed, an' I'm hard pressed to take my boots off hwenever I do sleep."

"Dem fears is all dat save' our necks. Dirk n' Rommy got haul' off right smart for havin' no doc'ments," said Johnny.

"Yes, sir. That they did." Caleb shook his head in dismay. "Anyhows, I just laid low in the woods, buried myself under leaves, an' watched as they lined everybody up. Soldiers went inside the lodges, chased everyone out, took what they wanted, then torched 'em to the ground. In twenty minutes the whole place was a pile of ashes. Snow on Ground, Little Deer an' the rest gathered up hwat little they could on their backs an' were marched out. They didn' take much. Soldiers helped themselves to hwatever they wanted, which was most everything they didn' burn. I watched 'em take the skins right off women's backs an' leave them to stand shakin' in the cold."

"How many days past?"

"Mus' be six by now."

"Snow on Ground an' Little Deer—they hurt?"

"No. They looked fine, but it wasn' a good thing, Taa. Soldiers were real pushy an' cared little about anybody's feelin's or well bein'. Grey Rabbit stood up to them an' he got a right good beatin'. There wasn' much anyone could do, too many soldiers. They must have planned it for late in the year. Woods are too thin to hide in, the ground is open an' the snow hasn't come. Good time of year for roustin'. No place to run or hide."

481

"I find them. I go tomorrow night."

"You should Taa. Sooner the better, they need you. I didn' hear much about hwere they were off to, but I got the idea they were headin' west past Indiana, maybe into Illinois country or farther. Maybe across the Mississippi, hard to say."

"Yah, I leave tomorrow night. I find them." The men grew silent. They stared blindly into the flames and lost themselves to thoughts of despair.

"Caleb."

"Hwat?"

"White woman speak. Ask for you."

"Hwat hwite woman?" Caleb was immediately on guard.

"Ezlbeth, woman with gift for Little Deer."

"The woman who rode into camp?"

"Yah."

"She asked for me?"

"Yah."

"By name?"

"Yah."

"That don' sound good. Hwat does she want with me?" Caleb was nervous. He shifted his weight and looked into the darkness with concern.

"She say she have Rachel."

"Hwat!" Caleb's eyes snapped directly back to Taa'sooma'hane. "Hwat! Hwat did you say! She has Rachel? Hwat do you mean she has Rachel? Are you sayin' she bought her? Did you see her? Taa', did you see Rachel?"

"No."

482

"No?" Caleb stopped short. "Hwat do you mean, no? You didn' see her? Is that what you're sayin'? You didn' see her? Was she with the hwite woman or not? Hwere were you? Hwere 'd you go? You must tell me hwere you went. You must tell me hwere she is. Tell me hwat happened. I can't believe it. Oh, thank God Almighty she's alive. Thank God Almighty!" The rush of the news overwhelmed Caleb, cresting before a long deep breath, whereby he finally settled down.

"Taa, I never thought I would ever see Rachel again. I don' know how this can be, but the Lord has surely blessed my worthless black ass. Tell me what happened. Please, I need to know everything. I just can't believe what I am hearin'. Rachel's alive, Rachel's alive an' she's here in New York. I can't imagine how she made it this far north. Maybe she's free. Maybe she saw my signs." He shook his head. "Tell me about this hwite woman. Tell me hwat the hwite woman said, Taa."

Taa'sooma'hane lifted Caleb's medallion off his chest.

"Rachel in Buffalo. White woman look at this. She say bring Caleb to me. This make Great Spirit happy."

"She was lookin' at the medallion?"

"Yah."

"She'd said bring Caleb to me."

"Yah."

"She'd said my name? She actually knew my name?" Caleb offered the Indian a cup of hot chicory.

"Yah."

Caleb stared at Taa'sooma'hane. He had given him the medallion with a heavy heart in return for shelter and food. He had been weary and in a bad way. How ironic that the medallion should leave his breast to rest upon the chest of another and return with word of his heart's desire. If God had cursed him with loss

483

and pain, He too, blessed him with hope and a sign that maybe the Almighty had a design for him and Rachel after all.

Caleb was distracted by these amazing thoughts as Taa'sooma'hane arose from the fire to head back into the darkness. Caleb jumped to his feet and followed him. The Indian went for his horse, which he brought back and tied up so as to keep an eye on it. He retrieved his pipe and tobacco pouch. Caleb's mind continued to race.

"Can you take me there, Taa? Can you take me to her?"

"No. I go to my people. I find Little Dear and Snow on Ground."

The refusal quieted Caleb. Taa'sooma'hane sat back down before the fire and filled the pipe. He pointed the stem first to the stars, then the earth and finally the four directions before lighting it. He inhaled deeply of the smoke and passed it on to Birdie, who ironically enough was sitting at his left rubbing his burnt hands to warm them.

"You go to Buffalo. She there."

"I don' know Taa'." Caleb was hesitant. "A black man gets in a heap of trouble if he's caught on the road durin' daylight let alone after dark. It's mighty dangerous. Bad enough durin' the day an' all, but after dark, I don' know. I have no papers an' that could get me killed quick."

It was a depressing reality that made moving about almost impossible for a black man unless he knew the backwoods and trails. Caleb couldn't pressure Taa'sooma'hane because Taa'sooma'hane had no concept of what being pressured meant. He would say yes or he would say no—and he said no. Caleb sipped at his coffee, took a turn at the pipe, and while the conversation turned to the plans of Johnny and Birdie, he dropped into thoughts filled with frustration and disillusionment.

The following morning came in hard and cold with heavy frost. In the wee hours before sunrise, the three men closed in tight next to Taa'sooma'hane, who laid claim to the only blanket. He voiced no complaint in sharing it as they huddled together for warmth. They turned the blanket's length across their chests and pointed their feet toward the fire. Every hour or so, either Johnny or Birdie, who slept on the outside of the group, would toss fresh wood onto the coals. By morning all were up searching for firewood, stoking the fire, and trying to drive out the cold with a pounding of fists and sips of hot chicory. There was nothing left to eat that might warm a man.

"I'm gonna walk da traps."

Birdie almost disappeared into his coat as he walked away in the cold morning air. Taa'sooma'hane was skillful with a bow and always kept one with him. He preferred its silence, and he could shoot a dozen arrows in the time an experienced musketman could pound down a second ball. He strung it.

"I go hunt. You look in camp for things."

"I think we got about everything, Taa," said Caleb.

"I hunt, you look."

"Hwatever you say. I'm starved. Hwen will you be back?" Taa'sooma'hane looked up into the trees. He pointed to a large branch overhead.

"When sun there."

With that Taa'sooma'hane stood up. He wrapped his blanket about him, and after reaching for his bow, stalked off through the woods heading for a thicket of berry briars.

True to his word, the sun touched the overhead limb, and he came back with three rabbit. Birdie had returned with another armful of firewood and a couple of rabbits from the traps. Everyone went to skinning and skewering the fresh meat. It was roasting over the fire by the time Taa'sooma'hane headed back into the woods for a second time.

He reappeared moments later with a slain deer draped across his shoulders. The men ran out to take the weight from him. He was close enough to camp that he decided to gut it in the warmth of the fire. Caleb and Johnny had spent their time scouring the ashes, and as Taa'sooma'hane had predicted, a number of useful items were discovered, badly discolored but entirely useable.

The best find, a good size cast iron pot, was sunk in the fire pit at the lodge of an elder. It had been deemed too hot or too heavy to carry off on such short notice. Now it was full of boiling creek water and pieces of rabbit and venison. Johnny and Birdie made a pass through the garden and found some half rotten winter squash and pumpkin, which they placed into the coals to bake.

The men ate well and feeling the energy of hot food and drink, they spent the day talking, relaxing and attending to the business of cutting up what remained of the deer, roasting and drying the meat. Caleb tried hard to cover the anxiety he felt knowing Rachel was in Buffalo and that it was almost impossible for him to get to her. He considered the fact that winter season was fast approaching and many blacks had headed north of Tonawanda and Buffalo to work in logging camps. He could pretend to be a logger, but he was tredding on thin ice.

"Taa?"

"Yah."

"Taa, I was thinkin' about you leavin' tonight. I was thinkin' that we both have to go in the same direction, but it is goin' to be very difficult for me to move freely toward Buffalo, be it day or night. I was thinkin' that I suspect your people are bein' driven westward along the Great Turnpike, an' it might make sense if we traveled together.

"I know you would move faster by yourself, an' I know I can't offer you much of anythin' worth value, but if you would consider takin' me along, I would give you the other half of that medallion once we reached Rachel. It's good gold an' silver, not cheap. It was a heartfelt present from the owners of the plantation where we lived. It's yours if you'll take me along. It also might help that I can read an' write. That may come in handy when looking for news of your people."

Taa'sooma'hane listened to what Caleb had to say, and as much as he liked the medallion, he was just as interested in the payment offered by the white woman. The idea that Caleb could read might or might not be helpful, but at least he was experienced at traveling on foot, this proven by the fact he had gotten as far north as he did.

Taa'sooma'hane was having a change of heart. Buffalo wasn't exactly *'going his way'*, but then who could say whether his people went west or not. It was just an assumption, although a good one. Going to Buffalo meant going north at some point. On the same hand, his people might be going north as well. What did he know? All things considered, it made more sense to take Caleb to Buffalo and take a chance on gaining a reasonable reward, then move on.

"I take you."

"Yes! Yes! Thank-you Taa'sooma'hane. Thank-you very much." Caleb tossed a burning stick into the fire and rose to his feet, unable to contain his excitement. "Yes!" He hollered into the wood. "I'm on my way Rachel! You wait for me! You hear! You wait for me!"

By the time nightfall arrived, it was decided to leave the traps, and utensils with Johnny and Birdie. Caleb and Taa'sooma'hane would pack the horse with all the food they could carry in order to sustain them as long as possible. The men pushed and pulled at each other, gave hugs, handshakes and said their good byes.

Johnny and Birdie remained behind. Standing before the glow of a fresh fire, they turned into paired silhouettes, swinging arms and waving farewells, until they meshed with the trees. Caleb finally turned his back on them and looked forward, beyond Taa'sooma'hane, beyond the mist of their breath and into the spread of western stars.

487

THIRTY-EIGHT

Thanksgiving it was. A day of thanks and yet, it was the worst dark kind of day with no hopes for even a hint of sunshine. The world was submerged in the shadows of thick low-slung clouds that seemed to soil their bottoms by scraping the ground while forcing us to keep the cabin lamps aglow. A cold nor'westerly was coming in hard, blowing, and bringing with it a horizontal spray of sleet freshly scraped off the turbulent surface of the Great Lakes.

While waiting for Jack and Kenneth to finish getting dressed for the weather, I stood peering out a small larboard window that offered a limited view toward town. I could choose not to see these foreboding signs of winter, but there was no escaping the roar of the gale as it peppered the window and decks with intermittent blasts of ice and debris. The sound of wind was constantly in our ear, and the boat jerked back and forth against the restraint of its lines.

At least we were no longer traveling on the end of a towline. We had arrived in Buffalo with the last of the canalers, leaving scant time to spare. I shuddered at the thoughts of the freezing rain and what Buzzy might have faced in such a storm a week earlier while still on the towpath, especially in places like Rock Cut.

A silent prayer expressed my gratitude for our safe arrival and the warmth and coziness of our cabin. It was a comfortable place to live, for we anticipated in advance that the SCHOOLBOAT would be a home to mostly children, and planned its overhaul and fitting out accordingly.

Our cabin enjoyed certain comforts rarely if ever found on an ordinary canal boat. The best example was in the galley where sat a sizable stove. Few homes, let alone a canal boat, might boast having such an item. I had purchased it as much for its potential heat as its room for pots and pans. When it came to boats, whether in a harbor or basin, there was always a problem

488

with damp chilly quarters, and a stove of this size could put a respectable amount of heat into the cabins when needed. It was well suited to keep comfortable children and adults alike.

At breakfast time, the woodburner could serve any number of people fried eggs, bacon, hot cakes, potatoes, fresh bread and more, all at the same time—and all hot. Cold dinners were a thing of the past, and a considerable chunk of the chore in preparing meals was history. Needless to say, Dorrie was beside herself at first sight of it, for only the wealthy could afford such luxury.

On this particular morning, I fully appreciated the heat of coals glowing within the stove's big black belly, and I would add, the wisdom of my decision to buy it. As I backed away from the worrisome weather beyond the window, I soaked up the stove's heat, storing it in the fabric of my garments, while contemplating how much I dreaded the idea of going outside.

Unfortunately, I had made a promise to Jack and Kenneth that I would take them up to the trading post and buy them each some sweets if they would help me bring back foodstuffs for our dinner. Unlike me, or any sane person, they were raring to go. Sleet meant nothing to them, and the more I hesitated to venture out, the more they were filled with impatience and childish threats.

Dorrie's husband and son had been with the Lord for some time now, and although it was to be a day of thanks for us all, the loss made it difficult for her to enjoy much of the good fortune that had come her way. Jack and Kenneth, on the other hand, were too young to appreciate the meaning of marriage, its bonds, the dependence, and especially the heartbreak and loss that often went with it.

To Dorrie, the boys seemed painfully oblivious to the passing of their father and brother. They lived only for the future, unable to repress the energy and explosive impulsiveness of their young hearts. It was disheartening for Dorrie to see the distance growing between her boys and the memory of their father, but it was a reality Dorrie understood was best. They were ready for a good time, and the idea of a walk to the store easily surpassed the monotony of a morning confined to the cabin and the concerns of a cleaning chore that might crop up unexpectedly.

With a sigh of desperation, I donned my coat and led the boys out into the icy blast. The door was wrenched from my hands by the force of the wind and slammed hard against the cabin side. The cold air stole my breath and forced me to bury my chin deep into my woolen scarf. My blood had not yet thickened enough to prevent winter's first calling from reaching right to the bone. Of course, the boys were immune to winter and not about to be delayed, so we were off at once stepping lively along the bank of the abandoned canal.

Most everything was closed down either for the holy day or for the season. The most important concern, the trading post, always remained open for business, and so having no reason to fear otherwise, the boys left me far behind as they crossed the bridge and ran for its door.

About the time Jack and Kenneth disappeared into the store, a rag-tag assortment of children wandering about outside in the street grouped together and positioned themselves to intercept me. They numbered six or seven, ranging from about five years in age to about twelve or thirteen.

Quickly, they surrounded me, and I could see the effect of the cold upon their reddened cheeks and hands. They were poorly dressed for the weather and stood wet and covered with beads of melting ice. The sight filled me with compassion as though I might have been a mother worried about my own.

These street orphans most certainly lived by thievery. I knew their kind well, having seen and worked with many since the first time I laid eyes upon the mudlarks back in England on the River Thames. They were constantly bumping into me and I clutched my bag tightly to foil their sometimes and sometimes not so inconspicuous attempts to steal me blind.

"Good day, ma'am." One of the older boys spoke out.

"Good day children. Why are you all out here in this cold wet?"

"We have no homes, ma'am," he answered.

"Don't you have some place to go where it's warm and dry?"

"Not really, we live in the street," said another.

"The livery. We sleep in the hay pile. That's warm." Said a little girl with a filthy face.

"Sometimes we crawl under a foundation and can feel the heat of a hearth," said a young boy.

"What is it you want with me?" I brushed off the groping hands and prying fingers.

"Just a bit of change so we might eat." Said the older one.

"Please, please, please." They began to cry out in unison.

"Hold still, now!" I snapped. The children grew silent.

"I will offer you something better than change. I will give each of you a fine dinner if you want it. Their eyes grew wide. "But you all must bathe, wash your clothes, and make yourself clean before you sit down at my table."

The boys withdrew at once. The girls looked at each other. The youngest of the girls, maybe six years in age, looked up at me.

"Why do we gotta do that?" She asked with the utmost sincerity.

"Because you are all a filthy stinking lot, and I'll not have you sit at my table in such a state. It would only serve to ruin dinner for the rest of us."

"Baths make you sick," exclaimed one of the boys. "Nobody takes baths. That's stupid."

"Can't you just give us some money?" The oldest of the disgruntled boys asked.

"I'll give you all a grand dinner; I have already said so."

491

"But how are we supposed to get cleaned up? We can't jump into the canal. It's too cold." A younger boy protested.

"I agree, but you could heat water at my place, soak in a tub, and scrub yourself down good with a bar of soap and a stiff brush." The boys looked at each other clearly frustrated by prospect. The whole lot presented me with a collection of facial expressions ranging from curiosity and astonishment to torture.

"Well, what's it going to be? I haven't got all day to stand in this freezing rain. Is it yes, or is it no and go hungry? I know what you rascals are up to, and I promise you won't be stealing anything of value from me. You might just as well put those adventurous hands back into your pockets and keep them warm."

"I will." Said the youngest girl. "I'm hungry an' I'm cold an' I'll take a warm bath, an' I want something to eat. I'll sit at a table. I'll do it, ma'am. I'll wash up."

"What's your name, honey?"

"Maggie."

"All right then, Maggie, you come with me." I started to walk away with this youngest of the three girls. She was soon followed by the other two, and after a given amount of grumbling and protest, the four boys finally came around and fell in behind. By the time I reached the front doors of the store they had closed ranks and remained most sullen.

"Now listen up children. I have another proposition for you." They were not too eager to hear what else I might have to say, fearing I could be drawing them into some form of work or other undesirable situation.

"I know you are all a scruffy and unruly bunch, but if you can keep a promise, if your word is good, then I offer you this. You may each pick out ten pieces of candy, whatever kind you wish, but I will only pay for the candy held by a child who acts with favor and respect whilst inside the store. If I see anyone running amuck, I'll pay for nobody's. Do you understand?"

Of course, they all swore to show only the best of behavior, and of course, they all lied through their teeth, unless you understood they had little or no concept of what best behavior even meant. Following the same path of Jack and Kenneth, the orphans scrambled inside and surrounded the candy jars trying to get the best pick of the sweets that were available.

I nodded to the storekeeper, who appeared not only to know each and every one of the little thieves, but also to be absolutely mortified at the sight of the miniature gang storming into his establishment.

"Good day, sir, and happy Thanksgiving to you."

"And to you as well, ma'am. Hey! Hey! No! No!" The storekeeper's arms flew outward as if to cast a paralyzing spell.

"Sir, don't worry about the children. I know they are a riotous and unruly lot, but I will cover all expenses including damages, which I pray will be minimal." This seemed to ease the owner's complaint somewhat.

"What a bunch of hooligans they are!" He looked at me first with an expression of blame, then one of exasperation, and finally one of question. "Aren't you one of the ladies on the schooboat?"

"Yes, sir, I am. Elizabeth Claussen." I extended my hand.

"Bernard. Pleased to make your acquaintance. I usually see Miss Whipsman. She mentions you at every visit. I gather she must be a clever one to have you out on a day terrible as this. It is bad enough for December, let alone November."

"Isn't that the truth, sir. To be honest, Dorrie is the better of cooks, and I promised the boys sweets for Thanksgiving. Unfortunately, along the way I encountered this miserable lot." I shook my head in dismay. "It troubles me to see them in the cold. I have decided to take them back with me for dinner, after all this is a day of thanks, and for me what better way to show it than by feeding the hungry?"

493

"You must have the heart of a saint. I suppose I spend so much time chasing the brats out of my store, I forget their plight in life. Maybe this is a reminder from above. How would you feel if I donated the meat for your meal?"

"My word, sir, how generous of you to offer." I was genuinely surprised.

"It's a small gesture, but it will ease my conscience. Take what you want and feed them well. There will be no charge, besides I have been paying for their thievery all year as it is."

"I don't know what to say. I am afraid I feel as though I have imposed upon you."

"No, nothing of the sort. Please, I insist, take what you wish. I've got milk and butter hanging on a rope in the well; take what you need. As you said, it is a day of thanks."

"I am not sure how to thank you, Bernard. You are too kind."

"I'm not really as kind as you might think, believe me. Just ask any one of these little horrors. Them hooligans have cost me more in stolen goods than I care to know. Let's just say somehow you've put a sense of sympathy in my heart for the moment, for whatever reason I can't imagine. Truth is, I long since forgot they were kids; I only see them as trouble. Make 'em a good dinner, Miss Claussen, but keep a sharp eye on the silverware or you'll spend the rest of the year eating with your fingers. I guarantee it."

"Good advice, and that I will, sir."

I went on about my business, selecting the things I needed for the evening's dinner. I saw to it that the children thanked Bernard for his generosity. Indeed, there must have been a long-standing relationship between the parties because they were utterly astonished, speechless in fact that he should give them anything. Their opinion of him was reflected in the way they cautiously slithered up to the counter in order to snap up their candy before making a quick retreat.

494

THIRTY-NINE

"Oh, my word! What is this?"

Dorrie's eyes went wide with surprise. The rambunctious lot of kids poured down into the boat fast on the heels of Jack and Kenneth, who were loving every minute of it. All the pushing, shoving and stomping of feet, all the howling and laughter within our close quarters made the level of noise near deafening.

"There's been a change of plans." I hollered above the din. "No! No! Girls! Stay out of those! Boys! Boys! Whoa! Whoa! Now hold on a minute."

"Get your filthy fingers off o' that!" hollered Rachel as she threatened to snap or slap probing fingers. "Nobody's eatin' yet!"

"Alex! You keep those younger boys in line!" I ordered.

"Yes, ma'am."

"Jack! Kenneth! Settle down!" hollered Dorrie, who then turned to look at Rachel and me in disbelief.

"A change in plans, indeed," said Rachel, trying to get a word in edgewise. She and Dorrie both started laughing in resignation amid the pandemonium.

"If the two of you possess anything dear to heart, you best put it up now, and make sure nobody leaves the boat without being searched or you'll likely regret it. I have been fully forewarned," I advised.

Dorrie took a deep breath and sighed. "Well—what do you want us to do?"

"I suggest we clear the stove for now. Obviously, we'll be eating later than we planned. We need hot water, *lots* of hot water. There's a good deal of scrubbing to be done before we sit to eat. That is the deal that was struck, *right children?*" The question was lost in the noise.

"Alex! Alex!" I hollered.

"Yes, ma'am."

"We're going to need water brought on board. I put you in charge of filling the tubs. There are a couple of buckets in the bowstable and a wellhead just up the canal. You see to it that the boys get the water, and I'll see to it that the girls wash your clothes. Fair enough?" Alex first looked outside at the freezing rain and then at me. He hesitated.

"If you prefer to wash the clothes, then the girls and I will get the water."

"No, no." He shook his head. "We'll get the water."

"Good."

"Here." Rachel handed Alex a bucket from alongside the stove.

"C'mon lads, I'll find you some more buckets," said Dorrie as she grabbed a shawl. "Jack, Kenneth—you boys give a hand, you hear?"

"You best have them boys roun' up some extra firewood," said Rachel as she stuffed the stove's cast iron belly with split wood.

Amid all the commotion, the preparation of food was impossible. Whether good or bad, at least the children had eaten enough sweets to tide them over for the time being. Baths were now the order, and as the boys busied themselves fetching fresh water and firewood, Rachel filled her pots atop the stove and set them to boil. Bucket after bucket of hot and cold water was sent into the largest cabin, where they were dumped and mixed together inside two large tubs that when stored upside down served as tables in a space soon to be a classroom.

As Rachel stoked the stove and watched over the heating pots, Dorrie and I set off to strip the girls of their clothes, and start them soaping and scrubbing their garments on the washboards.

"Let's go ladies, get out of those filthy clothes. Hurry up now, we have much to do before sitting down to eat."

"What are we s'pose' to wear?" asked Maggie.

"You aren't supposed to wear anything, sweetheart. Now get them clothes off and stick 'em in this tub and when they're good and clean, you can march that little butt of yours over there and plop it in that tub and scrub yourself down."

"But I'm cold."

"Then you better get to scrubbing. The harder you scrub, the warmer you get." I studied the wisp of a thing as she stood all covered in goose bumps. "Lord, I can hardly tell what color you are child." I looked at the others. "And look at those mops atop your heads. What are you all growing, stable straw?" The girls laughed. "Oh my word, Dorrie, look at this hair!" I tried to run my fingers through the tangled mess, but it was impossible. "I swear these girls have never seen the likes of a comb or brush."

"Ain't the same as boys," said Dorrie. "I just whack their heads, dunk 'em, an' dry 'em."

"Amen. I guess we'll just have to see what we can do for this lot. Let me look at you, Ellen—mmm; yours isn't much better. Why don't you give Dorrie a hand with the clothes while I fetch you girls some brushes."

"Yes, ma'am."

I stepped out of the classroom and into the galley.

"Alex!"

"Yes, ma'am."

"Take this money to Bernard and bring me back a couple of brushes and combs from the store. You may keep the change if you're quick about it," I whispered.

"Yes, ma'am!" he whispered back with enthusiasm.

"Remember, be quick about it! We still need a lot more water."

"Yes, ma'am." Alex flew out the hatch and broke into a run.

In truth, I would have been happy to give the girls something with which to cover, but there were no extra clothes and so the three remained as naked as the Good Lord created them. There wasn't an ounce of fat upon their bones to keep them warm, and a lack of nutrition and weight suggested them to be younger than their years. Together, their three small frames would easily fit into one tub, and so once their clothes were cleaned, they plunged hand in hand beneath the warm sudsy water if only to escape the cold.

As lather and laughter flew this way and that, I collected from Dorrie the washed garments ready for rinsing in the forward stable. From there, I brought them to Rachel, where we draped the articles across a web of clothes lines to dry as quickly as possible in the heat of the stove.

Considering all the fuss about taking a bath, once in the tub, the girls were in no hurry to climb back out into the cold air. We pretty much had to yank them out by their hair and force them to follow Dorrie forward to the bowstable. The mules that were normally kept there during the summer months were absent, as the animals wintered in a nearby stable.

In place of mules, the girls stood shivering atop the left over straw. They stomped their feet and hunched over with teeth a-chattering in complaint as Dorrie poured buckets of barely warmed water over their heads. They gulped air from shock of the cool rinse. Once the soap was rinsed out of their matted hair, we wrapped them tightly in fresh towels and turned them loose to stand alongside Rachel before the heat and comfort of the stove.

Of the three girls, Maggie was about six years in age. Louisa was nine, and Ellen was eleven. Ellen was the last to step out of the tub and last out of the stable. Being that she was the oldest, she tended to mother the two younger girls. I was heartened to see a caring trait within the wildness of her character.

As for the boys, Alex was the oldest and clearly ruled the roost. He took charge of the situation as he saw fit. He wasn't bashful about cuffing one of the others if they crossed him or slacked off. He made sure a fresh supply of rinse water was always at the ready.

Dorrie and I next hung a drape between the two tubs. The boys were left on their own to strip down and bathe, being given a simple but stern warning to clean behind their neck and ears. Their clothes were passed over the drape to Dorrie or myself, and in turn passed on to the girls who were now warmed and called back to further soap, scrub, and rinse.

It was a fair trade, for the boys had faced the freezing sleet while working the well pump and fetching water and firewood for the girls. Now, Rachel heated the water so the girls could wash the boys clothes in return. By the time they were finished with the garments, their own dresses were dry enough to wear. They slipped into the warm clean clothes, and draped the boys' outfits to dry in turn.

The girls were confined to the galley while the boys waited for their clothes and busied themselves by emptying the tubs through the stable scuppers and then dry-mopping the deck. They stepped lively and called impatiently for the blankets and towels to protect them from the cold winter air that swirled about the unheated bowstable.

In the meantime I returned my attention to the girls.

"All right, ladies. Let me have a look at you."

The three girls faced me, and although their clothes were clean and dry; I was saddened to see the state of their garments. Such need, I thought to myself. I wondered how God could allow these tragedies to be. Most certainly, God was a he.

"I want the three of you to sit in a line, one behind the other. Maggie, you first; then you, Louisa; then you, Ellen; and I'll be last. Here—everybody gets a brush."

We passed combs and brushes back and forth, all working together, and all working out knots to make something presentable of the mops atop their three heads. They were a snarled, matted, knotted lot that needed scissors more than not, but to my amazement—few lice.

"No lice. What a blessing." I said aloud. I couldn't believe it.

After the boys donned their clothes, they were sent back into the stable to warm up by splitting additional wood for the stove. That was a chore given squarely to men. In the meantime Dorrie and I worked on the girls, attempting to transform them from street rats with fewer manners than stray dogs, into beautiful young ladies with fewer manners than stray dogs. One could do only so much in a morning.

For Dorrie and me, it took one meal to chance, one to question, and one to confirm that Rachel was a cook extraordinaire. Having served in the kitchens of two southern plantation owners, her training in the culinary arts placed her in a league all her own. Dorrie and I both could both put out a respectable spread, but it was embarrassing to say as much after sitting down to Rachel's table.

In any event, Rachel easily assumed command of the galley and stove, and all boiling water unused for baths was put back to cooking. Dorrie, the girls, and I, sat about the table to begin peeling, slicing, and dicing the vegetables and potatoes. Rachel concentrated on making dough for bread and pastries.

It was a bittersweet experience as I looked into the hopeful faces of these three young girls. How obvious it was that they needed a mother. How obvious it was that I had no children. They thrilled to sit alongside me and perform the simplest tasks with joy. They were angelic in appearance, innocent in certain ways, and yet could make a grown man blush with the words that crossed their lips.

'Wasted miracles.' The term came back to me from my past and weighed heavy on my heart. I embraced the girls, talked to them and fussed over them with heartfelt tenderness. So starved were they for the attentions of a mother's love, that they returned my every affection twofold.

The boys tired of their labor and returned to warm their hands by the stove. They had done a fine job of splitting wood and stacking it in the stable, providing us enough to last us for a couple of weeks. They re-entered the cabin rosy cheeked and thirsty, bringing in with them a blast of winter air. I welcomed them to sit across the table and join us for a cup of hot chocolate or cider. This they did, and by the look of amazement upon their faces, I concluded that we had done a good job with the girl's hair.

As we resumed our wait for dinner, Dorrie and I sat at the table with our hot drinks and listened to the heart-rending stories of these children and the hardships they faced. I was drowning in sympathy when all of a sudden Rachel let out a scream that drove the breath of life from us all.

Badly startled, we jumped up from our benches ready to dash off, fully expecting to see some immediate danger.

"Lord! What's the matter?" I asked no one in particular. I turned to see nothing amiss, other than the last of Rachel disappear out the hatchway and into the storm. "What on earth—?" I started for the hatch and turned to face Dorrie who was as wide eyed as me, and equally nervous about what might happen next.

"Is there something wrong with the stove?" she asked me.

"I...I...."

I shrugged my shoulders having seen no sign of fire. I didn't have a clue. We moved to the hatch with the children close behind. A quick escape was foremost on our minds. I had just set foot upon the top step when we heard another scream from outside.

The children stopped short as I looked outside in fear of Rachel's well being.

It all happened so fast; I could hardly venture if the trouble was on the boat or off. Were we supposed to run or stay put? The children were watching my every move, waiting nervously for direction. Above the roar of the wind I now clearly heard Rachel either crying or laughing. I looked along the canal through the freezing rain.

"Wait." I said in a lowered voice as I raised my hand to hush the others.

"What is it?" said Dorrie as she eased up the steps to stand alongside me.

We stood still and strained only momentarily to make sense of what was before us, for there across the way was Rachel swinging around and around, feet off the ground in the crushing embrace of a man. She was crying uncontrollably. She was crying so hard, and the sound of her joy was so pure, it brought a flood of tears to my eyes.

"What's going on Elizabeth?" Dorrie whispered. "Is that Caleb?"

"I do believe so."

"Oh! Imagine that!", she whispered. "How on earth did he find her? How could he possibly know she was on this boat? Must have been talk about town."

"The Indian brought him," I said as I observed Shadow Hunter standing in the background.

"The Indian?" said Dorrie as she turned to look at me fully confused. "How did he know she was here? Do we know him? I don't get it. Who is the Indian?" She cupped her hands over her eyes and squinted, hoping for a better look at the figure. I filled her in on a few of the details.

502

"Remember that little Indian girl that I was telling you about, the one who was injured by the horses?"

"Little Deer?"

"Yes."

"Well, he was the one I met in that camp. He was the same one that rode out here to give me the amulet. What I never told either of you was that he was wearing the same medallion that Rachel wore, only it was the other half."

"Huh!" Dorrie covered her mouth in surprised shock. "And you never told us?"

"I figured there had to be a connection, but I didn't want to make issue of it, for fear of raising Rachel's expectations. You wait; I bet it all comes out at dinner. For now, I'd say we have more guests to feed." I stepped out onto the deck and called out.

"Those men are freezing, Rachel! He'll be dead of cold if you don't stop hugging him. Bring them inside! Come on in Caleb, you too Shadow Hunter!" Shadow Hunter barely acknowledged me, and then only with certain suspicion.

"Don't you even think it! You will come in and eat! The last time you didn't, this time you shall. Now get in here where it's warm! Rachel, bring him in. Come on, all of you!" I waved them vigorously toward me.

Rachel took both men by the arm. She and Caleb came down the steps first, and their faces were awash with melting ice and tears of happiness. Shadow Hunter half-entered about as wary as a cat going into a sack. Only his head appeared for the longest time. He would have been content just to stand there letting out the heat while looking around inside the boat at all of us. I reached up and gripped his arm firmly.

"Come in. It's nothing but cold and wet out there, so you might as well sit at my fire." I tugged at his wrist.

"Yeah, Taa. Get warm. We've had more 'n our fair share of the cold for sure," said Caleb.

Shadow Hunter was persuaded enough to let me lead him across the cabin. I seated him at the table and handed him a blanket with which to dry and wrap himself.

"Alex, Jack, do you think you might be able to fix us up with one more hot bath?"

"Another bath!" They were utterly put out.

"Boys?" I said nothing more, but my tone was sufficient.

"Yes, ma'am."

With that, they were up and off, fetching fresh water.

Bucket after bucket came on board and only stopped when the boys entered with two wayward souls in their company.

"Buzzy! Carter! What a surprise!"

"Good morning, Miss Dorrie. Miss Claussen, Mrs. Cook, happy Thanksgiving on this miserable November day."

"Happy Thanksgiving! Come in! Come in and sit down." Dorrie was elated to see the two men. "I was worried you might not have a hot meal today. Have you eaten? Are you hungry?" Before the men could answer Dorrie continued. "Oh! You must meet Rachel's man, Caleb, and his friend Taa." The four men exchanged greetings and no hint of animosity toward Negroes or Indians was noticeable in Buzzy or Carter's manner.

The younger boys went to hauling the tubs back into the middle of the classroom all the while shooting glances toward Shadow Hunter and Caleb. They were passing whispered secrets, for they were curious about the Negro, but thoroughly captivated by the Indian, as was I. Meanwhile, Dorrie switched the remaining pots back to boiling water for Rachel, and in no time Caleb was driving the chill out of his bones in one tub, and Shadow Hunter in the other. Both men, when sufficiently cleaned and relaxed, returned to the galley with a broadly smiling Rachel.

504

Dorrie and I remained in the classroom to wash Caleb's clothes. We stared at each other and shared our smiles in silence as we listened to the bliss in Rachel's voice. The song of her heart could be heard in every corner of the boat, in every word spoken, and her joy raised the spirits of us all.

When Dorrie and I turned to the garments of Shadow Hunter, they were mostly leathers, and generally no man liked his leathers laundered. It caused the skins to become uncomfortably stiff. We were given a choice of putting up with the smell or loaning him a blanket. We chose the latter. Caleb was also given a blanket to use, but only until his clothes were dry.

By now, it was no longer possible to further delay dinner lest it be ruined. Not to mention, the growing hunger of the children who were starting to complain. They could hardly be blamed for their growling stomachs after enduring a full morning of tantalizing aromas and promises so far unkept.

"Miss Elizabeth?" Rachel signaled me to come to her side at the stove.

"Yes."

"I've stretched this dinner out as far as I am able," she confided in a lowered voice. "—But, by the look of hunger on them kids, an' now four grown men... " She shook her head. "We don' have enough to go aroun'."

"I know. I've been fearing the worst myself," I whispered in return. "You've done a handsome job, Rachel. I would have bought more at the store, but Bernard donated the meat, and that made me hesitant to buy additional or take what I thought we might truly need. I didn't want to insinuate he was stingy. Let's see to it that the children are first fed, then Caleb and Taa, then Buzzy and Carter. You, Dorrie and I can work out something for ourselves later."

Rachel nodded in agreement and commenced to filling bowls and handing them over for placing on the table. Silverware was sorted with the usual last minute gives and takes, and everyone

505

settled into place. Four grown men, three women and nine children made good of any extra space on the benches.

Privately, each adult must have realized there was not enough food to go around, but no one uttered a word of concern. Instead, we all anticipated the pleasures of what was surely the best smelling, best tasting food to be found on any boat, every morsel appearing fit for a king. What was missed in quantity, was made up for in quality, and Rachel was showered with due praise.

"Lordy, lordy, lordy, Rachel." Caleb dropped his face into his hand to hide his emotion. With a breaking voice, he expressed his feelings. "I clearly remember the last time I ate a meal this fine. You, me, an' Isaac…. It's been a long, long, time, Rachel—a long, long, time…."

"Elizabeth, would you say grace?" Dorrie asked. It was a request to respectfully break the silence and ease the attention now being paid Caleb, who was emotionally overwhelmed.

"By all means." I stood up at the head of the table. The cabin remained silent, but all faces turned my way. I took a brief moment to think about the amazing things both good and bad that had happened as of late.

"Beloved Father—."

"Miss Claussen?"

I looked up, my thoughts having been interrupted at the start.

"Miss Claussen?"

The boat suddenly rocked from the weight of callers upon the plank. Everybody turned to face the hatchway. A flurry of voices seeped into the cabin from outside, followed shortly by a quick rap on the hatch.

"Elizabeth Claussen," came the call again.

Puzzled, I walked over at once to unlatch the hatch, whereafter it was immediately opened from the outside to reveal four of my favorite people. The faces of the Schuellers and Gunninks were huddled together and attempting to ward off the sleet as they looked down at us. They came with greetings and great warm smiles in spite of the weather. I was genuinely surprised.

"Aggie! Opal! I can't believe it! Why would you be out on a day such as this? You are all foolish, foolish, foolish!" I scolded them in jest. "Come inside at once! Get out of the wet! Alex! Jack! Find us seats, hurry!"

"No. No. You needn't bother, boys," said Opal as she reached out for Alex. "We can't stay. We have only come by to bring you some holy day fixin's. Hams and hens, breads, peas and pies, sherry, a general fare. We wanted to make sure you had plenty to eat, but we had no idea you had so many for dinner. Maybe, we didn't bring enough," she said, looking around at all the hungry faces.

"Nonsense! You've brought plenty. Truth be told, you've saved our day. Even we didn't know we had so many. We were just wondering how we might stretch such a fine meal, but now it's settled. Indeed, you *have* saved the day. It's so good to look upon you again. You must sit with us. You must. Say you will."

"Forgive us, Elizabeth, but we can't," said Aggie. "Truly, we can't. Our families insisted on awaiting our return before sitting to the table."

"Well, at least stay for grace and glass of good cheer. You must do that." I implored.

Opal looked at the others.

"That's fine," said Mr. Gunnink. "But let us not waste a minute more getting the food inside or it will be as cold as the day."

"Boys!"

* * *

507

"Beloved Father, we have come together before you this day from every walk of life. There are seated at this table, children of the street. There are broken hearts having lost the love of family, the love of husbands, of mothers and fathers, brothers and sisters. There are those of us traveling though life lonely and searching, wanting only to know the joy of a loving embrace. Together we face these and all the trials of mortal life that bend us painfully before the storms.

Almighty Father, we make no claim to being better or worse than others in your flock. And we pray you save us from jaded thoughts and hearts crippled by the inability to see how these tempests are short lived. There has always been sun before the storms, and sun long after their passing.

How often the smallest setback blinds us to all that we possess. How often we fail to give thanks for the Schuellers and Gunninks, the Sawyers and Claussens, and all the other good people who play a minor part in our lives. How often we fail to give thanks for the food and shelter that comes our way. How often we forget to give thanks for the thousands of little things that we take for granted, the song of birds, the sound of baby's laughter, the smile of children, the color of a setting sun or a flower opening beneath a bright blue sky.

It is for these failures that we have chosen this singular day to unclutter our minds and express clearly our gratitude for the blessings that you have bestowed upon us. On this day we ask only for your patience, your understanding, and the light to lead us to eternal happiness at your side, in your glory forever, amen.

"Amen," came a chorus of voices.

I looked up and saw Rachel and Caleb weeping silently in each other's embrace. Dorrie's stare was fixed upon the two of them and tears filled her eyes as well. Shadow Hunter was lost in his thoughts, leaving me to wonder if he understood any of the words to my prayer. The children were definitely dumb-founded, not by the prayer, but by the sight of Rachel, Caleb, and Dorrie, all adults who appeared on the verge of bawling aloud. I started to laugh realizing how confused they must be.

"Good Lord, I hope we are all crying out of happiness at this table."

The three began wiping their eyes and laughing as well, and tears quickly gave way to merriment. I raised my glass.

"A toast to the Schuellers and Gunninks who are now pressed to return to their families!" I said. "To their dinner, their endless efforts, and their generosity beyond measure."

"Here, here!" chimed Buzzy and Carter.

I barely swallowed my drink when midway through my gulp came an unexpected announcement from Dorrie.

"I would also like to propose a toast. This one to Elizabeth."

"Here, here!" Again from Buzzy and Carter. "A toast to Elizabeth! A toast to Elizabeth!"

I had little choice, but to remain standing uncomfortably before all as the cabin grew suddenly quiet, my awkwardness made all the worse by the amount of time Dorrie took to choose her words. Holding her glass to her chest, she stared into its liquid then looked up at me, her eyes meeting mine.

"Curse us all should we ever forget the near miracles you have worked. I have no idea why I was so blessed as to have you come into my life, but I know in my heart of hearts that God has chosen you not just for my sake, but for something grand, something greater than all of this. You are special, Elizabeth. I believe you have always been special. You may never know what it is you have done or yet will do, but I am certain you were chosen to be the instrument of God's design." Dorrie's eyes never left mine as she slowly raised her glass in my honor. "To God's chosen one."

"Oh, Dorrie —."

"It's true! It's true, every word. It's absolutely true. To the chosen one!" said Rachel with utmost conviction.

"To the chosen one," said Mr. Gunnink.

"To the chosen one!" all replied. "Hurrah! Hurrah!"

I was shocked. I purposely said nothing further so as not to extend my embarrassment and discomfort. I tipped my glass with the rest, but the drink passed my lips to find my stomach on the floor.

'The chosen one!'

'The chosen one!'

They had no idea how words of an old soothsayer rang in my ear. It had been strange enough when Jack, the horseman uttered as much at the stage office in Albany, but this was something else again. I was mortified by Dorrie's toast and worked to quickly dismiss it, burying it beneath the din of a cabin filled with gratitude, resumed conversations, and voices of excited children. I retreated to a place where the air was filled with a feeling of family and togetherness. I distracted myself by wishing the Schuellers and Gunninks the very best on this holy day and seeing them safely on their way. The feast was now in full swing and with a little work, the incident passed from my mind.

I took up my seat next to Shadow Hunter and saw to it that he ate his fill. It was hard for me to take my eyes off this man, for he represented so much of what I had been raised to fear. I tried to see him for what he was—a man, nothing more and nothing less. As I sat next to him and we talked, I found him to be of few words, but when he did speak, his words were not wasted. They were deep and thoughtful and made my fear of Indians suddenly seem abstract and unfounded.

I didn't know anything about Shadow Hunter or Taa, as Caleb called him. I looked at the people seated about the table and contemplated how little I knew about any of them, and yet at this moment, in my heart, they were as close to me as kin.

It was a Thanksgiving dinner of good will equal to any I had known.

We ate well and talked late. Most of the conversation was centered on Rachel and Caleb, for their story seemed to give us the greatest pleasure. It offered everyone a sense of hope and happiness. The children played in the classroom and stomped about raising the dickens. I doubted the orphans could remember a night free of hunger or worry, and although we often scolded them for being so unruly, it was wonderful to hear their laughter.

Eventually the need for sleep overtook the last of us, and we called it a night. The youngest children were picked up from the floor and placed upon blankets and pillows about the stove. Rachel and Caleb were given the privacy of a make shift room partitioned off in the classroom. Buzzy, Carter, and Shadow Hunter grouped together beneath a thick stack of blankets in the bowstable. Dorrie and I took a free corner in the classroom.

My closing thoughts for the day were on Mary, Allen and the boys. As I drifted off to sleep, I wondered how they spent their day. I wondered if they were in good spirits. I wondered if they missed me at the table. I wondered if Christopher ever dreamed about me.

FORTY

It was mid morning before our lot came back to life. Shadow Hunter was undoubtedly first on his feet, but most certainly last to follow Buzzy and Carter back into the cabin. I supposed in spite of the fact he had gotten his best night's sleep in weeks, his only motivation to reenter the galley was a craving for hot coffee. The three had stirred Dorrie and I from our slumber while stoking the stove afresh, and we arose at once to greet them.

Maggie, Louisa, and Ellen were still slumbering soundly in their places upon the floor and making the best of a dry roof overhead. Rather than step over them time and time again, the men gathered up their small frames and tucked them into the still warm blankets that Dorrie and I had left uncollected in the classroom.

Alex, Jack, and the boys were looking about the galley dull-witted, and watching our movements during those last fleeting moments of silence and innocence when 'half-sleep' kept them yet adorable. I persuaded the whole lot of them to dress and fetch us some fresh eggs and bacon before they regained enough of their senses to argue.

Rachel and Caleb remained asleep within the privacy of their make-shift room, and no one wished to see them anytime soon. I vaguely remembered hearing the whispered sounds of laughter and tears during the dead of night. I wasn't sure if I heard it for real or if it was just my dreams. Maybe the tears were my own but for thoughts of love.

Dorrie dumped a couple handfuls of coffee into a boiling pot, and soon after inhaling its aroma with anticipation, cups were filled all around. Once the boys were returned, breakfast was begun and soon served up to satisfy their hunger and that of the men.

The conversations and smell of breakfast brought a guilt ridden Rachel into our midst apologizing for not having helped with the morning meal. We promptly banished her from our company. With a sound scolding we ushered her back to her bed and husband. It was about the only time Shadow Hunter clearly participated in anything with the rest of us. The feeling was unanimous; we wanted them to have all the time they needed. Dorrie and I made the two of them breakfast and presented it with a strict reminder they were to remain in bed all day. Privately, I wished Rachel to enjoy all the unrestrained love I imagined in my fantasies. We closed the door behind us.

When we did next enter the classroom with breakfast for Rachel and Caleb, the commotion brought Maggie, Louisa and Ellen back to life. They cast off their blankets and huddled their way into the galley to sit and eat with Dorrie and me. It was very nearly noon by the time we last five finally settled ourselves to breakfast.

Everybody laid about yawning, dragging their feet, and losing the battle of wills to make something of the day. Talk was small and sparse. Even the children were quiet. Only the voices of Buzzy and Carter could be heard, as they were discussing winter plans between themselves while the rest of us ate and listened.

As always, I continued to glance up from my plate and observe Shadow Hunter who, *as always*, knew when I was watching him. It was pointless for me or anyone else to pursue a conversation with the man—even over coffee. It just didn't happen. He had a way of bringing any question to an answerless end with just a look. He was clearly uncomfortable in these surroundings and it was often so obvious that it was funny. Even he laughed about it once or twice to our amazement. Except for a few words with Caleb, he barely spoke at the dinner table, and he had been the first to retire.

Shadow Hunter brought to mind the memory of an old dog nicknamed 'Toothy' that belonged to Mary and Allen. The animal had spent its entire life out-of-doors leaving them to worry forever about its health, especially in its later years. But try as they might, there was no talking that dog inside where it might be safe and dry. The animal would rather lay buried in the snow and face freezing death, than settle down before a warm fire. And so it seemed with this Indian.

* * *

513

The day moved along faster than did any of us. Breakfast ended well past noon. The meal was mostly for the benefit of the children, who were always clamoring for something to eat, as their youth suffered them with insatiable appetites. They were asking for second rounds before any of the adults ever left the table. Against all our feigned contempt, Rachel and Caleb eventually entered the galley for want of a fresh cup of coffee.

At that point the children were urged to go into the classroom where they played their games and slowly wound themselves up into an irrepressible mob. Dorrie and I joked about needing the old double-bottomed hull to handle the beating. At least they were clean, well fed, warm, and happy for a change.

The weather broke late in the day. The sleeting stopped, but all was left miserably cold and dripping wet outside. It took but little effort in convincing ourselves to remain camped around the table huddling over hot tea and warm biscuits. Even Shadow Hunter's horse was left to enjoy the shelter of the forward stable and fresh hay.

The day looked to end almost before it started. There seemed only enough time to stuff a log or two into the stove for heating up leftovers. It was an afternoon of picking and nibbling that eventually ended up in a half-hearted attempt to serve up a late dinner for the same slothful faces. It wasn't long after, the young-uns were told to settle down and undress. They were tucked into bed without much complaint after my promise to read a bedtime story.

* * *

The third day began with a good hearty breakfast of hot fried cornmeal cakes, bacon, and eggs. In spite of such tempting fare, the children were impatient to breakfast, preferring instead to head out of doors, for their spirits soared with a sun that rose bright in the sky and a fair wind that was determined to blow

514

the fields dry. Buzzy and Carter were fast on their heels, even kicking up a little dust themselves as they teased the lads.

The rest of us made best of this first peaceful opportunity in days to discuss matters of importance without children underfoot. The future of everyone at the table was in question, and there was plenty that needed to be addressed. Fears and concern filled the minds of all. Over coffee and tea, one by one, reservations were expressed; and one by one, remedies put forth.

"I would really prefer to remain on the boat," said Dorrie. "The boardinghouse will be much too cramped for all of us, and I can only imagine the complaints I will have to face. Here, all I need do is open the hatch and cut the boys loose. They'll be out of harm's way. Besides, here I might even keep Maggie and the girls if they should choose, at least for the winter. Same goes for the boys. The boardinghouse would never stand to have the likes of their lot running about the place bothering patrons."

"I think that's a wonderful idea, and the stove should keep you plenty warm," I injected.

"I would think so, and we have plenty to eat. The Schuellers and Gunninks will probably be quite happy to have someone watching over their investment in the boat, *and the stove,*" she laughed. "I like it here, Elizabeth. I've lived most my life on a boat, and this is where I am comfortable." Dorrie looked to me for understanding. I had no objections.

"I support your decision, Dorrie. I say, stay on the boat, and I'll see whatever provisions you need will be made available. I'll talk to Bernard before I leave and set up an account in your name."

"Thank-you."

"Has Buzzy or Carter made mention of their plans?"

"Yes! They did well for themselves. Both of them found jobs as snow wardens."

"Wonderful. That's good to hear."

"Hwat's a snow warden?" Rachel asked of Dorrie.

"Well, in this part of the country all of the heavy hauling, especially things like logging, take place in the wintertime. That's when the ground is snow covered and frozen solid so that large sledges can be piled high and dragged by the teams. If a farmer owns one wagon, he's bound to own three sleds.

"Trouble is, a few passes down the road might draw up the dirt and stone. That stops the sleds dead. It is up to a snow warden to cover the bare spots. They call it snow paving. Snow wardens are the only people alive that bemoan the thought of a sunny day in the dead of winter. They hate covered bridges as well, and pray for blizzards to fill them from the ends. I can't say I blame them. I for one would hate to shovel a bridge full of snow. Lord, it must be backbreaking work, but someone has to do it. Needless to say, the pay is excellent so long as you can stand up to both the cold and the sweat."

Dorrie turned to me. "Buzzy promised they would come by every now and then to check on the children and me, and to fix what might need fixing. I promised them hot dinners in return, not up to Rachel's fare I admit, but hot nonetheless."

The news did much for my peace of mind. It assured me that most likely Buzzy and Carter would be around come next spring and willing to work the SCHOOLBOAT for another season.

As for Shadow Hunter, he had a mind of his own. He was determined to leave tomorrow, and take his chances searching Ohio, Indiana and Illinois. He was deeply dismayed at having seen nothing, nor hearing anything of his people during his four trips between Albany and Buffalo. It was Caleb who said there was much talk of Indians being forced to relocate west of the Mississippi River, and he feared that Taa's people were marched south of the canal. It was hard to pry anything out of Shadow Hunter other than to say he feared time spent in Buffalo only added to the suffering of those he sought. He was ready to leave at nightfall.

As for myself, not unlike Shadow Hunter, I too was ready to leave. I had posted Mary and Allen with trepidation as I

516

revealed not only my lack of desire to winter-over in Buffalo, but also my decision not to return east.

I had never anticipated actually heading into the far west, and made no mention doing so in my letters to Mary until now. In Boston, I had never planned anything more than a journey up the Hudson River to Albany and even though I packed a trunk full of books, I only half-heartedly expected to see Jennifer Laketon or Julia Tonazzo. In truth, I never envisioned myself standing anywhere near the shores of Lake Erie, but here I was.

Here too, was the season of gales. Any travel from this point farther west was an undertaking of no small measure, especially across the water of the Great Lakes. The territory of Michigan lie upon the opposite shore and aside from Monroe and Detroit, it was as barren as the moon. Ague and sickness ran rampant within its swampy borders, and I couldn't imagine Christopher or anybody spending much time in such a woeful place without very good reason. Not more than a handful of white people lived in the whole of the territory. It was a land of Indians, and there were some rumors of unrest.

I further considered my desire to pay Julia Tonazzo a visit. Word returned that she was living a few miles west of Detroit along the Sauk Indian Trail. It seemed by Divine design I should pass by her way if I followed the path and advice given me by Randolph at the lumber mill. Again, I felt the sensation of being drawn to something of which I little understood.

The only thing for certain was my inclination not to return to Boston as of yet. I even began to settle my sights boldly on far-away St. Louis, something that would have been unthinkable when dreaming up my itinerary back in Boston.

This may all have been insanity at best, and my dearest Mary would die of fright once she received my latest letter, but by then I expected to be well on my way, hopefully departed by the first of December, hopefully before the worst of winter set in. Like Dorrie, Buzzy and Carter, I was too was comfortable with my decisions.

517

Only the plans of Rachel and Caleb were now to be known. I saw how the fear of uncertainty increased upon Rachel's face as Dorrie, Shadow Hunter, and I exchanged well thought out objectives. We had direction in our lives, whether foolhardy or not, we had objectives.

"What about you Rachel? What are your intentions?" I asked. She looked at Caleb and then back to me. She attempted to be strong and decisive, however....

"Well, I...I'm not sure at the moment. Caleb an' I haven' really had time to—ah—I suppose we'll be havin' to find a place to stay. We'll have to look for Isaac. Yes, of course. Isaac comes first."

"Isaac come first," said Caleb, nodding his head to assure her.

"Everything will be based on that so I couldn' possibly know hwat our plans would be. They will change day to day. I...I...I don' know exactly, Miss Elizabeth. We'll manage, I'm sure. Caleb is here now, an' it may seem hard at first, but we'll work it out. Don' worry about us, we'll be fine." She placed her hand on Caleb's shoulder. "He's good at barberin'." She smiled.

"They're doin' some loggin' up north of here," Caleb said. "It'll be in full swing come the freeze. I was thinkin' of headin' that way to find work as a roustabout. They're always needin' people to start fires in the mornin', or cook, or sweep out the bunkhouses an' things like that. Or I might be able to find work as an ice-cutter. I hear they don' ask too many questions up that way an' a black man can get by."

My heart went out to Rachel, to both of them. Caleb never looked directly at me when he spoke. He couldn't meet my eyes. He didn't want me to read his inner apprehensions. I suffered to know the pressure he faced worrying about Rachel's well-being. She was frail in many ways and looked to him as her absolute savior.

Neither did I wish to humiliate Rachel, for she was a woman who had pride and knew the meaning of respect. But I knew she would never find a place to settle free of worry and want as she followed Caleb from forest thicket to forest thicket, stumbling from one band of vagrant Indians to another in search of a place where they might be welcome. It was a pitiful situation. They had no papers, no promise, and no future.

"I would like you three to listen to me," I said, as I looked away from the table and worked to choose my words carefully. "I have a proposal to make that may benefit us all. I must stress that I mean no one disrespect and that my thoughts are only for the well-being of those I address. Is that understood?" I was given assurances and undivided attention.

"I would propose that you, Rachel; you, Caleb; and you, Taa, present yourselves as my slaves. If you did so, you would be able to travel openly and without worry of slave catchers or soldiers so long as you remained in my company. I would gladly pay your way to accompany me to Michigan and maybe as far as St. Louis, for I would appreciate the company. It would be safer for me than traveling alone.

"Caleb, you and Rachel should find St. Louis a much more hospitable place to make a living. At least the weather would be a good deal more agreeable than New York or Canada. I would even do my best to obtain a new set of papers for the two of you, legal or otherwise. I promise you would be free to leave at your will."

"I hear they are more open minded about freed men, an' that jobs are plentiful that way," said Caleb as a ray of hope shot across his face.

"That is what I have heard as well. I hope you will give it serious thought, Rachel, for I fear that you and Caleb might have to face winter in the hardest manner should you stay.

"As for you, Shadow Hunter, know my promise to reward you still holds true. I know you plan to leave this evening, but if there is to be any information on the movement of your people west of the Mississippi, you should know it at once in St. Louis.

519

It is a gathering place of voyagers and trappers. It is a place where information is certain to be traded freely. I am told there are often more Indians than whites about the settlement. If your people are crossing the Mississippi, I am certain you will hear of it in St. Louis."

I looked back at the others.

"I only ask that you sleep on my suggestion and let me know your answers in the morning so I can plan accordingly."

* * *

The following morning at breakfast, Rachel and Caleb raised the issue in order to say that they would be happy to travel to St. Louis as my slaves for real or pretend, whatever was safest and caused least trouble. They lived their lives only to escape fear and if this arrangement would ease their burden then so be it.

In something like three or four words, Shadow Hunter stated basically he would rather die first, but he would agree to go as my hired scout.

At that point we engaged in discussions to iron out a plan agreeable to all at which point the atmosphere of the cabin was notably improved from the day before. We set our departure for the day after next as I had hoped, it being the first day of December and much to the delight of Shadow Hunter who was most impatient to get underway. The rest of the afternoon was spent packing and procuring goods from Bernard. Shadow Hunter went off with Buzzy and Carter to sell his horse in hopes of getting a good sixty dollars.

That night, Dorrie was a flood of tears and gratitude for all I had done in her behalf.

"I can't believe how desperate I am to have you stay."

"I'm sorry, Dorrie, but either way I would never be able to stay. Even if I didn't continue on, I am long past my time in New York. I should have been back in Boston ages ago. Mary and Allen are beside themselves. Their last letter to me was full of worry and that was before I broke the news of my heading into Michigan."

"When will I see you next, Elizabeth?"

"I can't honestly say."

"Please, Elizabeth. You can't just leave me and say I may never see you again. Not after everything you've done for the boys and me. You must come back to see us."

"Well, if it's to Michigan and back, let's give it a couple of weeks. If you don't see me back by then, figure I've gone on to Chicago or worse yet, St. Louis, and in that case give me at least two or three months before you start worrying. St. Louis would be a fair ways to go, Dorrie, and could easily change everything, but I can't imagine returning this way later than mid-summer next. However, if by chance I don't come back through New York, I promise to write as soon as I am able. That I promise."

"You promise?"

"I promise. I will even give you an address to post Mary and Allen in Boston, should we lose touch. Don't fret so, Dorrie. Things will be fine."

Dorrie and I were the last to retire for the night and being that we slept together, I was kept restless by her troubled heart. She tossed and turned the whole of the night. I shared her anxiety and prayed for her future as well as mine before finally giving way to fatigue.

* * *

Dorrie, Buzzy, Carter, Aggie, Opal and their husbands, Rachel, Caleb, Jack, Kenneth, Maggie, Louisa, Ellen, Alex and the boys, Bernard the storekeeper and a sizable party of supporters for the 'SCHOOLBOAT', friends and acquaintances, old and new, came by to see us off. Even Shadow Hunter remained within the group instead of disappearing from sight.

After a good deal of hugging, well wishing and farewells, it came down to just Dorrie and I. We had been through so much together. She was utterly depressed and a whirl of sobs and tears at having to face this final farewell.

"I love you, Elizabeth. I will never forget all that you have done for my boys. I will never be able to thank you enough for helping me through Robert's death. I wish I knew how to thank you, but I will never be able."

"You'll find a way."

"I'll be waiting for you, and I'll be looking for your postings. I swear I'll learn how to read. I'll miss you Elizabeth, the Good Lord knows I miss you already. If you need anything, anything, anything at all, write me. Whatever is in my power, I will do. I promise. I owe you so much. I love you, and I will pray for your safekeeping."

I looked at the children, nine in all that stood about to wish me farewell.

"Dorrie, judging by this bunch, I think in a month you'll probably hate me more than you can know."

"Never."

We kissed and embraced one final time at the dock as the chill of an easterly wind tried to separate us.

"Go. It's too cold to stand out here. Take the kids inside before they catch their death of cold. Hopefully, I'll be back when it gets warmer."

"Promise."

"I'll do my best."

"Good-bye Rachel, good-bye Caleb, bye Taa."

"Good-bye, Dorrie." They waved from the boarding plank.

Dorrie turned away and led the troupe of rascals back toward the comfort of the SCHOOLBOAT. I pulled my collar up tight about my neck and felt a sense of satisfaction as I watched her walk down the street to take charge of her new life.

"Come on, Miss Elizabeth!"

I turned toward my companions who were facing the plank and plenty nervous to board the sloop.

"Hurry! The captain's ready to cast off."

"I'm coming!"

Where Credit is due...

As with Volume One, the richness of this second work must be credited in part to the direction and opinions offered me by the following good natured friends. Mary Van Heck, Donna Hunter, and Jon Hunter. A very special thank-you to Nancy Smith

To my wife, Nancy, who has accepted my obsessive daydreaming in dark corners while our house continues to crumble.

To Maria E. denBoer, my editor, whose limitless support remains but a phone call away.

A special thanks to Frederick Biller, whose bloodline, background, and willingness to assist, made perfect my German characters. Thank-you, Fred.

Not to be outdone, a special thanks to Anthony Van Berkum, whose bloodline, background, and willingness to assist, made perfect my Dutch characters. Thank-you, Tony.

Again, to Martha Hart, whose generosity, advice, and encouragement made this 'MH' edition possible.

Finally, to my daughters, Britany Michelle and Tawnie Allison, who taught me how make-believe is properly presented with conviction.

I thank you all.

C. John Coombes

www.ingramcontent.com/pod-product-compliance
Lightning Source LLC
Chambersburg PA
CBHW020823030726
47496CB00001B/61